Dear New Friend,
Please help the Earth.
Send her love every day.
She needs you.
In peace be
Claude

Other Books

Presented by Claudia Helt

She got the messages for 25 years to share messages

Seeking Our Humanity, Part III
2020

Seeking Our Humanity, Part II
2020

Seeking Our Humanity
2020

The Answer in Action
2020

The Answer Illuminated
2019

The Answer
2018

The Time When Time No Longer Matters
...Continues...
2018

The Time When Time No Longer Matters
2016

The Book of Ages
2016

Messages From Within:
A Time for Hope
2011

Messages From The Light:
Inspirational Guidance for Light Workers,
Healers, and Spiritual Seekers
2008

Love Thy Neighbor

Claudia Helt

BALBOA.PRESS

A DIVISION OF HAY HOUSE

Balboa Press books may be ordered through booksellers or by contacting:

Balboa Press
A Division of Hay House
1663 Liberty Drive
Bloomington, IN 47403
www.balboapress.com
844-682-1282

Print information available on the last page.

ISBN: 978-1-9822-6588-5 (sc)
ISBN: 978-1-9822-6589-2 (e)

Library of Congress Control Number: 2021906163

Balboa Press rev. date: 03/23/2021

Introduction

Dear Reader, thank you for turning to this page. You see this is a first step. As you enter into a phase of knowing without knowing what it is that you are knowing, rest assured that you are in good company. Others, including people just like you, may already have taken a similar first step, and these good people still have many of the same questions that you currently have. The process of "knowing without knowing how or what you are knowing" is of ancient beginnings. You are following in the footsteps of Those Who Came Before, and in similar fashion as your ancestors; you seek answers to questions that rise from within you.

Take a deep breath, Dear Reader, you are not alone. The transitional phase that you enter into is one that is intended, and it is the journey of a lifetime…your lifetime! So as you hold this book in your hands, remember why you reached out to it. Remember why you were drawn to this particular book, and trust the inner knowing that brought you and the book together. The pages ahead were prepared just for you. Although your story may not coincide exactly with the story presented, you may be surprised by the similarities of your inner journey and the one that unfolds within the chapters of this small book.

It is time, Dear Reader, for you to take the next step. Begin with a deep breath as you open your heart to the story that is about to be told. Accept and be grateful for the part of you that knows you are intended to turn this page and begin the next phase of your eternal journey.

$$\dots \quad 1 \quad \dots$$

Once upon a time on a planet in a distant galaxy, a spark of light glistened in the darkness. As happens when an event such as this transpires, witnesses from afar observed the occasion with great delight.

A passage from
The Word
(Chapter One)

"On the day of your beginning, Existence was filled with joy. So grateful and pleased were all in existence that you joined the Family of Existence. Such was the beginning of your existence and this remains the truth of your existence for all time to come."

"Good Morning, Deb! How are you today?" As usual a wave of the hand accompanied the greeting that was exchanged between these two collegial acquaintances. Good wishes were typically included as well, and they were sincere and heartfelt, but the morning routine rarely allowed for more than this quick interaction. Invariably at the same time, the same thought would race through their respective minds. Each truly desired more connection and inwardly committed that she would suggest an early morning get together with the other, but the commitments made separately never seemed to reach fruition. And as each rushed to their private offices, a sense of loss was experienced, yet barely noticed because of the internal To Do List that directed them. Once inside their personal spaces, another sense of a missed opportunity was realized, but again, there wasn't time to dwell on the unusual feeling of emptiness that overcame them. After all, the workday had begun.

I relieved myself of the briefcase first, then placed the stack of folders on the edge of my desk, and then immediately grabbed my favorite office pen from its assigned space strategically located along side the pale blue

Post-it pad. In large print, I wrote myself a reminder to call Deb about an early morning confab. "This is ridiculous!" The words announced my frustration to the empty office. "This is not how relationships should be treated. For goodness sake, make the effort!" With the written note quickly scribbled, I retreated to my Sacred Space for time with Self and Others. This area of my office was especially created for contemplative endeavors. The favorite chair awaited me. Nearby and easily accessible was the amber sandalwood scented candle, which brought me great satisfaction. And there at its side was the Tibetan bell that makes my heart sing. Just seeing these cherished items prepared me for the entryway into the Silence. The candle was lovingly lit, the bell was gently sounded, and a deep breath overtook me.

A smile came to my face as a memory surfaced from the past. With hands in prayerful position situated just under my chin, I bowed to honor the memory. It was a gentle thought: a sweet reminder of when this regimen began. I breathed the memory in, accepted it as the gift it was, and released it. A sense of peace engulfed me. Soon the chair was no longer noticeable. I felt suspended in midair, neither coming nor going…simply being. The peaceful moment expanded and I rested, simply rested, without anticipation or expectation. Time passed, or so it seemed, but one is never certain when resting in this place of timelessness. At some point during the indescribable experience, awareness came that it was time for me to return to the time in which I existed. A breath was taken and I found myself comfortably rooted in the favorite chair. I repositioned myself to reach for the revered journal only to find that it was already resting in my lap. The journal lay opened with the preferred pen nicely nestled in its crease. The pages, filled with an entry dated with today's date and current time, indicated that my time in the Silence was much more active than I realized. Another deep breath was necessary. "Oh goodness. It seems another interesting experience has been had."

My thoughts rapidly assessed the moment and wisely led me to focus upon my work. Although I was eager to read the journal entry, it was obvious that I needed to prepare for the first client of the day. Because of an old habit, this actually required very little of me. Some time ago, I learned that rushing to the office to freshen it up before the first client arrived served only one purpose. It shifted my quiet nature into a frenzied state. That wasn't a good way to start the day for the client or for me. Once that behavior was recognized, I shifted my pattern. At the end of each day, I took time to connect with my Sacred Space. Sitting quietly within this space that was a sanctuary for me, I was able to express my gratitude for the lovely environment that I was privileged to enjoy and share with others. It was a special time for honoring one's blessings. I truly love this setting; it is a wonderful space to do my work. From that perspective of tender connection and gratitude, it was a pleasure to put the office in order and ready it for the next day. That little adjustment in my daily routine significantly improved my state of being. Rather than beginning my day from a hurried place, I actually had time to come in and attend my own personal and spiritual needs. A quick glance about the room reassured me that it was looking its best. As that assessment was made, I heard the opening and closing of the front door of the office.

"Good Morning, Jan! The office is ready for us! Come join me!" Jan's smile revealed that she was in very good spirits, which she elaborated upon once she was positioned in her favorite chair in the office.

"Sit down!" Her declaration, a mixture of confounding thoughts, revealed both a plea and a command at the same time. The tenor of Jan's voice surprised her. "Oh goodness! That sounded very authoritative. Sorry, about that, but I am so excited to be here. So much has happened!"

"Tell me everything!" My response tickled Jan, but also delighted her. She accepted the invitation and eagerly began to share her story.

"Well!" she announced, and then quickly stopped herself. I waited for her to continue, but she remained silent. Typically, I am not inclined to rush someone's thought processes, but Jan's reaction puzzled me. I waited a bit longer before leaning forward in my chair.

"Jan, Dear, are you okay?" My question seemed to startle her, and her reaction took me by surprise. "I'm so sorry, Jan. I've interrupted you. Please take a deep breath and try to remember where you were when I reached out to you." She followed my instructions. Several deep breaths were accessed before she slowly opened her eyes.

"Not to worry," she whispered. "In fact, I think you intervened at just the right moment." Jan paused for a few moments before posing several questions. "Were you led to reach out to me when you did? Were you afraid that I was in trouble? Or was I silent for so long that you thought it necessary to check on me?"

"I'm not exactly sure how to answer your questions. I remember feeling concern about how quickly your mood shifted. My first thought was to honor your process, but as time passed, my uncertainty grew. I'm really sorry if my intervention disrupted your inner work. Can you share with me what was going on?" She nodded her head, took a very deep breath, and closed her eyes again. I assumed she was trying to center herself before she entered into the conversation. Jan was a person of deep faith. She had diligently followed her spiritual path for decades and was capable of tackling any situation. I trusted her sense of timing and wondered if my earlier reaction was premature.

"Oh, don't start doubting yourself! As I said, your timing was perfect." Jan's response to my doubting thoughts was duly noted. "Did I just respond to your thoughts again?" I nodded, and she simply accepted her behavior as if it were normal. And it was, for her.

"So let's strategize for a moment. You came in eager to share recent events, and then something happened to stall that process. So what's your preference? Which situation do you wish to discuss first?" Jan's energy was back and she was eager to start at the beginning.

"I've had another unusual experience, and as we both know, you cannot share these interesting experiences with everyone. So I was over-the-top excited about coming today. You are such a breath of fresh air. I always know this is a safe place to discuss my spiritual escapades. But this time the most peculiar thing happened. When I shut my eyes, fear overwhelmed me. It was bizarre! I don't understand what brought this on, but I refuse to fear my fear. So, let me begin at the beginning." I quietly clapped my hands in support of her courage and reassured her that I was eager to hear her story.

"I doubt this will surprise you, but my unusual event happened on one of my early morning walks. I awoke earlier than usual that morning and felt compelled to head out to the path south of town. As you well know, I am an early morning person. Sunrises are always a draw for me, but that morning was different. I felt as if I was being summoned to the trail and that time was of the essence. Well, you know me! I was dressed and out the front door in minutes." The image brought a smile to my face. For those of you who have not met Jan before, it might be helpful for you to know that she is tiny woman with exceptional energy who quietly refers to herself as a person of age. Those who know her well refer to her as a woman of wisdom and eternal youth.

"So was it still dark when you arrived at the entryway to the trail?"

"Yes, it was, but you know how that trail is. Even at the darkest hour it seems to emanate a dim light that makes it perfectly safe to trek." I nodded in agreement and she continued. Jan openly admitted she had entered the trailhead with a slight bit of apprehension, but she was so clear that she was intended to take that particular path at that particular time that she pushed herself forward. "I just knew something or someone was waiting up ahead, and that belief was so profound that the idea of turning around simply wasn't an option."

So what happened? My curiosity was becoming unruly. I took a deep breath in hopes of squelching its exuberance.

"I'm sorry, Dear. Let me see if I can walk us down the path more quickly." Once again, Jan responded to my unspoken words and I hastily reassured her that she did not need to take care of my curious nature.

"Oh, I understand. You are as excited about these unusual experiences as I am. We are peas in a pod, you and I." We both giggled about that. Jan and I were very similar in our openhearted approach to unusual possibilities.

"What unraveled, Dear, was a new perspective of our world. As I said before, the trail itself emanates a dim light, but that wasn't all that I witnessed. As I proceeded down the trail, the plants glowed as I came near to them. Some were more brilliant than others, but all gave off some level of light. And that marvelous colony of ferns that we are both so smitten with was spectacular. It was as if an entire community switched on their lights for the outsider passing by. I selfishly thought that they recognized me and that this magnificent light display was their way of acknowledging my appreciation for them. I guess that sounds corny, but I do believe the experience was interactive. Even as I continued along the trail, the ferns seemed to be the most exuberant. Their response seemed to be inter-relational. As my eyes peered further into the woods, singular ferns would brighten when I looked in their direction.

"And then, a lovely family of deer came out of a heavily wooded area, and what I witnessed was amazing. As the family of three walked through the area, the plants shimmered, lighting the way for them. The plant life was providing light for all who passed by, including a great horned owl who flew high up into that old towering white pine. As she flew upward, the branches sparkled, lighting the way for her until she landed comfortably on a large limb. Then the tree dimmed so that the owl was hidden safely by the darkness. It truly was a marvelous sight to behold. This adventure continued from one location to the next until the morning sun took over responsibility for bringing light to the area.

"It was such a privilege to witness this reality that was totally unknown to me. And of course, as I share it with you, I doubt myself and the experience. I wonder if this was an exceptional experience or if this is how our world really operates. I wonder if I can trust what was seen? Was it real or did I just imagine it? What nonsense the mind creates! Instead of becoming suspicious, why can't the mind just enjoy the experience and be grateful for this remarkable opportunity?" Jan sighed loudly before posing a question. "So, Dear, tell me what you think about this latest adventure?"

I took a deep breath and asked her to join me. "I am so grateful you shared your unusual encounter with me. How fortunate you are! I understand your frustration with the suspicious mind. After all the wonderful experiences you've had the good fortune of witnessing, why does the mind still question the validity of these blessings? The two questions that always come to mind for me are 'Why Me?' and 'Why now?' The first answer for you, Jan, seems apparent. You have these experiences because you are open to them. As you said, you felt summoned to the trail that morning. I trust your intuition and I believe you were summoned because you are one who is capable of accepting the truth of that which you witness. Now, the second question remains a mystery. Why now? So what do you think, Jan? Why was that experience presented to you that day?"

"Hmm! That's a very good question. And what comes to mind

immediately is that I do not believe in coincidences, and I know you don't as well. So, let me see if I can sort through this. Because I do not believe in coincidences, I am inclined to trust myself as you suggested. I believe the summons truly was a call for me to bear witness to that wonderful unfolding of a reality that I've not been aware of before. Assuming my assessment is accurate, then the next 'all purpose' question would be... what am I to learn from this?"

"Yes! I agree wholeheartedly, Jan. You were extended an invitation to experience that new reality for a reason. What a privilege! And what an incredible opportunity! So, take a deep breath, Jan, and open your heart to another phase of that experience. Envision yourself on the trail again, and enjoy the connection you experienced with those other Life Beings. Remember what you felt, what you sensed, and what you intuited. Just be with that moment in time again. What were those Life Beings trying to convey to you? What were they wanting you to learn from the experience?" Jan closed her eyes, while she listened to my words. I knew she was taking advantage of the moment, trying to reunite with the experience as it was and also as it is now. The experience on the trail was still alive within her, and as she quieted her mind, the sense of being in that setting returned and her connection with the other Life Beings grew vibrant again. I sat quietly as Jan calmly engaged with the experience.

Eventually she opened her eyes. They were sparkling. She was sparkling! "I get it. What I witnessed was real. The Life Beings of Mother Earth are reaching out to us, trying to remind us that we are not alone. They are here, mutually coexisting with us on this beautiful planet, while we live our lives as if they are insignificant.

"We are so unaware of our place in existence. We act as if we are the only species that matters on the planet, and that all other species are here for us to use as we please. Our scope of existence is so limited. These Life Beings reached out to me. They initiated the contact, and they were the ones that revealed and demonstrated their abilities. These remarkable Beings want us to know that they are real and vibrant and equally essential to the Earth's well being. They are already doing everything they can to maintain her health, but they cannot do it alone. They need our help. As was demonstrated, these different species mutually coexist together. The plant life was graciously assisting the deer and the owl. And they do the same for us, but our ignorance and disrespect of their existence makes us unable to see the assistance they provide. If we cooperated with them and joined their efforts to assist the Earth, She would greatly benefit from our contributions, and we would benefit from her improved health.

"Goodness! This was a huge download of information, which I missed until just now. Thank you for helping me to retrieve that incredible message."

"Well, I'm glad my presence was helpful, but I'm the one who is grateful. Jan, thank you so much for sharing that experience with me. I am blessed by your story, and witnessing your retrieval of the message that you were intended to receive was absolutely exhilarating. We must remember this experience, Jan, for it was a beautiful example of a delayed recognition and understanding of a gift that was received. And doesn't it make sense? At the time, your senses were so enlivened by the actual experience that you were totally engulfed in the moment. As you stated, it was an enormous download of information and it required time to digest and assimilate. By sharing your story, you awakened the moment again and were able to receive the fullness of the message that was presented to you. And just look at what has happened, Jan. Because you were willing to share the story, not only did you access more information from the experience, but another person, in this case me, also benefitted from your extraordinary experience. The beauty of this natural process of sharing our stories is vital to our continued growth. I am so grateful that I was here and able to learn from your experience. Thank you!"

Jan took a deep breath and embraced everything that was said. "It is another lesson for us, isn't it? These so-called unusual experiences that we keep encountering are real, and in the moment they seem to be absolutely extraordinary. But we both know that these events are actually ordinary experiences that we have been oblivious to in the past. Oh, thank you so much for being here. Some day, I hope there will be others that we can share these experiences with, but for now, you are definitely my 'go to' person. Just saying thank you doesn't touch the depths of my gratitude for your kindness. It is such a gift to have someone who believes in and trusts these unusual happenings."

Before Jan left, we concluded the session with a prayer for the Earth. A strong advocate for healing the Earth through prayer and energy work, she took the lead. "Dear Old Friend, once again, you have honored us with gifts of awareness regarding the incredible ways of your residents. We accept these gifts with gratitude and appreciation for all that you do for all of us. Please accept our gift now as we ignite the healing energy that exists within us. We gladly share a particle of this Source Energy with you. Please use it for yourself, Dear Friend. We know how generous you are, but you must accept this sustenance for your own good health. Thank you for your tender care of us. In peace be, Old Friend."

Hugs were shared before we wished each other well. As always, it was a privilege to be in Jan's presence. She is a model for everyone who has a desire to help the Earth.

A passage from
The Word
(Chapter One)

*"In the time of your beginning, Existence was filled
with other existences and all in Existence were Beings
who abided by the Way of Existence. The Way of Existence
was, is, and always will be founded in peace, goodness,
and mutual respect for all Beings by all Beings. Through
this manner of being, All in Existence became consciously
aware of the presence and needs of those around them.
This awareness enhanced and solidified the connection of
All in Existence and created a familial bond that exists to
this day. All in existence came from the same Existence,
and All in Existence are One. This is one of the many
truths that exist in Existence. It is the foundation from
which All came and it is the truth for All in Existence."*

"Well, Dear Room of Mine, that was a remarkable experience. We are
so very blessed to bear witness to the wonderful stories that are shared here.
Let us express gratitude for the privilege of being present during this recent
important moment." Bowing my head to honor the prayerful occasion, I
moved toward the nook on the far side of my office, which was designated
as my personal Sacred Space. Even though the entire room clearly was a
Sacred Space for those who came to explore the meaning of their lives, this
small area truly was sacred to me and for me. Here in this setting of less
than fifteen square feet was where I came to seek the meaning of my life.
It was a place for exploration, worship, and wonderment.

The journal, which held secrets from my earlier quiet time, called to
me. A quick glance at the clock indicated that there was sufficient time
for an adventure. I carefully thumbed through the pages, passing by the
most recent entry, to a clean fresh page. Although my desire to review
the morning entry was keen, I decided it was best to seek guidance with
the precious little time that was available. The decision was driven by a
wisdom not of my own making.

*"Thank you, Dear Friend, for joining us after the exciting time spent
with Friend Jan. She is one who has much to offer and her energy to serve*

is a gift to All who assist her." The words poured from my pen as if they were my own, which was not the case.

"Yes, she is a dear person who openly shares her gift with others. I am truly blessed by her presence in my life, as I am by yours. Thank you for coming. How may I be of assistance?" During these unusual, yet ordinary periods of connection, I record everything that is heard, including my own part of the dialogues, so that the full essence of the conversations is saved for later opportunities. How this came about is a story in itself, which can be discussed at a later time, but for now, let me bring forward the conversation that is underway.

"Old Friend, thank you for focusing your attention upon the moment. We come for a reason and ask that you listen with the ears of your heart. The information shared by Friend Jan is most significant. The Friends of the Earth are increasing their efforts to connect with the human species. It is critical that the civilization of humankind recognizes and accepts their role in the declining health of the planet Earth. All other species are aware of the consequences of Earth's failing health. It is hard to conceive that the human species is unaware of the obvious.

"The cooperation that Friend Jan witnessed among various species along the trail during her early morning excursion is evidence of the loving and respectful nature of other existences in existence. What she witnessed is the way that Beings of Goodness exist, and it is the way that the human species is intended to exist as well.

"For the sake of the Earth and all her inhabitants, the human race must awaken to their role in this tragedy, and they must become part of the race to save the Earth.

"We are sorry to burden you with the truth of Earth's crisis, but you are here to help her. Your ability to hear messages from Others in existence will enable us to assist the peoples of Earth. Because other species are well acquainted with the circumstances endangering the planet, they have been diligently attempting to assist her for millennia, but the extreme damage caused by blatant negligence and intentional misuse of the planet's natural resources has taken a toll. Compound this extraordinary abuse of another existence with the vicious violence perpetrated by the human species upon their own species and towards other species and the impact of humankind upon the planet Earth becomes very clear.

"Efforts attempted by people of goodness give us hope, but much more is needed. The efforts of a few cannot overturn the damage created by billions. When a small child spills a glass of milk at the table, the family can quickly correct the mishap. But when a mishap of such proportion as the destruction of a planetary Life Being occurs, a small collective cannot resolve the incident. That requires the cooperation of all the inhabitants

existing on the planet as well as other existences, who also are impacted by the calamity in progress.

"*Your intuitive skills are keen, Old Friend, and the sense of urgency that you experience is accurate. This is a matter that demands immediate action. Differences must be laid aside. There is no time for debates or denial. The evidence is clear and calls for unification of all peoples for the sake of the Earth. Old Friend, we are sorry that we must be the bearers of this unthinkable news, but it must be done. The time is now.*"

I waited quietly wondering if more information would come forward, but the messengers remained silent. Eventually, in written communication I inquired about their health. "Dear Friends, your silence puzzles me. Are you okay?"

"*We are fine, Dear Friend. We simply grieve the circumstances of the Earth and we pray that the Children of Earth will come to her aid. And we are concerned for you, Old Friend. You bear the brunt of this tragic information. This will weigh heavily upon you until you unite with others of similar awareness. Please know that we are always here. If you desire consultation or reassurance, we are but a breath away. Your logical mind begins to strategize, wondering how you are to serve. Rest with this information. You are one who will bring the messages of truth forward, and many will assist you with this task, but in this moment, we desire that you simply hold this information in your heart. Be present to your daily activities. Observe what is transpiring about you, and listen with the ears of your heart. Already this morning, you were gifted with information that validates the harmonious nature of various Life Beings that inhabit the Earth. This encounter happened for a reason. Friend Jan experienced the event for a reason and she shared it with you for a reason, and more is coming. You are keenly aware of the so-called coincidences that transpire about you, and you know from deeply within that these unfolding events carry information that you are intended to receive. Be consciously present at all times. Whether you are engaging with another or if you are seemingly alone, maintain your conscious presence. Be vigilant about this, please. Practicing being consciously present creates conscious presence and this will enhance your ability to be in alignment with others, including those of your own species as well as other species, some of whom you are acquainted with and others with whom you are not. Dear Friend, there is so much more in existence than you are presently aware of. Becoming consciously present will greatly expand your perspective.*"

"Our unusual conversation is evidence of limited awareness. In my world having a conversation with someone who is invisible is regarded as suspicious, even diagnosable. And if I were to boldly speak out about this experience with others, I might create a very uncomfortable situation for myself, but I know this experience is real and I trust what is happening.

Just as I know that Jan's experience was real, I know this interaction is real as well. I am very grateful to be a participant in this process, and I will definitely practice being consciously present.

"Your news is indeed unimaginable, but it validates what our scientists have been reporting for years now. Obviously your perspective is much more expansive than ours, and you well know that it will not be easy to change the minds of people who are determined to cling to misguided disinformation. But we must try, which is exactly what you are doing now with me. I wish to assist in any way that I can. Thank you for being present and sharing the truth with me. I trust you will connect when it is necessary. I will strive to be consciously aware of your presence."

"We are most pleased with your openness to our presence and to the reality of the planet Earth. We will most definitely call upon you again. In peace be, Dear Friend."

With that said, the encounter was over. My body of its own accord immediately sank deeply into the chair. My mind attempted to take liberties as if it were in charge, but the mind was as confused about this wonderful reality as was I. The internal conversation commenced. *How is this happening? Sometimes, dear mind of mine, the inexplicable does not require explanation. What is transpiring is real. It is simply real, and I know without knowing how it is known that this unfolding relationship is real.*

The remainder of the day came and went with ease, which was typical for me. The lovely people who came for a variety of reasons were a delight to be with. Each one brought new insights into my life and expanded my awareness of the world in which we live. I was acutely aware of the blessings of my chosen career, although in retrospect, I sometimes wonder if the career choice hadn't been made long before I even arrived here in this particular lifetime. But that's another story to be discussed at another time.

My focus turned to freshening up the office for the next day. Fortunately, in attending this task, I came across the scribbled note written earlier this morning. The commitment to call Deb had completely been forgotten. Part of me wondered if this was an age thing, but another part of me completely resisted such a ridiculous idea. *Call her now before you leave for the house or you will forget to do this again.* My internal authoritative voice knew me well.

Just as I reached over to grab the cellphone, it rang. It was Deb! "Oh my goodness! I was just reaching for the phone to call you. We must be on the same wavelength!"

"Well, perhaps we are," she laughed. "I was just straightening up my office and came across the Post-it note that I wrote to myself this morning. So I'm calling to see if maybe we could meet early some morning to have a visit!" The circumstances, which looked like and sounded like a coincidence, were evidence as far as I was concerned.

"Deb, you probably won't believe this, but I was having the same experience just now, but you reached the phone before I did. And yes, I do want to meet. Are you available tomorrow?" Arrangements were made to arrive an hour earlier at the office. We decided to bring our own preferred breakfast treats. After goodbyes were expressed, I chuckled about the unusual circumstances of the telephone call. *Such is my life*, I mused.

... 2 ...

The drive home was brief, but pleasant. Because my home is very near the office, I enjoy the luxury of walking to work, but today my early morning activity left me running late. Thus the rarely used car, which often feels neglected, embraced the opportunity for an outing. As we pulled into the driveway, the car seemed disappointed. For a brief moment, I entertained the idea of driving out to a nearby overlook so that the car could extend its playful moment of joy, but selfishness overcame me. I was glad to be home. "Sorry, Old Girl. I'm so grateful for your patience. I promise we will go for a long drive this weekend. I know you don't get the attention you deserve, but this weekend, we will do something speedy together. Maybe we can race around the back roads! I know how much you enjoy that. Thanks for getting me to and from work today. Rest well this evening."

Before entering the house, I strolled about the backyard in awe, trying to telepathically acknowledge each individual plant for its contributions. *Goodness! How did all these different specimens come together to create such a sweet, amicable family? You are all Divine!* Eventually I landed where I often do, sitting upon the top step of the deck overlooking what I consider to be a Sanctuary. This preferred sitting spot, often referred to as the throne, allows me a clear view of every angle of the garden. "Oh, how blessed we are, my Dear Companions! All of you bring such grace and beauty to this wonderful piece of heaven. I am so grateful to all of you."

My mind returned to the story that Jan shared regarding her summons to the walking trail. It was a fascinating experience, and I believed every word she shared. She really did witness a part of existence that most of us are oblivious to. For a brief moment I felt envious of Jan; this is embarrassing to acknowledge, but unfortunately it was true. "Dear me!" My thoughts startled me. I was not happy with myself. I did not want to feel such an emotion, even if it was quick in its coming and going. "You are blessed with so many gifts, how can you slip into envy? And don't you run away from this question. You sit here and work through this nonsense."

My eyes turned back to the garden. An appeal was made through unspoken intentions. *Oh, Dear Ones, please forgive me. I do not do you justice. If Jan were here right now, she would be noticing responses from you that I am unable to see, and I know she would be able to see your luminescence when darkness falls. There is so much more for me to learn.* A few tears were shed, as it became obvious to me that I simply was

13

not investing myself fully enough. "Envy for Jan's abilities is a waste of energy," I announced to the backyard. "I am behaving like an impudent child. My Friends, I intend to work on this. I firmly believe we are all intended to see what Jan witnessed. She has reached a level of openness and acceptance that allows her natural gift to actualize. And I was blessed today to hear her story, so now I know what to aspire towards. Oh, Dear Ones, soon I will be able to see your full beauty. Thank you so much for tolerating my limitations. Although what I see of you in this very moment is more than anyone can hope for, I know there is more, and I humbly desire to see your full essence soon." Just as I finished professing my beliefs to the garden inhabitants, a familiar face landed on the bird feeder. She pretended to be feeding, but as this sweet one often did, she waited for the perfect opportunity for connection. It was late for the chickadee to make an appearance, which made her presence all the more delightful. I tried to monitor my excitement, but honestly, how can anyone restrain themselves when this precious creature enters into your range of vision? She was gorgeous and I felt compelled to do what I always do in her presence. I reached out with open palm hoping she would join me. Unfortunately, every time this happened, I had no seeds readily available, so I just hopefully wished she would come to join me anyway. To date, that wish has not come true. But hope burns eternal. Convinced that some day she would accept my offer of friendship, I sat there on the top step hoping she would intuit my desire. And then it happened. She pecked a seed from the feeder and flew in my direction. My heart raced as she neared my hand. When she gracefully landed, the old adage, light as a feather, came to mind. It was a brief moment in time, one that I will never forget. We made eye contact, and then she carefully placed the sunflower seed in the crease of my hand. I remained perfectly still, thinking that she would consume the seed, but that was not her intention. It was a gift. She glanced again as if to confirm my awareness and then she flew away.

The interaction transpired in seconds, but felt like eternity, and it was riveting. Once again, an extraordinary experience happened, but it was not a coincidence. This encounter happened for a reason, and I am certain that the experience with my sweet little neighbor was recognition and acknowledgement of the mutual respect that was shared with my Beloved Companions living in the backyard Sanctuary. My heart was full. I bid my Friends a peaceful evening and retreated into the house.

As I locked the back door, I stole another glance at the garden. It truly was a Sacred Space.

A few blocks away, Deb, still at the office, prepared for the following day. Similar to her next-door colleague, she did not like arriving to an office that was not fresh and ready for action. As she straightened up the waiting room, she wondered about the early morning meeting that was scheduled for tomorrow. She was excited, but also anxious for reasons that eluded her. Their morning exchanges were always cordial and sincere, but little more had developed between them. The few times when they had visited at professional events, it had been very pleasant, and she had been interested in pursuing a relationship, but starting a new practice was time consuming and she never seemed to follow through with her good intentions. Deb sensed there was much more to her colleague than she currently knew, and she was very curious…and hopeful.

Deb was a believer in the concept of Oneness and she eagerly wanted to make new friends who also had similar beliefs. Relocating to a new community was difficult enough, but trying to find likeminded people was even more complex. She recognized her needs demanded action on her part, but she also felt compelled to build her practice. So the balance that everyone seeks between a social life and a professional life was taking a toll on her. In truth, the social aspect of her life was much more rooted in her spiritual life, which also compounded the need for connection. Deb wanted to meet folks who were deeply committed to a spiritual life that embraces the idea that we are all One. Her personal journey was taking her deeper and deeper into awareness that acceptance of and mutual respect for all Life was absolutely necessary for a peaceful existence.

Deb's thoughts wandered as she continued cleaning her office. She wondered how the conversation would unfold tomorrow: if the conversation would be professionally related or if it would turn more personal and intimate. She hoped for the latter. *Well, if that's what you're seeking, why don't you be the one to initiate? It isn't fair to expect the other person to read your mind.* "That's a good idea," she announced aloud. "It's an opportunity to challenge my shyness!" Deb's entire body shivered in response. "Oh, this is such a nuisance. Will I ever grow out of this ridiculous inclination?" She paused for a moment, as if she were anticipating an answer to her question. The moment passed and she continued her conversation with herself. "Deborah, you are way too old to be victimized by shyness. Grow up, for heaven's sake."

"Heaven is very happy with you, Dear Friend, but perhaps, for your own sake, you might choose to address this annoying and complicated issue." The voice that had been anticipated earlier finally arrived.

"Any suggestions?" Deb's response was unemotional. Clearly the voice that appeared to have no visual embodiment did not startle her.

"Yes, several suggestions come to mind; however, your undivided attention is requested. Will you please join me in your Sacred Space?"

Deb replaced the dust rag with a pen and notepad and quickly moved towards the small nook where she had created a personal place for her own inner work. The similarity of Deb's creative use of her space with her colleague's would open the door for conversation between them at their morning gathering.

Instinctively, she turned one of the client's chairs around as she passed through to her quiet space enabling her visitor a comfortable place to sit. "Welcome, Dear Friend, thank you for coming. Would you like to sit down today or do you prefer to remain as you are?"

"I am comfortable in my present form, but I will be happy to position myself in the chair so you have a focal point of reference." This response was not unusual for Deb's Friend from unknown origins, but her penchant for hospitality demanded that she make the offer.

"So, you have words of wisdom to share with me regarding this ongoing, never-ending proclivity for shyness?"

"Words of wisdom are not necessary for this situation, my Friend. But acceptance of self is! Those who are your oldest friends love you just as you are. We do not judge the moments of shyness and never will. However, we encourage you to love you, as do we, and we invite you to engage with the issue of shyness that continues to disrupt your appreciation of self. Old Friend, your understanding of shyness is less expansive than it might be. On your plane of existence shyness has become a word that triggers a negative connotation. So unfortunate this is. One who has experienced incidents of shyness remembers how uncomfortable it can be in the moment, and once it has been experienced, the fear that it may happen again perpetuates the fear that lies within the shyness. It is an insidious cycle of a fear-based reaction that incites more fear, because of the fear that similar reactions will occur. Fear is the issue of relevance. Old Friend, assist the child within you who continues to have an open wound. Accept her and the wound she incurred, and healing will finally transpire." The words softly spoken made it sound so easy.

"My Friend, please allow me to interrupt your thoughts. Correcting what has transpired is a choice. You are one who embraces the idea of Oneness that includes acceptance of and respect for all equally. You are devoted to this truth, but you have forgotten to include you in the truth. Would you not immediately reach out to a child who was in tears even if you did not understand the reason for the tears? You would reach out and hold this child near to you regardless of the incident that caused the reaction. This is the response that every child needs regardless of the present form that he or she exists in. My Child, I am holding you in my heart now, and I repeat to you that you are very loved by all your friends in existence. This was true when you came into our awareness and it has been and always will be how we regard you for all eternity. We see you as you truly are: a

Child who is equal to all others and who deserves to be loved, cherished, and tenderly cared for in all the days to come. The days that lie ahead would be easier if the old wound could be released. My Friend, may I be of assistance?"

The question called Deb to task. The choice was hers. Would she choose to accept this generous offer or would she shy away from the invitation for fear of something that was yet to be understood.

"My Friend, as you ponder your options, I stand by your side. I am here to assist you in all ways possible. That is the task that I am most privileged to have. Since you came into existence, watching over you has been my reason for being. It has been a most delightful experience thus far, and I continue to desire to be of usefulness to you. The part of you that fears this opportunity is here as well. Just as you in your adult form listen to this discussion, so too does the one who is trapped within you. She does not understand that she is trapped, but she is nonetheless. I wish her to know that I am also here to help her. She is a very brave child who has maintained a secret for you for a very long time, because she believed it was her task to do so. It is time that she is relieved of that task. She must accept you as much as you must accept her. She must come to understand that you have grown well because of her assistance, and that you are now ready to move forward on your own accord. You must accept that she has protected you since the forgotten incident transpired. She is not the handicap that you sometimes believe she is; but in truth, she is the backbone of your strength, and because of her courage, you are who you are today.

"Without this child within you, you would not be. And without the adult that you are, she could not maintain her strength. Each has served the other extremely well, and now, you are both ready to continue on with your respective journeys.

"My Friend, please embrace this small one within you. You need not remember the incident that harmed her. You simply need to accept that she was wounded and she needs you to acknowledge her pain, express your appreciation for her protection all of these years, and offer her freedom from the task that she so devotedly attended on your behalf."

Tears streamed down Deb's face. She knew this interaction was happening for a reason, and she believed every word that was being shared. "The time is now," she whispered. The words that she had heard repeatedly throughout her life once again were guiding her to take another step forward. She whispered again, "Do not allow fear to be your guide, Deborah! Accept this assistance. Help yourself and help the child within you." A brief moment of reflection was necessary before she could continue.

"Yes, Dear Friend, I do want your help. I accept your offer of assistance." Deb leaned back in her chair anticipating some type of healing ritual to be performed. She was not surprised when the invisible Companion requested that she close her eyes.

"My Friend, please rest your heart in mine and allow me to release the wounds of the past. As I embrace your heart, I also embrace the heart of the child, for you are both one. Each lives with the other's company, and will continue to hold each other in the highest regard, but now the time of separation must occur. Do not fear this next step for it benefits all involved. Each has played a role in the developmental process of the other, and now, another evolutionary leap will be made. Your circumstances are not unique. This is and always has been the way of the evolving existences within this Great Existence. You come into existence, you experience existence with the assistance of other existences, and you continue to evolve, expand, and experience more experiences forevermore. The process is ongoing and never-ending. All who enter into existence continue even when the existence emerges differently than what is commonly perceived by those who reside upon your plane of existence. The child within you gained consciousness while experiencing your existence, but she grew separately as you continued to pursue your path of intention. Now you must bid each other adieu so that both of you can continue your personal pursuits. Please breathe deeply, Dear Friends, and be grateful for the time that you spent together, each serving the other, even though you did not fully understand the presence of the other. As you prepare for separation, please know that you will not be alone. Each of you has and always will have the assistance of Those Who Came Before. As you are assisted now by your Companions, so too will that continue in the future. Remember this, Dear Ones, for it is one of the greatest gifts of the Great Existence. No one is ever alone; we are always held in the embrace of the Ultimate Presence.

"I speak now to the one who is still a child. Open your heart my young Friend. So much is awaiting you, and the time ahead will be filled with blessings. You will not live within another from this time forward, but you will live freely and effortlessly in your new evolutionary process. Always will there be Companions about you, who have waited for this next phase of development for a very long time. They will care for you as if you were their child and they will assist you during your time of expansion. Breathe deeply, my Child. You are free to live your own journey." With this said, Deb gasped for air. For a brief moment she felt the absence of the other part of her. It was an odd experience, a mixture of grief and excitement. She felt sorrow for the misunderstanding she had regarding the child's role in her life, and she was truly happy for the future that awaited her. And she was grateful...grateful for how the child had cared for her, and grateful that she now had greater understanding of the mystery that was hidden within her for so long. She closed her eyes again, took several more deep breaths and tried to assess her feelings.

"How are you, my Friend?" The gentle voice emanated loving concern and kindness.

"I'm fine! Part of me wonders if that is okay. I wonder if I should be depressed by the release of this small child from within me, but it truly feels like a miracle for both of us, so I find myself feeling grateful and excited rather than maudlin and wounded from the loss.

And I wonder how one can be so oblivious to the inner-workings of oneself. I suspect there is much, much more for me to learn about this situation, but in this moment, I am simply filled with gratitude for both of us. I believe she is headed for a life filled with happiness, connection, and fulfillment. And I believe the same for me. At this moment, my life feels like a realm of ecstasy. There are no words to fully express my gratitude, Dear Friend. I know you are responsible for this healing. Thank you!"

"My presence merely facilitated what you and she were ready to create. I am most grateful for the privilege to be present. Please return home now, Friend, and rest well. In peace be!"

A passage from
The Word
(Chapter One)

"When you entered into existence, those who had come before you were most excited about your arrival. They accepted responsibility for your development and vowed to watch over you for all time to come. Their fondness for you and your descendants was and remains everlasting."

Another deep breath was taken as a single tear escaped the outer edge of Deb's left eye. The words 'In Peace Be' filled her with compassion and contentment. How could three small words have such extraordinary power? She pondered the question on her drive home. In Peace Be. If only the human species would embrace these words as we were intended to do. Can you imagine what life would be like on this planet if we all just behaved according to this small message?

... 3 ...

"Good morning, Master Sun! You are looking glorious as always. How do you manage to pull this off day after day?" No response was heard, but I felt certain that the desired connection had been achieved. Rarely did a day go by without this morning ritual. It began in childhood. One morning, I was awakened by faint noises coming from the kitchen. As curious children will do, I scurried towards the mysterious sounds and found my Dad sitting in front of the bay windows staring out into the darkness. He was surprised to see me up at that early hour. And I was surprised to see this part of my father's daily routine. He was always gone when my brother and I began our day, so I was not aware of his morning ritual. I discovered that morning that my Dad had a fascination for greeting the sun. The bay windows facing east were all opened, which was the noise that had awakened me. Dad's hot cup of coffee was conveniently situated on the windowsill. I asked him what he was doing and he picked me up and positioned me on his lap and pointed to the windows.

"Watch!" he whispered. "Something great is going to happen. You're just in time!" So there we sat, waiting together, and Dad was right. Something great really did happen. The sunrise was spectacular! It was like nothing I had ever seen before, because I had not seen one before, and the fact that it was going to happen again every day was simply unbelievable to me. That was the day I became a sunrise enthusiast. To say it was a life-changing event would be the biggest understatement ever. That moment solidified my relationship with my father and with Master Sun. The love affair with sunrises continues to this day. My preference for viewing the morning event changed over the years as my life circumstances were altered by responsibilities, locations, and relational obligations, but the need to bear witness to the Grand Ascension, as my father referred to it, never waned.

At this point in my life, rising early and going for long walks suits me well. Although I typically walk alone, I never feel alone. After years of pursuing the inward journey I have come to believe that we, meaning all of us, are never alone. We are all One, living individual lives, yet intrinsically linked from the moment we enter into this amazing existence. Being in nature is my preferred space for worship.

My affinity for the company of Mother Nature is another gift from my Dad. His love for the outdoors taught me to be a good steward of the

Earth and her wildlife inhabitants. So, on my walks to greet the rising sun, I am always hopeful for some surprise encounter with a delightful creature of nature. Mother Nature has so much to offer! And today her gifts were many. On the trail leading to the bay, I enjoyed several adventures. The first included visiting with a mother deer and her two adorable fawns. The fawns are extremely curious, one more so than the other. I tried, with little success, to monitor my lust to touch them, but who could possibly resist the opportunity to converse with this lovely family? Clearly, not me!

My second blessing of the morning occurred further up the trail that follows along the seacoast. The view of the sea at this particular point is spectacular, and with camera in hand, I vigilantly keep an eye on the horizon waiting for the grand event to occur. But this morning I had the surprise of all surprises. About twenty feet up ahead, there was activity just off to the side of the trail. I stopped immediately. Unable to discern what was going on, I advanced several more steps, and then the prize was seen. The cutest, most adorable creature pounced out from the tall grass and landed on the trail in clear view. It was love at first sight…for me, but not for the weasel. We did make eye contact, and for a brief moment, I thought there was potential for a relationship, but my new friend, yet to be, was not ready for such an encounter. He or she quickly disappeared back into the tall grass, leaving me ever hopeful for future opportunities. When I reached the location where the incredible four-footed friend had disappeared, I spoke softly in his or her direction. "Not to worry, Dear Friend, we have plenty of time to work on this relationship. I promise you I will respect your boundaries, but I can give you references if you would like to check me out. Your neighbors, the family of deer down the way, can vouch for me." With that said, I bid my new friend yet to be adieu and rushed toward my favorite viewing site. I arrived just in time.

"Oh, Dad, I hope you can see this from your present location. I am so grateful for the gift that you gave me that morning so very long ago. Because of you, I have appreciated this spectacle for decades now. And every time I witness this moment, the overwhelming essence of Master Sun's presence captures my heart anew. Thank you for sharing your love of sunrises with me, Dad. And thank you, Master Sun, for bringing joy to my Father all those years while he was here on this plane, and even now when he watches you from wherever he is."

Time passed, as I stood mesmerized by the constantly changing view. Each moment, surpassed the previous, and no words will ever adequately express the experience of being in the presence of such beauty. My heart was happily content, but my hand intuitively reached into the side pocket of my windbreaker and found the phone that was just seconds away from sounding its alarm. I turned the device off and enjoyed one more look at the best sunrise I had ever seen. And then the trek home began. There was no need to hurry. Ample time had been allotted for the walk, and still there was plenty of time to get ready for the early meeting with Deb. I was looking forward to our time together. It was time for us to really get to know one another.

... 4 ...

"**G**ood morning, Sweet Beauties! What a treat it is to see you all of you! I trust you had a peaceful night." Deb loved this time of day. Nothing was better than spending quality time with her feathered friends before leaving for the office. Her days actually began much earlier. She rose early every morning so that she could enjoy the quiet time of the day. Her routine varied. Some days, she rushed out the door for a sunrise walk, and other times, she headed directly to the smallest room in her house that was designated as the 'At Home Sacred Space.' Deb enjoyed many sacred spaces, because she is one who recognized and experienced the sacredness in all places.

This morning unfolded, as did most of Deb's mornings. The internal clock, which she totally relied upon, awoke her at a very early hour as usual, and she immediately knew that she needed time with her journal. There was no struggle about what she was to do. Deb simply knew, without knowing how she knew it, that her presence was needed in the Sacred Space.

"Good morning, everyone," she declared as she entered the room. "I hope you are all well, this morning." Her routine was simple and brief. A small lamp was turned on, her favorite amber incense was lit, and a deep breath was taken. No more was needed. So skilled was Deb at centering herself that she very quickly moved into the silent space that enhanced connection. With an open heart, she focused upon the blank page of her journal. She was ready. "How may I be of assistance, my Dear Friends?"

"We are most grateful to be in your presence, Dear Friend. Thank you for responding so quickly." This unusual means of communication no longer seemed unusual to Deb. For her, it was no different than speaking to a friend on a telephone. In the situation with her friends, she heard the person at the other end of the line, but she didn't see the individual. What she experienced during these so-called unusual situations was exactly the same, except that a device was not necessary. Although she realized this form of communication seemed strange to those who have not had such an experience, for her, it was simply an every day ordinary experience.

"Are you here for conversation or is there a task that needs to be addressed?" Although Deb's question may have seemed forward to an outsider, it was in fact a sign of her dedication to the work that she did for these Friends from afar. "I know you are here for a reason, my Friends, and I cannot imagine the length of your To Do List. So I am ready to be of assistance whenever you are ready to begin."

"We prefer to begin with conversation. After our discussion yesterday regarding your issues with shyness, we realized that an error was made that must be corrected. Old Friend, we were remiss in our reassurances. So certain are we regarding your capabilities and your strengths that we forgot to affirm your concerns about the bouts with shyness. Although you may not be aware of the need for reassurance, the truth is, when one is in human form, reassurances are needed on a regular basis. For some individuals, pride does not allow them to accept this reality; however, it is true nonetheless. For others, there is simply no awareness that this need is a reality. Only a few are aware of a need for reassurance, and unfortunately, even fewer know how to ask for assistance when they recognize that they need reassurance. As you can see, it is a complicated situation, which demands attention.

"As with many complex emotional reactions, it is best to explore one's possibilities, before actually experiencing the situation.

"Old Friend, it is a widespread misunderstanding among the peoples of Earth that requiring assistance is a sign of weakness. When one fully understands the shame associated with this misunderstanding, then one also gains clarity about this contributing factor to humankind's reluctance to accept help from others. We are all One and we are intended to assist one another when one is in need. To assist a society that denies the needs of its people is not an easy dilemma to resolve; therefore it is wise to strengthen their self-confidence in their early formative phases rather than waiting until the dreadful misunderstanding of self has become deeply entrenched within them.

"Accepting the truth that everyone requires reassurance at various stages of his or her life diminishes the issue; however, until this misunderstanding is fully corrected, reassurances must be readily available for everyone whenever it is needed.

"Therefore, my Dear Friend, we come to reassure you that you are loved and cherished by all those who came before you, and we are most grateful for everything you do to assist the wellness of the people of Earth. We are also grateful for the tender care that you provide the Earth and her other inhabitants. Your kindness and your open heart are most appreciated"

Deb sat quietly for a moment trying to assimilate the received message. She was humbled by the gesture and bewildered by the information regarding humankind's misunderstanding of their needs.

"Your thoughts take you in many directions, my Friend. May I be of assistance?" Deb was acutely aware that the pronoun had changed from plural to singular, which validated her sense of recognition.

"Thank you for coming, and for the lovely messages of reassurance from you and your Companions. As you undoubtedly already know, I was not aware that reassurances were needed, but your heartfelt communiques are very comforting. It is an amazing realization to know that one is loved and cherished. I wonder how many people on Earth actually believe this." Deb released an audible sigh, as did her Companions, and she realized that she wanted reassurance that her fears were not true.

"Regrettably, my Friend, only a few truly accept this truth as their reality."

"Is there anything I can do to help? Obviously, the information you've share with me is life-changing if one is willing to believe it. But how do you convince an entire civilization to accept this incredible reality? As you well know, humans are a complicated species. We have problems dealing with each other. Can you imagine how humans will react when we are confronted with the reality that other beings in existence are actually involved in our existence? One would hope that we would be pleased that these other beings hold us in high regard. One would hope that we would be grateful that these other beings love and cherish us. One would hope that we would respond with open arms and hearts. If that were the case, we would not be having this conversation now. I am certain that you have made every effort possible to reach out to us, and still the complexities of our species interfere with the possibilities that await us. I am so sorry, my Friends. And I am so grateful for everything you have done for us, and for your continued efforts. I am humbled by the challenge of this endeavor, but if I can help in anyway, please call upon me."

"Your response warms our hearts. We so desire to rescue the Children of Earth from the crisis that engulfs them. Our time with you, Dear Friend, gives us hope. The challenge before us is indeed large, but it is not beyond our means to achieve. A successful transformation of the misunderstandings that impede the growth of the Children of Earth is possible. Rest assured this is possible, and do not allow your fears to dissuade you from this truth.

"The one that you are meeting for breakfast is a person of similar understanding. She is also one who accepts responsibility for saving the Earth and her children, and she is one who believes that there is more in existence than is presently known. She is a person of goodness, and she is one who will provide you friendship and support as you continue to adapt to your way of being. Old Friend, the two of you are intended to provide assistance to one another. Please open your heart to this reunion of Dear Old Friends. You have been and always will be Friends of the Heart.

"I am most grateful for this time we have shared, as are all who participate in these interactions. In peace be, Dear Friend."

"And to you and yours, my Friend. This has been a very important conversation. Thank you, and peaceful travels." Another deep breath was inhaled and released as Deb relaxed into her chair. She dozed briefly, but when she awoke she was totally refreshed and ready to view her lovely feathered friends.

... 5 ...

Greetings were exchanged from a distance as the two early risers waved at each other while approaching the office complex from different directions. "Oh my goodness!" exclaimed Deb. "Don't tell me you're a walker." I reassured her that walking was a passion created in childhood.

"Heart be still!" she replied. "We haven't even reach the office yet, and we've already discovered we have something in common." We both chuckled at the immediate connection and continued the walk into the complex.

"I suspect we have much more in common than either of us ever imagined."

Deb agreed and inserted another comment. "Yes, and I am really excited about getting to know more about you this morning. I've wanted to spend time with you for a long time, but I've been distracted by the evolution of my practice. It seems overwhelming at times, even though it is basically going well. But one never really knows how to assess one's success when you work alone. And some day I would like to talk with you about that, but not today. Today, I want to get to know the real you, not the professional you."

"Yay!" my reply was short but sincere. I was delighted to see that we were on the same wavelength. "That's my preference too." Arriving at our offices, I suggested that we spend time visiting in both settings. "I would love to see your space and to share mine with you, as well. Who wants to host first?" Deb quickly asked for the privilege, and away we went.

As we entered into the waiting room area, my reaction was uncontrollable. "Oh my goodness! You are not going to believe this, but I feel as if I have just come home. Your space is wonderful, Deb! And more importantly, you have created a Sacred Space for your clients and for yourself." My response, which was sincere, truly pleased Deb. She was beaming with delight.

"Well, needless to say your response thrills me, but let's visit in my private office. I really want your feedback about that space. As she opened the door, I came to an abrupt stop. I was taken aback by the similarity of our offices. The look on Deb's face indicated that she was misinterpreting my reaction. I quickly grabbed her arm to reassure her.

"Please forgive me. I am flabbergasted. I cannot believe this!" She led me into her private space and urged me to sit down, but I couldn't. My eyes

29

continued to move from one area to another as I attempted to assimilate everything that I was seeing. "Deb, I love your office. You have created an exceptional healing space. Just walking into this room alters one's sense of being." As I took in a deep breath, the energy of the good work Deb was doing became obvious. "Oh, my goodness, the people you work with are very fortunate. You're a healer! The essence within these walls exudes peacefulness and safety. Deb, thank you for sharing your space with me. My heart and soul are filled with the positive energy that is alive in this room. It is a privilege to be here!"

It was Deb's turn to take a deep breath. She closed her eyes and just sat quietly on the edge of her chair. "Excuse me," she finally found her voice, "I had no idea how nervous I would be sharing my office with another colleague. Your lovely feedback really is comforting and validating." Her reaction reminded me of the first time I invited another professional to visit my office, and the memory help me to understand what Deb was going through.

"Deb, you really have created a setting that will facilitate people's inner work. And it's obvious that you are already doing good work because the energy in this room is palpable. The reason I was so shocked when we first entered the room was because it feels so familiar to me. You and I clearly have very similar inclinations and our offices demonstrate that. I actually had forgotten that our offices are the same floor plans only reversed, and we've furnished and decorated them in a fashion that you have to see to believe. I think you will have a similar reaction when you see mine."

"Okay, my curiosity is over the top," declared Deb. "Let's go see your office now." We both jumped up to do so. Within minutes, Deb understood.

"Oh, my goodness! We are so on the same wavelength." As Deb moved from one area to another, I knew she was having a similar feeling to the one I had just experienced. She looked towards me and with complete sincerity and asked, "Are we twins separated at birth?"

"I think we may be Soul Sisters!" was my response.

"Even better!" Her reply was little more than a whisper, but everyone present was pleased by the mutual recognition. "Hmm! I believe our Companions are smiling and giggling. Another task completed!" My wide eyes and big grin revealed my agreement.

"Oh yes! The Sisters are reunited again!" We both hugged and laughed as if no time had past since our last lifetime together. I suggested we return to her office to continue the conversation, and that we did.

We made ourselves comfortable in Deb's private space, and both of us took a deep breath at the same time. "No coincidence!" We both declared simultaneously.

"Did you know this was going to happen?" Her question preceded mine. I paused before answering, knowing without knowing how I knew that our conversation was headed for a deeper dialogue.

"There are several answers to that question. First, I will admit that I've thought for a long time that we were intended to meet, and I apologize for not initiating sooner, but life often seems to have a life of its own." Deb nodded in response to that comment. "And I certainly believed when we both initiated getting together essentially at the same time that it was evidence that we were moving in the right direction, but I did not anticipate this office situation. I mean this is a hoot!" We both started giggling again. "It certainly appears to me that more is happening here than either one of us is aware of at this moment in time."

"That's my interpretation as well! And I must tell you that I've been praying to come across someone who is of like mind, and judging from our offices, I think it is safe to say that my prayer has been answered." Deb turned pensive from a moment, and then looked me in the eyes. "I know we are just getting to know one another, but I can tell that neither one of us believes in coincidence. This unusual situation begs me to wonder, why now? We've been office neighbors, saying hello and goodbye to each other for a long time, and now this is happening. Why now?" She paused, but it was obvious that she was not finished, so I remained silent.

"Thank you, for your patience. Sometimes, it takes me a while before I know how to articulate what it is that I want to say. This may sound trite, but I am quite sure you will appreciate the significance of what I am about to say. What's going on here is not a coincidence. Sister, you and I have been brought together for a reason. And we need to pay attention to what is happening here. For over a year, we've just been faces getting accustomed to each other, but now, out of the clear blue sky, we are discovering that we were brought together for a reason. This is important, Sister! This is very important."

I tried to respond, but my mind was reeling from the experience just shared, so I suggested that we enjoy a moment of silence. Deb handed me her beautiful Tibetan bowl and invited me to take the lead. In appreciation, I bowed to her and sounded the bowl with its wooden mallet. We enjoyed the silence each in our own way, but comforted by the presence of the other. At some point, it occurred to me that it was time to end the session. I had no idea how much time had passed. We both returned to the present and glanced towards the clock. Less than ten minutes had been consumed by our time in the silence. We were both surprised.

"Goodness," remarked Deb. "I felt as if I were gone for a lifetime. These expeditions into the silence are predictably unpredictable."

"Anything you would like to share?" My question was selfish. I was very curious to know about her experience. "Yes, but I'm warning you. This will take a lot more than ten minutes to discuss. Are you up for that?" I assured her that she had my full attention.

"Well, I think we, you and I, have many things in common. One of which is visiting the silence." My smile encouraged her to continue and she did. "A deep breath accompanied by the resonance of the ancient sound, and I'm a goner. Rarely do I know where I've gone, but the destination is always fascinating. Such is true for today as well. I remember slipping away and then entering into what seemed another realm of existence. Please excuse my limited vocabulary, but it is very difficult to find words that adequately honor these adventures." Deb looked deeply into my eyes and knew that I understood her frustration. "Oh good!" she continued. "I can see that you understand the circumstances. So this other realm was both familiar and at the same time like nothing I had every seen before. I was alone, or so it appeared, and yet I knew that someone was overseeing my adventure. Although there was no clarity about the purpose of this overseer, I found it comforting to know that someone was near. As is often the case during these explorations, there was a path that was beckoning me, and of course, I accepted the invitation. Sometimes I wonder if these scenarios are a result of my fascination with investigating every trail or pathway that I encounter. Perhaps, I will never know the answer to that, but the reality is…I find it very difficult to resist the opportunity to discover where a path might lead me.

"I looked down the path, took a deep breath, and paused. I knew the next step would take me to a place of new beginnings. It was an exciting thought, and I was eager to proceed. So, I carefully and boldly took the first step, and then the next. That was all that was necessary to ground me into the new phase of the adventure. No longer was I on the path. Now I was on a mountaintop with a view that few have ever witnessed before. Standing on the edge of a precipice overlooking miles and miles of incredible beauty, I experienced unity with the forest. It was breathtaking! I wasn't just looking at the forest that ranged for thousands and thousands of acres. I was one with the forest. As I felt my feet grounded to the Earth, I sensed the interconnectedness that stretched from one tree to another to another and to another. And I was one with all of those trees and with the Earth herself. There was no separation. No division among different species. Everyone was working together as one. The plant life was serving the Earth and She was serving them. Cooperation was gladly provided by all existences for all existences.

"As I think about it now, I wonder what my role was other than being an observer. Even though I felt in Oneness with everyone, I cannot say that I was contributing, but I know that I was there for a reason." A quick expression of worriment crossed Deb's face. A faint prayer was heard. "Oh, Dear Friends, please help me to understand the lesson of this experience. I do not want to fail you. Please assist me." She closed her eyes for just a brief moment and then the expression of relief swept across her face.

"Oh, thank you, Dear Ones. Now, I understand. Please excuse me, Sister," she said looking directly at me. "For a brief moment I was afraid that the lesson had slipped by me. But all is well. My memory is refreshed. My role was to be a witness to the cooperation that transpires among most species on our planet. They already live in harmony with the Earth, and we must learn to do the same. So, what I have learned from this adventure is multifaceted: I am to accept responsibility for learning how to live in unity with Mother Earth and all her other inhabitants. And I am to speak the truth about her needs with other folks around the globe. I don't exactly know how to achieve that at this moment, but I sense that more exploration is in my future.

"The Earth is trying to educate us and we simply aren't listening to her. While other species are already in alignment with her, we continue to live in ways that are not in her best interest. She needs our help. She needs everyone, all species, including the human species to live in a manner that is mutually beneficial for all the inhabitants on the planet.

"There's probably much more to learn from this expedition than I discussed, but for now that's enough about me. I'm sure more will be gained from the experience when I sit down and do some journaling." Deb's travels were indeed exciting and I could not help but think of the story that Jan had relayed the day before. This was no coincidence.

"Deb, thank you for sharing your experience. The commonalities that we share are mind-blowing. You're receiving information about assisting the Earth, aren't you?" She nodded in agreement. "Is this happening on a regular basis?"

"Yes, almost daily!"

"You know there are others who are also receiving information, don't you?" Her earlier comment about wanting to find others of like mind was the basis of my question.

"Well, I assume that is true, but so far I haven't linked up with anyone yet. But truthfully, I've been so focused on establishing a practice that I really have been rather reclusive. Sister, are you telling me that you too are on an Earth Trek?" Her manner of speech tickled me and I started to giggle.

"Oh, Deb, please forgive me, but you make my heart sing. This is an Earth Trek, isn't it? We are on a Trek to save the Earth. And yes, I am definitely having unusual experiences that are associated with assisting the Earth. And Deb, we are not alone. I am hearing wonderful stories from other folks who are also seeking camaraderie in this journey. We really have been brought together for a reason. This is so exciting."

"Yes, it is, and now I want to hear your story. Did you have an adventure during your time in the silence?" Deb welcomed me to share my story. I knew that she was as curious about me as I was about her, so I decided this was a good time to reveal a secret that I was hiding.

"Well, if I may, I wish to tell you about another part of life, first. For some time now, I have been receiving messages during my meditations. Let me back up here. What I mean is this. Before I go into meditation, I place my journal on my lap, and when the meditation is over, my journal is filled with messages that were received during the meditation. Needless to say, this was a shock when it first happened, but now I've adapted to the process. Truth is, the messages are so kind and gentle that there simply is no reason to be upset by the experience. And the messages themselves are of ancient wisdom, which I am incapable of producing, so it is obvious to me that this is real. It's really fascinating, and as I said, it's real.

"So at this point, it seems that I am being trained to receive these messages so that I can share them with others. It's a bit daunting to think about this, but I assume the way will be shown to me. I'm sure you understand that this is not something that I share with many folks. In fact, you're the first colleague that I've told. But since we are Soul Sisters, I feel absolutely safe to share this unusual story with you."

"Thank you, Sister, I am honored to hear your story, and I will hold it in confidence. In fact, now that you have brought this up, I'm sure my reluctance to actually seek others of like mind is because I am concerned about coming out with the experiences that I'm having. Well, that's a reality that I've been in denial about. I must tell you this is a godsend. It really is such a comfort to have someone to confide in. Thank you, so much."

We both fell silent again as we thought about the consequences of our expanding abilities. Neither one of us really wanted to face the reality of what we might have to deal with at some point in the future, and yet, we knew that we would do whatever was necessary to assist the Earth.

A passage from
The Word
(Chapter One)

"Although you are unaware of the commitments made on your behalf, they were indeed made and are faithfully attended to this day. You are not alone, Dear Friend. You exist in an existence that is filled with other existences, all of which cherish your existence."

"May I ask you a question?" Deb's request was so soft I could barely hear her, but I knew what she wanted to know.

"You want to know if I ever doubt the messages." She nodded. I understood the importance of her question. I knew why she was asking it.

"Deb, when the messages first began, I was concerned. I was hearing voices, for goodness sake. As we both know that can be indicative of a diagnosis, but the information that I was receiving was so profoundly important that I could not accept that those experiences were the result of some type of delusional circumstances. So I persevered, and I am so grateful that I did. I know with all that I am that these experiences are happening for a reason, and I also now know that many other people are having similar experiences as well. So, no, I do not doubt the messages anymore. They are of goodness. They are intended to assist the Earth and the peoples of Earth. Therefore, I will continue to present them as long as they are provided to me."

"Oh, thank goodness!" sighed Deb. "Thank you for every word you just spoke. I so needed to hear that. I am so grateful that you had the courage and the strength to speak your truth, for your truth strengthens me. I cannot tell you how important it was for me to hear that. This truly is a godsend. We have been brought together for a reason and I am so, so grateful." Tears streamed down Deb's face, and mine too. We finally had someone with whom we could feel completely safe.

When the time was just right, we both inhaled deep breaths simultaneously. No coincidence. We truly were in alignment with one another.

"Well, my new Dear Friend, my Soul Sister, I am so grateful for you. And I am excited about the future. I think we have many adventures coming our way." My heart was so full that I started to giggle. "I so wish we could just go out and play today, but I know that we both have work to do. And it's time for me to get to my office!

Thank you for hosting today, Deb. I'll do so next time." And with that said, we shared a huge sisterly hug. The day had begun well.

... 6 ...

The front door chimes were heard just as I put the finishing touches to the day's To Do List. Once again it was much longer than anticipated—all the more reason to have the reminder strategically located so that it could not be ignored. One more look at the office reassured me that I was ready for my next visitor.

"Evelyn, how wonderful it is to see you again." Hugs were in order. It had been a long time since her last energy session. We walked arm in arm back to the private office chatting about her recent happenings. She quickly informed me that many unusual things had been transpiring in her world.

"Everything is good," she reassured me, "but I need a sounding board. I'm actually very excited about what is taking place, but I'm also out of my depth. So, I need to be sure that what I perceive is happening is actually happening. If not, I need a wakeup call." Evelyn was a strong, independent woman who rarely experienced a lack of confidence, but I could tell by the sound of her voice that she was questioning herself.

"Well, I'm curious and eager to hear everything, and it seems appropriate that we do a brief relaxation technique before you share your story. Does that suit you?" Evelyn seemed relieved.

"Yes, that's a great way to begin. Let me get myself positioned." She wiggled about in the chair creating the position that she was most comfortable with and then announced, "I'm ready!"

Once again I found myself enamored with my work. *I am so blessed to work with the most delightful people. Thank you, my Friends, for bringing this dear, wonderful woman here today.* As with many of my clients, Evelyn was a skillful meditator. The mere suggestion of an act of self-care was all that was needed for her to delve into the inner world of her being. With a few deep breaths, the level of peaceful serenity that she desired was acquired. She truly was ready. Her eyes opened. She thanked me for my assistance, and declared that she was eager to share her recent events.

"Evelyn, you are a marvel! I did nothing, Dear One, but hold the Sacred Space for you." She rolled her eyes and I reacted by tapping the end of my nose to get her attention. "Hear my words! You created your readiness, and you did it so quickly, it was amazing to witness. You are very skilled at realigning yourself, Dear, and I am most grateful to be in your presence. So, Evelyn, please tell me everything!"

"Thank you for challenging me," she replied. "I really am fortunate.

A few deep breaths and I'm a new person. But," she elongated the three-letter word to capture my attention. "You are the one who taught me how to do this! Thanks to you, I have a tool that will help me for the rest of my life, and I want you to know how grateful I am to you for that incredible gift." I accepted her kind words and we both agreed that we were grateful that our paths had crossed. I urged her to return to her recent happenings.

She began with another deep breath and then launched into her most recent experience, after first emphasizing that several other events had occurred previously. "Well, a few days ago several of my dearest friends came over for a visit. We've all been very busy lately, and as a result, we were starving for each other's company. You now how it is when good women friends come together after prolonged absence from one another. We start sharing our lives as if no time has gone by whatsoever. Our connection is so strong that the separation doesn't diminish the strength of our relationships. At first, we did the small talk thing, just catching up on the day-to-day stuff, but then we quickly moved into a deeper conversation. It began when Mary, whom I've known since grade school, announced that she was going to relocate at the end of the month. We were all very surprised, because she hadn't indicated anything about this in previous gatherings. So, the bottom line to this story is that Mary, for over a year, had been studying long-distance with an animal whisperer and she decided to move closer to this person so that her studies can be intensified. Of course, this news was also a surprise. We all knew how fond she was of animals, but never had she mentioned any interest in this type of work. It turns out that she has been able to connect with animals most of her life, but she was reluctant to tell people about it, because she was afraid that they might think it was odd. Well, what she learned at our meeting was very comforting for her. Everyone there was extremely supportive of her decision and incredibly curious and interested in the field. She explained that interspecies communication was actually an ancient ability that we all have, but have forgotten.

"She also elaborated upon how extensive the field has become. Undoubtedly, all across the globe there are people who are actively gathering information from animals and plants that is relevant to our endeavors to assist the Earth back to good health. These Beings to whom we rarely give any notice have always lived harmoniously with the Earth, and it seems that there is much that we can learn from them. Isn't this fascinating?"

"Yes it is, Evelyn, and it validates several other stories that I've recently heard. It seems that more and more people are waking up to the Earth's health issues, which is good, because she needs all the help we can give her. Tell me Evelyn, how does Mary's work personally effect you?" Her response was slow in coming. She appeared to be assessing how to proceed.

I assumed she had so much to say that she couldn't narrow her thoughts into a single thread.

"I have so much that I want to share with you that I don't even know where to begin, but let's stick with Mary's story a while longer. As you've probably already intuited, Mary's courage to pursue this new endeavor has really challenged me. She's found her dream! All her life she knew that animals knew more than most humans do, but she had no one to share that knowledge with; and now a whole new world has opened up for her. I've already read two of the books that her teacher has written, and they are fabulous. Breathtaking! And I believe every experience that she conveyed. So, Mary's life long passion has blossomed into fullness, and it challenges me." The look on Evelyn's face revealed her sadness. "I am so ashamed to acknowledge this, but I must. Please believe me when I say how happy I am for Mary. She is radiant. I've never seen her so filled with joy. I am truly excited and happy for her, and at the same time, I am envious. She has found her purpose! And I want to be where she is. I want to feel passionate about something as well, which brings me to another experience recently had.

"Another woman in our group is also on a Save The Earth journey, and she is learning how to do energy work so that she can help the Earth by sending her positive energy everyday. She is as excited about her new passion as is Mary. So, again I feel enlivened by both of their personal pursuits, and I also feel left out. Please forgive me for sounding like a brattish child, but I feel like an outsider looking in, and I want to be inside the circle doing something important for the Earth. I want to help, and I'm here today because I have a thousand questions, and I need answers." Evelyn's heartfelt appeal filled the room. It was a mixture of despair and sincere intentions to be a better steward of the Earth. I invited her to take some deep breaths with me. Composure returned to her face, which was my cue to take the lead.

"Thank you, Evelyn, for sharing your stories and also your deepest fears and desires. I am honored to bear witness to your truth." A look of puzzlement washed over her face. I was not surprised. The bewilderment encouraged me to continue. "Tell me, Dear, which of the thousand questions do you wish to explore first?" Her mind started to race again, and I invited her to join me in another deep breath. "Just relax, Evelyn, and quiet that mind of yours. The question you are most concerned about will surface, if you just give it the space it needs to manifest." Her response was faster than I anticipated.

"I want to know if you think I'm an awful person because I am envious of my friends." Her eyes quickly turned downward. So well I knew the shame she was feeling.

"Evelyn, please look at me. I want you to see my face as you hear my response." It was not easy, but she managed to make eye contact. "You are a person of goodness and integrity, and never will I think that you are an awful person. Never! Please breathe that in before I continue." The sigh of relief was a good sign and she appeared prepared to hear more.

"The enthusiasm of your friends has sparked the same in you. You witnessed their robust excitement and you desired to feel that passion within you. Please do not shame yourself for having a natural human reaction. Instead be grateful for the fire that your friends ignited in you. Their willingness to share their stories with you and your friends was a gift to all of you, and because you were ready to hear your own call through their stories, you are now ready to pursue and expand your own spiritual quest. My Dear Friend, this is not a shameful act on your part; it is an awakening to a new adventure for which you were already longing.

"Another way of saying this is that your friends served as messengers. You were longing for something that remained unknown, and your friends unveiled the mystery and made it known to you."

"That's a beautiful way of reframing my thoughts and it rings true for me." Evelyn's manner was gentle and calm. I could see the relief that she felt. She accepted that my version of her experience was more accurate than her punitive perspective. "How did you know that would be my first question?"

"Because it would have been mine. It is our nature to judge ourselves negatively. Hopefully we will learn kinder ways to assess our behavior in the future. And by the way, I also want you to know that I share your excitement about your friends' pursuits. It is wonderful to hear that more and more people are searching for ways to help the Earth. Wherever your path leads you, Evelyn, trust that it will be something that will inspire you to expand into an even better person. You are here for a reason, Dear Friend, and it appears that doors are opening for you. Trust your intuition and have compassion for your impatience."

A passage from
The Word
(Chapter One)

"If these statements of truth puzzle you, rest assured you are not alone. Others before you have also wondered about similar statements that were made by those who came before them. Always it is the same. New ones enter into existence and are welcomed into existence by those

who came before, and those who hear the messages about their place in existence wonder about the messages, the messengers, and all those existences purportedly existing in this Existence. Who are they? Where are they? And exactly where do they exist and how? The questions about existence lead the new ones to question their own existences, which inspire the journeys to seek all there is to know about everything in existence. This was true in the beginning of existence and it continues to be true now to this very day, and so shall it be for all days to come."

"Thank you. That is wonderful guidance. I don't know how you manage to put a positive bent on all my flaws and leave me feeling good about myself. But you do, and I am very grateful." Evelyn's appreciation was duly noted and it opened the door for another learning experience for both of us.

"Actually, Evelyn, I'm not doing anything that you don't already do for your friends. What you view as a flaw within you, I see differently, and that is true when you are the listener for someone else. When we are the listener, we have a kinder perspective than does the one who is revealing what feels like a shameful secret. Thank goodness that we can be of service, and that there are others who do the same for us. I feel privileged to assist in this way, and I know you do as well. Our goal, Dear Friend, is to strive to remember our inclination towards negative self-judgment when we are in the process of punitively evaluating ourselves. Let's remember to remind each other about this in the future." We both giggled about that idea, knowing full well when the next incident came about, we would most likely fall victim to our judging nature.

"Do you really think that we can overcome this tendency? It is extremely persistent and insistent, and at times it seems insurmountable." Evelyn's comments were well taken. Our inclination towards self-judgment would not be an easy habit to break. If that were the case, we would have done it a long time ago.

"We must persevere, Evelyn. Let's make a pact. I promise you that I will be accountable for my judging behavior. Essentially, what I am committing to do is this. I will strive to be a better person, for the sake of self and all others. As long as we continue to bow to self-judgment or participate in the judgment of others, we are harming all who are around us, including the Earth. So, if we choose to tackle this unkind behavior, we will assist humankind and become better stewards of the Earth at the same time."

Evelyn sat quietly with hands in prayerful position. Her thoughts invited her to many places, but she chose to remain steadfast, pondering the commitment that she was considering. "Wow! This is no small task, but I love the challenge. I will spend some time with my journal when I get home and set up a strategy for myself. This is important, and I don't want to have it slip away from my attention. I think this is a commitment that has life-changing possibilities. I'm in!"

"My goodness, this feels like a transformative experience for both of us, and I thank you for bringing this opportunity forward today. But now, let's return to your need for a thousand answers. Which question do you wish to tackle next?" Evelyn did not hesitate.

"I want to know what you think about interspecies communication. You mentioned earlier that you had recently heard similar validating information. Is this something that you know about first hand? Are you able to communicate with other species?" It was my turn to take a deep breath. I needed to consider what was appropriate to share because of confidentiality issues. And then one of those unusual moments came about, and the answer became clear to me.

"Evelyn, Dear, I'm struggling a bit, because the incidents that came to mind when you were sharing your story were actually stories that were also shared in the privacy of this Sacred Space. So, obviously, I am limited in what can be revealed. However, I can affirm that this is not the first time I've heard of the exciting work being done by animal whisperers. Quite honestly, I am fascinated by the possibilities, and nothing that I've heard thus far surprises me. I'm just so excited that people are now feeling safe to openly talk about this type of communication. So, my first response to your question is yes, I absolutely believe that we have the ability to communicate with other species, even if I have not honed that skill within myself. However, that brings up another thought that I believe is in the same range of possibility. Obviously, you come here for a variety of reasons and you are aware that I am often assisted during these sessions." Evelyn nodded her head in agreement.

"Yes, I am aware of that and I would love to hear more about it."

"Well, I personally believe we are speaking about a similar means of connection. It's difficult to elaborate upon a process for which we do not have a language. Some people refer to these so-called unusual types of communication as intuition, insight, and/or telepathic communication. I also know that the term existential communication is frequently used, but the truth is, I do not have the words to adequately explain what happens.

"All I can say is that there are times when I receive messages as clearly as I can hear you speaking. It simply happens. And the literature that has crossed my path regarding animal communication sounds very similar to what I experience. When this first started happening for me, it was worrisome, as you might well imagine, but not anymore. I am as accustomed to this unusual type of connection as I am to the conversation that you and I are having now. It's real, and I simply don't doubt it anymore.

"Evelyn, there is so much more going on in the world than we can currently explain, and whether we can expound upon these unknowns or not, does not mean that they do not exist. Even if we don't have the words to describe what is transpiring, we still need to be open! It's time for us to start opening our hearts to all the possibilities that are waiting to be acknowledged and accepted."

The words quickly came to a stop, leaving me perplexed. *Were those my words or another's?* The truth is I wasn't sure, but in going silent, it occurred to me that another question needed to be asked.

"Evelyn, may I impose upon you?"

"Certainly," she responded. "Please do!

"Well, I'm curious about your interest in interspecies communication. Obviously, Mary's decision to relocate brought this topic to the surface, but has it also stirred a realization within you that needs to be discussed." She shook her head in disbelief.

"How do you know these things?" she asked. "We've never discussed this before and yet somehow, you are tuned into me and you know things that I still do not have clarity about. How do you know this?" Evelyn's reaction surprised me. I hadn't realized her discomfort until this moment.

"Dear One, once again you have witnessed how alike we are. I am simply following a thread of thought that you would also follow if the table were turned. Obviously, Mary's announcement aroused your curiosity, and I chose to pursue the possibility that there might be more to this experience than you had already shared. Perhaps, I am totally off the mark. I frequently am!"

"Of course, you're on target. And yes, it is time for me to come out about this. I guess in many ways, Mary's story is my own. The difference is that she is actually doing something about it and I am just lingering in my confusion."

"Are you being hard on yourself?" In light of our previous conversation, it seemed appropriate to bring this topic up again. But Evelyn's perspective differed from mine.

"Actually, I think my reaction is realistic, but I appreciate your concern. It is respectfully noted, and I will try to speak about this issue in a manner that is not harsh or critical. The truth is I don't have the courage that Mary has. I cannot imagine packing up and moving to another area where I know absolutely no one. It's beyond me." I nodded in agreement and then made a suggestion that grabbed Evelyn's attention.

"Let's back up for a minute, if you will. We need to tackle this from another angle. Evelyn, I'm going to ask you to take one of those deep breaths that are so revitalizing for you, and if you like you can express your gratitude to Mary for the lesson that she is providing you. But once that is done, from that point forward, I want you to refrain from comparing yourself to Mary.

"We're going to continue with a different approach. Rather than focusing upon Mary's story, let's focus upon yours. When you're ready, Dear Friend, please tell me your story?" She sighed loudly and I could tell from the look on her face that she was relieved. We were back on track now, and she was ready.

"Thank you, for helping me to get centered. Avoidance is a sneaky character that often slips my notice. Thank you for bringing its presence to my attention. And thank you, Mary, for leading me into another opportunity for growth." Another deep breath was enjoyed and Evelyn met my eyes with a smile on her face.

"We may be more alike than you think," she laughed. "First, I should apologize for not telling you about my unusual experiences a long time ago, but every time I've come for a session we became so deeply involved in the moment that it literally slipped my mind. And actually, I think the real reason it never came up was because it wasn't time." Her comments made sense to be. Timing is critical to the awakening mind.

"A lot has happened since we last convened, all of which now seems to have been beautifully orchestrated so that Mary's message would capture my attention. And of course, it did! But let me backtrack and give you some information that you may already know, but never revealed to me. My unusual experiences began in childhood. I was able to see auras around other kids, which was really cool, until I found out that the other kids didn't see the same beautiful colors that were clearly visible to me. As you might imagine, it didn't take long for me to realize that this was a topic not to be discussed. I cleverly broached the subject at an evening meal one night by insinuating that I had heard some older kids at school discussing the topic, but my family's reaction was so dismissive that I never brought it up again. I had to be very careful, because it was so exciting to see the amazing colors that engulfed people, and it was hard to remain silent about it. And I was very sad for the other kids who didn't get to enjoy this incredible experience. At some point, my unusual abilities expanded and I became able to see the energy emitted by plant life. It was spectacular to see how they would react as people approached them. Over time, I was able to connect with them and they seemed as delighted about the connection as I was. And this remains true to this day.

"Obviously, my abilities were not something that could be shared with others, which left me feeling like I was on the outside looking in. Oh, I tried to be like the other kids, and for the most part I succeeded, but there was always an emptiness that was felt, because no one really knew who I was. The kids didn't know. My teachers didn't know. And my family didn't know. I don't really know how I managed to maintain this secret all of my life, but I did. When I think about it now, I realize that my young self was a very strong individual. In fact, my younger self reminds me of Mary. I doubt that my experiences are much different than folks who have similar gifts, but it is such a shame that we grow up not knowing that there are others like us. Even into adulthood, I led a secretive life. It's sad and a lonely way to live." Evelyn's story wasn't unusual. My work allowed me the good fortune to hear many similar stories, and always it was the same: the secrets, the heartaches, and the fears of not knowing how someone would react to you if you spoke your truth.

"And where are you now, Evelyn? Now that Mary shared her experiences and you witnessed how supportive your friends were, can you see yourself coming out and sharing your story with these folks?" Her response was cautiously stated.

"I don't think Mary's announcement was a coincidence. She feels called to pursue her passion, as does my friend who signed up for a Reiki class. Both of these women have been reaching out to learn more about themselves and about ways to improve the conditions upon our planet. Their stories are inspiring, and I was in the right place at the right time to hear their stories. This is not a coincidence! The time is now. And I need to take action." I remained silent, attempting to give Evelyn the space that I assumed she needed.

"Okay," she eventually continued. "I assume you're trying to give me space to process my thoughts, but I'm done now, and I actually need feedback."

"Oh, goodness, here I am assuming again!" We both started giggling... it was a wonderful release for us both. I finally resumed my role as facilitator with a bold announcement. "Well, my Dear Friend, I suspect your gifts are more expansive than you know, or perhaps you do already know and you just haven't shared it with me yet." A puzzled look crossed her face and she indicated that I should proceed. "Evelyn, are you aware that you are tuning into my thoughts, and probably others' as well?" She looked surprised.

"Are you asking me if I am reading your mind?"

"No, I'm asking if you are aware that you are hearing my thoughts and responding accordingly?" The puzzled look remained. I chose to remain silent, once again, assuming that she needed time to soothe her over functioning mind.

"Well, that's a fascinating thought, and it seems that you have witnessed this behavior before. Is that true?" My eyebrows raised and a smile came to my face.

"Yes, I've been meaning to bring it to your attention. Are you aware this is happening?" My question seemed to create some uncertainty with Evelyn and once again I was unsure if she needed time or if she needed me to intervene.

"Actually, I would love it if you took the lead," she replied to my thought. I looked into her eyes and grinned again.

"Are you demonstrating your gifts, Evelyn?"

"Oh gosh, no!" she answered. "But, I definitely noticed what just happened. And it explains a lot." She took one of her big breaths, which seemed to serve its purpose. Evelyn went on to explain that recently she had noticed people looking surprised when she responded to what she thought was a spoken question. She found it curious.

"Now I understand why I've been getting these odd looks from people. Jeepers! What must they think of me?"

"No one has confronted you about it?" She indicated that no one had mentioned anything. "Well, that's a good sign! Your friends are curious, but they obviously are not worried about you. Dear One, you may find that you are surrounded by people who are as fascinated by unusual experiences as are you. Judging from the way your girl friends responded to Mary, I would say that you are in very good company. But this means you will need to speak up and take action as you said before! Oh joy! You are having a growth spurt! I am so excited for you. This is a time of great discovery. Just open your heart to every possibility you can imagine...and take lots of deep breaths. I'm very happy for you, Evelyn."

"Well, I appreciate your enthusiasm. I must admit I'm a bit antsy about this, but judging from your reaction, I guess there's nothing to be afraid of. There really is nothing to be afraid of, is there?" We both took deep breaths at the same time.

"Evelyn, we all know that life happens and sometimes we are pleased with the events that happen and other times we are not. I encourage you to trust yourself. The same way that Mary is trusting herself with her big decision. In fact, I think it would be a great idea if you talked with her about this. I'm sure she is also having fluctuating emotions about her process the same way you are right now. This is normal, Evelyn, but trust yourself to be able to handle whatever comes along. Try to look forward with hopeful optimism and don't linger in the moments of fear. I feel such joy for you! You are taking the next step forward!"

A passage from
The Word
(Chapter One)

"The truth of Existence lies within the mystery of existence. Before existence came into existence, existence existed, and to this day, all in existence seek to know the mysteries of existence."

7

"**H**ello there!" Deb and I declared at the same time. It was a first for us to exit our offices at precisely the same time. Some might think this was a coincidence, but neither of us believes in such ideas. "What a nice surprise!" We spoke simultaneously again, which brought about a round of giggles.

"I don't think we've ever ended our day at the same time before," Deb noted and continued with what seemed a typical exchange for two colleagues. "Did you have a good day?" I told her my day had been fascinating and inquired about hers. She paused briefly, as if my question took her to another place in time.

"Actually, I had a fascinating day as well, and I would love to discuss it with you. Would you like to join me for a walk?"

"Seaside or countryside?" I tried to restrain myself, but the idea of walking in the sea breezes while watching the sun bring the day to a close particularly spoke to me.

"That's a great idea!" Deb's response to my unspoken thoughts did not surprise me, but her behavior made me wonder how many other people around the planet were also becoming increasingly more telepathic. "A stroll along the seacoast would be the perfect way to end this day." We agreed to meet at the nature preserve parking lot in thirty minutes.

The five-minute brisk walk to the house was invigorating. I was so excited about meeting Deb for our walk that I rushed through the living room without even addressing the house. This was unusual for me. A quick change of clothes and off I went rushing through the house again on the way to the garage. "Excuse my rudeness, Dear House of Mine, I'm off for a walk. Will be back soon." With no awareness of the three miles just driven, I arrived precisely at the same time as did Deb. We greeted one another with mutual excitement and immediately agreed to head towards the west side of the peninsula.

"Oh goody! We should arrive at the point just in time to get some great photos." Deb seemed to be excited about that as well. It was fascinating to witness our similarities. "So, Deb, tell me everything! What transpired in your beautiful office today?" The question made her shiver with anticipation.

"First, I must admit that I am absolutely delighted that you were able to join me. Is this one of your favorite places?" Nodding that it was validated another shared likeness. "Well, I'm not surprised. This is such a lovely place: seacoast vista, wonderful wildlife, and magnificent views of the sun rising and setting. As far as I'm concerned, this is heaven." We strolled a bit further and then the conversation turned inward. "In answer to your question, I had the most interesting session today. Not with a client," she quickly inserted. "It was a private session shared with my Companions. And of course, once again, the depth of their love for us, and of course, for the Earth is absolutely stunning. As they speak their truth, you can physically feel the sincerity that emanates from them." Deb's story validated my own experiences; it was comforting to hear her perspective. "I can tell," she continued, "that you understand what I'm saying. You have similar reactions when you receive their messages, don't you?" I reassured her that our situations were indeed very similar. She wrapped her arm in mine, and released a loud, deep breath.

"This feels like a miracle! I am so grateful you are here. It is such a relief to have someone to share these experiences with...thank you!" We walked arm in arm, filled with gratitude and joy for the gift of our newly developing friendship.

"I suspect there is more to the story that you were about to discuss. Please tell me more!" My behavior was that of child wanting more and more and more. And it was true, I did want more and it appeared that Deb was going to be a person who might be eager to share the mysteries of the unknown with me. She already was someone who was expanding my awareness of the more that I was seeking.

"Yes," she softly replied. "There is more." Deb's mind took her elsewhere for the moment: a behavior with which I was acutely familiar. In moments like this, I believed it was wise to just send loving energy to the one who was exploring his or her inward journey. Deb clearly was someone who was extremely capable in this realm of exploration. Patience and positive energy seemed likely gifts to offer.

"Thank you, Soul Sister! Your patience and your lovely energy are most appreciated. I find myself searching for words to describe the fullness that presently resides within me. I feel blessed, as if the goodness of All That Is fills me with love and grace. It's a remarkable experience, one that everyone should have. I feel joy, gratitude, and peace. And I feel accompanied and cherished. Isn't that amazing? How can one feel so much, and still be in this plane of existence?" Deb fell silent, but she was not finished. She just needed breathing room and this trail certainly provided that.

"I wish everyone could experience what I am presently feeling, because if they did, there would be peace on Earth. It saddens me that our distractions impede our abilities to feel this ever-present connection. How sweet it is! How can the people of Earth be so unaware of this remarkable, yet ordinary experience? This is real! It's right here surrounding us, and yet, most of our people have not opened their hearts to that which is their birthright. This cannot continue! Somehow the people of Earth must awaken to the reality that they live in. These delusions that distract them are just that...distractions that prevent them from seeing, hearing, and feeling the real world in which they live. How sad this is!"

"Dear Friend, you are speaking your truth beautifully. I understand the ache to find the exact words to glorify what you have experienced, but simply stated, there are no words that will satisfy the recipient of the experience. The existential connection that you feel is inexplicable. But do not despair, because your intentions were felt and the depth of your connection touched me. I will never know exactly what you experienced, but what I gained from hearing about it makes me also feel full. I am blessed because you spoke your truth. Gratitude abounds!" We both fell silent and each in our own way processed what had just transpired. Deb returned to center before I did and quietly asked if she could interrupt my thoughts. I assured her that her thoughts would be welcomed.

"Actually, I need a sounding board, if you are up for that?" Again, I reassured her that I was ready to reengage. "Well, first, let me thank you for your kind words. They have given me pause. They seem to be a message, and I want to be sure that I am interpreting them correctly. I believe, and please correct me if I am wrong, but it seems that our goal is multi-purposeful. First, we must speak our truth, as clearly as we can, and secondly, we must trust that the intention of our truth will reach the listener in a way that is suited for that particular person. The presentation of the truth is more about our sincerity than it is about our descriptive abilities. Does that ring true for you? Am I interpreting this correctly?" She looked to me for clarity, but all I could provide was my own interpretation.

"Deb, I do think your interpretation is accurate, and I would like to tag on another idea that I think complements what you are saying." She was eager to hear my perspective, and urged me to do so. "Well, I believe the reason it is impossible to perfectly describe these exceptional encounters is because each person's experience is uniquely exceptional. Therefore, there is no single description that will completely illuminate the essence of the encounters that take place. However, each story that is shared with another gives the listener of the moment more information to assimilate into the breadth of his or her own experience; thereby, expanding the exceptional experience even more fully. Now, it is my turn to ask you if my interpretation rings true for you?"

"Oh yes, it does, and it validates what we both just experienced. My story expanded your own personal experiences as a receiver of messages, and your interpretation of my interpretation expanded my experience." The conversation reached a point of rest just as we arrived at the point of the peninsula. I encouraged Deb to join me at my favorite bench overlooking the bay. Pointing westward, I whispered the words my Father had said to be so very long ago, "Something great is going to happen!" And so it did! Many photos were taken in between the oohs and ahs. As the sun slipped beneath the horizon, we both sighed.

"Look at all those stars that are coming into view!" Deb's gentle voice was a pleasure to hear. "There is so much more, Soul Sister! And I want to know every secret that lies here and beyond. I sound like a selfish brat, don't I?"

"No, you sound like a seeker; a curious seeker who wants to know all there is to know."

A passage from
The Word
(Chapter One)

"Long ago, before you had any awareness that there was an existence, Existence was expansive and it was populated with countless numbers of existences, all of which shared a similar curiosity about the beginning of their existences. Since existence came into existence there has been confusion about the origins of existence. Some have traveled far for answers; others have not. Some have pursued scholarly endeavors, while others have not. Some have followed ancient traditions to explore their beginnings, while others simply ponder their existence. And to this day, the mysteries of existence still remain elusive. The mystery of old is an intricate element in the development of each new existence that comes into existence."

8

I was surprised upon my return from the seaside to find the house in darkness. This was odd and evidence of my earlier neglectful behavior. So excited was I to join Deb at the nature preserve that I truly forgot my manners. When the house was purchased years before, a decision was made to create a special relationship with the house. So from day one, I began engaging with the house as if it were another important being in my life. And essentially, this is what a house really is. For me, it is the container for my heart and soul. The house knows everything about me, including those not so pleasant things about self that no one else gets to see or know. *Yes, the house holds many secrets and I am very grateful for the tender care that it provides me.* In my effort to have a healthy relationship with the house, I made it a point to speak to her on a daily basis. I praised her, apprised her of my activities, and always asked her permission before having guests. It just seemed the courteous thing to do. After all, this was her living area, and as a resident within her space, I felt obligated to take her best interests into consideration.

"Hello, Dear House of Mine, I'm home!" The silent response was not new to me. Over the years I've grown accustomed to the reality that the house is a being of few words. "I apologize for rushing in and out earlier. That was rude of me, as was the fact that I forgot to leave the lights on for you. My behavior was unacceptable! I'm not exactly sure what has come over me. I seem to be distracted. Oh, by the way, the walk with Deb was lovely...expansive. I think you will enjoy her company. She's very grounded in Mother Nature and she is a seeker! Yes, I think you will find her most intriguing. I would like to extend an invitation to her. Would you be amenable to that?" It was probably my imagination, but I thought there was a slight flicker of the living room light. One never really knows about one's own interpretations of such things, but I chose to believe that it was a positive response to my inquiry. "Oh, thank you, Dear House of Mine. I will invite her over sometime earlier next week." With that said, I wished the house well, and retired to the bedroom. It was definitely time for some solitude and perhaps an engagement with the journal.

A few blocks away, Deb was already located in her bedroom, sitting in her favorite chair with the unopened journal resting on her lap. With eyes closed, she reviewed the day and the evening walk with her new, old friend. *Yes,* she thought, *she is a new, Old Friend. Thank you everyone who was involved in helping our paths cross!* She opened one eye to check if she was alone or not, which was typically a fruitless endeavor; but nevertheless, she couldn't restrain herself.

"Hello!" she addressed her seemingly empty room. "Is anyone here? Well, let me reframe that question. I assume you are here, as you have often reassured me of your ever-present presence, but I wonder if you might desire conversation this evening?"

"Indeed! Conversation would bring us great happiness. We are very pleased that you are happy with the new acquaintance of a very Old Friend. Many adventures have you shared in the past and many more will you have in this life experience."

Curiosity overcame Deb. "Okay, stop right there, please. Before you go any further, tell me more about these past adventures. Elaborate, please! And perhaps, you might wish to materialize for this discussion." As if she were watching a science fiction movie, the presence of a visible individual appeared in the chair across from her. This was not a new experience for Deb to witness, but it was one that always delighted her. And it was an experience that she very much wanted to have.

"Old Friend, it is good to be in your presence once again." His smile altered the energy of the room. Deb immediately slipped into a deeper state of relaxation, but she struggled against it. She had a thousand questions to ask and she didn't want them to be forgotten.

"Shall I answer the most fervent question first?" Her thoughts were speeding so swiftly about the racetrack of her mind that she could barely keep up with them. She wondered how he could possibly identify the one that was most intense for her at the moment. A soft, gentle chuckle came from the direction of her guest. *"You wish to know if and when I am going to teach you how to come and go in the way that I do."*

"Yes!" she replied with great gusto. "Let's do it now! Teach me how to materialize and dematerialize. Let's do it now, please!" Deb's passionate reaction tickled her companion. He took a deep breath knowing that his response had the potential for deepening their relationship. This was his intention, as was agreed upon a very long time ago. She, who is now called Deb, had agreed to return to this plane of existence on a mission of extreme importance, and he had agreed to assist her efforts from his plane of existence. Much depended upon the development of their present relationship. Trust between them was essential if they were to achieve the goals that were recommended so long ago.

"My Old Friend, your enthusiasm for life has not changed throughout

the ages. Always, you are eager to learn and always are you quick to take action. My Friend, hear me with the ears of your heart. That which you seek, you already possess. Trust these words and know that they are information. Presently, you do not need to practice multi-locating. You are here on this plane of existence and this is where your work unfolds. In my present form, multi-locating is a necessity, for I must work in my plane of existence and also on yours. Rest assured, Old Friend, you have enjoyed this means of transportation many times before. You excel at multi-locating, and if a situation arises that requires you to access this form of relocation, rest assured it will transpire instantaneously. I know this is not the answer that you desired to receive; however, it is the truth regarding your fascination with my means of mobility." Deb's disappointment was apparent, but she was not one who dwelled in negative energy. Her mind quickly moved on to other topics.

"No need to worry about me," she declared. "I can manage my disappointment. I'm grateful for the information that you shared, and as you might imagine, it raises many more questions. The idea that we have known each other for many lifetimes is very comforting to me. I have wondered about that and it's gratifying to have it confirmed." Deb paused briefly, as if she were sorting things out in her mind. A deep breath was heard, which seemed to calm her. "Am I correct in assuming that we have played many different roles in these various life experiences, and for reasons that I cannot remember, we continue to pursue more opportunities to be in each other's company?"

"Yes, you have described our situation well. We share similar passions and we do indeed enjoy working together. And a very long time ago, we agreed to work on a project that captured our imaginations; and since that point in time, we have devoted our life experiences to fulfilling the commitments that were made. Our experiences have brought us to this time and place, and once again, we are confronted with the tasks before us. This is also the reason that you and the new Old Friend have crossed paths again." A puzzled, but excited look flashed across Deb's face.

"I see," she mused. "So all three of us know each other and have had numerous experiences together. Right?"

His smile could not be contained, nor did it need to be. In many ways, they were enjoying an unusual reunion. *"Your paths have crossed for a reason, Old Friend. What has transpired in the past is done, but what is coming awaits your attention. Much work remains to be done in the days ahead, and time is of the essence. I come this evening to affirm your intuitive sense regarding the new Old Friend. She is indeed a person with whom you are to develop a lasting relationship. Both are here for a reason and together you are more influential than separately. Pursue this friendship! Already you are witnessing commonalities and similar* preferences. *Much more will be discovered in the days to come, and your connection will become self-evident.*

"*Revel in the beauty of this reunion and express gratitude for the companionship of a Dear Old Friend.*"

The two Old Friends from different planes of existence sat quietly enjoying the moment together. It was a sweet time of remembrance and acknowledgement that there is more in existence than we allow ourselves to believe.

A passage from
The Word
(Chapter One)

"*You, Dear Friend, are similar to all others who entered into existence before you. You ponder the universe about you and you wonder what your place is in this magnificent expansiveness. This wonderment is true for all others. It is so for all the species on your beautiful planet, and it is so for all the other species that fill the vast spaces of the never-ending existence within which all exist.*"

9

"Oh, what a wonderful surprise! It is so good to see you!" My enthusiasm was obvious and equally shared by the couple walking towards me.

"And you!" My neighbors, who live in the house directly across the street from mine, replied in unison. Even though we were very close and fond of one another, we rarely spent time together, which was a disappointment for all of us. "It seems like ages since our paths have crossed on this spectacular trail," Pam noted and we all agreed.

"We need to do something about that," Gary pronounced authoritatively. His eyes were twinkling in the most delightful way, as he boldly stood with arms akimbo. "So, I am going to speak my truth. I want the three of us to get together and I want it to happen SOON. If we don't schedule a date, we all know what will happen."

"You're absolutely right," I replied. "Let's get together this evening. Are you available?" The couple offered to host, but I reminded them that it was my time. "Light meal at six o'clock?" We all agreed and exchanged hugs before parting. As we went our separate ways, I heard the couple declare simultaneously that they were very excited about our date. It made me wonder how often this pattern happened between with them. *Note to self: ask Gary and Pam if they are aware of their telepathic abilities.*

As I was putting the finishing touches to a small veggie tray, the doorbell rang. Rushing towards the front of the house, I could see my neighbors happily waving through the French door. They appeared as excited about our gathering as I was.

"Yay! We're actually doing this!" squealed Pam as we all enjoyed a hug fest. Gary, sporting a lovely arrangement of freshly picked flowers, asked permission to place it on the table.

"Absolutely! And thank you for sharing your garden wonders. As you can see, the table is in need of your able handiwork." Always thoughtful, Gary had prepared a low-lying arrangement that could sit in the center of the table and still allow easy viewing of one's dinner companions.

I invited my friends to join me in the kitchen while the quiche was reaching the perfect temperature. "Shall we just sit here at the breakfast table and enjoy a few snacks while we're waiting." Pam quickly grabbed the tray of goodies and placed it in easy reach for all of us and Gary began pouring the wine, which he had uncorked and allowed to breath for thirty minutes before they advanced to my front porch. "You guys think of everything! Please sit and make yourselves comfortable, and dig into the spinach and artichoke dip." It didn't take long for the yummy sounds to circle the table. Enjoying treats together was definitely one of our favorite pastimes.

"Geez! I really miss you two." I wondered briefly why the three of us had such a difficult time connecting. We just lived across the street from one another. It didn't make sense.

"I think we take each other's presence for granted." Pam's response to my unspoken thoughts was so blatant that I could not let it pass.

"Pam, your intuitive skills are incredible. Are you aware that you just replied to my thoughts?" Before she could respond, Gary acknowledged that her skills were increasing in accuracy and frequency.

"I'm not sure she even knows when she is doing it now," he said gently. "It's become very commonplace in our house."

"It's not just me," responded Pam. "Gary is doing it as much as I am."

"I noticed!" My reaction seemed to surprise Gary, but he was also very excited about my observation. They both were. "So tell me! Are you deliberating trying to develop this ability or is it just happening?"

"The latter," they replied simultaneously.

"We've talked about practicing, but then life happens and we forget. You know how it is." Pam's comment reminded her of the previous comment she had made. "Back to the statement I made earlier," she continued, "about us taking each other for granted, I think we should talk about this."

"Let's do! I'm intrigued by your comment. Tell me more!" The couple glanced at one another, as if they were checking in to see who would address the situation first. I wondered if this was just a typical couple reaction, or if they were actually communicating telepathically. Gary took the lead.

"We've been talking about this off and on for quite some time, but after our surprise connection this morning, we gave it more thought throughout the day and what we came up with is the idea that our close proximity is actually impeding our relationship rather than facilitating it. We find comfort knowing that you are just across the street, and as a result, we feel connected whether we connect or not. And we've decided that we want more. Now that we realize what we are doing, we recognize that we want to enrich this relationship by actually spending time together. So, we hope you may want the same."

"Yes, I do want more, and I'm so grateful that you took the time to sort through this. Like you, I feel a very strong heart connection with both of you, and it simply didn't make sense that we were seeing so little of each other. Well, I'm glad that misunderstanding has been corrected."

Just as the last word was spoken, the oven timer went off.

"Perfect timing!" announced Pam. "How can we help?" Instructions were quickly given and within minutes we, and the food, had relocated to the dining table. Gary was given the privilege of serving the quiche. They were surprised and delighted to see that I had made a stop on the way home from my morning walk at a mutually appreciated bakery and grabbed one our favorite treats.

"I've been craving one of these for weeks!" Pam grabbed her fork and made tapping noises and she impatiently waited for her serving. "Come on Gar, make haste! We have things to talk about." Her wish was soon granted.

As we each stared at our respective plates, the impulse to dive in was hard to resist, but Gary managed. "Shall we begin this wonderful meal with a prayer?" Both Pam and I, slightly embarrassed, put our forks down and gestured that he should take the lead. Our invitation seemed to surprise him. His face blushed a bit, but with a deep breath he was ready to proceed. Reaching out to both of us, he grabbed our hands and we completed the circle. "Blessed Ones, thank you for bringing us together. Our hearts are full as we sit here as One. Thank you, for the chance encounter this morning. Thank you for the clarity we gained today regarding our desire to enhance this relationship. Thank you for having situated us in such close proximity. Thank you for all the similarities that we share, and for the differences that enrich our lives. Thank you for the love we share for our wonderful planet, and thank you for our beautiful Mother Earth. Thank you for all that you do for us, and for all others. And thank you, Dear Ones, for this incredible quiche sitting here before us. Amen!" A sweet moment and a deep breath were enjoyed before all three of us announced, "Let's eat!"

The first bite of quiche was taken and bliss overtook us. We laughed at ourselves and at each other. We were hopelessly lost in our passion for this exceptionally delicious quiche. "I vote we meet every week if for no other reason than to share one of these big beauties. My goodness! This is truly the best quiche in the world!" Gary immediately seconded the idea, and Pam closed the matter with another vote of confirmation.

"Okay," Pam continued. "We have the meals planned for our upcoming gatherings. Now, let's focus on this evening conversation. You," she said pointing her fork in my direction, "need to bring us up to date. What have you been up to lately?" I reacted with fork in hand, pointing it at both of my guests, and declaring that they needed to tell me everything.

"Oh no," interjected Gary. "We went first last time. You're up to bat! So, tell us everything!" Our playfulness was so natural. We simply enjoyed each other's company. It was obvious that we were brought together for a reason, and both households were aware of this.

I pretended to be miffed, but couldn't maintain it. "Okay, okay, let me think about this. What has been going on?" The question gave me pause.

My life seemed full and yet, in the moment, I was at a loss. I sat quietly staring at my plate and then an idea occurred to me. *Speak the truth!* The words were heard with such clarity that I wasn't sure if they were the creation of my mind or the voice of another, but it truly didn't matter. The message was clear! *Speak the truth!"*

Pam reached across the table and gently touched my hand. "Just speak the truth, Friend. We are eager to hear whatever you have to say." Her kindness brought tears to my eyes.

"Pam, before you so lovingly told me to speak the truth, I heard those words from within. Did you hear them as well? I'm just curious; because, so many unusual experiences are unfolding around me lately that I'm trying to understand everything that's going on. And what just happened here at this table falls into the unusual experience category. So, can you share with me what just happened with you?" Pam straightened up in her chair, and closed her eyes. I knew she was taking my request seriously, and I was very grateful.

"I honestly don't know how to answer your question, but I suspect it has to do with us being in sync energetically. I don't have any memory of encouraging you to speak the truth. So, I think that message either came from you or from another who was nudging you to do so. As we both know, sometimes we nudge ourselves forward, and other times, we are actually being assisted by someone else. Regardless of the source, you were definitely urged to speak the truth, and somehow, I intercepted that message, and was led to act on your behalf as well. Is this message one that you have been receiving frequently lately?"

"Yes, it is. My life seems incredibly busy currently with unusual connections, messages, and encounters. So, I was trying to discern what to share when the 'speak the truth' message came through loud and clear." Pam, nodding in agreement, validated my experience. She repeated her belief that we are energetically in alignment.

"Well, I guess the best way to start my update is to say that the experience we've had today is part of a bigger sequence of similar experiences that have been unfolding for what seems like weeks and more. I simply do not believe that we just happened to cross paths this morning and that we were all available to have dinner tonight and that your gracious invitation to speak the truth were coincidences. I don't believe in coincidences!"

"We don't either!" interjected Pam and Gary. The couple exchanged glances again and then Gary continued.

"So, what is it that you are supposed to speak the truth about? Is it just one particular topic or many topics?" Trying to sort through Gary's question made me chuckle.

"I'm sorry, Gary. Your question should be easy to answer, but it isn't. I think the best I can do is say, yes! Yes, it entails a specific topic, and yes, it includes many other topics within the central theme." I took a deep breath and my Friends joined me. It was wonderful to be in their presence. We were so comfortable with one another that it made me wonder about our histories. But that was another topic for another time.

"Let me begin by creating a starting place, which in itself is not easy. But I will begin by saying that my spiritual journey is becoming increasingly more expansive, and recently I have been receiving messages during my meditations that I am recording in my journal as they transpire. I know this isn't a unique experience; people all over the world do this, but it's new for me. It's fascinating, and it's odd, but I'm having so much fun that I do not care that it is odd. I'm not capable of writing what is showing up in my journal, so it is obvious to me that something unusual is happening.

"I believe it is my calling to speak the truth about this so that other folks who are also having similar experiences recognize that they are not alone. Hopefully, if we all start speaking the truth about our experiences, the world might realize that something really important is happening that needs to be acknowledged and explored, hopefully with open minds and hearts."

Although my thoughts were still racing in response to Gary's question, I felt complete for the moment. It seemed to me that my update had taken a great deal of time, and I wanted my Friends to have time to speak about the happenings in their lives.

"Don't worry about us! We can take care of ourselves." Once again, Pam had responded to my unspoken response. I wondered if all humankind was headed in this direction. My intuition led me to believe so. "Excuse me, Dear," interjected Pam, "but my inner ears are really highly in tune with you this evening, and it makes me wonder if this isn't happening for a reason. May we talk about inner communication for a while?" Both Gary and I indicated that we were very interested in pursuing the topic and invited Pam to continue.

"Well, over the years, I've learned to rely upon and trust my own intuitive abilities. This came with maturity. As a young person, I didn't pay much attention to the unusual experiences I was having. My focus was elsewhere; i.e. boys, dating, acne, etc. Now, looking back on some of the things that happened, I am certain that my intuitive skills were already highly functioning, but it wasn't until I became interested in homeopathy that my intuition seemed to blossom to a point that it could not be ignored. My development as a homeopath transformed my acceptance of the reality of intuitive wisdom. Too many incidents transpired over and over again for me to deny that something unusual was happening, and whatever the unusual factor was, was reliable. My confidence in my intuitive abilities crystallized during that period of growth, and I still trust it to this day. And speaking of today, you Dear have witnessed, both this morning and here tonight, the advancements that are happening for both Gary and myself in the field of telepathy. We're participating in telepathic communication on a regular basis, and we aren't even practicing. It's just happening within and between us, and as you can attest our skills are expanding.

"True confession here!" Pam's hand gestures indicated that she was about to reveal a truth. "It's becoming so natural for me at this point that I am not always aware when it's happening. You can attest to that as well. I find it absolutely delightful, and like you, it makes me wonder if humankind is moving in this direction. I think it's our next great evolutionary step. Having said that, I also think that the human species has a lot of growing up to do before we can shift to this type of communication. With this new skill comes responsibility." Pam's comment grabbed my attention. Clearly, she was aware of potential concerns that had not reached my limited consciousness.

"This sounds very fascinating, Pam. Please elaborate, if you will." She paused for a moment and I sensed that Pam was deliberating how much she should say. I reached out across the table and placed my hand on hers.

"Speak the truth, Pam. I'm ready to hear whatever needs to be said." Deep breaths circled the table as our conversation continued to go deeper and deeper.

"Well, Gary and I have some serious concerns about this ability being misused. Let's face it! Just because you can hear or intuit another person's thoughts doesn't mean you have the privilege to invade another person's privacy. We believe one must be exceptionally responsible when accessing this remarkable ability. Hopefully wisdom will come with the refinement of this skill. Another true confession!" The same hand gesture was made as before to alert her listeners that an important statement was forthcoming. "One of the reasons I worry about this is that I see my own transgressions when using my ability. A couple of times tonight, I was showing off. I knew what was going on within you, and I wanted to show off. Truthfully, I was confident that you could handle what was going on, but the fact that I allowed my pride to act out is not appropriate. This is a small example of how telepathy might be misused, but I'm afraid there may be much more destructive opportunities that some might seek to orchestrate."

"Goodness, Pam, I am so naïve. Thank you for that wakeup call. You're right! This topic requires a great deal of consideration. I hope we can continue to discuss this in the future."

"So do we!" exclaimed Gary. "We haven't discussed this with any of our other friends. Perhaps we are being disrespectful, but we don't think they are ready for a conversation about telepathy or unusual experiences. Maybe we need to rethink that assumption. It is possible that our own fears are interfering with our decision-making process." Gary turned to his wife of over thirty years and suggested that they should strategize other options. "I would hate to think that we are shutting folks out of these marvelous conversations because of own fear-based conclusions." His sincerity touched my heart and made me realize the seriousness of their concern.

"This is a very important topic! In my work, I hear many stories from folks who are afraid to share a part of themselves because of fear. They are afraid of being misunderstood or judged or ridiculed, and the list goes on and on. And we, the three of us, did the same here tonight. We all stopped in our tracks when we were revealing a part of ourselves that we thought might be seen in a negative manner. Thank goodness, we supported one another! We must be sure to support others in the future, and we must confront ourselves regarding the influence of our fears. Wouldn't it be a shame if the mission to speak the truth was stifled by fears? Wow! My Friends, you have given me much to think about."

"As have you!" exclaimed Gary. "And this takes me back to our earlier comment about taking our close proximity for granted. These conversations are riveting, at least they are for me, and I think it's true for both of you." He looked for confirmation from Pam and me, and quickly received it via big smiles and nods of reassurance. "Well, I want our relationship to become a priority. I feel so energized and excited about these discussions that the kid in me wants to stay up all night, leaping from one topic to another, but at my age that just isn't possible. Also, I need time to digest all of this information. But I want more!" He stated insistently.

"Me, too!" Pam attempted to mimic her husband's demanding posture, which brought laughter to the table. "As you can see by our childlike antics, we want to spend more time with you and we are hoping that you may want the same. The truth is we are desperate to have another person with whom we can share our thoughts and our concerns."

"Count me in!" My response, which continued the childlike manner, quickly changed to a more serious one. Reaching out to both my neighbors, a circle of hands instantly formed around the table. "I need this! Today has been the most wonderful day because of our reconnection. What a blessing! My day began with your happy faces and now it draws to a close in the safety of your companionship. This is no coincidence! My Friends, I vow to make our relationship a priority!" The three neighbors reveled in the beauty of the moment. Each enjoyed the special intimacy that transpired as a result of their shared vulnerabilities and their mutual interests in topics of a so-called unusual nature.

"Before we bring the evening to an end, I have another question for you, Friend. Are you up for another brief discussion?" I assured Pam that more conversation would be welcomed. "Well, I'm curious. Obviously, you have a lot going on in your life presently that falls into the 'unusual experience' category, and I wonder if you have other folks of similar interests with whom you can talk?"

"Pam, the answer to that is yes and no. I am meeting more folks who seem to have similar interests. At this point, it is fair to say that there seems to be potential for more in-depth conversations with them. And I'm also discovering that some people that I already know are as interested in the topics as I am, but like me, they have been hesitant to bring the subjects to the forefront. So, the point is, I do think there are opportunities for us to expand our conversation group if and when we want to." This news brought another round of excitement to the table, and a tiny bit of apprehension.

"Well," admitted Gary, "I look forward to meeting the others eventually, but for the time being, I selfishly want to dig deeper into the conversations with just the three of us. My fears are clearly acting out, and I promise to monitor that, but I'm also very sincere about wanting the opportunity to explore these heartfelt topics with the two of you." Pam nodded and admitted she was in the same frame of mind as her beloved.

"Yes, I agree. I felt extremely comfortable and safe here this evening, but I'm not ready to venture out just yet. At some point, yes, but not now." Sighs of relief circled the table.

"Yep!" declared Pam. "We definitely have some fear issues sprouting up that we are all going to need to face. That's okay by me. We can handle this. But isn't it interesting," she mused. Her beautiful mind swiftly led her down several pathways of hypotheses. "I find it fascinating how easily and quickly fear is able to squelch our curiosity and excitement. It makes me wonder how many ideas and dreams are lost in an instant flash of fear." Pam's comment made me have similar thoughts. I wondered how many people even have awareness that they have fears, much less know that their fears are influencing their lives. The three of us went silent as our minds traveled in many different directions. Even now while we were lost in thought, our fears were affecting us.

Gary was first to break the silence.

"As you said, Pam, this is fascinating! Our mood has shifted from exhilaration to timidity. Why? Are we really afraid of what people will think about us if we speak openly about our experiences? You know we keep referring to our experiences as unusual, but I'm not sure that they are. We don't really know how many other people are having similar experiences, and we won't know until we start taking some risks. So, I'm revising what I said earlier. I still prefer to have several more gatherings with just the three of us. But then, I suggest that we expand our circle. We need to move out of our comfort zones and explore these topics with other folks. If we don't, we will be limiting ourselves, and I don't want to be limited. And I certainly do not want my fears to be controlling my life.

So, I say we schedule some more meetings with a goal of increasing our numbers within three weeks."

"Wow!" Pam's response and mine sounded like an off-tune duet. "Good for you, Gar!" she added. "I'm really proud of you! Thank you for taking charge and leading the way." Pam's comments touched her husband deeply. His face blushed as he attempted to fully receive her praise. Then Pam responded to his unspoken fear. "Now Gary, don't doubt yourself about taking action. You did the right thing, and I am personally very grateful. I'll be the first one to admit that I can be very comfortable in a low profile zone. But we cannot be satisfied with such a lackadaisical manner. Something important is happening in the world, and I want to be a part of it. So, I appreciate your ambition to move forward and I'm on board." As I witnessed these two lovely people in action, I realized why our paths had crossed early this morning. We needed each other. Each of us brought a special quality to the whole, and together we had more potential than individually. My eyes moistened from the gratitude of the moment. Reaching out to my Friends, our hands again formed a circle.

"Dear Ones, this is happening for a reason. A better script could not be written. Thank you! Thank you! Thank you!" The evening ended with hugs, more expressions of gratitude, and a date for the next gathering. I watched my Friends walk arm-in-arm across the street to their home. We waved good night from our front porches.

... *10* ...

"**G**oodnight, Dear House of Mine. I hope you enjoyed the conversations this evening. It was a very remarkable event. We are very fortunate to have such good neighbors and friends. I think it is fair to say that we will be seeing more of them in the future. Thank you for being so welcoming. You are a lovely setting for intimate conversations. I am blessed to live within your walls, Dear House of Mine. Rest well, Old Friend." I waited for a moment just in case a reply would be forthcoming, but as always, the house kept her thoughts to herself. After this evening's conversation, I wondered if the house was actually communicating with me without my awareness. As I turned off the living room light, I chuckled at myself. *If the house ever replies to me, I will probably faint. Oh well! That too would be a new experience.* I shuffled down the hallway marveling at my imagination. *Dear Mind of Mine, you are a wonder!*

It was way to early to retire so I headed towards my favorite chair in the house. The conversation with Pam and Gary had been so rich that I felt the need to write about it. Leaning back into the chair, I briefly closed my eyes. My mind continued to whirl about rushing from one curious experience to another. *Whoever is orchestrating this is certainly doing a remarkable job!* Concerned that I might fall asleep, I opened my eyes and straightened my posture. My thoughts continued to wander to the notion that my life truly seemed to be unfolding as if some thing or some one was orchestrating events that led me in a direction that was intended. *Can this really be happening?*

Grabbing my journal, I turned to the first blank page. The date and time were carefully entered at the top of the page. For some reason yet to be known, it seemed imperative that this habit be maintained. My entry began with a question. 'Why is this happening?' was printed in large capital letters, and then my hand went limp as my mind went silent. It was an odd sense of confusion, anticipation, and acceptance all wrapped into one. I had no idea what was going to happen, but I assumed it would be something positive, and I was willing to wait for the event to unfold. And then it happened.

My right hand resumed its writing position, poised and ready for action. The event began. Words began to be heard as clearly as if someone was sitting before me, and at the same time, the words streamed through my hand and were penned upon the page. As odd as this sounds, the action was seamless and effortless. The entry that follows is the message that was received and recorded:

Beloved Child of the Light, please be at peace. What you experience now is what you are called to do. Be not afraid, for the communication that you now participate in is one that many others have experienced throughout millennia. Although this experience seems unusual to you at this time, rest assured that you will soon be as comfortable with this form of communication as you are with your present means of connecting. What you experience is ordinary for those with whom you will be working, and soon, it will feel ordinary for you as well.

We come forward now at this point in time, because we must. The time is now! For ages, messages have been delivered to the Children of Earth apprising you of a most unpleasant situation that was developing upon your beautiful planet. Unfortunately, our efforts have not been successful. You, Old Friend, are one of many who is being contacted to assist us in our efforts to help the peoples of Earth. Please hear this truth. You are needed! With your assistance, the messages of truth can be spread across all nations so that the cooperation of all the people of Earth will be attained. Rest assured, you are not alone, Old Friend. Others, much like yourself, are also being solicited to participate in similar ways. The messages of truth must reach the masses. Time is of the essence. Old Friend, in days ahead, much will be asked of you. We will require your attention, your assistance, and your patience. We will strive to communicate with you on a daily basis so that your skills advance quickly. Already, you make progress, and with practice, you will reach maximum performance very rapidly. We are so very grateful for your assistance, Old Friend. We recognize that your daily routine will be interrupted with these extra duties, but we will help you to adjust and manage the new regimen.

You will find the work most invigorating, and you also will receive information that will be difficult to hear. The challenge will be to sustain a sense of balance so that you maintain your wellness. We will monitor your health and see that you are provided with everything that you need during this process. At times, your days may seem lonely, but you will never be alone. Always you will be accompanied by those who are here to assist you with this vitally important project. As relationships develop between you and your Companions, the sense of loneliness will fade away.

Old Friend, your work will be consuming at times. Unfortunately, the circumstances demand your attention. We apologize for the inconvenience, but it is necessary. As you listen to the words flowing through you and see them form upon the page, you must realize that what is happening is indeed happening for a reason. As one with a psychological background, your instinct to question this experience is understood, and yet, you must trust what is happening. Deep within you is a memory of the process that you are now experiencing and awareness that this method of communication is not one that is new to you. You have had many lifetimes, Dear Friend, that required you to be a listener and a receiver of existential communiqués. This is who you are. Simply stated, you are a messenger. Your gifts are finely tuned and await the moment that they will regain full vibrancy. That process is in motion as we speak.

As you bring messages of truth forward for the people of Earth to read, you will also find yourself in situations, such as your gathering this evening, where you feel compelled to speak the truth. Initially, you will feel cautious about doing so. Fear will stir within you, and your mind will strive to convince you that silence is a better path. Have compassion for that fear. No need is there to scold the fear, but do not abide by its guidance. When these moments of doubt disrupt your intentions, take a deep breath, let the moment subside, and remember who you are. You are a messenger who is intended to bring the truth forward. As you read the previous statement, you may have felt another wave of doubt move through your body. If that was the case simply sit still, enjoy another deep breath, and accept the truth that is now delivered to you.

As a messenger of truth, you are here to present the messages as gently and lovingly as you possibly can. That is the goal of your mission. You are not here to convince others of the truth. You are here to provide the information so that the reader or the listener can have his or her own experience with the message. Old Friend, please remember this message for the future. It is essential for a messenger to thoroughly understand her or his purpose. Many more discussions will we have regarding this topic, but for now, please accept that your first task is to bring the messages forward.

My Friend, the hour grows late and the day has been long. I am most grateful for your presence, Old Friend. It is a pleasure to be in your company once again. Rest well, Dear Friend. In peace be.

"Thank you! I'm not sure if you are still here, but thank you." My heart was full, and my mind was racing about in many directions. "Mind, be still! We are not going to explore every question that you are creatively manifesting. Look at this journal entry, for goodness sake. Isn't this enough to ponder about? I am satisfied with what just happened. I am grateful for what just happened and I intend to hold this experience in my heart for as long as I can. So, please quiet yourself, Old Mind of Mine. It's time to go to bed."

... *11* ...

"**G**ood morning, Master Sun! I am so grateful to be in your presence!" Sitting on the rocks overlooking the bay, I waited patiently for the great aha moment. I had awaken earlier than usual this morning and felt totally refreshed, so I jumped out of bed to race with the sun. It was such a treat to reach my favorite viewing spot while the hour was still very young. With the help of my tiny, but powerful flashlight, I was able to find the preferred boulder to park myself. Similar to the preferred chair in my home, this boulder perfectly suited my body. I took my usual position. Leaning forward with elbows on my knees, waiting in anticipation, I simply enjoyed the moment. The world seemed very peaceful. The seaside noises were minimal; only a few geese were discussing their plans for the day. And the fishermen, who usually arrived before me, were not yet on the scene, so for a brief moment in time, I had the illusion of having the sanctuary to myself.

"Wow! What an amazing gift!" My words were barely a whisper. It seemed rude to disturb the silence. For me, this moment felt like a magical experience. I reveled in my breath, the silence, the faint sea breezes, and the notion that I was alone. It was one of those times when time seems to stand still. Although I was not aware of time passing, I was grateful for every second that was provided. I sat for what seemed an eternity, and still the sun was not near ready to peek over the horizon. I basked in the blessing of time standing still.

"It is an exquisite view, is it not?" The question took me by surprise. I had not heard anyone advance in my direction. I turned around to respond to the greeting, but no one was there. Then I looked in another direction and still no one was to be seen. I appeared to be alone, which was exactly what I was delighting in just seconds before the voice came onto the scene.

Curiosity rose within me. My mind raced in many different directions, attempting to determine what had happened. Was it my imagination? Was it an encounter? And then, an image from the night before flashed through my mind. The reminder to take a deep breath and speak the truth guided me. The deep breath was easy. Although I didn't feel as if I had a truth to speak, the decision to speak honestly was instinctively made. "Hello! The answer to your question is yes. It is an exquisite view. We are most fortunate to share this moment together. Would you like to join me?" The words flowing from my mouth surprised me. I quickly glanced up and down the coastline and was grateful to see that no one else was around.

71

It was worrisome to think that someone might be alarmed if they saw me speaking to no one.

"You need not worry," came a reply. *"For the moment we are blessed with privacy. And yes, I would be most grateful to be in your company. May I join you on your preferred ancient stone?"* My body instantly scooted over to make room for my invisible visitor. I patted the empty space, as I would do for anyone, and invited the unknown guest to make herself comfortable. A peaceful sigh was heard nearby.

"It is breathtaking, isn't it?"

"Indeed, a lovely setting and a lovely time of day. You choose wisely, my Friend. It is so delightful to be in your presence once again. It has been a very long time since we have been together in this way." I turned to face the visitor, which is difficult when one does not really know where to look at someone who is not visible.

"Thank you for your kind words. You speak as if we are Old Friends and I wish to honor you as such, but my inability to see you makes it difficult for me to recognize you. I take it that we have known each other in other lifetimes."

"Yes, many lifetimes, many different places, many different adventures. Are you well, my Friend?" I assured her that I was and asked the same of her; she too expressed that she was in good health. *"Would you be more comfortable if I took on my current form so that you could experience a visual encounter with me?"* She explained that great energy was required to facilitate such an appearance, but she believed it would be advantageous for both of us. My excitement overpowered good manners. With childlike exuberance, I encouraged her to do so, before a more mature response came forward.

"Oh, excuse my selfishness. Please do not expend your energy; it is not necessary. I know that you are here, and even though I would love to be able to see you, I trust what is transpiring between us. Please do what is best for you." The friend whom I cannot recall was a remarkably gentle soul. In her kind, peaceful way she shared her truth with me.

"As much as you wish to see me, I wish to be seen by you. And as much as you wish to see my visible form, I wish to see your form through the eyes of my visible form. I am with you often. I am only a breath away, but when I am in my invisible form, my perspective of your form is not as clear as when I see through my visible form. We most certainly will both benefit from this experience. With your permission, I will come forward." And this she did. My heart filled with joy.

"I am honored to be in your presence."

"As am I to be in yours."

"You must be here for a reason. How may I be of service?" The interaction that transpired was as natural as any between two Old Friends. Mutual respect. Mutual tenderness and care. And mutual purpose.

"Old Friend, the time is now! Although you heard these words last night, I come to confirm the urgency of our mission, and to remind you of commitments made long ago. Old Friend, the efforts made in the past have not altered the tragedy that is unfolding upon the planet Earth. Our messages have not been heeded and the Earth's declining health is rapidly nearing a point of no return. Although recent developments have shown the resilient nature of this Life Being, the brief reprieve that she experienced is not enough for her to regain her strength. It is promising that more people are taking her warning signs seriously; however, a few changes will not stop the catastrophe that is unfolding. The Earth requires immediate health care, which demands immediate changes in human behavior. As has been witnessed in this most recent crisis, the human race is not inclined to assist one another even when a global health incident demands cooperation from all citizens of the planet. This disgraceful display of negligence and disrespect for their fellow human beings demonstrates the radical lack of conscience that must be addressed. The Earth is in need. And what she needs most is love, respect, and tender care from those whom she has provided a space to live, grow, and evolve since they came into existence. She has provided a home to countless species that mutually coexist together collectively working for the good of the entire planet. These species are acutely aware of the crisis that is underway and they are working on her behalf, but they cannot save her without the cooperation of the human species.

"Old Friend, time is running out. I apologize for speaking so bluntly with you, but the truth must be told. If the Earth's health continues to decline, protective measures will become necessary. Because of her love for all of her inhabitants, she is desperately trying to avoid such actions, but her strength is waning. She will not be able to continue this battle for much longer. The thought that this beautiful Life Being might lose her vibrancy for centuries is incomprehensible. This is not intended to happen, and it does not have to end in this way.

"The peoples of Earth have the ability to reverse this situation and they must take action now. The actions of sustainability and responsible care for another Life Being are indeed necessary, but these actions alone will not be enough to alter the present course of her demise. The human race must face their reckless, selfish ways and they must change. No Life Being has the right to presume dominance over another. No Life Being is better than another. The misunderstandings that misguide the human species can no longer be the guide for their behavior. What we speak of does not apply only to a few of the human species. All who are members of the human race must face their negative behaviors, their ill will, and

their aggressive nature. And they must change! For this to transpire, it requires the cooperation of the entire species. There is not time for debates about this reality. There is no time for blaming and shaming others. There is no time for nations to point fingers at other nations. There is no time for more human antics. The time for action is now. Above all other matters, saving the Earth is the priority of this moment. Each person must accept responsibility for his or her own behavior. They cannot wait for governments to take the lead. Each person must honestly assess their behaviors and they must make appropriate changes that will eliminate ill will from within and foster good will towards all others.

"The task before us is not easy, but the human species is capable of making these changes. For too long have they been living a delusional reality that fostered foolish ideas of grandiosity. Greed and selfishness have been their guides. This is not who the people of Earth are intended to be. They are so much more than recent history indicates. The human species is capable of change and they are capable of healing the Earth so that her recovery period is lessened.

"Within every species resides the ability to heal self and others. This is a truth about existence that the human species has forgotten. A few humans still remember this truth, but because of her enormous size, it will take the masses to heal her. She will naturally regain her strength when the ill will perpetrated by humans on a daily basis diminishes. The toxicity that accompanies ill will is draining her energy and soon she will not be able to sustain her inhabitants. Eliminate ill will from seven plus billion humans and the Earth's situation will rapidly improve. Her progress will be even more rapid when the peoples of Earth actually start treating her with love, kindness, tenderness, and respect. As the human species begins to generate positive energy, the Earth's vitality will return at an unbelievable rate.

"The recovery of the Earth is possible, and the human race is the factor of relevance. If they choose to participate and cooperate collaboratively, the Earth will survive. If they choose to continue as they now operate, she will have no choice but to seek refuge through an extended period of dormancy." Deep sighs were heard from the two Old Friends sitting side by side on the ancient stones of Mother Earth. Silence persisted for what seemed an eternity, but in truth was only a moment in time. Then a question was whispered.

"Do you believe the people of Earth will come to her aid?"

"Yes! I do!"

"But how can you state that with such certainty. Your own words speak of the irresponsible nature of the human species. What makes you think that they will take appropriate action now?"

"The Children of Earth are a remarkable species. They have lost their way, but they are not lost to those who have loved and cherished them since

they came into existence. They are more than they presently appear to be, and with assistance, they will find their true selves once again. I believe they will regain their humanity, because I have faith in them. Those who are their forebears will never lose faith in the Children of Earth.

"We are here to assist, and we need your assistance to facilitate our rescue of the Children. Please remember they are but Children, and Children need to be treated with tender loving-kindness. Indeed, much work lies ahead, but with commitment and perseverance, our goals are attainable. Old Friend, I am so grateful for this time together." She pointed to the horizon. *"Look! "Something great is about to happen!"*

"Oh, my goodness! Master Sun never fails us. How can one not believe when you bear witness to this incredible event?"

"Yes, the beauty of existence is breathtaking. How can one not believe in all the wondrous possibilities that are available in existence? My Dear Friend, I must bid you adieu. Please know that you are never alone, and remember, I am but a breath away. In peace be."

The Friend of Old faded away before my eyes. It was a sight to behold. I sat quietly trying to assimilate everything that was just experienced. It was a lot to take in. I wondered how and when my world had become so odd, and so wonderful at the same time. "Can this really be happening?" My question, offered to the universe, was interrupted by a familiar voice.

"Hey there! Is that you?" I turned around and saw Deb waving from the trail. "May I join you?"

"Yes, please do!" Hand gestures welcomed her to come sit beside me. "This is a delightful surprise. Did you catch a glimpse of the sunrise as you were walking along the trail?"

"Yes, I did! In fact I was viewing the glorious moment from the bend down the way, when I noticed you and your friend sitting out here on the rocks. The sunrise was spectacular, wasn't it?" I heard her question, but my mind had fixated on her comment about seeing my friend and me sitting on the rocks. She had witnessed the event. A wave of relief washed through me. The experience was real! It wasn't just my imagination.

"Friend, are you okay? Your face just turned white." Again, I heard her question, and this time, the concern in her voice brought me back to center. I placed my hand on her knee in a lame effort to quiet her concern, and found that the physical contact centered me even more fully. I was able to take a deep breath and regain my sense of presence once again.

"Oh, excuse me, Deb. It seems that I went away for a moment, but I'm back now, and so happy to see you. What a wonderful coincidence this is!" The minute I voiced the ridiculous statement, we both began to laugh.

"Not likely!" she replied. "Seems to me you've already lived a lifetime this morning. Are you in need of a listening ear?" Although this was a perfect opportunity for a deep breath, I sat there rigidly not knowing how to reply. My thoughts left the starting block and raced about the pathways of my mind. This technique that my mind developed years before was a skillset that rarely resulted in any assistance. I eventually closed my eyes and took the deep breath that should have been taken before.

"I truly do not know what to do." My truth was spoken, but it did not resolve the questions of the moment. "Do I want to talk? I think so. Should I? I'm not certain. Do I need to? Probably." Turning to Deb, I continued. "As you can see, I am confused. I just had the most remarkable encounter, and it's left me somewhat bewildered."

"Does this have to do with the Companion that was sitting with you earlier?" I nodded that it did. "What a privilege it must have been to be in her presence. She is a remarkable Old Soul. Have you encountered her before?" Needless to say, her comments captured my attention.

"No, this was a new experience for me, but it sounds as if you are familiar with this type of event. Is my assumption correct?" Deb smiled and gently shook her finger in my direction.

"Your intuition is correct, and I will gladly share my experiences with you at another time. But you just had a remarkable event; and if and when you are ready to discuss it, I would love to bear witness to the occasion." Deb's gracious invitation was irresistible. I did want to share the experience. I wanted validation, and the fact that she had seen the Companion sitting by my side was a gift from heaven.

"You know when individuals have an unusual experience as you just had, they typically need to talk about it. Of course, you already know this, but the question is: will you allow yourself to seek comfort from another person in human form? Our professions teach us how to assist others, but sometimes we forget to take care of ourselves." Her assessment of the situation was indeed accurate and I wondered why I was hesitating. Then I realized that my reticence was what needed to be discussed.

"Ah, I think an idea is brewing in the cavernous pit of my mind. Let me see if it will come to the surface." I paused briefly as the machinations of my thoughts seemed to crystallize. "This is rather interesting and it gives me insights regarding some of the folks with whom I work. First, let me say that I am so grateful that you witnessed the experience. Validation is a blessing! And I know it was intended. No one will ever convince me that your arrival on the scene was a coincidence. What confuses me now is my hesitancy to discuss what has happened. Obviously, this was a huge unusual event, and I am someone who loves unusual events, so my hesitation surprises me. But I think clarity is evolving. As you know, this was a very special experience. It was a privilege, as you said, and I do not take that lightly. So part of me wants to savor the moment and to protect the intimate nature of the encounter. Please forgive me, but I am struggling for words. Perhaps, it is accurate to say that I want to honor the privacy of that moment. I want to remember it exactly as it occurred. I do not want to have even a word of the interaction changed." A bit of frustration entered as I attempted to find the perfect words to describe my feelings regarding the incident.

"I'm so sorry, Deb, but I seem incapable of speaking clearly about this." She quickly interrupted my negative self-assessment and offered reassurance.

"No, please don't discount your description of your feelings. I will never know exactly what you experienced, but I feel the heartfelt connection that was shared and I understand why you do not ever want to lose the memory of that remarkable moment in time. Please just take a deep breath and trust that what happened was real and that you will remember what was intended. These blessings transpire for a reason. We both know that, and I am so grateful that I was guided to be in the right place at the right time this morning. Please hear me. I saw you sitting on this ancient stone in conversation with a very Old Friend, who loves and cherishes you. While I do not know what transpired in your conversation, I do know that you have been called to service. If there is any way that I may be of assistance to you in the days ahead, please let me know." The sincerity of Deb's offer made me weep...for her kindness, for her witnessing the event, and for the event itself. She wrapped her arm in mine, as the tears flowed through me. My heart was full.

Time passed as I collected myself, and all the while, Deb sat patiently with me. Eventually, a deep breath instinctively happened and she responded with one of her own. "You're a champion! Thank you so much for being here."

She sported a raised eyebrow and replied, "Champion? I don't think so. You're the one that's been doing all the hard work. I just had the privilege of holding the space for you. It was a pleasure."

"And it is much appreciated!" We sat quietly for a bit longer before we both became antsy. "I think we both need to get to the office, don't you?" A quick glance at the time caused us both to jump up from the favorite rock, which would soon come to be called the Sacred Stone. We rushed back to the parking area, exchanged hugs, and off we drove to our respective homes.

... *12* ...

"**S**hall we gather for a moment, Dear Friends? I wish to report that connection was made this morning, and it was successful. As always, the Old Friend is ready to serve. Her willingness to be of assistance is as fervent now as in the past. She is a most gracious messenger. Am I correct in assuming that her training is progressing rapidly?"

"You are indeed! She has moved into the second phase of recall and she is adapting easily. The ancient memory is strong within her. Couple this with her openness to what she refers to as 'unusual experiences' and she is enabled to accept new experiences readily. As you say, she is a very gracious messenger and is able to encourage others with their personal journeys. Her present vocation is advantageous for advancing our messages outwardly. People who come to her for assistance feel safe sharing their stories in her presence. Her confirmation of their experiences enables them to move forward more rapidly. She is a gift, and a pleasure to serve."

"And what of the colleague? May I assume that she too is advancing as desired? And how is the relationship progressing?"

"Once again, you assume correctly, Old Friend. The relationship is progressing as intended and both parties are mystified by their similarities. Indeed, their personal skills are beautifully complementary. They will be an influential force capable of inspiring the masses. As will the neighbors who are also conveniently located. Their enthusiasm and openheartedness will create a means for strong connections."

"Yes, we now have a Circle of Four that will expand quickly. My Friends, your assistance is most appreciated. As we all know, the time is now; therefore, we must push forward. Please continue! I am so grateful to be in your presence. Your contributions are indispensible. In peace be!"

... 13 ...

My first client was running late, which was very unusual for her, and a relief for me. I needed a moment to gather myself. My thoughts took me to an inner conversation. *Dear Mind of Mine, please stop whirling about! We've enjoyed a remarkable morning, and we will have time later to process everything, but for now, please be quiet.* I took a deep breath, and the mind politely did as was asked. We sat comfortably in the preferred office chair and remained silent for what seemed like a very long time, which was eventually interrupted by the arrival of my client. *Another gift of time! Thank you so much for the moment of respite!*

"Therese! So good to see you!" We exchanged hugs as she profusely apologized for being late. I reassured her that it was not a problem, without elaborating upon the timing of her tardiness. Never once in all the years that we had worked together had she ever been late for a session. I doubted it was a coincidence.

"Not to worry, Dear. You are here now, and I can hardly wait to hear what's going on in your life since the last time we met. You've been traveling, if memory serves me."

"Yes, I have! And we definitely need to talk. I need your help in processing the interesting events that were experienced. As you know, I love all of these unusual incidents that seem to follow me around, so don't worry about me. I'm having a hoot of a time. But I want and need to hear your perspective. I have an inkling of what is going on, but I suspect you will have a more expansive understanding of what has happened. And don't roll your eyes at me!" Therese was an absolute delight to be with. Her curiosity was unlimited, as was her energy. She wanted to know everything about everything, and she was willing to travel anywhere to find answers to her never-ending list of questions.

"Well, you know how much I enjoy hearing about your adventures, so please take the lead. Tell me everything! I'm ready!" She took the necessary deep breath that all my clients tend to do, and she was off and running. I sometimes felt as if I should have a seat belt installed into my chair just for Therese's adventures. She was a marvel.

"Okay, fasten your seatbelt!" she announced with great vigor. As you might imagine, Therese's statement seized my attention, but I refrained from making a comment. "So," she continued, "my first adventure was a four day silent retreat that took place a few hours north of here in a heavily wooded area in the mountains. The setting was beautiful beyond words and the participants were…well, they were silent, so that's about all I can say about them. We arrived in silence and we departed in silence, so basically there was no communication other than the written material that was received when we registered.

"We were informed, via written instructions, which small sparsely furnished cabin we were assigned to and we were given a bag of groceries suitable for a four-day stay. We were also informed that several spiritual advisors, whose names and photos were provided, would be available to any one who was in need of consultation. Oh yes, and a map of the property with its various walking trails was also provided. So, what I'm telling you is this was a very solitary experience. Other than the check-in person, I never had contact with any of the other retreatants.

"So, with groceries in hand, I headed for my cabin and was quite surprised to see how refreshing it was to have the small space all to myself. It was indeed small, but had everything that was needed for a few days of silence. It reminded me of the wee houses that are becoming increasingly more popular. Once my groceries were properly stored and personal items were put away, I curled up in the comfy chair that was situated in front of a very large, over-sized window. The window feature was brilliant. It made the space seem much larger than it really was, and it provided a beautiful view that included a close-up encounter with a highly frequented birdfeeder. Within minutes, I was completely relaxed. My thoughts attempted to take me to many places, but the birds zooming in and out successfully kept me focused on their joyous escapades.

"At one point, I wondered if my presence was an intrusion upon their privacy. They are such lovely creatures, and we humans just take it for granted that we have the privilege of spying on them. The thought that my behavior might be disrupting their routines really bothered me. And what bothered me even more was the fact that it had never occurred to me before to question my behavior. Although this may not sound like a big deal, it was life changing for me, and you will understand why, as I continue with the story.

"My concern continued to grow, so I decided it was time to do some self-exploration with the assistance of my trusty journal, which had been carefully placed on the small table that was intended to double as a desk. Again, the efficiency of this tiny space became evident. As I got up to retrieve the journal, the birds frantically escaped in different directions. My action, albeit unintentionally, caused these beautiful feathered creatures to panic. This was an awakening for me. We humans are so clueless about the impact we have on other species. Let me rephrase that statement. I am so clueless about the impact I have on other species. And let me be totally truthful here, I am also clueless about the impact I have on other members of my own species. I walk through the world oblivious to what is going on around me. Anyway to conclude this part of the story, I did grab the journal and return to the same chair, because I wanted to see the full impact of my presence. Not one bird returned to the feeder for sixteen minutes. Finally, a large blue jay took a chance, but even this audacious character was cautious. He swooped by the feeder several times before actually landing, and even then, he was vigilantly on guard. Once again, I witnessed the effect of my presence upon these lovely beings. This experience gave me great pause, and it continues to weigh heavily upon me to this day. Although this event may not seem like a big deal, it was! And the fact that most people would not typically regard this as an extremely important experience is evidence of how significant it really was.

"So," she said with a sigh of relief, "that was the first hour of my retreat. Needless to say, many pages of my journal were consumed by that experience. It left me wondering what might happen next."

"Goodness, what a way to start your retreat. How blessed you were! I share your perspective about this incident; it was a life-changing event. And your precise description of the birds' frantic response to your movement helped me to understand the breadth your experience. It truly does awaken one to the reality that our mere presence has consequences. We are so oblivious. Your experience was indeed significant, Therese. This is the type of event that I refer to as a teaching opportunity. Because you shared this story with me, my awareness has expanded. Thank you so much! And please share this story with others. It's important." Therese nodded and shared her appreciation for my feedback.

"One of the reasons I am so grateful that we met is because you have taught me how important it is to share our stories. I didn't understand your insistence about that when we first started working together, but I do now. And I know this recent chain of events needs a bigger audience."

"Therese, tell me more. What happened next?" She elaborated upon the rest of her first day at the retreat center, and emphasized how upset she had been by the incident with the birds. While the time spent with her journal was important, it didn't quiet the guilt and shame that she felt. She attempted to distract herself from that mindset by doing a few word games, which normally worked for her, but unfortunately, that tactic wasn't altering her present situation. She admitted that her mood was bothersome and she was concerned that her retreat experience was going to be a bust. So, after a brief mid-day snack, she concluded that a walk was necessary.

"You know how I am," she declared. "Walking helps me to process things, and I really was having a very difficult time accepting my lack of regard for other Life Beings. Just getting out of the cabin became an issue for me, because I didn't want to disturb the birds again. I literally sneaked out and skirted the feeder as quietly as I possibly could." Therese's description helped me to understand just how affected she was by this experience. She indicated that the trail was easily found, which was a relief, because she didn't want to cause any more disruption to the inhabitants of this forest. "Once I got away from the cabin, I finally started to breathe freely again. It was shocking to see how wound up I really was." She indicated that she had never felt that out of sorts before and she didn't know what to do other than to keep walking.

"The trail finally grabbed my attention and I became enamored with the diversity of the terrain. At one point, a small opening in the trail provided me with an unexpected view. While lost in my mind fog, the trail had led me upward to an altitude that truly surprised me. It overlooked a large heavily wooded gorge that had a robust creek running through it. The view was breathtaking, and the roar of the creek was so loud that it could not be missed. And yet, on my trek up the trail, I had been oblivious to it. Once again, I was confronted with the fact that I was not consciously present to my surroundings. Fortunately, this particular recognition did not come with a litany of self-criticism. I was able to have compassion for my situation. When the walk began, I clearly was still distracted by the earlier event, demonstrated by my walk up the mountain without conscious awareness. Isn't it fascinating that the body can continue to function adeptly even when the mind is actively engaged elsewhere?" Therese shook her head in disbelief and then continued with her story.

"So from that point on, I deliberately attempted to focus my attention upon being present. I tried to notice everything! What I learned from this experience was how difficult it is for me to be present. And, I also learned how much I do not observe. Oh my goodness!" She declared. "It is shocking how much I've been missing! I'm really taken aback by this, because I am someone who tends to be very aware of my surroundings…or so I thought. That assumption about myself is totally delusional." Therese gently laughed at herself. She wasn't harsh or disrespectful; she simply was acknowledging how humbling her self-discoveries were.

"What these two experiences helped me to understand is that we all need to take a good look at ourselves and honestly assess how we are functioning in the world. My personal impression of my relationship with the Earth and her inhabitants needed a wake-up call. Not only was I unaware of my impact on others around me, but also, I was astounded by how blind I am to my surroundings. This truly was a surprising experience. I've always considered myself to be such an avid nature lover, and in many respects I am; however, I now realize how limited my involvement with nature really is. Thinking that you are a lover of Mother Nature isn't good enough. With that title comes responsibility! It requires commitment, activism, perseverance, loving-kindness, respectfulness, and dedication to the world around us. And at a base level, that means getting to know the

Earth and her inhabitants, really getting to know them, not just pretending to yourself that you know them. It means being consciously aware of other species and developing relationships with them, so that you actually know what their needs and preferences are. It means learning about and being aware of how to mutually coexist with these other beings that also live on this beautiful planet.

"Needless to say, I was inspired by these experiences. The new awareness that seemed to flow through me stimulated optimism and replaced the guilt that was earlier experienced. My heart was filled with gratitude and I was hopeful: hopeful that I could make a difference, and hopeful that I could establish relationships with these other life beings.

"I returned to my small cabin determined to start anew. On the trek back, I managed to maintain a consistent level of conscious presence, which truly pleased me. I knew there would be ebbs and flows to developing this skillset, but I was adamant about achieving my goal. When I reached the clearing around the cabin, I paused, took a deep breath, and offered an unspoken, special prayer to the beautiful beings that I had disturbed earlier.

"My Dear Friends, I am so sorry that I interrupted your morning. I meant no harm. I promise you that my manners will be more considerate of your needs in the next few days that I will be here. Please know that I will not approach your eating area, except to refill the feeder, and I will inform you when that is about to happen. You may see me moving about in the cabin, but rest assured, I will not approach you. Thank you for being here and thank you for being such good neighbors. I am most grateful to be in your forest.

"And with that said, I carefully and quietly skirted the area and reentered the cabin. From that moment on, the birds did not seem to be bothered by my presence. I actually think they heard my appeal and accepted my sincerity. Do you think that is possible? Do you think these birds could understand my intentions?"

"Yes, I do." My response was stated calmly, respectfully, "Actually, I think we humans are the ones who are lacking in communication skills. I believe our Friends of many sizes, shapes, and colors have much to teach us, if we will only open our hearts to the possibility that they are more advanced than we are." Therese ended her session with a quick overview of the remaining time spent at the retreat center.

"The entire retreat was a lesson about relationships: relationships with self, with the Earth, and with all the wonderful life beings with whom we coexist. It was a time of awakening. I now have a better understanding of the concept of Oneness. We truly are all intricately linked with each other, and every action we take effects those around us. The truth is, we cannot really appreciate this if we are not actively, consciously engaged in this reality. What I learned in those four brief days was how oblivious I am to life around me. I have been so absorbed in my own life that my awareness of other Life Beings escaped me. It's shocking to recognize this truth, but now that I have, I actually can change my ways. Until we realize this truth about the world, we do not know there is a profound need for change." Therese released a loud sigh. "How could I be so oblivious for so long? There is so much more to learn about this great existence of which we are such a tiny part. I am so excited about learning more…about everything!" Her eyes were sparkling. She was a ball of energy sparked by hopefulness and curiosity.

... *14* ...

"**G**ary, what are your plans for the day?" The neighbors, situated across the street from the narrator of this story, typically begin their mornings in silence. Each enjoyed rising early and then spending time in their respective Sacred Spaces. It was a tradition of long standing and one that was mutually cherished and respected. There, in the quiet, they each accepted responsibility for exploring their personal inward journeys. The time dedicated to this spiritual ritual varied from day to day and eventually concluded with the couple gathering in their small kitchen nook for a light breakfast and conversation. This was their favorite setting in the house, with the exception of their Sacred Spaces. Here in this small nook, they could enjoy the view of their backyard, which was a sanctuary for the neighborhood birds and small four-legged creatures. It brought them great happiness to share the property with their outdoor friends. The setting was so lovely that Pam and Gary had to be careful. Frequently, they would get lost in their observations of the backyard activities and lose track of the time, which could be most inconvenient.

Of course, the kitchen nook was more than just a wildlife entertainment center. It was also a place where grand ideas came into being and wonderful adventures were planned. It was a place of connection, strategizing, and birthing. And today, Pam had a plan forming within that remarkable mind of hers. Gary, whose mind was equally sharp and creative, knew that his beloved's question indicated more than just casual curiosity.

"Well, Dear, I haven't really made a plan yet, but I sense you may have an idea in the making." The twinkle in Pam's eyes revealed that she was indeed up to something. Gary encouraged her with his favorite phrase. "Spill the beans, Girl!" Pam rubbed her hands together in a fashion with which her husband was very familiar. This action meant that she was having an exceptionally brilliant idea. She opened the discussion with another sure-fire indicator that something big was brewing.

"Gary, I've been thinking a lot about something and I wish to discuss it with you." For those of you who have not met Pam personally, let me expound upon the meaning of this statement. As her husband well knows, this means that a plan has already been conceived and is ready for implementation. He responded perfectly by sitting as erectly as he possibly could and looking on with ardent curiosity.

"I believe we must take action," she began calmly. "We can no longer remain silent about the communications we are receiving from our backyard friends. For years we have known that the Earth's vibrancy was diminishing. My homeopathic work was the first indicator for me. The intuitive messages I received from various specimens were warnings signs, and as you well know, it wasn't just me that was concerned. My colleagues were as well, but for reasons I am yet to understand, I ignored the severity of what was being received. Sometimes I wonder if I deliberately forgot the information because it was too difficult to bear. The point is we cannot continue ignoring the information that plants and fauna are providing us. Our neighbors in our backyard and beyond are reaching out, and we have to pay attention. Gar, I know we're old and the idea of taking on a project like this feels overwhelming, but we've got to do something."

"I agree with you, Pam, but I'm not exactly sure how to proceed. What is your idea?" She looked into the bottom of her teacup trying to get the courage to speak out. And then she started to chuckle.

"This is so fascinating. I'm sitting here observing myself trying to claim the courage to tell you that I think we need to start speaking the truth about what we have learned. My reluctance to speak the truth to you in this moment is evidence of the fearfulness that we will have to face. Why is it so frightening to speak out about things that are actually happening? Our experiences are real. Even if they are unusual, they are real, and we are not the only people on the planet who are having connections and communication with other species. I just know that we have to do this. It's important, Gar, and we have to step up." Her husband remained silent briefly, giving Pam a moment to catch her breath. He was not surprised by this conversation. Ever sense they had met their neighbor on the trail, the realization that action needed to be taken was on his mind.

"Dear, this will come as no surprise to you, but I've been having similar thoughts, and I am totally in agreement with you. My thoughts about speaking the truth have led me to the written word. I've been wondering about the efficacy of writing articles about our experiences and also about the possibility of producing a book. My thoughts brought up many questions, which I would like to explore with you." The excitement at the small table was palpable. The couple shivered with delight.

"Of course, you would be on the same page. It was inevitable. So why was I fearful about bringing the topic up? We talk about everything." Pam shook her head in frustration and made a declaration. "You know what, let's put our fear on the To Do List. We can mull through that later. But for now, let's keep sharing our ideas. As you might guess, my mind went to the written word as well, and I think there are numerous avenues for publishing some articles." She grabbed a notepad that was always left on the table for occasions such as this. In large printed letters, she wrote TO DO LIST. The first item, Fear, was duly noted. And the second, Publication Resources, was recorded as well. And then she added another entry. Third, Options for Presenting Messages of Truth. "You know, Gary, there are many different ways of delivering the truths that we are learning. They don't all have to be presented in scientific journals. In fact, we probably have a much greater opportunity for reaching a larger audience if we try other outlets. Social media is an option we need to explore." Her husband nodded in agreement and acknowledged it was a much faster means of communication.

"I realize one of the reasons that fear has come up for me," continued Pam, "lies in the idea of hosting gatherings. I agree with our neighbor, we need to start connecting with friends, neighbors, and friends yet to be, and hopefully spread the truth by word of mouth. I believe these conversations would be very beneficial, but the idea of standing up and telling folks that we've been communicating with a bumblebee gives me the shakes, which takes me right back to that fearful place. For goodness sake, what is this about? At our age, what does it matter? We're retired, so our professional licenses are not in danger."

"That's true, Dear. But on the other hand, will our age be a detriment? Some folks may discount us because we are old."

Pam asserted herself back into the lead. "You're right, that may happen, but we cannot allow that possibility to stop us. I believe more people will respect our years of credibility rather than disregard us. Every person who listens to our experiences has the option to believe or not. We have no control over that aspect of speaking the truth, but we do have a responsibility to speak out. And we have an obligation to act. The Earth can no longer be ignored. We must come to her aid. From what we've learned, Gary, the human species is the biggest offender of the Earth. Other species work collaboratively with her. We are the ones who are causing her health issues. This cannot continue." Pam paused and took a deep breath. "Excuse me for going off on my save the Earth spiel. I got carried away." Her husband and best friend reached across the table and placed his hand on hers.

"I think you have the potential to inspire others to get serious about the Earth's crisis. So don't stop spouting about the Earth. She needs more folks like you to speak on her behalf. You're amazing."

"So are you, Dear!" responded Pam. "I think we can be a good team with both the spoken word and the written word. And I know our Friend across the street is going to be part of this project." The couple sat quietly for a moment mulling over their situation.

Before returning to their conversation, Gary reached over and added another item to the To Do List. Number 4: Go For A Long Walk. "Let's continue this conversation on our walk, and let's take the list with us."

"You're reading my mind," accused Pam. The two Old Friends giggled with delight.

"Gary, I love this trail! Thank you for selecting this walk; we are so lucky that we live only a few minutes away from this incredible sanctuary." Her walking companion nodded in agreement. "Did you read my mind again?" Pam asked. "Did you know that I was hoping that we would come here for our walk?" She wrapped her arm in his and poked him in the ribs. "You did, didn't you?"

"No, no, I don't believe this is a result of an intuitive reaction," he responded with great sincerity. "I wanted to make you happy and I know this is your favorite trail, so I just drove in this direction."

"Well, thank you. You have made me very happy. We have so many beautiful areas to explore that are nearby, including our own neighborhood, but this one just speaks to me. You're absolutely right: this is my favorite spot. It feels like coming home. Does that sound crazy?" Gary didn't answer at first, not because he wasn't paying attention, but a visitor on the trail ahead had grabbed his attention. He came to a stop and pointed ahead.

"Look, Dear, there's a friend of yours." Pam focused on the trail and a smile crossed her face.

"Oh my goodness. Isn't she looking well? Do you see any of her fawns?"

"I haven't located them yet, but surely they must be on the scene. Shall we attempt to approach her?"

"Let's reach out to her first so that she will understand our intentions. May I take the lead?" Gary nodded and encouraged her to do so. Very softly, Pam began to address the large doe about thirty feet ahead of them. "Hello, Sweet Beauty! It is so good to see you again. We are delighted to be in your neighborhood and would love to approach, if you are agreeable to that. We will move slowly and as quietly as we can. We do not mean to disrupt your morning feeding. Please inform your children that we are coming." With that said, the couple slowly moved forward.

The doe remained still with head held high as she vigilantly watched their approach. At one point she took one step forward and then braced for action. In response, Gary and Pam came to an abrupt stop. "Not to worry, Dear. We mean you no harm." Gary's softly spoken words were barely audible, but they didn't need to be. The deer understood his intentions.

Pam projected her intentions telepathically. *"Old Friend, we marvel at your beauty and would love to come closer. We will stay on the other side of the trail. We will not come any closer than that. May we continue?"* The female deer, mother of two fawns, snorted as if responding to Pam's question. "I'm not sure how to interpret that. Gary, do you have any idea what that sound meant?"

"Not a clue, but let's do as you said. Let's walk caravan style while hugging the left side of the trail." And this they did for several more steps. Then they paused again, giving the deer time to adjust to their close proximity. She snatched a sprig of wild berries and munched away as if their presence was irrelevant, so they took a few more steps, and then one of the kiddos appeared from behind a bush. This youngster was more curious than alarmed and bravely advanced forward to see what was going on. The doe, in motherly fashion, took another step forward to provide more protection.

Pam immediately intervened. *"Don't worry Friend! We honor your boundaries. Your little one is growing rapidly. You must be very proud of him!"* Once again, the doe responded with a snort followed by a flicker of the right ear. And then the other fawn came into view. It was a sight to behold. The three of them were a picture post card. Gary wanted very much to take a photo, but knew this was not the moment. Any sudden movement might frighten them. He decided to converse aloud with the family.

"Well, your family is just looking lovely. It's obvious that you are taking very good care of your children. We are most grateful to be in your presence. Is there anything we can do for you?" The couple stood quietly hoping for some type of response. As they waited, the young buck took several more steps towards them. "You are a very handsome young fellow," Gary's voice was but a whisper. The youngster made eye contact with him and took another step forward. Gary responded by very slowly moving his hand, palm up, toward the young deer. Curious, and wisely cautious, the fawn sniffed the air, but did not come any closer. The experience was precious. On one side of the trail stood two old members of the Human species and on the other side of the trail stood three beautiful specimens of the Cervidae species, each sizing up the other.

"Gary, what is your sense of all this?" whispered Pam. "Are you receiving anything?" He indicated that he wasn't and suggested that they attempt another telepathic connection. Pam nodded and took responsibility for the task. *"You have a beautiful family, Dear One. It is such a pleasure to be in your company. We would love to connect with you, but we do not want to overstep your boundaries. Is there anything we can do for you?"* Instantly Pam internally saw an image of a sprig of berries similar to the ones the doe had nibbled on before. Turning her head to the bush to her left, Pam saw a collection of berries in arm's reach. Slowly and gently she raised her hand, plucked a sprig, and turned back to the family of deer. She made eye contact with the mother who pointed her nose towards the young buck. Pam interpreted this gesture as an instruction that was to be followed. Since Gary was nearer the designated recipient, she handed the sprig to him, who in turn gently reached out to offer the berries to their new friend. The gift piqued the young one's curiosity. He clearly was interested, but turned to his mother first. She snorted again, which undoubtedly was her way of giving the buck permission to accept the offering. And this he did. Carefully and gently, he stretched his long neck closer to Gary's hand and tasted one of the berries. It met with his approval. He relieved Gary of the sprig and thoroughly enjoyed the treat. Of course, Pam and Gary wanted more time with this wonderful family, but the doe was satisfied with the exchange as it was. She nosed her children back into the bushes. Before she followed them, she turned to her new Friends and flicked both of her ears.

"Thank you!" exclaimed Pam. "We so enjoyed our time with you. Please take good care and we will see you again soon." The doe turned towards the bushes and flicked her tail as if to say goodbye. "Oh my goodness! That was awesome!"

"Yes, it was!" agreed Gary. "In fact that was incredible. We really had an interactive experience with them. She understood our intentions and took the risk to interact with us. Pam, this is really happening. Oh, my word! We really do need to record these experiences so that we can share our stories precisely as they transpired. There is no need for embellishment of these incidents. Communication is really occurring. We are not just making this up. By the way, when you turned around to reach for those berries, had you received a message about that?" Before Pam could answer, Gary asked another question. "Did you see an image of a sprig of berries?"

"Yes, I did. Did you see it as well?"

"Yes," he replied. "It was clear and in color. The minute you turned around, I was certain that you had received the message as well. Pam, this is remarkable!" The two old friends were as excited as children. They continued down the path giggling with delight and noticing the various sites along the way.

"Every time we come here, we see something new, don't we? It's hard to believe that such a small area can hold so many surprises. We are so fortunate to have access to this property." Pam nodded in agreement as they continued walking and enjoying the views. Eventually, they returned to the earlier conversation shared at the breakfast nook. "So, Pam, I have a thought about our To Do List." She looked on wondering if his idea would be the same as hers, but she was surprised. His creativity had already inspired another idea to add to their list. "Actually, I thought about this earlier," he said, "but I lost it momentarily as we engaged with our other ideas. You know how that is. Anyway, I think we should each begin an Invitation List. I have a few folks that may be curious about our findings, and I'm sure you do as well. If we're really going to pursue this notion of speaking the truth, then we need to have people with whom we can share the message. And personally, I'd rather do that with folks we already know. Guess that takes us back to the fear issue. The truth is if we begin with friends, we will have an opportunity to gain confidence." Pam readily agreed and suggested that they compose their list of names before the next scheduled meeting.

"You know, Gary, I just sense that we are entering into a phase of huge changes and I think we need to be prepared. Our To Do List encompasses a plan of action. My day is rather flexible, so my goal is to tackle the items on the list. I think it would be great if we could present these ideas to our Friend when we meet up again. The tasks are not tedious, but the fear issue remains puzzling. Let's grapple with that as we continue our walk." Gary agreed and committed to the task as well. He also acknowledged that his concern about speaking the truth regarding their interactions with nature and her friends kept him awake for some time after they went to bed.

"You know how I am," he admitted. "I tend to ruminate about a topic until I have the illusion of conquering whatever the subject is. My deliberations were somewhat successful. And by the way, while experiencing my mind's repetitious deliberations, I realized that it might be beneficial to create a small handout that addresses various perspectives on people's fear regarding the notion of sharing ideas that are very personal to them. For some folks the idea of speaking out may feel very risky, even threatening, while others may not be bothered by it at all. I envision this as a continuum: easy for some people and not for others!

"Growing up as a shy person, the idea of speaking out about any topic was challenging for me at times. I've released most of that anxious energy over the years, but not all of it. There are times when shyness still remains an obstacle for me.

"My reaction to our specific topic brings up my need for approval. This too has been an issue since childhood. I recognize that it is perfectly normal for it to rise up now. We are, after all, considering taking a risk by exposing our truth about our experiences in and with nature. I am aware of how silly this sounds, but I still want people's approval, and I do not want to be teased or criticized about my thoughts or my beliefs. The thought of experiencing that type of reaction at this age is almost unbearable. Pam, I'm embarrassed to admit this, but childhood shame runs deep, and I suspect that anyone who has had similar experiences will also have similar fears.

"Having said that, I also believe having these conversations would be very healing. As you said earlier, you and I really don't have anything to lose because of our retirement status, but that's not the case for people who are still actively engaged in sustaining their livelihoods. Perhaps, my imagination is taking me places it doesn't need to go, but I think we need to consider as many avenues as possible. And people need to feel safe. If we can create a safe place for people to explore these issues, then that will open the door to more expansive conversations."

"Great work, Gary! Take a deep breath with me. You need it and so do I." They did as Pam suggested and both benefitted from the simple process. "I am so proud of you, Dear Heart. Forgive me for sleeping through all of your hard work last night and thank you for the effort. I so appreciate your own self-disclosures about the debilitating effects of shyness and also about the fears of loss of approval. Well, my Dear Friend, you have my approval and my respect. The idea of a handout is brilliant, as is the image of creating a safe place. In fact, Gary, let's consider giving the handout the title of Creating a Safe Haven." Her husband's eyes began to twinkle.

"I rather like that idea! And thanks for all those words of kindness and support. It really does help to share these painful realities. Having spoken my truth to you gives me a sense of peace. Now, I must acknowledge that our relationship facilitates this type of response. If other folks had been present, I would most likely still be anxious about their reactions, but every step made diminishes the effects of the original fear. Dear, it appears to me that our conversations from the heart have the potential for being very emotionally and energetically therapeutic." Hands joined as they continued along the path. Gary was aware that his companion's energy shifted.

"Pam, what's going on with you? I sense a disturbance in your quadrant of the universe." His choice of words tickled her.

"Oh, there does seem to be some microscopic activity whirling about in the cosmos of my mind." She admitted.

"Having a bout with fear?" The question was indeed on the mark. Although he had no idea about the specifics of her discomfort, he was aware that something was amiss.

"You rascal! Your intuition is growing exponentially, and you're right of course. While I'm wrapped up in the activity of problem solving and strategizing, I'm in a very good place. I feel useful, productive, and hopeful, but when I return to the reality of Earth's dilemma and the complexity of uniting people on her behalf, then I feel very small, inept, and ill-equipped to grapple with the magnitude of her problems. It takes my breath away, and I just want to run away and hide. I suspect this is exactly how most people feel, at least among those who actually are aware of her declining health. I just want to curl up in bed and throw the covers over my head when I think about how many people still refuse to accept the truth. And then, I watch my mind move into all kinds of outrageous judgments about people I don't even know. My negative reactions towards these unseen people just add to the problem. Even now, as I think about these scenarios, I'm aware that my energy is off kilter. You felt it! And so does the Earth. The point of this little scenario is this. I have no power or privilege over someone else's behaviors, but I do have a responsibility to monitor and control my own behavior, including my reactions to others. Gary, I am a walking, talking example of one of the ways that humans misuse and waste energy. My righteous indignation towards people who do not believe in our environmental crisis serves no purpose. It is a waste of good energy. Judging other people is the equivalent of manufacturing negative energy. We must remember this! Our negative energy affects everyone around us including Mother Earth. It doesn't matter where we are, she is there feeling the effects. We must be careful, and we must learn ways to express our emotions responsibly." Pam quickly turned her attention to the Earth, softly expressing an apology and prayer for her recovery.

"Oh, Dear Friend, please forgive me for spewing negative energy. I exposed you and Gary, and God only knows how many other life beings with my burst of frustrations and arrogance. I am so sorry. I promise to monitor this inappropriate behavior, and I will make changes. And now, please allow me to attempt to reverse my error. Dear Friends, far and near, please assist me with an energy transfusion to our Beloved Earth. I have been remiss and need assistance in correcting my mistake. Please join me, everyone, with your deep breaths and your good intentions. Let the source of all energy that resides within us heighten our reach. Wherever you are located, please send a particle of your pure energy to the Earth at this time. Send your powerful healing energy to her and accompany it with your prayers. Thank you all for assisting with this healing session, and please continue to attend her on a daily basis. Thank you so much for your help." Tears streamed down her face as the couple continued to take one step after another.

Gary wrapped his arm in hers. "That was lovely, Dear. I know the Earth appreciated your kindness." Pam nodded in agreement.

"This happened for a reason. I'm not saying that to excuse my behavior because it does not do so, but the timing of my questionable behavior was significant. Gary, this scenario is one that teaches. If we share this story with others they will grasp the importance of monitoring their behaviors and their speech. They will bear witness to the impact of my negative behavior upon you and the Earth, and they will see how we attempted to amend the consequences. Sharing these stories is such a good way of demonstrating what we need to convey. Thanks, Gar! You pulled me out of that downward swing and helped the Earth as well. You see we really are a good team!" Her husband accepted the words of gratitude and shared his own.

"I too am grateful for this experience because it showed me how quickly we can turn an event around. And by the way, the disruption that I felt coming from you was minor; I simply knew something was brewing. I'm telling you this so you realize that it wasn't as extreme as you think it was. But your point is well taken. We must be vigilant and careful at all times, because our actions have consequences. I was very impressed by your ability to step away from your discomfort with your behavior and quickly move into a state of action. It was exceptional Pam, a wonderful demonstration of accepting responsibility for one's behaviors. Goodness! This has been a remarkable morning, and it's still young."

The sanctuary parking lot came into view as they strolled around the bend. It had indeed been a very productive morning.

... 15 ...

Deb was surprised when she heard someone enter the waiting room of her office. Initially, she thought time had escaped her, so she began organizing her paperwork, but a quick glance at the desk clock indicated that her next client wasn't due for another thirty minutes. Before she could push her chair away from the desk, she saw a familiar face peeking around the door.

"Hello Friend! What a wonderful surprise this is!" We exchanged hugs and Deb welcomed me into her private space, briefing me that she was in between sessions.

"Me too!" I replied. "I just wanted to check in with you to see if you might be available for a walk this evening?" Before another word could be spoken, Deb responded.

"Yes! I'm done at five o'clock. How about you?"

"The same! Does the wildlife sanctuary suit you or would you prefer another trail?" We both agreed that we wanted to enjoy the sunset from the coastline, and then learned that we had both brought our walking clothes to the office in hopes of a quick escape.

"We are so in sync." The response, voiced simultaneously by the two of us, made us laugh. Even though these so-called coincidences were amusing, one couldn't help wondering about the purpose of our paths crossing. We exchanged a few more pleasantries and then mutually agreed that we should freshen up our respective offices now, so that we could leave immediately after our final session of the day.

I quickly returned to my office and addressed the daily cleanup routine. The thought of enjoying Deb's company again brought a smile to my face. It will not surprise you to know that Deb was sporting a similar smile as she neatened up her office.

Both Deb and I noticed that our clients arrived promptly on time. Our entry doors opened at the same time, the sessions began at the same time, and our clients departed at the same time. It would be very interesting to know if our sessions focused on similar issues, but that was not to be discussed. Other topics would be addressed on the trail.

Minutes after our sessions concluded, we both exited our offices at the same time. "Who's driving? No reason to take two cars!" We came to an abrupt halt and just burst into laughter. I started to say something but quickly put my hand over my mouth, only to hear Deb state exactly what I was intending to say.

She looked at me and immediately understood what had just transpired. "Okay, Friend! This is just too unbelievable to comprehend. As I just said, I'm happy to drive. Let's go see the sunset." The drive took seven minutes. The chit-chat that we shared on the brief commute shifted the minute our shoes hit the trail. Deb moved us from inconsequential to in-depth conversation immediately.

"Please forgive me for my forward behavior," she began, "but I have many questions to ask you and I want to take advantage of every minute we have together." I assured her that all questions were acceptable and that I would try to field them as best I could.

"Deb, I am very excited that you were available for this walk, because I too have many topics I would like to explore with you. So, please take the lead. I am eager to hear which question is at the top of your list."

"Well," she chuckled, "I wish they could all be asked at the same time. Each one is equally important to me. I've been having a fantasy since our recent encounter that some day we will have an opportunity to sit for hours and hours talking about all the mysteries of this beautiful planet and of the entire universe. Wouldn't that be grand?" Deb quickly clarified that the question just asked did not count as her first question. I wrapped my arm in hers and suggested that we just breathe together for a while. And this we did. As the sea breezes welcomed us back, our bodies slowly aligned with the locale. The sea birds squawked acknowledging our presence, and the coastal views captured our hearts. We were in paradise! And we were one with the land and the ocean. Eventually, my new Old Friend asked her first question.

"My first question is deeply personal, and if you prefer not to answer, please know that I will honor your boundaries, but I would like to know when you realized that you were more than you appear to be?" Deb's question was a surprise. For once my intuition totally failed me.

"Goodness, I wasn't expecting that. And it isn't an easy question, but you're aware of that." She just smiled and patiently waited for a response. "The simple answer is this. Some time ago, I won't mention how many years ago, my life profoundly changed. I became aware that there was more, much more going on in the world than I had ever imagined...and let me tell you, my imagination was expansive.

"I suspect you have heard similar stories before, Deb, so I'm not at all uncomfortable sharing this with you. What transpired began slowly. I started hearing a message that repeated over and over, and the message I heard was, *you are here for a reason.* Well, as you might imagine, it was intriguing to hear such a message, and it was also a bit disconcerting to be hearing a voice that was not accompanied by a body. As a licensed psychotherapist with many years of experience, I was acutely aware of the implications of hearing voices. Fortunately, there were no other signs of health issues, so I simply continued to observe the unusual appearances of the repetitive message. Over time it became rather annoying. I would fall asleep hearing the message and wake up to the same. As a result of this seemingly significant message, I started attending workshops on topics that I would never have considered prior to hearing the message and devouring books that previously would not have been of any interest. The insistence of the repetitive message pushed me to seek more.

"And then one weekend, as I was sitting in my home I realized that my focus was not in alignment with the intentions of this message, so I visited the small library that was located in the upstairs attic. As I stood in front of the shelves of books, my eyes immediately were drawn to two books that had been sitting there unread for years. An intuitive knowingness came over me. I knew that these books were essential to my future. Grabbing them from the shelf, I returned downstairs and spent the entire weekend absorbing the two books. My life changed that weekend. I think it is fair to say that my spiritual journey of this lifetime birthed during those hours of going back and forth from one book to the other. At the end of the weekend, I was aware that my journey had begun. I knew that I was here for a reason." My mind raced back to that weekend as if it were yesterday. It was an exhilarating time. The memories made me chuckle at myself. "Deb, I didn't even know what a spiritual journey was at that point; I was totally clueless. But I can vividly remember the joy that was experienced. I felt embraced by a Presence that I had not given credence to before. Although the destination of the journey escaped me, as did the role that I was to play in it, I knew with absolute certainty that it was the intended path to pursue.

"As I look back on that weekend now, the phrase Blind Faith, comes to mind. My behavior was so unlike me, and yet, I was more alive and more content than ever before. It was an exceptional weekend."

"And does the journey still continue to this day?"

"Oh, yes. As far as I can tell, the journey is ongoing, never-ending. Countless experiences, countless lifetimes, countless destinations."

"Do you have any regrets?" Deb politely inquired. Her question puzzled me, but I refrained from dwelling in my curiosity.

"None whatsoever! I sometimes wonder how my life might have unfolded if I had not chosen this path. Obviously, our decisions can take us in many different directions. But if I were granted the opportunity to relive that moment in time, I would make the same decision. My life has been blessed and I am very grateful. Trusting that there are many more opportunities ahead, I just try to be present in this one, so that I can fully enjoy it and learn whatever it is I am here to learn. Of course, my ability to do that varies from one day to the next, but it is a worthy goal to pursue.

"Actually when you believe in eternal life, Deb, which I do, it makes life so much easier. I don't feel the need to experience everything in this lifetime. I don't worry about missing out on a particular event or experience, because I have faith that there will always be another opportunity. In my younger days that was not true for me. Then, there was a sense of urgency about seeing everything and doing everything. It was an exhausting and chaotic way to be. When you live life hurriedly and frenetically, you don't absorb the fullness of what is transpiring. The abundance of stimulation is too much for us to process. Once I let go of that unrealistic need to experience everything, life became less stressful...and much more meaningful. It took me a while, but I eventually learned that one must live in the present to truly be alive. You cannot fully appreciate what is happening around you if you are not present for the experience. When one focuses on the future, the next event, the next experience, you are not fully engaged with the present. Now is the moment of relevance." A deep breath overwhelmed me accompanied by a flitting embarrassing thought. *Have I gone on and on again?* Enmeshed with my own story, I had lost track of time. The fear of monopolizing the conversation stirred within, but before I could address the concern, Deb clarified the situation by responding to my unspoken thoughts.

"Oh, Dear Friend, you have not monopolized our conversation. On the contrary, I have enjoyed every moment of your story. When I hear stories such as yours, I find it so comforting. It soothes my soul. As you well know, the spiritual journey can be a lonely experience at times. That's actually a misperception, but being aware of that doesn't make it seem any less lonely. So, while I was listening to you, I felt fortunate and grateful for the opportunity to get to know you better. I'm actually doing what you just addressed. I'm living in the moment and fully appreciating this time with you.

"In fact your story reminds me of some of my own experiences, and it's nice to review them occasionally. Thank you for sharing...my heart is full." Deb's words were comforting. I looked forward to hearing more of her stories. I suspected that we had many similar experiences.

"Look Friend, there's your Sacred Stone! Isn't it lovely in this light? I would love to know all the secrets that it holds. I wonder how many other folks over the ages have had transformative experiences there. My imagination takes me in many directions. I suspect heartfelt emotions of all kinds were shared with this grand stone: magical moments of proposals, vows of commitment, celebrations, as well as difficult times when confessions were heard, sorrows were released, and relationships were healed. Yes," she mused, "this Great Mother has witnessed many, many passages." We debated whether we should stay with the ancient formation or continue. Both options were alluring, but the setting sun was awaiting our presence on the other side of the small peninsula so we expressed our gratitude to the Sacred Stone and took our leave of her.

"Deb, I am aware that you are a woman with many questions," my tone was humorous, "but would it be possible for you to share one of your memories now?" She laughingly poked me on the arm and accused me of backing out of my commitment to field all her questions. I assured her that my commitment was steadfast, but my curiosity was as strong as hers.

"Like you, Dear, I want to get to know you better as well. And I am so glad that you are a storyteller. It's such a wonderful way to communicate." Deb acknowledged that she too preferred to connect by sharing stories, and she was very happy to reveal more of her life.

"Let me think for a minute," her voice was so soft and faraway that one could almost picture her lost in the recesses of the mind, trying to select the perfect memory to share at this time. As we neared the bend at the point of the peninsula, she suggested that we take the small, infrequently used path that leads to the rocky coastline. We stepped across several large boulders, whose geological features were stunningly different than the setting that was home to the Sacred Stone. Deb noted how remarkable the Earth was. "Here we are less than a quarter of a mile from the other area, and this formation is a completely different terrain...and equally beautiful! How blessed we are!" Her eyes embraced the seascape and tears trickled down her face. I would not have noticed if the setting sun hadn't glimmered in one of the teardrops. I put my arm in hers.

"You're having a moment!" I whispered. She nodded, but remained silent. As we stood side by side a vision crossed my mind of another time and place. Two people, a man and a woman holding each other very tightly, stood in this exact place gazing out over the ocean. Their emotions were intense, but no other information came into my awareness. I wondered if Deb was recalling some event in her life that related to this imagery. I remained silent. Time passed in its inevitable way: for me it was a brief moment, but for Deb it was a lifetime.

Eventually, Deb indicated that she was ready to leave. When we reached the main pathway again, she paused, turned around, and stared at the ocean view again. She quietly stated, "I've been here before." A cold shiver went through me. "I can't explain it," she continued, "but this setting is so familiar. Every time I reach this point on the trail, there is an intense sensation that comes over me. I feel pulled to those rocks, but for reasons that are not clear to me, I've resisted. Thank you for accompanying me today. It was very comforting to have you by my side. It's so strange, but I just know that I've been there before." We continued strolling around the bend heading towards the same bench we had occupied the week before. Our timing was perfect. The sunset was exceptional, as always. We parked ourselves on the bench and absorbed the moment.

As I sat staring at the sunset, my mind returned to the vision that was experienced near the point. I wondered if it was a topic that should be brought up for discussion, or if it should wait for another time. Since my understanding of its relevance was limited at best, it seemed wise to let the issue rest.

Deb reached over and patted me on the knee. "Please don't worry about me. If there's something you would like to discuss, please do so." Her intuitive abilities continued to fascinate me. Responding to unspoken thoughts was normal for her. I could no longer resist the temptation; the question needed to be asked.

"Deb, your intuition is right, again. I would like to discuss a vision that was experienced while we were at the bend, but before we take that topic on, I simply must ask you a question or two."

"Did I do it again?" Her question was another demonstration of her intuitive acuity. "Geez! I did, didn't I?" She apologized profusely accusing herself of being rude and inconsiderate. "I am so sorry. It happens so frequently now that I'm rarely aware of it."

"I'm not offended, Deb. On the contrary, I'm curious…and fascinated. And by the way, this is not my first experience with this type of communication. I know several other folks who share your ability to hear the unspoken word. Have you always been able to do this, or is it a recent development?" My questions were many, but I tried to refrain myself. Deb would probably intuit them anyway.

She giggled and admitted that she had just heard my inner comment. "The answers to that question are more complicated than you might imagine. Let me attempt to clarify my experiences with telepathy, if you are okay with me using that descriptor. I know some people don't believe that it is real, but it happens nonetheless. Regardless of what descriptor is used, the ability to hear others' inner thoughts exists. Since this has become a reality in my life, I have learned that many others experience this as well. And I realize now that it was within me as a small child, but it wasn't vibrant then. I look back and remember some incidents that occurred, and they were clearly telepathic experiences, but when you're a kid, you don't give much credence to that type of thing. It passes you by, and you're on to the next adventure. But the actual development and honing of the skillset started about five years ago. It began slowly and continues to progress as we speak. As you've witnessed, it is so common for me now that I really am attracting attention. People, like you, are beginning to notice. Frankly, it's a bit embarrassing. And I am afraid that some people will find it very intrusive. I really need to be more careful."

"You're right, Deb, I had no idea how complex this could be. I assure you that I was not offended in any way, but I see your point. Some might react in that manner. Quite honestly, I'm too excited about it to be offended. I want to know everything!!" My fingers gestured quotation marks around the last sentence. She laughed at my gesture, but understood the curious nature regarding this unique skillset.

"So do I!" she replied. "I want to know everything there is to know about telepathy or existential communication, or whatever title one wants to give to this ability. Actually," she emphasized assertively, "I think the best way to refer to this little known ability is to call it as it is…an innate ability." She looked to see how I would react to her statement and a smile crossed my face.

"I agree with you! In fact, I think this ability exists in all species, not just ours. I'm not sure why or how this communication style was lost in our evolutionary process, but I believe it is just waiting to be reignited within us. And I think it is happening! I witness it in you and several others, and I am now enjoying its resurgence in me as well." Deb's eyes lit up.

"Yay! We do have much to talk about. I am so glad to know that you too are having these experiences." I quickly acknowledged that this was new to me, and she shook her right index finger at me. "Remember, Dear Friend, it's been within you since your beginning, and now you are here nursing it back to full vibrancy. Oh, how wonderful. This is majorly exciting!" We turned our focus west as the sun slipped beyond the horizon.

"There is so much beauty in the world," I whispered.

"Yes!" Deb replied. "And so much curiosity!" We both chuckled and continued to admire the twilight moment. It was the peaceful time of an ending day, a sweet moment between daylight and darkness. It was lovely. We sat in silence for what seemed like a long time, which of course, was not the case. Only minutes had passed before Deb returned to the topic of the vision that I had mentioned earlier. Her curiosity was getting the best of her; she was eager to hear more.

"Actually, I would love to talk about it, Deb, but perhaps we should head back to the car now before it gets too dark. Would you like to join me for a light meal? I made a huge pot of chicken vegetable soup yesterday, and it's just waiting to be devoured."

"I love chicken vegetable soup! It's comfort food! And now that we're talking about food, I'm starving. Let's go," she commanded, and off we went. Within minutes, we were in my small kitchen heating up the soup and slicing a loaf of fresh sourdough bread. Even though it was Deb's first visit to the house, we worked comfortably together in the small space, and in no time at all, we were sitting at the small table enjoying the first spoonful of soup. "Oh, yum! That is delicious!" Her response was so instantaneous that she was embarrassed by her outburst. We both giggled and I graciously acknowledged her delightful reaction.

"I'm taking that as applause to the chef!" Deb gave me the thumbs up as she indulged in another bite. Conversation paused briefly as we sated our appetite in silence with the exception of a few oohs and ahs. As we each grabbed for another slice of bread, she invited me to proceed with the discussion about the vision that occurred on the trail. I had decided on the drive back from the trail that I needed to prepare Deb before just launching into this conversation. It seemed the proper action to take since I was unsure if my vision and her experience were related.

"Deb, before I share the experience with you, I need to let you know that it transpired at the same time that you were engaged with your experience at the point. I don't know if our experiences are related or not, but I want you to be aware that they might be. So, are you up for this discussion or would you rather delay it to another time?" She paused and appeared to give my question a great deal of consideration before she made her decision. With a long deep breath, she encouraged me to continue. Because I had so little information about the situation, some protective feelings arose for me. "Are you sure, Deb? I don't need to do talk about this now. It can wait." She appreciated my concern and reassured me that she was ready to face this very old issue.

"I think this is a very important issue for me to address. It's still very vague, but there is something that is nagging at me, and I believe whatever it is needs to be released. I think this is important for both of us," she added. "And please forgive me, because I have no idea what that last statement means. It's just a deep knowing within me, which at this point is still unknown to my conscious self. As you can tell, Friend, I'm confused, but I am ready to face whatever unfolds." Deb placed her hand on mine and leaned forward across the table, her eyes staring deeply into mine. At first I was taken aback, but then her eyes grabbed mine, and the message was received. *"Are you ready, Old Friend?"*

I returned her stare and replied to her unspoken words, "Yes, I am." A deep sigh came from Deb's side of the table, as she relaxed back into her chair.

"Please tell me about your vision, Old Friend," Deb's referral to me as an Old Friend touched me deeply. I had sensed that to be the truth since we first met, but it now penetrated my soul.

"The experience was barely a moment in time, but it seems so significant that I cannot ignore it. While you were looking out over the ocean a few tears escaped and streamed down your face. One caught the setting sun and glimmered brightly. When that sparkle captured my attention, I witnessed a man and woman holding each other tightly standing exactly where we were standing. Although I had no understanding of what was transpiring, I felt their emotions. They were deeply intense…so strong that they almost bowled me over. I don't know if this means anything to you or not, but the timing of the vision seemed relevant." Deb sat quietly while I shared my experience, listening with the ears of her heart. Then she closed her eyes. I remained silent knowing that she was processing at a level that was not yet known to me. At that point my role was to be patient and to hold the space while she engaged with her inner work, or so I thought. But my intuition was not as sound as my Friend's. Soon the vision previously experienced returned, and again, the emotions were overwhelming. Heartbreak and despair overcame me. The vision became more tangible, when I heard the words: *Please don't leave me. I cannot bear your absence.* The words broke my heart. Tears streamed down my face as the memory of that day flooded into awareness.

"I am so, so sorry. Please forgive me, I am so sorry." Deb's hand grabbed mine.

"Stay with me!" she demanded. "Don't go away! Stay with me!" Her words spoken in the present were the same words she spoke so long ago. Then, she begged me not to leave on an overseas assignment, and now, she begged me to stay in the present. "Do not get lost in this memory," she stated firmly. "I know what happened now. I remember. Please come back so we can both heal from this old injury. I still love you, Old Friend. There are no regrets!" Deb talked me through the moment, urging me to take deep breaths, until I was finally back into my body. The experience left me in shock. Sitting rigidly in my chair and gasping for air, I held on to the table with both hands. And then, the reality of what had transpired sank in. Shame and embarrassment washed over me. Unable to face Deb, I stared at the empty soup bowl in front of me, while a repeated message raced through my mind. *I left her! I left her! I left her!* Deb was not able to get my attention until she loudly pounded her hand on the table. The noise and the rattling of the dishes successfully brought me to the present.

"Old Friend, please be with me. Let go of this pain! Your ship went down at sea. You did not desert me. Please release this pain." Her gentleness calmed me. Finally, I was able to meet her eyes. My emotions poured out again.

"I'm so sorry. I tried so hard to survive. I held onto a piece of the wreckage for days, but I was so tired." The tears came again, as I remembered my last breath and my last thoughts. "Please forgive me." Deb left her chair and wrapped her arms around me.

"There is nothing to forgive, My Love. You did what had to be done; you served your country. I have no regrets. I never stopped loving you. My biggest concern was that you would punish yourself for eternity. I knew that I was the last thought on your mind. I knew how much you loved me, and I still do. And now, my Dear Old Friend, our paths have brought us back together. So, please stop worrying about the past. Let it go, and be with me in the present." My emotions slowly quieted. I was exhausted, but there was another task to complete before the conversation ended. I requested that Deb sit down again, so we could see each other face to face.

"You have literally saved my life here tonight, and words fail me, but this discussion isn't over yet. You've been holding this memory within you for ages. Tell me how you are. I'm okay, now. Let's focus on you. Please tell me what you are feeling." It was Deb's turn to take a deep breath. She knew the importance of this exercise for both of us.

"You're right, of course. I have been carrying this heartache without knowing what it was. And as you well know, events from the past affect our present lives. Some folks wouldn't believe our story, because they don't believe in eternal life, but we are living proof that it exists. In this particular situation, the heartache has been an underlying source of mild depression for as long as I can remember. It didn't make sense, because there were no incidents in this lifetime to explain the pain. Sometimes I would wake up in the middle of the night pining for someone and for some place, neither of which I had any inkling about. But when I relocated to this community and walked that trail, it called to me. Now, I realize why I was resistant to respond to that calling. I was afraid to experience that unknown heartache again. However, today, when we were together on the trail, I felt strong enough to engage with whatever was waiting for me...for us.

"I'm so glad this has happened. It feels like a huge weight has been lifted from me. I feel free. And I am so glad that you are as well. We are so blessed! Someone is truly watching over us. It must have taken a tremendous amount of orchestration to bring us together so that this old wound could be healed. Wow! It's beyond comprehension, and yet, I know this is our truth. Someone has gone to a tremendous amount of work to take care of us. We are so fortunate." She closed her eyes in prayer. "To all of you who made this possible; thank you, thank you, thank you!"

"Amen!" we expressed conjointly. Just as the prayer ended, the doorbell rang. It took us by surprise. I excused myself to answer the door and Deb started cleaning up the kitchen. As I approached the door I could see Pam and Gary waving from the front porch.

"My goodness, this is a surprise. Please come in!" The couple was beaming with excitement.

"We don't mean to interrupt your evening, but we were just finishing up our evening walk and saw the light on over here. So we made a spontaneous decision to stop in and give you a hug," Gary's eyes were sparkling again. The hugs were exchanged while I thanked them for their impulsivity.

"You two are just full of life this evening. I can tell that something is brewing!" They responded with laughter.

"We've been higher than kites since our evening together," announced Pam. "And we can hardly wait until our next meeting." Deb strolled out of the kitchen just as I was offering similar sentiments to my neighbors.

"Oh my goodness," expressed Gary. "We didn't mean to crash your evening."

"You didn't! In fact, this is perfect timing!" I introduced everyone and steered them into the living room. "I am so glad that you dropped by because the three of you need to meet. Trust me, my Friends, we all have a lot in common." We shared pleasantries for a few minutes and then Pam blazed the trail.

"So Deb, am I to understand that you and this one over here," she pointed in my direction, "are of like minds and hearts?" Pam had no idea how closely we were connected, or then again, perhaps she did. Her keen intuitive skills never ceased to amaze me. I was curious to see how Deb would respond to Pam's question.

"Well, Pam, I think your understanding is correct. I think it is fair to say that we are very Old Friends, who have crossed paths again. Fortunately, we are both aware of this and we're having a good time getting to know each other again. It such a blessing when both parties remember the previous connection." My neighbors, who also believed in eternal life, did not flinch at Deb's response. In fact, they were intrigued. Gary acknowledged that his curiosity was piqued, and that he looked forward to hearing more about our connection.

"I would love to hear more about this as well," inserted Pam. "Would you two like to join us for supper some time soon?"

"Yes, soon, please!" added Gary.

Deb and I exchanged a glance and then responded simultaneously. "Would tomorrow evening work for you?" This brought a round of laughter to my living room.

"Oh my!" declared Pam. "We really do have a lot to talk about." She turned to Deb and in a matter-of-fact way apprised her that she and her husband did not believe in coincidences. "It seems very clear to me that this impromptu gathering has happened for a reason. Shall we meet shortly after six o'clock tomorrow?" Deb and I agreed that we would come over after our last clients of the day. And with that said, my neighbors headed for home leaving Deb and me alone to say our goodbyes for the evening.

"I am still stunned by our adventure today, and so grateful. Thank you for loving me for all these lifetimes and thank you for joining me in this one! You are a blessing!" The words flowed from my heart.

"Thank you for the most remarkable experience of this lifetime! And this time," Deb spoke softly, "this is not farewell! I will see you tomorrow, Old Friend!" Our hug was tender and loving. I walked her to the car and waved as she drove away, knowing full well that we would see each other the next morning.

... *16* ...

"**W**ell, Dear House of Mine, did you have an enjoyable evening? I assume you overheard the conversation that transpired in the kitchen. Wasn't that amazing?" Once again, the house remained silent. I waited a bit longer hoping for some type of response. A squeaky floorboard, the dimming of lights, a moan in the antic! Anything would be deeply appreciated. "Oh, well! Hope burns eternal...goodnight, Old House!"

Although the hour was not late, I was exhausted. The emotional expense took a toll on me. My inclination was to go straight to bed, but with all that happened throughout the day, I felt compelled to record a small outline of what had transpired. I could elaborate later, but I needed to get the basics down so that they were not forgotten.

"You need not worry, Old Friend! What is intended to be remembered will be remembered." My exhaustion seemed to disappear.

"Are you just passing by, or do you desire conversation?"

"I am here to encourage you to rest now. The day was full. Many memories returned and old wounds were released. Although you do not recognize it as such, you have had a transformative experience. Because of the great release of pain and suffering, you are now more able to participate in the work that you are here to do. Blockage impedes one's abilities to receive messages. Healing and cleansing facilitate the receiving process. Old Friend, you expended great energy during your healing session and rest is necessary. Please release the compulsion to chronicle your experiences at this time. Tomorrow is another day. Now is the moment for rest! In peace be, Dear Friend. I bid you good night, my Friend."

The precious moment passed and I was overcome by my fatigue again. Within minutes I was sound asleep.

A few blocks away, Deb was still wide-awake and in conversation with her companion. *"Old Friend, much you have learned from this healing experience with the Friend of the Past and the Present."*

"Yes, I have, but I cannot help but wonder if there is more to learn. It was a tragic event for both of us that was long lasting. I so hope the suffering is over. Is that possible, Dear Friend, or will the memories of that event still linger and come back to create more hardship?

"Old Friend, a fear still lies within you. Do you wish to address it at

this time? The day has been long; it can be managed at another time." Deb was frustrated by this news. She was not aware that another fear was lurking and the idea that it might be true bothered her. She wanted the pain and suffering to be over.

"I prefer to address this now. I know the day has been long for you as well, but if you are available to continue, I would like to do it now. To allow fear to linger within me does not make sense. Can we just cut to the chase? What fear are you referring to?"

"Ah! Always you are one who wishes to make haste. Let me see if I can nudge you in the direction of intention. For lifetimes, you have held great concern for your Friend of the Past. You feared that he died in great pain because he was unable to return to you, and you were correct. He did suffer immensely. He promised that he would return, but alas, he was not able to fulfill the promise. Because of his love and devotion to you, the suffering lingered. But now, because of your openhearted conversation this evening, his pain is at long last gone. You successfully assisted the release of his pain.

"Now, my Friend, you must seek within and discover the underlying pain that burdens you. Indeed, your need to assist the Old Love penetrated your inner being, but there is more. What of your deep-seated pain that continues to this day? What is the fear that underlies this pain that demands your attention?" As Deb listened to the words of her Companion, awareness surged through her. She gasped for air as the pain was dislodged from her. She literally felt the release happening.

"Please leave me! I cannot bear your presence!"

"The pain is ready to release, but it needs your permission. It must know that you have learned the importance of its presence, before it can take its leave of you. Dear Friend, do you understand?" More information surfaced, cleansing the pain, and clearing space for her heart to open fully again.

"Yes, I understand! I've been terrified that I would lose another love again, which explains my avoidance of deep heartfelt relationships. Of course," she sighed. "This makes so much sense. The pain has been protecting me, keeping me from being hurt again. Oh, Dear Pain of Mine, I am sorry it took me so long to realize what was going on. Thank you for taking care of me all these lifetimes. I am so grateful. Now that I understand how much you've been assisting me, I will probably miss you. But not to worry, I can handle this now. Because of you, I am strong enough to do so. Please release yourself now. Let go! And thank you again, for your protection and your concern for me." A vision, brief, but jolting, abruptly stopped Deb. She breathed deeply while assimilating the information. "Oh, my goodness! That was his energy. My Beloved was lingering within me, waiting until I was ready to let go of him." Tears overcame her. The reality of his love rushed through her. She wept.

"My Dear Friend, at last the past is behind you. The memory of true love that rushed through you is the memory forevermore. The Beloved is at peace, and so are you. Rest is necessary, My Friend. Please go to bed now, knowing how deeply loved you have been."

... 17 ...

"**W**elcome! Please come in! We are so happy to have you in our home!" Gary's excitement was obvious. As he welcomed Deb and me into their home, Pam was echoing the greeting from the kitchen. We followed Gary down a small hallway and found Pam putting the finishing touches on what appeared to be a spectacular meal.

"We made an executive decision in our meal planning this afternoon and we hope that it suits you both," she clarified. "We had planned to serve some treats first, but then thought you might be famished after a day's work, so we decided to go straight for the full meal deal."

"Wonderful idea!" The words popped from our mouths simultaneously.

"Oh my!" declared Gary. "And the fun begins!" His boyish grin brought a smile to everyone.

Pam looked on with great expectations. *This is going to be a very interesting gathering.* Her thoughts did not go unnoticed. Deb debated whether or not she should respond to her thoughts and decided it was the right action to take.

"I agree, Pam. I think this is going to be a very interesting evening." And then, she quickly turned her focus towards assisting in the kitchen. "Do you need some extra hands, Pam? How may I help?"

"Yes," she replied, "all hands on deck, please!" Pam paused briefly as if she were strategizing, which of course she was. "First, I want to note that our new Friend here just responded to my unspoken thoughts. You're very talented and I cannot wait to hear your stories. And secondly, I need everyone to grab a dish and take it to the table. Gary, will you please take the tray of glasses? And I'll bring the platter of roasted chicken!" Appropriate oohs and ahs were voiced about the meal's centerpiece, which included a beautifully baked herb rubbed chicken surrounded by an assortment of fresh vegetables, also roasted with a special blend of spices. We all did as instructed and soon were gathered about the table that overlooked the backyard.

"This is a wonderful view! You've created a beautiful sanctuary." Deb said admiringly. "You must have a very difficult time leaving this setting." The couple enjoyed her compliments and concurred.

"Well, the truth is," responded Gary, "it is very difficult to venture elsewhere, but as you know, there are so many beautiful places nearby. We are blessed with an abundance of beauty, so we try to take advantage of all of it. In fact, we had a delightful encounter just recently at the wildlife sanctuary, which is just one of the stories that we wish to share with you this evening. But before we begin, shall we start with a blessing?" Hands immediately reached out and created a circle about the table. Deep breaths were enjoyed, as Pam took the lead.

"Dear Ones, from far and near, thank you for this reunion of friends. We are grateful that we have crossed paths again, and we are grateful for the helpers who made this possible. Please guide us this evening to share the most salient stories for this gathering, and please assist us as we hold each other in our hearts. And please bless all our beloved creatures in the backyard and around the globe, and take special care of the Earth as well. Thank your for everything! Amen!"

"That was lovely, Pam. It always warms my heart when someone acknowledges the Earth and her lovely creatures. And, thank you for mentioning our reunion! It does feel like a reunion of Old Friends. Aren't we lucky?" My words, sincerely stated, successfully validated Pam's feelings about the gathering. The excitement around the table was evidence of significant moments to come.

"So, how shall we begin this evening?" asked Gary. "We enjoy eating, talking, and sharing stories at the same time. Does that work for you two?"

"Gary, that sounds lovely, and I would like to invite you to continue with the story that you just alluded to. It sounds like a good place to start." Pam and Gary were delighted to take the lead, but urged us to fill our plates before the conversation commenced. And this we did!

"Oh, my!" declared Deb as she stared at her plate. "This is a feast!"

"And it's all healthy!" Pam proudly announced. "So enjoy a guilt free meal!" For a few minutes, the meal became the focus. The first bite is always the most fascinating to witness. The different facial expressions and the marvelous yummy sounds that are made are just delightful.

"Hmm! Well done, you two! And thank you for all the time that it took to prepare this feast."

"No, no, no!" Pam said excitedly. "That's the really great part about this meal. All it takes is about fifteen minutes of preparation and then miracles happen in the oven. This is my favorite meal to make because it is so easy. We are both so grateful that you have joined us. We really have been looking forward to this." There was a sense of camaraderie among us. Everyone seemed at ease.

"Yes, that's true," Gary added, "and I'm afraid we may be a bit overbearing this evening, because we are so excited about sharing our stories with you." He placed his hand on his beloved's and sought her permission to elaborate upon recent conversations. "Pam, Dear, shall I begin by summarizing our recent concerns?" She nodded her agreement and gave him a quick wink to confirm that he had once again heard her thoughts.

"Well, the truth is, as excited as we were about meeting with you this evening, we went through a moment of anxiety about sharing our rather unusual stories. Actually our experiences are not unusual at all, but for folks who are not familiar with such notions, it might be perceived as such. We believe you two are people who will actually embrace our stories. So in essence we are coming out to you!" Deb and I immediately put our forks down and applauded their courage.

"Good for you!" praised Deb. "You are going to speak your truths! Hallelujah!" She looked towards me, and intuitively affirmed my permission, "I think it is fair to say that we are definitely interested in hearing about your experiences." It was my turn to reassure everyone at the table that none of us believed in coincidences.

"I think we all know that we have been brought together for a reason." Hands clasped around the table again. "Let's take advantage of this opportunity!"

Pam and Gary took turns apprising us of their communications with various life beings in their backyard and elsewhere. Their stories were heartwarming, delightful, and encouraging. We particularly enjoyed the recent encounter with the doe and her two fawns at the sanctuary that Deb and I both frequented. But the tale of the Bumblebee was mesmerizing.

"So," stated Pam, "there I was removing a few dead heads from the zinnia garden, when I heard the familiar buzzing nearby. I turned to greet our visitor who was busily checking out the fresh smorgasbord of the day. Of course, I welcomed her and praised her beauty, which she normally accepts without fanfare, but that day, she surprised me. She flew upwards towards my face, but kept a very respectable distance so as not to frighten me, and just hovered there. At first I was taken aback, then amused, and then a brain cell fired. I realized she was trying to communicate. So, I quieted myself, which for me is not the easiest thing to do, but I managed! I took a deep breath, relaxed into the moment, and spoke to her telepathically. I let her know that I was listening and asked her to repeat what she had just said. And she did! She was so endearing. First, she complimented my beauty as I had done hers, and then she announced that she had been trying to get my attention for a long time. She told me that I have a very busy mind," Pam rolled her eyes. "She nailed me there. But then she went on to compliment my mind. She was very polite, and told me that my mind was wonderful, but it interfered with her attempts to connect with me. She acknowledged that she was most grateful that we were finally communicating. And then the important message was provided. She confirmed what Gar and I have already suspected. The flora and fauna are trying to reach out to us. They are trying to get our attention so that humans will awaken to what is happening to the environment before it is too late. The bumblebee made her appeal with such tenderness and concern for the Earth. She referred to the Earth as the Mother, and she eloquently spoke of her situation." Pam relayed the words as precisely as she could. "Here are the bumblebee's words: 'The Mother is in great pain and she needs our help. We are doing all that we can, but it is not enough. We make headway, but one human can come along and destroy everything that we have achieved in a matter of minutes. Your species does not realize how destructive they are, or perhaps humans simply do not care. We hope that is not true. That is not our perception of humans, but humankind's lack of awareness has catastrophic consequences. We need your help to save the Earth. Will you please help us? I know that you are of goodness. I see how you take care of this garden. The Earth is everyone's garden, and she must be treated as well as you treat this small space. Thank you for taking such good care of us. And please help us by teaching others about the crisis that is occurring.' With that said, the messenger zoomed away to a nearby flower. She nourished quickly and then zoomed back again and thanked me for listening." Tears trickled down Pam's cheeks. "It was such a lovely encounter." Gary patted her hand and applauded through an unspoken compliment.

"Whew! I love that story!" My exuberance was not containable. I couldn't wait to share my chickadee story, but knew that now was not the time. "I cannot tell you how grateful I am to hear about your experience and also to be privy to the message. My word, this is so comforting. Thank you for taking the risk to share this with us. I know it took a lot of courage, and I want to compliment you both. Speaking the truth is essential! And you both did a wonderful job." Deb's comments were similar. She was as enamored as was I, but she opened the door to another adventure.

"I have an idea that may be very beneficial for all of us." Her companions were intrigued and encouraged her to continue. "Well, when you shared your concerns, I was right there with you. I too have similar apprehensions, and I respect your desire to want to practice with folks whom you think might be accepting of this type of exchange. I would like to practice another scenario. Are you up for that?" We are agreed that we were.

"Pam, what if I had not been in alignment with your experience, and instead of applauding you, I questioned the reality of your experience? Let's all think about this. What are some non-defensive ways of responding to someone who isn't ready to hear these messages at this time?"

"Deb, I'm glad you're bringing this up," replied Pam. "I'm afraid my first response would be defensive, and we all know that will not help the situation. So, what I would like to do is approach the person with loving-kindness. I would like to acknowledge his or her confusion, accept their doubts as reasonable, and then be lovingly candid with that individual, as

I would try to be in any other situation. Let's face it! We cannot expect everyone to just automatically believe our experiences. So, I would like to share the same surprise with them that I enjoyed when the experience happened." Pam sighed as she realized that her approach was worthy of attention. "Wow! I think I just nailed it. This approach has great potential."

"Yes, it does, Dear! It's a winner! I knew you were made for this adventure. You're going to inspire lots of folks and they will believe your stories, because of the openhearted manner that you have. Well done!" Gary's admiration for his long time friend and spouse was obvious. I applauded his comments and Pam's delivery of her story.

"Well, this has been an educational experience. Not only have you broadened my scope of our world, but you've also provided a gracious manner for handling these types of conversations. We just need to be steadfast in our perceptions of what is happening and be generous when it comes to sharing our stories. I will be the first to acknowledge that my stories are unusual, but I'm going to share then anyway. The more stories that are told, the less unusual they will become." I turned to Deb and thanked her for bringing this issue to the surface.

"This has been an education for me as well. Pam, your approach is the answer. Having similar fears as yours, I've thought about this a lot, and this approach tempers my concern. This is how we normally behave. Why would we change what is already a lifestyle? Be gracious, be kind, and be loving and accepting. That's a combo that has a great track record! Thank you both for opening your hearts and your home to us. This has been a fabulous way to begin our new relationships." We congratulated ourselves for a brief moment and then Pam brought us back to task.

"Okay, who is going to take the plunge?" Deb and I exchanged glances and each pointed at the other. My Friend of Old accepted the opportunity and began with a deep breath.

"Well, you three are very lucky because I just had an experience this morning, that I haven't even had a chance to journal about. This is a first-time share, so give me a moment to recall the specifics of the encounter." She paused, stared at her plate, which was still brimming with food, and remembered how the event began.

"Ah yes!" Deb began, "I awoke very early this morning. The moon was still aglow and it called to me. I just love walking by moonlight and this morning it was still high enough in the sky to enjoy to the fullest. I didn't want to miss a moment of its presence, so I just walked in the neighborhood. It was lovely: cool breezes, sweet silence, accompanied by the giant spotlight in the sky. My meanderings took me towards the small park nearby. I don't usually stop there, but this morning I felt compelled to do so. It's a lovely setting with sidewalks running throughout the beautiful grounds creating mystery after mystery. I was happily content.

My mind was quiet, which was a blessing, and I just seemed to be floating along. It was an unusual sensation. My footsteps were silent as was the surrounding area, and I just seemed to be carried in the direction of the pergola located in the back of the park. You know the place! It's so cleverly hidden by the grove of trees carefully planted decades ago. Well, as you might imagine, the setting was lovely. The moonlight cast shadows about the area making the pergola even more enchanting than in the daylight. I stopped at one of the nearby memorial benches, not knowing if I should sit for a while or continue walking. And then I heard it. At first the sound was unrecognizable. First there was a hissing sound, followed by a louder sound that was more like a scream than the bark of a dog. And then movement was seen a few feet away, where a mother fox and four pups were huddled together. I immediately tried to communicate with the mother to reassure her that I meant no harm. I spoke softly at first while remaining perfectly still. I told her that I was just passing by the park when I felt a strong urge to enter and then literally felt directed back to this area. She hissed at me again and then I tried to connect with her telepathically. I told her that I would not come any closer and would leave immediately if she preferred it. She stepped in front of her pups, as if to make it clear that I was not to come forward. I took two steps back, and this seemed to calm her. She yipped at me, although I'm not quite sure that's how it should be described. The fox's voice is truly unusual. Anyway, she appeared to be less worried, so I again made an effort to connect, and this time, I received a clear message. She stared into my eyes, and I heard her convey that she appreciated my concern for her and the children. They are still very skittish, she acknowledged, and explained that they were having their first outing at the park. Then she said that she saw me passing by and reached out to me, and that she was very grateful that I responded. She also said that she had reached out to others without success, except for a young lad who was curious enough to respond. Children are innocents, she said, and easier to connect with than adults. I asked her why she wanted to connect and her answer was stunning. She expressed her concern for Mother Earth, and begged me to help. She said the human species had to accept that they were the primary cause of the Earth's crisis. She fears that we will not listen and that we will not act on the Earth's behalf. I commiserated with her fears, and I promised her that I would take action. This seemed to console her and she bowed her head. I was so touched by her gesture. It was so heart warming. I thanked her for the message, told her that I would share it with others, and then backed away from her and the pups. It was an exhilarating experience."

Everyone at the table was taken by Deb's story. "This is fascinating!" declared Gary and Pam simultaneously. They winked at each other, and then as if some inner decision had been made, Gary continued to speak. "It is so validating for us to hear this. We've been experiencing these encounters for some time now, but we were not willing to discuss it with anyone else. This is absolutely refreshing. Obviously, the messages are sobering and definitely demand our attention, but the experience of communicating with other species is still beyond my imagination. I am so grateful to be part of this. It's just extraordinary!" Similar comments were exchanged by everyone at the table, and then the excitement was overtaken by hunger. Food became the issue again as the yummy sounds echoed around the table.

Once our appetites were sated, our focus returned to the unusual again. Pam opened the discussion with an invitation for more stories to be shared, and everyone looked towards me. I debated what story would be best to share and decided to tell my Friends about the wonderful encounter with the chickadee. "It was a wonderful moment. She offered me the gift of a sunflower seed, made certain that I understood it was a gift, and then politely flew away. I was not able to hear her speak to me, but the eye contact that was purposefully made was definitely a message. I was and remain ecstatic about the experience, but now that I've heard your stories, I know that there is much more that must be pursued. These beloved creatures are definitely reaching out to us. It's exciting and it also requires us to take responsible action. Perhaps, that is the next topic that we should talk about."

"We're on the same track, my Friends! After our encounter with the family of deer earlier this week, we began to strategize a plan for action. We've discussed various ways in which we can share our experiences with other people, including word of mouth, workshops, small gatherings, and also through the written word. So far, we've made a list of folks who we think might be interested in these types of conversations, and we've been gathering information about possibilities for submitting articles, short stories, etc. Our gathering tonight is our first attempt at reaching out to other folks and we're hoping that you two will be interested in joining us in this adventure."

"Yes!" Deb and I replied. We shook our heads and pointed to the other to take the lead. Deb accepted the invitation. "Well, I'm stunned. You guys are moving forward and I am so grateful to be part of this. I've been trying to figure out what the next step was in this process, and you've done it. Thank goodness our paths have crossed."

"No coincidence!" replied the couple. This time Pam took the lead. "We are very happy about this as well. We've been longing for this type of connection and support. It's been wonderful having you here this evening. Being able to share our stories means the world to us, and to think that we can work together on future adventures is just a miracle. Our paths have crossed for a reason." Hands circled the table again. "Thank you, thank you, thank you!" Pam's prayer concluded with an exuberant Amen!

"Okay, so Deb and I need to catch up with you two by creating our own To Do List. When shall we meet again? I'll be glad to host the next gathering." Gary sheepishly asked if the next evening was too soon, and immediately received a positive response. His eyes began to sparkle again.

"Oops!" he declared. "I was going to say that I would bring the dessert for tomorrow night, but I just remembered we haven't had our dessert this evening." He jumped up, made a few noises in the kitchen and returned with a Key lime pie.

"My favorite!" sang out Deb and I.

"Really?" I asked.

"Yes! It's my all time favorite pie!"

"It's ours too!" declared Pam and Gary.

The pie was savored. Each bite better than the last! We were four very satisfied Old Friends. "Something very special is happening here," I mused. "May the Ones who brought us together continue to guide and support us! Dear Old Friends, we will need your loving assistance. And thank you for bringing us together. I think we are going to be a very good team." Another Amen circled around the table. The Circle of Four was aware that they were in the middle of something very unusual that was becoming increasingly strategic and purposeful. Even without full understanding of what lay ahead, they were resolved in their old and present commitments to assist the Earth.

Deb and I said our goodbyes and headed across the street. We were both tired from the night before and from the very long day. Although we didn't want to leave each other's company we knew that we would see each other the next day, which was a very comforting thought.

"Sleep well, my Friend," I said.

"And you!" she replied. I watched her drive away until she was out of sight. Then I went in and greeted the house.

"Hello, Dear House of Mine! You're not going to believe what happened this evening. It was amazing, and guess what? We're going to have company tomorrow night. The four of us will be gathering again. It should make for a lovely evening. I think you will enjoy it." The overhead light flickered so quickly that I was unsure if it had really happened. And then it happened again. A smile rushed across my face. "I thought you would be happy to hear this news. Sleep well, Dear House of Mine."

... *18* ...

"**G**ood morning, Deb! How are you this beautiful day?" A similar remark came from my new, old friend. Last night's gathering was still lingering in our minds and we spent a few moments chatting about it before we headed towards our respective offices. It was delightful to start the day in each other's company. We both admitted that we were very excited about having another meeting with Pam and Gary at day's end. Deb suggested that she arrive early to assist with the meal and I accepted her offer. Then we exchanged a big hug before opening our office doors and entering into our professional worlds.

I checked messages first to see that my day was on track before retreating to my Sacred Space. There was precious time for a moment of silence. The routine was followed as usual. The lighting of the candle came first and then the journal with preferred pen was carefully placed on my lap. Once that was done, the sounding of the bell echoed through the room followed by the long deep breath. The breath served me well. Without any effort, I found myself embraced by the silence. *What sweet beauty it is to be in this place of serenity.* The inner acknowledgement did not interfere with my experience. As always, time passes without one's awareness: a minute or an hour...one cannot discern one from the other. Timelessness prevails in this unknown, remarkable setting. *Am I within, or am I in another realm of existence?* The answer escaped me. I was. I simply was. And I was not alone. The essence of a presence was palpable. I was not alone. *How sweet this is!* I relaxed into the nothingness. At one point, a question raced through my mind. *Am I receiving messages?* Again, there was no answer to the fleeting question. I had no awareness of anything other than being, just being in the silence.

At just the precise time, five minutes before my first client was to arrive, I opened my eyes, refreshed and ready to face the day. Another deep breath was enjoyed as I marveled at the process. Many questions rushed through my mind. Sweet questions, not anxious ones. I wondered how the process actually transpired. I wondered where I went during these inward journeys. I wondered about the Presence that was so profoundly felt during these experiences. And I wondered if some day I might have greater clarity about the phenomenon of resting in the silence.

Many, many questions, Old Mind of Mine. Unfortunately, there is no time for us to converse about the wonderments of our most recent journey. Later, my Friend, later!

And with that internal comment made, the opening of my office door was heard. I quickly placed the journal, which was still closed, in its preferred location. Assuming that no writing activity had occurred during the meditation, I refocused and went out to greet my client.

Working with Bob was an absolute delight. His smile was infectious and he immediately did what Bob always does. He offered me a huge bear hug. Who could resist that offer? His heart was as big as the sun and his passions were bountiful. One of his greatest passions included helping college students to find their own way in life. I often wondered how many students Bob had actually touched during his long career. I suspected the number was much higher that anyone might imagine. One never really knows the influence of one caring individual, and Bob cared a lot about his students. Another passion that occupied much of his time was educating everyone who would listen to him regarding his concerns about the Earth's health. Bob was an enthusiastic voice for Mother Nature. I was excited to hear what he had to say. Like many of the people that I was blessed to work with, Bob challenged my limited perspective of the world.

After the bear hug concluded, I pointed to the inner sanctum, which was how he referred to my private space. "Get in there!" I said nudging him forward, "You know me! I want to hear every detail about your recent escapades." He hurried into the room, sat down in his favorite chair, and greeted me when I joined him.

"Okay Boss! Get your notepad ready!" His demeanor was so joyous, so playful that one could not have an unhappy moment when in Bob's company. I noted that we hadn't seen one another in many months and quizzed him a bit.

"What have you been up to? I know you're here for a reason, so something must be going on with you. Tell me everything!" He always chuckled when I made that remark, and then did exactly as requested.

"Well, first let me apprise you of the truth about retirement. It's great! If I had known it was going to be this much fun, I would have quit my job years ago."

"That's great to hear, but what about your students? Do you miss being at the University?" He paused briefly, sighed loudly, and then reiterated, "Retirement is great! I miss the energy of the students, but my focus has changed. As I grow older and become increasingly aware of my aging body, I have much greater compassion for the Earth. And I feel called to help her.

"That's the main reason I'm here today, because I need to discuss the spiritual journey that you so often brought up in the past. As you well know," he winked at me, "I wasn't ready to talk about such things back then. I was so wrapped up in my perceived self, that I just couldn't fathom being anything other than what I was, or what I thought I was. But so many unusual things are happening around me now that I simply cannot ignore the fact that there is more going on in this world than I've ever known before." He paused briefly and did something that Bob rarely did. He broke eye contact. When he reengaged with me, his eyes sparkled with tears. He tried to speak, but his childhood stutter surfaced and interfered with his attempt. We both took a deep breath at the same time, and he was able to quiet the old tendency.

"There's more!" he whispered and then tears streamed down his cheeks. This big jovial man just sat there allowing his tears to come forward. I knew he was fine, and sat quietly with him as the healing tears did what was needed. Eventually, they passed and he was able to regain his voice once again. "Thank you," he said softly. "I guess that's why I'm really here today. It makes no sense to me, but for whatever reason, the tears are able to flow when I sit in this chair. But goodness, usually the tears don't come until at least thirty minutes into the session. Have I even been here for five minutes? Guess I've set a new record." He grabbed a handkerchief from his pocket and wiped the few remaining tears from his eyes.

"I am honored by your tears, Bob. Undoubtedly, you needed to release an energy that's been weighing heavily upon you. I'm glad this setting is a safe place for you. Is it correct to presume that you've been having some rather remarkable experiences of late?" He nodded, and the joyful grin quickly returned.

"I've been traveling," he announced proudly. "You know I've always wanted to do that, so I finally did it, and it was a life changing experience. But don't get me wrong; one doesn't have to travel far to experience what I've encountered. I suspect most people don't! But after decades of being focused on work, I really wanted to see all the places that I've dreamed about since I was a kid delving into the National Geographic Magazine." Questions were racing through my head, but fortunately good manners overrode the impulse to take over the conversation. It probably will not come as a surprise to you that Bob immediately answered my first question.

"Well, I know you're just sitting on pins and needles wanting to know the first destination point. Do you want to guess?"

"Oh, you rascal! Just tell me where you went and what transpired while you were there?" Bob's laughter filled the room. He was such a playful fellow.

"Okay! Just brace yourself, because this is really going to be a surprise. Even though, my passion was and remains to see numerous National Geographic sites, I decided to go to another place that just captured my imagination a few years back. Have you heard of Bunny Island?"

"Oh my goodness! I've wanted to go there since I first saw a video about it on the Internet. Tell me everything?" My heart was racing! Bob was the first person I had ever met who had been to Bunny Island.

"It was glorious! You know, I've watched dozens of videos about this place over the years, and each time, I literally felt compelled to go to that Island. But then, life would take over, as it always does. Other things would distract me, and the urge would go away. So when retirement actually happened and I was making out my To Do List, a vision of the Island fleeted through my mind, and of course, I watched one of the videos again. And get this! I immediately got on the computer and scheduled the trip."

"And?" My manners fell to the wayside. The idea of being on Bunny Island was more than I could manage. I playfully reached out with a pointed index finger and demanded that he tell me everything. He, of course, loved my enthusiasm.

"It truly was wonderful! Seeing all those rabbits surrounding me is a memory that I will never forget. They were precious! And get this. I actually got down on the ground with them so that they could romp all over me. I'm telling you it was heaven. It really was heaven." Bob's demeanor shifted as he spoke of his connection with these delightful animals. His tender heart came forward in the sweetest way. And I was in awe.

"You know, I've always had a fondness for rabbits. They make my heart sing. Every time I remember the sensation of having them jumping all around me and on top of me, I just feel elated. But there is an interesting thing that occurred with one of the rabbits that really warms my heart. As you well know from the videos, the bunnies surround you until the goodie bag is empty, and then they go looking for another tourist who will happily feed them. Well, after the group left me, one little fellow stayed behind and just kept staring at me. I had noticed this one before. He was definitely a shy one and had cautiously stayed away during the festivities, so I was surprised to see him eyeing me now. Fortunately, my pockets were still full of bunny treats for precisely this type of occasion. I took out several niblets and carefully moved my hand in the direction of the small bunny. His ears perked up, but he resisted the temptation, so I decided to talk with this little fellow. I complimented his colorful coat, which really was exquisite and offered reassurance that I meant him no harm. He seemed to be listening, but I really wasn't sure if I was making any headway with this little guy. Then I grabbed a few more munchies and placed them in my hand, hoping that the increased quantity might capture his attention. And it did. He took a few steps forward, stood on his back legs, and stared at me. I waited quietly hoping that he would approach, but he seemed paralyzed in his upright position. And then, I whispered, please come join me, and he did. Initially, just a few steps were taken and then he came close enough to get a nibble from my hand. At first, I was so mesmerized by his presence that I couldn't do anything but embrace the moment. And then, he came closer and crawled atop my crossed legs and nestled himself in my lap. As you can imagine, I was ecstatic! I offered him more goodies and he did indulge a bit more, before settling in for a peaceful rest. He allowed me to stroke his back and seemed perfectly content to remain in that position. Eventually another herd of bunnies raced in our direction, and he retreated to a more distant location. I decided to refrain from feeding the new group, knowing full well that some other accommodating tourist would see to their needs. They left in search of the aforementioned tourist, while I remained sitting in my cross-legged position. The little fellow waited until the gang had moved to another area of the park and then came in my direction. He stopped a few feet away and stood up again as he had done before. I repeated the invitation for him to join me, and he responded immediately. He came forward, settled into his comfy position again, and just rested with me. He declined my offerings of food and seemed perfectly happy to be in the safety of my lap. Once again he was accepting of my touch and particularly enjoyed having his ears rubbed." Bob paused as he remembered the precious moments. His story was a beautiful example of two species treating each other with respect and trust.

"Bob, can I ask a couple of questions?" He encouraged me to do so. "When you invited the bunny to join you, do you think he understood your request?"

"Yes, I do! Of course, I'm biased, but the timing was just too interactive. What I really am curious about is whether or not it had to do with my whispering the invitation. Did my soft voice enable the connection? I guess I'll never be certain about the encounter, but I do know that it was a gesture of trust and acceptance."

"I agree! That little one checked you out while you were feeding his companions. He saw that you treated them kindly, which presumably emboldened his resolve to approach you. My goodness, Bob! What a lucky man you are! I am so grateful you shared that story with me. And I am so envious. Please forgive me, but I really have bunny envy." We both laughed about my confession before changing to another topic.

"Before we travel to the next adventure, there is one more comment I want to make about the bunny experience. This is going to sound weird, but I'm going to say it anyway. I honestly believe he was trying to reach out to me. When he stood on his back legs the first time, I truly believe he was trying to communicate with me. Unfortunately, his efforts didn't work, not because of him, but because of me. I just was not able to hear him. On the other hand when I whispered the invitation to join me, he responded immediately. I think he understood what I said, and I also think his gesture of sitting in my lap was part of his attempt to make connection. Not only did he validate my fondness for rabbits, but he also opened my heart to the possibility of connecting with Mother Nature and all her creatures. This may all be a figment of my imagination, or it may actually be an expansion of my imagination. Either way, I'm hooked. That little fellow inspired hope in me. I've always wanted to be able to talk to animals. He opened the door for more to come." His smile insinuated that his adventures held many more surprises.

"So, tell me Bob, where did the next adventure take you?"

"Well, the next adventure was truly a bucket list experience. And it probably was the most challenging for me, both physically and emotionally." A bird in the crape myrtle tree located just in front of the office window grabbed Bob's attention. He carefully observed it, which left me wondering what was going on. Then he casually turned back in my direction and commented that the bird, which was a Cedar Waxwing, enjoyed my work. "He said that you work with wonderful people, and he loves to come around and listen to their stories."

My jaw dropped. "Did he really communicate that to you?"

"Oh, yes! And he wants to hear my story now and he requested permission to stay. I, of course, invited him to. You don't mind, do you?" I reassured Bob that his decision delighted me and encouraged him to speak loudly so the beautiful Waxwing could hear everything.

"Well, I went to the other side of the globe for seven weeks." His boyish smile indicated more than words could ever express. He shivered with excitement. "It was amazing! Better than I ever imagined it would be. Actually, it was a dream come true. Obviously, I could spend hours talking about every little detail of the trip, but there is one incident that stands out that I wish to discuss with you. Let me give you a bit of background information. After a very long flight, I took an eighteen hundred mile train ride that provided a wonderful overview of the terrain. It was an excellent way to begin the trip. I followed that with a helicopter ride, which was extremely educative and crystallized for me the necessity of securing some sort of tour service. Fortunately, I found one that catered to older folks. That was a blessing for sure, because some of the available tours were way beyond my physical abilities. Fortunately, the perfect option for someone like me literally just seemed to find me. I had just concluded that a tour service was necessary when I looked up and saw a sign advertising exactly what was needed. It was the first of many blessings to come. Turns out that we were a nicely balanced and compatible group of people. Some were single, others were married, and of course, there were the introverts, and the extroverts: basically a very nice match of folks offering just the right amount of social engagement, and also ample alone time when it was needed." Bob paused briefly to check on the Cedar Waxwing just to be sure that he was still listening. The beautiful feathered friend had actually moved closer to the window. Bob took his relocation as a sign that his story was satisfactory and acceptable. "Lovely neighbor, you have here!" His remark seemed to please our companion.

He continued to tell me that the tours were primarily day trips, which started before dawn and ended at sunset. Some required traveling for several hours before reaching the day's destination. All in all, the experiences satisfied his need to know more about this area of the planet. "Each adventure brought joy to my heart," he said with a big smile. "It truly is amazing how beautiful this planet is. She's remarkable! Even in those areas that are arid and sparse, the variety of plant and animal life is stunning. I was surprised how taken I was by this hot parched scenery, but I was. On one of our rather lengthy walks, our guides were particularly cautious because of the heat. They vigilantly monitored our water intake, warned us about the signs of a heat stroke, and recommended frequent rest breaks. It was good advice! There was so much to explore and to investigate that you can lose yourself in the activity."

"And did you lose yourself, Bob?" My question came from curiosity and concern about this dear man, who had heart issues.

"Well, yes, I think it is fair to say that I did get turned around. There was no traumatizing incident or anything of that sort, but I was just so enamored with the landscape that I did find myself far off the path. The rule of these walking expeditions that we are all supposed to follow is that you always keep your fellow participants in sight. Well, at some point I paused to take a breather and to wipe the sweat from my brow, and that's when I realized that there was no one in my range of vision." He started to chuckle and admitted that his situation was a bit disconcerting. "I looked in all directions and saw nothing but more of the same. I must admit it was an eerie sensation. I was in the middle of nowhere. But as said before, many blessings happened on this journey. There before me was the reason I had stopped to take a breather. It was a very large rock that had broken my momentum. At the time the rock prevented me from getting even further off course, and then after finding myself in this rather ridiculous predicament, it became a place to rest this old carcass of mine." Bob took a deep breath and glanced over at his feathered companion again. I wondered what was happening between them.

"As you might imagine many thoughts raced through my mind. I wondered if this was the end of my adventures and thought how ironic that would be. After a lifetime of waiting to have these adventures would I actually meet my demise by getting lost in the outback of nowhere? Eventually, I got over the rush of fatalistic possibilities, and just started to laugh at myself and at the situation that I found myself in. The release of fearful energy was refreshing. I started enjoying myself again. The large stone upon which I was resting truly was a gift. It offered comfort and convenience, as I slowly repositioned a full three hundred and sixty degrees around the rock taking in the sights in each direction. When I returned to my original starting place, a very large lizard of some type was sitting in the path that had led me to this fine sitting stone. He was a marvelous creature and seemed curious about my presence. I must have been a sight to behold, scooting around from one position to another, on what probably was the lizard's favorite sunbathing place. I greeted him, but he didn't respond. At least I didn't see any signs of a reply, but then I remembered my encounter with the rabbit. I didn't notice any signs then either, but that bunny was staring at me in a very similar way that this lizard was staring at me. The situations were so similar that it gave me pause. I had to keep myself from laughing because I didn't want to frighten the lizard, but the truth was, I had no idea how one is supposed to approach a lizard. My response to the bunny was instinctual…just reached out and welcomed that sweet creature to come closer. Ah!" I thought to myself. "I felt comfortable reaching out to the fluffy adorable bunny. But this was a lizard." The reality of this situation struck me hard. "I was judging this creature differently than the bunny, because of the way it looked." Bob's facial expressions were telling. He was shocked and ashamed at the same time.

"Yes!" he replied to my unspoken perceptions of his reactions. "I was and still am ashamed of my instantaneous reaction to his species. I immediately judged it differently from the bunny that I perceived as a sweet, precious animal. That's shocking! And certainly relevant in today's world where we judge anything and everything for countless reasons. Obviously, I don't have a lot of experience with reptiles, but my reaction went in a negative direction rather than a positive or even a neutral one. This experience has really awakened me to my own behavior and also to the behavior of humankind. We make judgments about those whom we do not know. And then we stand by these knee-jerk judgments, as if they were justifiable reactions." Bob shook his head in disbelief. "This is so disheartening. That encounter with the lizard awakened me to an entirely new world vision: one where everyone respects and accepts everyone else. Regardless of our looks, size, shape, color, specie, preferences, or differences. We all live together on this planet and we need to figure out how to do that while honoring everyone else's needs." He glanced towards the Cedar Waxwing again, as if he was looking for support. I saw a few tears glittering in his eyes.

"Bob, that was a huge awakening. I assume you've been spending a lot of time with your journal since that encounter happened."

He smiled and nodded, then leaned forward with elbows on his knees. "You know, I've really had to look at myself. I'm basically a good guy, one that most people think highly of, but the truth is, I just don't measure up." He quickly raised a finger to keep me from jumping to his rescue. "Let me finish, please. I promise you that I'm not being hard on myself. I'm being realistic. I'm a work in progress, and finally, I realize how important it is for me to improve myself. That's not too much to ask of oneself. We all need to be actively involved in our own development, but we get so involved in the distractions of life that we forget the most important part of being alive. We're here for a reason."

Bob's announcement grabbed my attention. His eyes penetrated mine as he continued, "There comes a time when we need to face our truths. One by one, as we are able! I'm an old guy just now coming to realize that the world doesn't revolve around me. I am not the center of attention. I'm just one of billions of other life beings living on this planet. Well, it's time that we, meaning all of us, open our eyes and accept the reality of our situation. We're living on a Life Being who is in serious trouble, and we cannot continue pretending that nothing is wrong. We cannot survive without her, and she will not survive without our help. What I learned from my travels is this. Other species are already working on the Earth's behalf. It's the human species that is lagging behind in this matter, and we are the ones who are causing her health issues. We've all got to get on board with this, because everyone one of us has to participate. If some of us improve our ways, that will be helpful, but it will not be enough to change her downward spiral. She needs everyone's assistance and our good will. If we treat each other with loving kindness, she will benefit greatly from our good intentions. If we also treat other species with good will, the positive interactive engagement will profoundly shift the well being of the Earth. This may sound crazy, but it isn't. We can help her by changing our negative, careless ways. She will benefit and so will we. And by the way, I learned something else while I was traveling. I know this is old news for you, but I just wanted to acknowledge that you were right all along." I wasn't sure what Bob was talking about, but I was eager to hear whatever it was. "You were right about the power of energy work and prayer. Praying for the Earth and sending her positive energy are the most effective and efficient means of assisting her. If all the people of Earth would participate in these two healing modalities, her recovery process would be greatly hastened, and then there would be time for the necessary sustainability actions to be addressed." Bob took a deep breath and relaxed back into his chair. Then he turned and gave the thumbs up to the Cedar Waxwing. I waited for a moment to see if he was just taking a breath or was actually at a stopping place. He pointed a finger in my direction indicating that it was my turn to take over.

"My goodness, Bob, you really have had an incredible experience. I am so grateful that you shared some of your stories with me. I realize that there are many more to come, but what you shared today is a gift. Thank you!"

"I knew you would be pleased. I guess the main reason I wanted to see you was to say thank you. Because of our work together, I was able to be fully present and open to all the experiences that unfolded, and that's because of you, Boss! Your skills, your beliefs, your gracious way of being have helped me so much. As I said, there's a lot of work left for me to do, but I'm excited about it. I want to improve myself for me, and for the planet, and all my fellow beings. It's fascinating thinking of oneself as a member of a planetary family. That's what we are! We are all family. I like the feel of that. I like belonging to such a large family."

"Earlier, you said you wanted my opinion about your experiences. Was there something specific that you were curious about?" He searched in the files of his mind and then began to giggle.

"Well, if memory serves me, which it rarely does, I just wanted to know if you believe my interpretations of the incidents were valid. I suspect many people would think I'm crazy. Communicating with a rabbit, a Cedar Waxwing, and a lizard! And you're right, there are many more stories to share, but these two give you an idea of the direction in which I am going."

"This is easy, Bob! I believe your stories and your interpretations, and I am acutely aware that you are intuiting my thoughts with a keen degree of accuracy. I am particularly impressed with your description of our planetary family. I love that imagery and I totally agree with you. There is so much more that humans have to accept as their reality." My mind quickly reviewed Bob's stories and I remembered a question that came up for me regarding the lizard.

"Bob, by the way, how did things work out between you and the lizard? Did you have any communication with him?"

"Oh my goodness!" he pushed himself to the edge of his chair, smiling from ear to ear. "I didn't finish the story! There's more!" he giggled. "After finishing my meanderings about life and my limited involvement with it, I returned to the reality that was still confronting me. I was still in the middle of nowhere with an empty canteen and the midday sun beating down upon me. I stood up and looked in all directions again, hoping for some sign of life somewhere in the vast emptiness of my surroundings. I would love to tell you that I was feeling brave and confident about my situation, but I wasn't. In fact, my concern was rising, and my options didn't diminish my worriment. The alternative that seemed most viable was the path where the lizard first appeared and still remained. My footprints were clearly visible, so it seemed wise to back track and rejoin the main trail, and hopefully find my companions from the tour. With that decision made, I moved towards the lizard thinking that he would scurry away, but he didn't; so I attempted to walk around him, but he wouldn't allow it. Each time I changed my route, he raced in front of me and planted himself in front of me. I couldn't believe it, but it appeared that he was deliberately trying to keep me from going down that path. I was confused and a bit miffed. This reptile was wasting my time and my energy. It just didn't make sense. Finally, I returned to the rock and sat down again. The lizard followed and rested on the trail about two feet in front of me. We stared at each other for a while, and then an image flashed through my mind. I saw myself walking in the opposite direction with the lizard leading the way. It was the weirdest thing! And what was even stranger was that the vision seemed like the solution to my problem.

"So, I just looked at the fellow and softly said that I was lost and asked him if he could help me. Now, Boss, you're not going to believe this, but it really happened. The lizard immediately responded. He raced to the other side of the rock, turned around, and stared at me. So, I followed him!" Bob threw his hands up in the air and laughed at himself. "Can you believe that? Here I was lost in the wilderness, following a lizard that clearly was an angel from heaven. Even now, the event remains a mystery to me. I honestly don't know how I got lost in the first place. How can someone just wander away from a group of folks when you're on a tour? And how could I possibly decide that a lizard was going to guide me out of my predicament? Let's face it, Boss; this is a crazy story. And it's true! I followed the lizard for over thirty minutes, and then the miracle appeared. Up ahead, in waving distance, I saw my companions. The guides came racing towards me. The relief in their eyes was obvious. Needless to say, they had been frantic, not knowing if they should go on or back track. The reunion truly felt like Divine intervention. The guides were trying to steer me in the direction of the others, but I resisted, which was troublesome to them. I didn't know how to explain to them that I needed to say goodbye to the lizard, but I finally firmly told them to give me a moment. Well, I guess my voice was so forceful that they gave me some space. I quickly turned around hoping to find my guardian angel on the trail, but he wasn't in sight. Much to the chagrin of my guides, I backtracked a few yards and then the Angel appeared on the trail. It was such a pleasure to see him again. I got down on my knees to thank him, and he came a few steps closer. We stared at each other for a while, and of course, I shed a few tears. I wiped the tears away with my index finger and then reached out to my new friend. He came forward and licked the tears from my finger. It was such a sweet moment of connection. Sweet beauty," Bob whispered. "He allowed me to touch the top of his head, and then off he ran back down the trail. He stopped at one point, turned around, and stared for a moment. And then he was gone."

When Bob looked up he found me in tears. I couldn't help myself. "That was a remarkable story! Once again, you had a special encounter with another species. I love your description of the final exchange. Sweet beauty! Indeed, it was."

"Actually, that little fellow saved my life. If I had gone in the other direction, I would have been without water for several more hours. I don't think this old body would have made it. Fortunately, the guides had ample water for me and we were only twenty minutes away from the vehicle. So all was well. All is well! I'm a very lucky man." He paused, took a deep breath and sighed loudly. "There's so much more going on in this world than we know. And it's a shame, because life would be so much easier and far more expansive if we allowed ourselves to be a part of it."

"You're making a difference, Bob! Please keep sharing these stories with others. It's important! People will listen to your stories, and their hearts will open to the 'more' that you are presently experiencing. It's here! The 'more' is here at all times, just waiting to engage with us. But people need help to take that next step. You, Dear Friend, are one who can help a lot of folks! Just as you helped all those students, now you can help other folks to realize who they really are."

Next door, Deb sat quietly waiting for her first client to arrive. Rarely did she have this opportunity. Typically, clients arrive early for their appointments, and it was particularly unusual for this client to be tardy. She felt slightly guilty for enjoying the free time. It was unusual for her to have a moment of respite, and Deb forced herself to resist the urge to get up and do something. Instead, she allowed her mind to wander. She thought about the evening before, remembering various comments made by Pam and Gary. She was very excited about spending more time with them tonight after work. They were an enchanting couple and she was eager to learn more about them. Just as her mind scurried off in another direction, she heard the outside office door open. That brought an abrupt halt to the mind's meanderings. Deb took a deep breath before exiting the room to greet her client.

"Good morning, Barbara! It is so good to see you again." Many apologies were offered for the few minutes of tardiness that occurred. Deb reassured her client that it was not an inconvenience and invited her back to the private office. Barbara rushed in, sank into her chair, and collapsed into tears. Although Deb was concerned, she trusted Barbara's ability to take care of herself. She deliberately waited, giving Barbara time to regain her composure. After what seemed like an eternity, the flow of tears came to a halt, and Barbara took a deep breath. Repositioning in her chair, she sat up straight and faced Deb. "Thank you for not intervening. You have great intuition, Deb. Obviously, I just needed to release all that pent-up emotion. It is amazing how much the past can impact the present. Whew!" Barbara relaxed back into her chair and took another deep breath.

"That was a big release, Barb. What brought this on? Do you feel ready to talk about it?" Barbara reassured Deb that she was okay and immediately began to update her on the situation.

"Actually, I'm really doing well, but traffic was terrible this morning. As you well know, I am usually here early, but the traffic was backed up for miles, and there are no alternative ways for getting here, so I was stuck. And I left my phone at home, so I couldn't let you know what was going on. The longer I sat there in line, the more difficult it became to monitor my agitation. I knew exactly what was going on. This is old stuff! Punctuality was an edict in my family. There was no tolerance for tardiness. And here I am decades later, still feeling the impact of that family rule. Will this nonsense ever end?"

"You were only a few minutes late, Barbara. No harm was done."

"I know that, I really do. And I repeatedly reassured myself of that while the traffic was at a complete standstill. But it didn't matter! Even though I knew you would understand the situation and that you would not think that some huge offense had been committed, the incident still blindsided me. In my family, being late was unacceptable. In fact, being on time wasn't good enough. Punctuality meant you arrived early." Barbara started laughing at herself. "Do you believe this? Clearly, the past still plays a role in my life."

"Barb, let's both take a deep breath." And this they did. In fact, they enjoyed several deep breaths before Deb assumed her role. "Barbara, I think we should look at this incident from a different perspective. It's obvious that you have done a lot of work regarding this issue. You grasp the underlying trauma and shame, you're aware of the triggers that cause the pain to resurface, and you're aware that it was a family dynamic that is not useful in your life today. You have all this knowledge, and still the old pain holds significant power over you." Barbara agreed with Deb's summation and was eager to explore other possibilities for dealing with this annoying issue.

"Sometimes," continued Deb, "these old issues continue to resurface because they hold a message that hasn't yet been discerned. I've had the pleasure of witnessing this with other folks and it's been amazing. If you actually face the issue, as a gift, rather than an intruder, you may discover something very fascinating and beneficial to your present life." Deb had much more to say, but she wanted Barb to absorb the idea.

"I get it!" responded Barb. "So the point is to eliminate the knee-jerk reaction, and instead open my heart to the onslaught of emotions. Hmm! Well, can we try that now? The experience is still fresh in my memory. And I feel able to pursue this, so let's do it!" Barbara's response was exactly what Deb had hoped for.

"Actually, this is perfect timing, Barb. You've already experienced the rush of emotions, so you don't need to open that floodgate again. Instead, let's just sit here quietly, calmly, and take some deep breaths again." Deb gave Barb time to relax and settle into the idea of welcoming the fears from the past as a gift and a messenger. "Just relax, Barb. Don't try to make something happen. Just remember that the pressure from the old message no longer applies to your life today. The shame and punishment associated with tardiness belongs to a time gone by. That fear resided in your parents and they mistakenly imprinted it upon you. Their fear became your fear. It is sad to think that your parents were so fearful about punctuality, but they were. For whatever reasons, their fear was so large that they could not contain it and it became your burden. Take a few more breaths, Barb, and see where that process takes you." Both women simultaneously indulged in the deep breathing exercise. One escaped to another time and place, while the other protectively witnessed the process. Deb sat quietly, simply waiting for a sign that would nudge her toward the next step to be taken. Minutes passed, but she was patient; she'd been through similar situation many times before, and she trusted the process.

The sign came with absolute clarity...Barbara opened her eyes and immediately inhaled deeply. Their eyes met and a smile of curiosity united with a smile of sweet knowing. It was obvious that Barb's experience was noteworthy. Deb reached into a nearby drawer and pulled out a small container of nuts and passed it her way. "You might need a little protein, Barb. I think you have travelled far, and some nourishment may be helpful." She accepted the treat and leaned back in the chair holding the container in her lap. Her breathing was smooth and easy; she just needed a few moments to center herself. Eventually, she popped the lid off the nuts and enjoyed a few bites. She offered them to Deb, who grabbed a couple. It was comforting to hear the crunching sound coming from both.

"Well, Dear One, it looks to me like you just had an adventure. Would you like to share your story?" She snatched a few more nuts, before responding.

"How do you know that?" she asked. "How can you possibly know what just happened to me?"

"I don't, Barbara! I have no idea what transpired, but from the look on your face, it seems obvious that something did happen. I've seen similar reactions from other people who have sat in that chair and opened their hearts to new possibilities. Each one has his or her unique experience, and they return to that chair in awe and wonderment. They acknowledge a feeling of inadequacy in their ability to speak of the situation, and still, they know with absolute certainty that the experience was real. Does this sound true for you, Barbara."

"Yes, it does! And I presume that every one of those individuals was concerned about your reaction." Deb's smile and nod validated her assumption. "Well, I certainly understand that," she admitted. "Deb, we've known each other for a very long time, and I totally trust you. But I'm nervous about revealing my experience. I don't want you to think I'm crazy. I don't want to lose your respect. And I do not want you sharing this with anyone else, which of course, you wouldn't do anyway. I know you abide by your professional ethics, but the truth is, coming out about this experience makes me feel very vulnerable, and that vulnerability is bringing up a lot of nonsense for me. So, please forgive my neediness right now. I definitely want to discuss my experience with you, but, but, but." Barb started to laugh at herself. She understood herself very well. Deb reassured her that other clients were equally concerned about the same issues she just divulged.

"You're in very good company, Barb. I'm eager to hear what happened and grateful to have the privilege to bear witness to your journey. I do understand your reservations, but please try to let go of that. You've just had a remarkable experience. Share it with confidence, humility and gratitude. And I promise you that I will hold your story in my heart." Barb placed her hands to her chin in prayerful position. Deb bore witness to the transformation that transpired. The great concern that engulfed her face slowly dissipated and was replaced with an expression of strength and determination. It was a sight to behold. And then, she opened her eyes, and invited Deb to join her journey.

"Thank you for defining my experience as a journey, because it was. When I opened my eyes and saw that so little time had passed I was stunned. It felt as if I had lived a lifetime during that period of time. Actually, it felt like several lifetimes, because I actually visited different settings that brought clarity to the issue regarding punctuality. First, I was given the opportunity to understand my parents' fear, which had never even occurred to me before you mentioned it earlier; and you were on the mark, Deb. They were terrified about my safety, just as their parents had been for them and their siblings during the period of the Second World War. Even though they grew up in different countries, each family lived the horror of that period. Their parents, my grandparents whom I never knew, were rigid about time. They wanted to know their children's exact location every minute of the day. And when the air raids sounded, the kids were expected to be home within minutes, which of course was not always possible." Barbara stared at the floor imagining the agony of those times. The fears that surfaced every time the alarms when off and the ever-present fear that it would happen again, at any given time, must have been excruciating.

"No wonder my parents were so obsessed with punctuality. I cannot imagine what it was like to live through those dark times. Now, I understand why they were so overly concerned about my tardiness. Their frustrations were related to their fear of losing me. Isn't that sad, Deb? They loved me so much, but the fears from the past compromised our relationships. What a blessing it is to understand how much they cared about me! Isn't it a shame that this was never discussed? They probably didn't know how to broach the topic, and I'm certain they would not want to talk about their memories of the war. Who would? In essence, another way they tried to take care of me was by remaining silent about those terrifying times. They didn't want me to feel the burden that they carried." She paused for a moment, assimilating all the information that she had received in her first encounter of the journey. "I now realize how much they loved me. They really did. I'm sorry that I didn't understand that when I was younger, and that the opportunity for greater understanding and connection never came to fruition. But it has now. We had a chance to reconcile, Deb. I actually had a chance to see them again. They both were of youthful appearance, the way they looked when I was a kid. Their smiles were so kind and gentle, and I could see how proud they are of me. What a gift! And I was able to express my love for them. It just poured out of me. I'm so glad that I was able to tell them how much I appreciated everything they did for me. It feels wonderful to share this love fest with my parents. I am so blessed!" Barbara paused, while a teardrop escaped to honor the event. Once again, Deb had the pleasure of witnessing an incredible event.

"What a remarkable healing experience! You truly are blessed! And I am honored to be in your presence. Thank you, for sharing that experience."

"I'm very grateful that you are here. It helps to share this experience. I know it sounds crazy, but it really happened. I can't explain how, but it was pure grace. I wish everyone could experience something similar. Deb, this journey, as you called it, is confounding, but one of the reasons that I know it is real is because I am incapable of making up a story like this. It is simply beyond my creative abilities."

"I'm really glad that you're owning this encounter with your parents. I agree with you Barb, the 'how' of these unusual events is definitely puzzling, but the healing effects are profound. You can attest to that, and I can attest to what I am witnessing. These wonderful experiences must be shared. I believe these events are happening all around the planet, but many people are afraid to share them for all the reasons that you discussed and countless more, and this is a shame, because something very important is happening. These unusual events need to come out into the open so that everyone who is experiencing one knows that he or she is not alone. I suspect the number of these events that are transpiring around the world every day will stun the populace, as it well should. The time has come for this information to become public. People need to know about the special events that are transpiring throughout all the lands of this beautiful planet. The stories have to be told and shared. It's important, Barbara. I think if this information becomes known worldwide that life, as we presently know it, will change. This is happening for a reason." Deb's client looked on in awe. She was intrigued by what she was hearing.

"Oh, my goodness! What you are saying is beyond comprehension, and yet, it rings true. Deb, I need to share the next part of the story, because it relates to what you just said." Barbara placed her hands in prayerful fashion again and sighed. "I cannot believe this is happening, but it is, and you are a witness to it. Jeepers! This really is an amazing experience." Deb gently urged her to continue.

"So, after farewells were exchanged with my parents, I instantly found myself in another time and place. It was nighttime so my experience was more emotional than visual. I was running as fast as I could through a heavily forested area, as if my life depended on it. The sensation that overwhelmed me was that I had to be at a certain place at a certain time or something awful was going to happen. Of course, I didn't understand what was happening, but I knew the person, the man, who was desperately racing through the thick and very dark woods, was me. It was me in another lifetime. The sense of urgency and commitment that he carried was overpowering. Even now, I can feel the panic that he felt, and the more frightened he became, the faster he tried to run. My goodness, Deb, it was exhausting and painful." Barbara immediately waved her hands to negate what she had just said. "Let me clarify that!" she interjected. "I was not experiencing any pain, but I could sense his pain. Every time he fell down, it was a jolt, and he fell a lot because he couldn't see where he was going. His strength of will was unbelievable. He just kept pushing and pushing himself until he was on the verge of collapse, but he would not give up.

"Eventually in the distance, I could hear people yelling and screaming in terror. It was bone chilling to experience, but he, we, continued to barrel forward. When we finally arrived at the destination, the scene was utter devastation. The entire village had been destroyed. Bodies were everywhere, some were dead; others were terribly injured. Oh, Deb, it was dreadful.

"Undoubtedly, he felt responsible for the tragedy. I think he had heard that the attack was going to happen at a certain time, and he was desperately trying to reach his village before the marauders arrived. I'm not sure his presence would have made a difference, but clearly he believed that he had failed his family and friends. His agony was beyond words. Everywhere he looked he saw death and destruction. My heart ached for him. He blamed himself for being late. He was convinced if he had returned earlier that his people would have been prepared to defend themselves. Whether this is true or not, one will never know, but clearly he went to his death believing that his absence was the cause of this tragedy." Barbara stopped briefly to regain her center, but it was obvious that she had more to share.

"Fortunately," she said quietly, "I was whisked away to another location and time when I realized what his intentions were. I did not have to witness him taking his own life, but I understand his decision. His pain was inconsolable. There were too many losses to bear." Another moment of deep breaths were necessary before she continued.

"The new setting was the absolute opposite of the previous one. I went from darkness and hostility to the most beautiful and serene environment that I had ever seen before. The contrast from where I had been to this new area was mind-blowing. I literally felt as if I had come from hell and landed in heaven. My location was elevated, overlooking endless valleys and hills that reached far beyond my range of vision, and still I was able to see every detail clearly. It was amazing. I stood at the edge of the overlook just breathing it all in, when the sense of another's presence overwhelmed me. The realization that I was not alone was so palpable that it could not be denied. My body reacted so quickly to the sensation that it startled me. I don't even remember turning around. It just happened! One second, I was taking in the views, and the next instant, I was looking at the incredible views behind me, which were equally as spectacular as the ones that were now behind me, and to each side of me. I was surrounded by spectacular views! Only then did I grasp the reality of my situation. The landing where I was perched was smaller than this room. My mind immediately went into overdrive trying to figure out an escape route from this predicament, and then, a voice softly and gently told me to be in peace. The voice reassured me that I was in no danger, and in fact, my location was one of the most popular places in existence. And then, the voice explained that this was a location where heartfelt thoughts were pondered and significant decisions were made." Deb's curiosity was off the charts; her list of questions was growing longer by the second.

"Goodness, I'm going on and on. Am I boring you to tears, Deb?"

"No!" she replied. "Not at all, Barbara! In fact, I'm having a hard time monitoring my curiosity. Your story is compelling and greed is consuming me. I want to hear every last detail. Please continue."

"Thank you, I really do want to share my experience with you. It seems important to do so. The next thing that happened was indicative of what was to come. The voice respectfully asked my permission to join me on the precipice. Needless to say, I invited the voice to do so. I was very excited about meeting this invisible voice. And then it happened, Deb. This incredible glowing Light Being manifested before me. It really happened! There it was standing, or perhaps, it is more accurate to say 'floating' several feet from from me. I don't know how to describe the experience other than to say the light engulfing the Being was exceptionally bright with a mixture of gold and white colors. At first, the light was blinding, but very quickly, it dimmed and I was able to gawk at the visitor. Although I could not discern any specific features of this Light Being, its presence was indisputable. The essence emanating from this Being was pure goodness, and the apprehension that was initially felt disappeared immediately and I was indeed at peace.

"It is good to see you again, Old Friend. Welcome Home!" Those were the exact words that were spoken, and Deb, the words just reverberated within and through me. I knew this Being was speaking a truth that escaped me. I truly felt as if we were Old Friends, and even though I did not recognize the location, it really did feel like home. It was an indescribable moment of knowingness and confusion at the same time.

"Initially, I was uncertain about the gender of this individual, and even now, I am still not sure if my determination was correct. After he spoke, I sensed a masculine energy, so from that point on I addressed the Being as such. He explained to me that we had enjoyed similar encounters on many other occasions and each time we reunited, it was for the purpose of clarification and renewal of commitments previous made. He insinuated that commitments often entail numerous lifetimes to reach fruition. Essentially, one lifetime sets the stage for another, and each one builds upon the previous one. So, in my particular situation, punctuality and tardiness are the threads that weave these lifetimes together. It seems that it was necessary for me to experience the pain and suffering that can result from tardiness so that I will fully comprehend the necessity of being punctual. According to the Old Friend, my journey in this lifetime requires a commitment to punctuality; however, it must be approached openheartedly rather than obsessively. Undoubtedly, the lessons embedded in me regarding tardiness have caused me to overact to incidents that do not demand any other action than an apology. As you noted today, I was only a few minutes late, but from my perspective, the incident was unforgivable. Hopefully, now that I understand the lineage of this behavior, perhaps I will be able to manage my reactions in a more balanced and healthy manner." Barbara reached for her glass and took a few sips of water. I asked if I might intervene for a moment and she seemed relieved.

"Barb, this is truly a life-altering experience. To receive this amount of information in one session is remarkable. It seems that you are being prepared for whatever is unfolding in this lifetime." She nodded in agreement. "Did your guide provide you with any specific details about the days ahead?"

"Yes and no!" she answered. "It seems that I am to be prepared to relocate before the end of this year, which is unimaginable to me, but the Old Friend was insistent about it. He urged me to begin the relocation process now, starting with the release of excess accumulated items. Yikes!" Barb's reaction was comical. "Obviously, the Old Friend is aware of all those boxes in my basement." She chuckled about the situation for a moment, before reality sank in. "Deb, what do I do with this? I just had an incredible experience that I know was real, which includes a message about being prepared for *something* that's going to happen in the future. And part of this preparation process involves moving to an unknown destination. Goodness! This is a lot to take in!" Deb validated her reaction and suggested that they both just sit quietly for a moment. It was a good idea, but Barbara was afraid she might go off on another adventure, so she was reluctant to do so.

"Barb, just take some deep breaths with me. You're not going anywhere. Just relax with me. Your journey has been bountiful today, and now you just need to sit with the goodness that has transpired. You are not expected to clean out your house tomorrow. This is a process. And now, remember your Old Friend and the lovely setting that you enjoyed." Barbara did as suggested and soon a sense of immense gratitude washed over her.

"Whew! Thank you, Deb. Your calm presence is helping me to live into this experience, and I realize now that there is more to share. How could I forget this?" she shook her head in disbelief. "Deb, I've never felt such a strong sense of belonging before. I belong in that place. I came from that place. Even though I have no recollection of that beautiful terrain, I feel it in my bones. It is home. Guess, that sounds really weird, uh?"

"No, not at all. I've heard similar stories, Barb. Each adventure is uniquely different, but the gist of the story is the same. You're not alone in this experience. In truth, you're in very good company. You, like many other people, have enjoyed communication and connection with another life form." Barbara's eyes sparkled with excitement.

"That's very comforting to hear, Deb, and it brings up another facet of the experience that I also forgot to share with you. Deb, I knew that we were not alone. Even though, I only saw the Light Being, I was absolutely certain that others were also there bearing witness to the encounter. The same way you were here bearing witness, there were others honoring the event. We are not alone!" Deb, who was a true believer in this concept, nodded in agreement.

"And there's more!" Barb continued. "We are deeply loved by these 'Others.' They, whoever they are, are devoted to our well being. I'm sorry that my words do not adequately represent the deep heartfelt connection that they feel for us, but their love and concern for us is real. It's a wonderful experience to know that you are loved." Her eyes closed briefly as she reveled in the moment of awareness.

"I am so grateful for this experience. You do know that I will be calling upon you again. There will be ups and downs about this upcoming relocation idea, and I will need your help to keep grounded and on course. It's actually exhilarating to think that 'more' is coming." Barbara's smile lit up the room. Deb imagined the light she was emanating was as bright as the Light Being's that she had encountered on her adventure.

A passage from
The Word
(Chapter One)

"All who come into existence ponder about their existence, and each new arrival curiously seeks more information about their place in existence."

Pam and Gary were punctual as always, and they came bearing gifts, which Gary immediately placed on the dining room table. "Oh, my! This doesn't look like a light meal. I think we're in for another feast!" Deb and I both reassured them that the fare was sumptuous, but light.

"That may sound contradictory," explained Deb, "but it isn't! We've created a lite menu, and added some pizzazz. Come take a peek in the kitchen, and then, we're going to put you to work." The foursome immediately fell into a natural rhythm of chatting and playfully teasing one another. An outsider, looking in, would have thought that these four had been friends for ages. In truth, they were, but in this life experience, this was just the second time that they were gathering.

Within minutes, a decision was made to incorporate the appetizers into the meal. Everyone was ready to sit down at the table and begin the evening's conversation. Each person grabbed a dish or two and soon the table was fully adorned with a variety of healthy and relatively healthy treats. Everyone took a seat and Gary was invited to offer a prayer. He graciously accepted.

"Thank you, thank you, thank you!" he began. "We are so grateful to be gathered again. We are so grateful that the four of us have been brought together and our hearts are open to whatever tasks lie ahead for us. We thank you for the blessings of this wonderful meal, for the connection we share, and for the awareness we have been given regarding our beloved planet. And at this time, we ask for the Earth's healing. Please help her to regain her health, and please enlighten all of us, who call her home, to appropriately take care of her. We know there is much that must be done on her behalf. Please guide us to be good stewards of her needs. Amen."

"Amen!" replied the other members of the foursome.

"That was lovely, Gary! Thank you, for including the Earth in your prayer." My comments embarrassed him. Ultimately, he was a very shy person who had moments of extroversion. Deb also complimented his prayer, which brought on a few tears.

"Thank you, both. I must admit that your comments deeply touch me. I'm really attempting to be diligent about honoring the Earth. She desperately needs our help. And I find it very comforting to know that the four of us are of like mind. Pam and I were discussing this last night after you left. We were feeling hopeless and alone in our desire to help the Earth, but your companionship in this endeavor has totally changed our attitude." A big grin spread across his face and he giggled at himself. "I'm embarrassed to admit this, but I've been looking forward to seeing you two all day. And every time the thought entered my mind, this goofy grin popped up." With a silly tilt of the head, and a grin from ear to ear, he demonstrated his point. "I'm really looking forward to our conversation tonight."

"I love your boyish grin!" asserted Deb, as Pam nodded in agreement. "And I wonder, if you might like to be the initiator of tonight's conversation." At first, it looked as if Gary would accept the lead, but then, in a loving gesture, he invited his beloved to do so.

"Pam, Dear, I had the privilege of offering the prayer, would you like to begin our conversation?" She readily accepted the opportunity.

"Thank you, Gar, I would love to take the lead. My entire day has been spent in gratitude, and it is a wonderful way to live. So, if all of you are up for this, I would like us to begin with an expression of gratitude." The idea was well received. "And I'll be happy to go first. Gary just addressed some of what I've been feeling, but it needs to be elaborated upon. There is a truth that must be shared, but it is embarrassing to do so. I had no idea how lonely the two of us have been. It's perfectly reasonable when you understand the level of our compatibility. We are very happy together. Essentially, we satisfy each other's needs for socialization, and because we have so many similar preferences, that also makes life very comfortable for us. On a day-to-day basis, our lives are very content." She turned to her husband for confirmation and he respondeded succinctly.

"Oh, yes," he concurred. "That describes our relationship and our lives very nicely."

"The truth is we've been so content within our little world that we forgot that we needed other folks in our lives. We didn't realize there was a problem until recently when we became increasingly more alarmed by what we were observing on our outings. The signs of the Earth's struggles became more and more apparent every time we went for a walk. What we were seeing was confirming what we were reading, regarding the planet's environmental crisis. The more we saw, the more helpless we felt. And that's when it finally dawned on us that we had really become reclusive. We were just in the beginning stages of dealing with that new awareness when we coincidently ran into our neighbor," she pointed towards me. "It was such a delight to see you! We were invigorated by that initial contact and so excited about the date we planned, which turned out better than anyone could ever hope for. And then we met you, Deb!" Gratefulness exuded from Pam.

"I am so, so grateful that the four of us have been brought together. This is not a coincidence. I'm grateful for the connection, the camaraderie, and the possibilities that lie ahead. When Gary and I would think about tackling the Earth's health issues, we were overwhelmed by the problem. Essentially, the magnitude of her issues just stopped us in our tracks. But I don't feel stymied anymore. In fact, optimism seems to be stirring within me...and I like the feel of that." Pam reached her hands out, and within seconds the table was encircled by the four new friends. "I am so grateful for the two of you and we really are looking forward to working and playing with you in the days ahead. And I am also grateful to those who brought us together. I know you did this for a reason," she stated, "so thank you!" The hands clasped tightly together were resistant to releasing their grips. A strong bond was being established by these four friends of old.

"Okay, everyone, we really do need to relax back into our chairs now. And I wonder who would like to make an offer of gratitude next?"

"Well, I will take advantage of the moment, if I may?" Everyone nodded in my direction. I took the all-important deep breath and was instantly joined by my companions. "My list is long," I began. "I too am grateful for what is happening among us, and I agree with you, Pam. This is not a coincidence. Knowing that we've been brought together for a reason adds to the mystery of our connection. While I must admit that my memories are elusive regarding our previous times together, the heartfelt closeness that I have for each of you is all the evidence I need to accept this gift of reunion as a sacred event. I am so deeply grateful for all of you! I am also very grateful for my work and for all of the lovely people that cross my path. None of this is a coincidence. Everywhere I turn, someone is awakening to the Earth's crisis. I am so grateful to be here in this moment of time with all of you. We are blessed to have the opportunity of being here on the Earth at this specific time." As did Pam, I reached out to my companions as well, and again the circle of friendship was made. "Thank you all for coming this evening, and thank you for being in my life." The routine was now in operation. Deep breaths were enjoyed, then we all relaxed into our chairs, and then another took the lead. This time, Deb accepted the opportunity to share her thoughts.

"My gratitude has already been spoken beautifully by both of you," she glanced towards Pam and me. "So, I will simply say that I too feel the unique quality of our reunion. It is so good to be in arms' reach of old friends. I cannot explain this reality, but it needs no explanation anyway. Suffice it to say we have gathered once again. And I am so grateful to be with you." She reached out, the circle united, and then we relaxed and it was Gary's time to speak. He quickly reinstated the circle by reaching out before he even spoke.

"I am grateful for the opportunity to serve. Even though the specific plans still escape me, I know we are here to serve the Earth. And I believe that we are also intended to serve all the Life Beings that reside upon her. Too many stories about connection and communication with other life forms are surfacing for this to be a mere coincidence. This is happening for a reason. If we are going to assist the Earth, then all Life Beings must be taken into consideration. I know it may be difficult for some humans to accept this idea; nonetheless, we must seek cooperation and collaboration from all life species. I am so grateful to be a part of this rescue mission, as well as the transformational process that the planet is going through. I feel as if I've been preparing for this all my life. Isn't that strange?" He paused deep in thought, and then ended with another prayer. "Dear Friends, far and near, please help us to be what we are intended to be...good stewards of the Earth, of our neighbors, and of the universe itself. Thank you for giving us the opportunity to be of service." With that said, we filled our plates and enjoyed the meal. Rather quickly, our conversation returned to the mysteries that intrigued us.

A passage from
The Word
(Chapter One)

"Many similarities do you share with other species throughout all existence, but the one that is most delightful is this: Each of you is uniquely different. This is one of the greatest gifts and joys existing in existence. Diversity is deeply cherished by all existences in existence."

"Okay, you two, I have a question for both of you. It's obvious that you enjoy communicating with various Life Beings." Enthusiastic nods responded to her statement. "And you're certainly skillful in silent communication between one another." They grinned and both nodded again. "So, tell me, are you also communicating in this manner with other people on this plane?" Pam looked at her husband and a silent agreement was clearly made.

"Well, we're very glad that you brought this topic up, because it was on our list as well. As both of you have noticed, Gary and I frequently connect in this way. Truth is, it's easier than talking sometimes, and certainly faster. We're not even sure how it came about, but it did, and when we finally realized what was happening, we started practicing with varying degrees of success, but over time, we've learned to trust this form of communication. The reason we wanted to talk about this is because we've noticed how often you two speak in sync. That's when we started noticing that something unusual was going on with us. Let's say our curiosity was piqued. And now, we're curious about your exchanges as well."

"To be more specific," Gary interjected, "we would like to know if you two are aware of what's going on between you and if you have started practicing yet?" Deb and I sat quietly for a moment, when we simultaneously invited the other to speak. That caught everyone's attention!

"Deb, what's your perspective on this? I don't mean to put you on the spot, but I am very interested in hearing your thoughts."

"Hmm!" she murmured as she rubbed her upper lip with her right thumb.

The gesture took me by surprise. Manners escaped me, as I blurted out a question. "Deb, do you often do that?"

"Do what?" she responded. I immediately mimicked her gesture and she looked on pensively.

"Geez! Perhaps, I do. It's never been called to my attention before, but it probably is a habit of mine. Why do you ask?" She took a quick look at my face and answered the question. "Oh, my goodness, is this a habit that we share?" I nodded and then we both turned to our friends who started to giggle.

"Maybe you two really are sisters!" Pam declared.

"Have you ever seen anything like this before?" My question was not focused at anyone in particular and Gary raised his hand.

"Pam and I experienced simultaneous speaking, but I don't remember any duplication of gestures. This is new to me. And frankly, it's rather endearing. I think it is merely an indication of how aligned you two are." That made sense to me and to Deb as well.

I apologized for interrupting Deb and urged her to continue with her thoughts. She needed a moment to refocus and watched herself fall into the same habit. Her right hand slowly rose to the upper lip and the thumb started its comforting motion. When she noticed it, she just shook her head and smiled. "Okay, back to the question," she mumbled to herself. "Obviously, we are both intuitive people in general, but it does seem to me that we are more in sync than I've ever noticed with anyone else. Is that true for you, Soul Sister?" I agreed that it was, and also admitted that I was unaware if we were communicating silently, as Pam and Gary were.

"I'm not sure either, but I appreciate the head's up. Now, that you've brought this to our attention, we can both start tracking and see where it leads us." I nodded in agreement and was also very eager to see where we were headed.

"May I take this back to my initial question? I still would like to know if you two are communicating with any other people the way you do with each other." They looked at each other and it was obvious that they were communicating with one another again, and this time, Gary was the designated responder.

"The answer is no, we are not, but we're hoping that it might develop with you two."

"YES!!" We both replied in sync, of course. The room filled with joy. Everyone was excited about the opportunity to experiment with this delightful communication process. We chattered on about it while indulging in the dessert phase of the meal. When the meal was finally completed, we moved to the living area of the house. The night was still young and the conversation would soon move into other directions.

A passage from
The Word
(Chapter One)

"For those youthful existences who have not learned to appreciate the gifts of diversity, existence can initially be difficult. Obsessed with their own existence, they see only what is beneficial to their own presumed needs and they are developmentally incapable of recognizing and respecting the needs of others. This maturational passage is typically maneuvered through quickly by most species; however, for some species, the process is slowed by an uncharacteristic attachment to self-centeredness. Unfortunately, those who experience this inclination often linger in this state of self-absorption longer than is desirable. Much wisdom can be gained during this developmental stage; however, it is intended to be a passageway not a place to dwell. Species that persist in remaining in a phase that does not honor and respect the existence of others typically lapse

into a state of devolution that severely interrupts their evolutionary process. Unless their misguided behavior is profoundly altered, the consequences can be devastating. So unpleasant is it to ponder this, that we choose not to do so at this moment. Instead, Dear Friend, let us speak of possibilities."

As we shifted into the living room, I wondered where our conversation would take us. Pam and Gary chose to sit together on the sofa, and Deb and I selected the two chairs opposite their position. It was a lovely setting for an intimate conversation. Once we were all settled in, I stretched over to light the candle in the center of the glass coffee table. Oohs and ahs filled the room, and I secretly wondered if this pleased The House. I chose to believe that The House enjoyed the ambience as much as our guests did.

"Well, Dear Friends, here we are! What will be our next focus?" Looking about the room, it became obvious that everyone was having similar thoughts. "Okay, listen up! Let's all settle into the opportunity that presents itself. Take your essential deep breaths please, and as you do, open your heart and your mind to the ideas and thoughts that you would most want to explore this evening. We have lots of time, so let's all seek within." Less than a minute passed when Pam announced that she was ready.

"That's my Girl," Gary proudly said. "Can you tell that she came prepared this evening?" Pam rolled her eyes.

"Actually," she said in response to her husband's comments, "I came with great desire to learn more about each other. Last night, you let us go on and on about our various experiences and happenings, and I hope tonight you will share more about yourselves." Pam looked perplexed for a moment, and then acknowledged that she was feeling selfish. "You know, I feel so blessed that we've been brought together, and grateful for everything that has already been shared among us, but I selfishly want more. I feel like a small child who has just found two new 'best friends.' And I want to know everything!" She burst into laughter. "My goodness, I am behaving like a child!"

"Not at all," replied Deb. "In fact, your openness is refreshing and I think we all feel the same way. I love your enthusiasm and I share the joy of our reunion. I feel as if I am amongst very old friends, and yet, I am just getting to know you. So yes, I am happy to share some of my happenings with you. In fact, I really want your feedback about one of my deepest secrets." She had a captive audience.

"Okay," she whispered to herself. "You can do this!" Deb placed her hands in prayerful fashion to her lips: another endearing habit of hers. The rest of the foursome responded in like manner, honoring the space for Deb's moment of prayer. When she opened her eyes and saw that we had joined her, tears streamed down her face. "Oh, how kind you all are. Thank you! I need your strength and support. What I am about to share is deeply personal to me." Pam urged her to take her time and reassured her that we were a patient group.

"Yes, this is a safe space, a Sacred Space, for sharing matters of the heart. My secret is very similar to yours," she said gesturing to Pam and Gary. "Like you, I've been communicating with other beings as well, but these beings apparently reside in locations that I am not acquainted with; or perhaps it is better said that I do not currently have any memories of these other places. As you might imagine, this is a topic that I've been hesitant to discuss with other people for the same reasons that you were reluctant to do so. I don't want to be ridiculed, diagnosed, shamed, judged, diminished, etc. What is happening is real! And I so value these relationships that I've experienced. It is such a privilege and a blessing, but as you said last night, there are times when it is very lonely." A few more tears appeared, but Deb paid them no mind. She was not afraid of her tears, nor were her friends.

"These encounters are the most important experiences in my life, and I have felt it necessary to conceal their existence. Isn't that a shame?" We all nodded in agreement. "It's sad for me and also for all those other people who are unaware that these incidents are occurring. Everyone should know about this! They should know there really is more! Obviously, I cannot prove that these experiences really happened, but why would anyone lie about this? You don't get bonus points for announcing that you are hearing voices and visiting with beings that are not from this realm of existence." Deb inhaled another deep breath and her companions promptly joined the exercise of self-care.

"Oh, my word! Please forgive my outburst, but this is so exciting! Can you p-l-e-a-s-e tell us about one of your experiences? Actually, I want to hear about all of your adventures!" Pam's exuberance brought laughter to the foursome.

"Oh, Pam, how refreshing this is! Thank you so much for just letting your excitement rush forward. This is the best reaction anyone could hope for! Here I was feeling timid and anxious about sharing my deepest secret, and now look at me. I am joyous! Dear Friends, we must remember this. I think we are going to meet many more folks in the near future who also have stories to share and we must remember to embrace their experiences just the way you did now. Wow! Pam, your reaction was so spontaneous; it was wonderful. I am so grateful to all of you. This truly is a Sacred Space." Deb placed her hands in prayerful position again, and her friends immediately joined her.

"Isn't this amazing?" she whispered. "I haven't even shared one of my experiences yet, and I am totally at ease. Thank you for making this so easy." Deb paused again, enjoyed another deep breath, and then made eye contact with each of her new friends. "Well, I have a 'Once Upon A Time Story' that I would love to share, if you're ready to hear it!"

"Yes!" Her friends responded in sync. Pam and Gary quickly linked arms in anticipation, while I positioned myself on the edge of my chair. The silence, which seemed to endure for an eternity, passed within mere seconds.

"Thank you for giving me time to discern which event is best to be shared this evening. You are very kind." Deb's thoughts turned inward again and another pause allowed her pensive listeners time to relax into more comfortable positions. Gary and Pam still sat with their arms entwined, but they no longer tightly clenched one another, and I shifted back into a more relaxed position as well. Our movements did not go unnoticed. "Thank you, for relaxing, my Friends. I am so grateful to have someone with whom I can share this experience. This is not the adventure that I had planned to share this evening, but now, it is obvious to me that this is the story that must be told. This is a rather long story, but it will help you to get to know me better." Deb began by telling us that her encounters with an unseen voice began years ago when she first started hearing a message that she was here for a reason. At first, she was surprised, because nothing like that had ever happened before, but the repeated message continued to insert itself into her life. Deb laughed as she shared a few examples with us. She described standing in front of the mirror getting ready for work when she would clearly hear: *You're here for a reason!* Similar experiences happened in the car, in her office, at a conference. Always, the same words were heard, while no one around her heard them; at least, no one else ever confirmed that they had heard the message. What began as a curious event grew to be an annoying experience! Not only was the mysterious presentation of these messages confusing; but also, she didn't understand the meaning or the purpose of the repetitive message.

"Well, needless to say, after hearing the message repeated over and over again, I became quite frustrated with it."

"Deb, how long did this go on?" asked Gary.

"That's a great question, and some day, I'm going to dive into my journals and find the answer. All I can say, Gary, is that it felt like an eternity. I remember the first message gave me pause. It was a curious experience...and an inspirational one. After all, one likes to believe that he or she is here for a reason. But it was also odd! Where did the voice come from? Whose voice was I hearing? How was I hearing this voice? My questions were many, but the only answer I ever received to my many questions was the same message. *You are here for a reason.*

"The confusion continued to mount as the messages came forward in greater abundance. The messages invaded my dreams, awakened me every morning, and were the last words heard when my head rested upon the pillow at day's end. *You are here for a reason*, became the mantra of my days and nights, and occasionally even inserted itself when I was at work. My mood fluctuated with its comings and goings: surprise turned to monotony, anticipation turned to desperation. At one point, I decided the message was surely intended for another, but the thought of that reduced me to tears. When that happened, it became clear to me how emotionally involved I was with this unusual message. It tugged at me. I impatiently waited for each message, only to become exasperated when it occurred with no more information than the time before. And then my own repetitive questions would race through my mind again. Why is this happening? Why me? What am I to do?

"Then time would pass without any messages and their absence would bring me to a state of longing. And of course, the same questions as before would arise, but with a different tenor. The ache for understanding, the desire for answers, the need to know why this was happening would overwhelm me, and just before I reached a place of despair, the message would be presented again. Sometimes in a whisper, other times with great volume, the words would be spoken: *you are here for a reason*. And I would sigh in relief! Such great relief! The confirmation filled my heart. Even though I didn't understand the message or know how to proceed; I knew with all that I was that the message was intended for me. Those brief moments of awareness and acceptance gave me hope." Deb paused briefly and refreshed herself with a sip of sparkling water. Pam, Gary, and I did the same.

"Well, one Saturday morning, I awoke early as usual and felt compelled to retreat to my Sacred Space. Early morning meditations were the norm for me, but the sense of urgency that I felt was not. I didn't even get dressed, but instead wrapped myself in a robe and hastened to my favorite setting in the house. The blinds that kept the darkness at bay demanded to be opened so that the soon-to-come grand ascension could be enjoyed. No lights were turned on, but a nearby favorite candle provided just the right amount of ambient lighting. With these two small tasks done, nothing else was required. I sat down in my meditation chair, closed my eyes, took a few deep breaths, and opened my heart to whatever might happen. A response was immediate.

"You are here for a reason!" Deb spoke the words loudly, just as she had heard them.

"I jumped up from my chair," she stated excitedly, "expecting to see someone somewhere in the space. I looked all about the room, but saw nothing, absolutely nothing out of the ordinary. I couldn't believe it! I was certain that the voice, so clearly heard had originated from within the room. Tears streamed down my face. The room appeared to be empty except for me, but that simply wasn't true. Someone was trying to communicate with me. The messages were happening for a reason, and they were intended for me, but I had no idea how to reply to the unknown messenger.

"Standing in the middle of the room didn't appear to be getting me anywhere, so I returned to my chair hoping to compose myself. Instead, the tears took over and continued for an endless amount of time. Eventually, I dozed off and did not awaken until the rays of the sun were penetrating through the windows. It was a surprise! Time had escaped me!" Deb needed another sip of water, and again, we all joined her. The three of us were a captive audience. I noticed that Pam started to ask a question, but stopped herself. I think it is fair to say that many questions were racing through our minds, and we each decided that now was not the time. I checked in with Deb to see if she need some type of refreshment, but she reassured me that she was fine and ready to continue.

"I'm sorry this is such a long story," Deb began, but was immediately stopped by her friends' reaction to her apology. Needless to say, she received nothing but positive comments and encouragement to continue.

"Oh, thank you, Dear Friends, for your support. You are such wonderful listeners!" Deb's eyes turned downward as a thought came to mind. Then she faced us all again and continued. "You know, it is a blessing to have friends who lovingly listen to you. What a gift this is!" An exchange of compliments took place among the four friends before Deb returned to her story.

"So, where was I? Ah, yes, I had just awakened from my nap and found myself sitting in the chair with sunlight streaming through the window. A quick glance at the clock informed me that the nap had been lengthy. Though the message and its unseen messenger were still perplexing, I no longer felt the sense of urgency earlier experienced. In short measure, a decision was made to begin the weekend with a long seacoast walk. So, I stretched toward the nearby candle to blow it out, but before the task was completed, I heard…*you are here for a reason!* This time the words sounded more like an appeal than a directive, and I instinctively wanted to help this unknown messenger. So I replied to the invisible voice, as if its owner were right before me. My exact words were: Thank you for this message. Unfortunately, I don't fully understand what you are trying to convey to me, but I would like to be of service. How can I help?

"Well, Dear Friends, what happened next still gives me chills and thrills." The rest of us were now sitting on the edge of our seats. "Across the room, a Light Being materialized. My breath was taken away as my eyes fixated upon this glowing mass of white and golden light. It literally was a sight to behold. I honestly don't know how long I spent gawking at this

Being until good manners finally stepped up. I apologized for not having another chair in the room and immediately jumped up to get one when this gentle, loving voice was heard again.

There is no need, Old Friend. I am perfectly comfortable in this position. The voice, spoken so softly, filled the room. *I am most grateful that you responded to my call, Old Friend. I seized the moment to approach you. I hope my presence does not alarm you.*

"Oh, my Friends, again I must apologize. There simply is no way that I can emulate the sound of this individual's voice. It was love personified. I felt no fear whatsoever…there simply wasn't any reason for it. Although the circumstances were indeed unusual, the sense of peace that emanated from this Being's presence filled the room leaving me with a sensation of being embraced by a Dear Old Friend." Deb's eyes moistened as she recalled the blissful experience. No one in the room doubted her story; we all sat enamored by the experience.

"Eventually, I managed to move beyond the gawking phase, and was able to engage with the visitor. Utilizing the message that was so often presented to me, I returned it to the sender. Old Friend," I hesitantly declared, "obviously, you are here for a reason. How can I be of assistance?

"Unlike me, the Light Being's response was not hesitant at all. First, I was invited to make myself comfortable in my favorite chair, and then I was encouraged to access my journal. Of course, I did so without question. *You are one who prefers to take copious notes, my Friend. Having the Book of Memories nearby will help you feel prepared."* Deb broke out with laughter. "That Light Being certainly understood my habits." She took the long deep breath, which was also one of her habits, before she began again.

"So, basically what was shared was information about a commitment that was made long ago. His words were: *I am here, as was requested long ago, to remind you of a commitment that you made before entering into this life experience. This arrangement is not unusual. Often one desires to attend certain circumstances when they enter into a new lifetime. To insure that the experience unfolds as desired, it is customary to engage a Friend who willingly agrees to assist you at the allotted time. I am here to remind you, Old Friend, that you are here for a reason.*

"Obviously, the visitor's message was fascinating, but it still left me without any specifics. When I requested more details, the response was simple. *Old Friend, your desire for more information is understood. Our meeting today serves as an introduction. In actuality, it is a reunion of two Old Friends. I come this day to offer my services to you, as you move forward with your efforts to reclaim awareness of your mission of purpose. If you allow me, I will return daily to assist you with your endeavors.*

"Needless to say, I accepted the offer! Before the visitor departed, we agreed to meet early every morning until we mutually concluded that the services were no longer needed. I was then, and still remain, overwhelmed by the gentle nature of this Being." Deb paused briefly, made eye contact with everyone. "So, my Friends, that's how my unusual journey began and continues to this day. Obviously, there are many more stories, but this gives you the groundwork for my spiritual journey." For a very long moment or two, the listeners remained silent. We were still digesting Deb's wonderful experience.

"Deb, what a remarkable journey you are having! I'm at a loss for words, but questions are racing through the chambers of my mind. For the moment, I just want to thank you for sharing your journey with us. And I can't wait to hear more about it."

Pam's excitement could not be bound. "Well, you know me!" she declared. "I am rarely at a loss for words, and quite frankly, I have a million questions to ask you. Are you up for two or three of them?" Pam was grinning from ear to ear, and Deb was enjoying her enthusiasm, as was her husband.

"She's on a roll, Deb," Gary pointed at his beloved and giggled. "You might want to fasten your seatbelt!" The relationship these two shared was a delight to witness. Pam just rolled her eyes and moved forward with her first question.

"I'm curious, Deb. Do you still have daily contact with this Being?"

"No, I do not, but the opportunity is always there, which is very comforting. I have been encouraged to seek connection whenever it is desired, but truthfully, my ego often gets in my way. Of course, there is the classic ego nonsense of firmly believing that I should be able to make decisions on my own without having to seek guidance or clarification from another. And then, I go through various phases of feeling like I'm a bother or that I'm not worthy of this Being's attention. These are just the games that my mind plays on me, which of course are ridiculous.

"For whatever reason, I am blessed to have access to this remarkable Light Being who truly wishes to be of service to me. It's a humbling experience, but it's real, and I'm grateful beyond words." Deb's eyes moistened as she spoke of her Spiritual Friend. "Of course, I often revisit the 'Why me?' phase as well. At one point I posed this question to my Friend and the response was absolutely delightful. 'Why not?' was the simple, yet profound answer. That reply continues to have a huge impact on me. Whenever doubts about my worthiness come up, it reminds me that I am just as worthy as any one else to be blessed with this Companion. Naturally, my attitude about this varies from day to day, but most of the time, I feel solid about this truth. We are all blessed with Companions, but we have to open our hearts and minds to this reality. I'm just grateful that my Companion was so persistent that I finally got the message.

"Never once, when I've reached out for connection, have I been received in any manner other than gracious acceptance. And over time, I have come to accept that our relationship truly is mutual. We are both here for a reason. We serve each other. Granted, I am much more aware of how I am being served than I am of my contributions. Perhaps, it is just wishful thinking on my part that I somehow am of service, but in my heart, I know this is true. In some mysterious and beautiful way, we are a team." A few tears were witnessed as Deb shared this intimate moment with her friends.

"Oh, my goodness! That was well said." Pam and I immediately nodded and added similar affirmations to Gary's, and then he took the lead again in his gentle, soft-spoken way. "Actually, Deb, I think one of the ways you demonstrate your partnership with this exceptional Being is the manner in which you speak of your relationship. You have definitely honored this Light Being by sharing your incredible story. I want you to know that I deeply appreciate your willingness to reveal this experience. That took a lot of courage, Deb. And later on this evening, when your mind starts creating doubts and concerns about what you said and how you said it, please just remember what I'm about to say to you. You did the right thing, Deb! Your story profoundly touched me, and I will never forget this evening. I am so grateful!" Gary turned to Pam and they shared a silent communiqué. Both heads nodded in response to the internal exchange.

"A penny for your thoughts," my teasing remark received an immediate reaction from Pam.

"Oh, I'm sorry, Friends. We're doing it again, aren't we? Actually, we were just acknowledging that Deb's experience validates many of our beliefs...and wishes. We really do have Companions who desperately try to assist us while we're in these human shells; but like you said, Deb, too many of us are distracted by our daily activities. I hope you take Gar's words to heart. Your willingness to share your spiritual journey has truly helped us, and others will also benefit from hearing about your experiences. I'm really beginning to understand the importance of sharing these stories. There is so much happening in the world that we are totally oblivious about." I waved my hand and added my own account of the influence of Deb's story. She quietly took our words in and we all witnessed the sense of relief and gratitude wash over her.

"Deb, it is wonderful to sit here and observe what just transpired. I think it is fair to say that we witnessed the cycle of storytelling reaching its completion. You bravely opened your heart to us by telling your remarkable journey. Even though it was a risk, you did it anyway. We, the listeners, each benefitted from your story in our own unique ways, just as you did from the experience itself. And then, the feedback we shared with you allowed you to witness the impact of your efforts. Your experience has influenced others and will continue to do so as long as that story is told and retold to others. Thank you for trusting us! And thank you for expanding our awareness."

"Wow!" replied Deb trying to take in the complimentary remarks. "First, let me say thank you for your feedback and for your acute listening skills. I definitely feel heard and validated. And encouraged! We really must absorb what is happening here. Obviously, our simpatico relationships made this interaction easier, but it also shows us how significant these conversations can be. We really must embolden ourselves and reach out to others for similar encounters. I think we all agree that these experiences are intended to be shared." Deb looked towards her friends for confirmation and immediately received it. "So, Dear Ones, we must be the catalyst for more opportunities. I really believe we must accept responsibility for creating future opportunities where more stories can be shared."

"Agreed!" confirmed her the three companions simultaneously. The reaction brought a giggle to the Circle of Four.

"My Friends, before we continue, I must admit that our light meal has left me hungry again. But not to worry, I anticipated this might happen so another tray of goodies is already prepared. Gary, Dear, will you fill everyone's glasses while I pop out to get the next course for the evening."

"Thank goodness!" chuckled Gary. "I'm in the same state. These conversations are riveting. Bring on the goodies, please!" Within minutes, we were all settled in our places again each with a full plate of treats to munch on as we continued our discussion. Even though yummy noises were circling the room, I decided to check in with Pam.

"A while back, Pam, you mentioned that you had a million questions for Deb. I'm wondering if you have another one to pose now."

"Yes," she confessed, "I have many questions!" Pam finished off a piece of cheese before she turned in Deb's direction. "I'm so sorry, but I have an insatiable appetite about these topics, and I could stay up all night talking about your experiences with this Light Being. I can't even believe we are actually talking about a Light Being. Oh, my goodness, this is just the thrill of a lifetime! Deb, are you still up for another question?"

"Absolutely! If I didn't have to see clients tomorrow, I would be happy to stay up all night sharing our adventures with one another. So, tell me… what's the next question?"

"Well, I noticed throughout your story, you never once indicated if the Light Being was a male or a female. I guess it really doesn't matter, but I'm curious. Never having had an experience with a Light Being, I'm clueless." Gary and I both shared Pam's interest regarding the gender of the Deb's visitor.

"Trust me, I was clueless as well. At some point during that initial encounter, the question did come up. It was actually very awkward having a conversation with someone when you don't know his or her name or the

155

appropriate pronouns, so the question was asked, and the response was intriguing. You're just going to love this," Deb smiled. "The response was this: *I am what is needed.* The Light Being further explained that all names were gratefully accepted, but the one most enjoyed was Friend. So now, I call my Companion, friend."

"What a gracious demeanor, your Friend has," remarked Gary.

"Yes, that's true. I've never known anyone who is so loving and accepting. It's a remarkable state of being that we should all try to emulate. Pure grace!" Deb paused for a minute as a thought raced through her mind. "By the way," she added, "it took a while, but at this point in our relationship, I no longer find the gender situation problematic except when I try to talk about my Friend. Our society is so accustomed to using gender-related pronouns that it's challenging to describe my Friend without leaning in one direction or the other. The truth is both masculine and feminine characteristics beautifully blend within this incredible Being. I feel so blessed to have this relationship."

"You are, Dear, you truly are!" Gary and Pam once again responded in sync. This consistent display of their connection reminded me of the many questions I still had about their communication skills. A mental note was made to address this topic at an appropriate time.

"Deb, I must thank you again for sharing your experience and your wisdom. This has been an enriching conversation. Gratitude abounds, my Friend!" Pam had more to say, but decided it was time to make space for others. Her husband placed his hand on her knee and conveyed another message to her that was visibly witnessed but not heard by their companions.

I decided the appropriate time for bringing up their telepathic behaviors had arrived. "Okay, you two! Gary, you just communicated something to Pam. I don't mean to be intruding upon your privacy, but can you tell us what just transpired, if it isn't too personal?" My question clearly took them by surprise, but they handled it graciously as always. They both admitted that they were taken aback by the frequency of their exchanges.

"You haven't intruded at all. In fact, you're helping us realize just how often we are actually communicating in this fashion. I think we are both rather surprised by this." Gary turned to Pam who affirmed his statement. "What actually transpired, I think you both will find very interesting. After expressing her gratitude to you, Deb, this lovely lady here decided that she had taken up too much time and decided that she was going to step back for a while." Deb and I were both shocked, and reassured Pam that there was no need for her to do that. Gary then went on to explain that his communication to his beloved was exactly what we had just stated.

"So, this is going to be a stupid question, but just bear with me, okay?" They both nodded and then Pam began to chuckle. "Okay, what's going on?" Gary turned beet red, as Pam tattled on him.

"When you asked us to bear with you, Gar responded: Oh no, this is going to be a doozy! And it tickled me. But just ignore us, we're ready for your question."

Deb inserted herself into the conversation, "It's difficult to ignore you two. I mean really…you two are discussing things internally all the time. It's fascinating to watch, and I want you to know that I am envious!!" This brought laughter to the Circle of Friends. "Geez, I wish I could see the inner-workings of your minds."

"Me too!" The couple responded, which brought another round of laughter.

"So," I returned to my stupid question, "do you simply think the words, the sentences internally, just as you speak them orally, and the recipient hears the words, just as if they were spoken aloud?"

"Not exactly," replied Gary. "We do not hear the words as if they were spoken aloud, we hear them internally. Not unlike your experience, Deb, when you were hearing the repeated message of your Friend. Perhaps I'm being presumptuous, but I assume you were hearing the message within. Is that correct?"

"Yes, it was, until the Companion started materializing. Then it became confusing. I'm not sure how to explain this, but sometimes it felt internal, other times, it seemed to be like an ordinary exchange just like we're having now. And at other times, it seemed to be both. I'm sorry but at this point, I'm unable to be more precise about this. It is a topic I've often wondered about, and still do."

"Well, we have so much more to learn, don't we?" expressed Gary. "I'm so enjoying the similarities and the differences that we are experiencing. It's just fascinating." Silence overcame the group as we each thought about Gary's remarks and our own appreciations of everything we were learning through these conversations.

A passage from
The Word
(Chapter One)

"Many truths exist in the existence in which you exist, and one relates to the remarkable powers that exist within you. Old Friend, this message has been delivered to the peoples of Earth for millennia, and still it remains a truth that only a very few acknowledge. Please breathe deeply, for the message is going to be revealed again.

You are a Being with exceptional abilities and with these abilities you have the power to heal self and others. Before the mind negates what has just been announced, please take another deep breath. Old Friend, your undivided attention is necessary. Do not allow the mind to steer you in directions that take you away from this purposeful moment in time.

You are a Being with exceptional abilities, and with these abilities, you have the power to heal self and others.

The words are boldly repeated and accentuated so that they will make a proper impression upon you. Please read these words over and over again until they are sufficiently imprinted upon your consciousness. This message is not a ruse. There is no time for such foolishness. The message is delivered because you and all the peoples of this planet are endowed with this ability. You are apprised of this truth once again, because you must accept this truth for the sake of your future."

"What about you, Soul Sister?" inquired Deb. "You've been a wonderful hostess and facilitator for our evening, but tell us one of your stories. I know that you have some! Are you up for changing roles for the moment?" The instinctive deep breath was taken as I prepared myself to take the lead. Many thoughts surfaced of course, but it was difficult trying to latch upon just one.

"Before I share one of my adventures, let me thank all of you for coming. We are so very fortunate. We have similar interests, we live in close proximity to one another, and we are all good listeners. Isn't that wonderful? And best of all, we are comfortable with each other! We really are blessed!"

"No coincidence!" declared Gary and Pam in sync again.

"You two are just showing off!" I said, shaking my finger at them. "Okay, let me think." I turned my thoughts back to the task at hand and decided to follow Deb's lead. Her idea of choosing a story that would help everyone to understand her current spiritual journey had proven to be a great avenue to pursue.

"Like you, Deb, I am going to share an experience that will hopefully be informative and give everyone an idea of my present situation. Words may fail me, but please bear with me. I think most of you know that meditation is a regular part of my life. My practice varies from day to day. Sometimes, it seems very successful and other times, it is not; but in general, I think it is fair to say that meditating helps me in many ways. Typically, I meditate and then follow it with some time with my journal. Well, recently, my process has changed." My mind started racing, so another deep breath was necessary. My wonderful friends accompanied me, which was such a loving gesture. I've come to believe that we are all so intimately linked together that these incidents are as natural as our own individual breathing experiences.

"Thank you for helping me to quiet myself. It's interesting to experience this anxiety even when I know it is absolutely unnecessary. I trust all of you and know you will receive my story positively, and still, it is difficult to formulate the words. But here is my truth, as best as I can articulate it. Recently, I've had several incidents of falling asleep during my meditations. The first time this happened really surprised me. Upon awakening, embarrassment gripped me. I know that must sound ridiculous, but there was a brief moment of feeling that I had done something very naughty. In childlike fashion, I literally looked around the room praying that no one had noticed this transgression, and in so doing, I realized my journal was resting on my lap. I was dumbfounded and had absolutely no memory of accessing the book before entering into my meditation, but there it was! With pages opened and my favorite writing pen carefully situated in the crease of the book, the journal was sitting there on my lap, as if it had been in use. And much to my surprise, it had been." Before continuing, I made eye contact with my friends and saw the support they were offering to me. What a gift it is to have friends who simply believe your stories.

"Thank you, Dear Ones. I can see your acceptance and my heart is comforted." Taking another deep breath, I continued. "So, needless to say, I quickly thumbed through my journal and found the latest entry coincided with the time and date of my meditation. It was pages long! Words of wisdom filled the pages and it definitely was my handwriting. But I had no idea where the messages came from. Since then, this has happened numerous times. It seems that I am being trained to receive and record messages. And now, I've reached another phase of the process. I'm actually receiving the messages while I'm awake, which also just takes my breath away. It's exciting to be a part of this, but as you can imagine, it isn't something that I'm sharing with everyone. So, that's my story!" The room remained quiet briefly as the listeners were absorbing the story. Deb replied first.

"Thank you, Sister. I just want you to know that I believe every word that you shared and I'm grateful that you let us know what you're experiencing. This is big, Sister! You're channeling messages!"

"Channeling?" Deb's comment took me by surprise. "I'm just taking dictation!"

"That's what channeling is, Sister. You're hearing a voice from unknown origins and you're recording the words that you hear. Is that correct?" I nodded that it was, but the descriptor still seemed foreign to me. "You know I've only been doing this for a short while, so I'm still adapting to the oddity of it all. The only thing that I'm certain about at this point is that I'm really grateful to be involved. The messages that are received are beautiful, literally words of wisdom. It is a privilege to receive them, and at some point, they will be shared with others. They have to be. These messages are not meant for just one person; they are intended for everyone!"

"Can you give us a clue as to the content of the messages?" asked Pam.

"They are filled with goodness, Pam. They bring me to tears as I'm receiving them. Messages filled with support and acceptance that make you feel as if you are lovingly embraced by a Presence of infinite kindness. While receiving these messages, the experience feels very personal and intimate, but I know with all that I am that they are intended for everyone. We all need this type of unconditional approval and support. The messages take you deeper than I've ever been before while at the same time leaving me feeling as if I could soar with the angels. If we could all embrace the depths of these messages at the same time, we would have peace on Earth."

"Oh, Sister, what a lovely image that is! It's absolutely inspiring." Gary immediately tagged onto Deb's comment.

"I agree!" he asserted. "In fact, I had the most fascinating reaction as you spoke of your experiences. This may sound crazy, but a deep sense of connection overwhelmed me, and it made me wonder if the Presence that you were speaking of was actually with us. Is that possible?"

"Gary, I don't have the definitive answer, but my understanding, albeit limited, is that the Presence is always with us. Everything is possible! Maybe, we are witnessing another aspect of sharing our stories. If my story enabled you to experience the powerful Presence that I enjoyed, then we are witnessing another validation of our mutual purposes. Goodness! Isn't this exciting?"

"Yes, it is!" responded Gary. "And it makes me want more, but I don't want to be greedy. It seems to me that Pam and I are blessed in so many ways. Our relationship is enviable, and we have the most delightful adventures together, as you two are beginning to realize, but there is more. We all know that! And what I just felt as you spoke, Dear, renews that awareness within me. There definitely is more...and I want to know everything there is to know about it." A huge grin spread across Gary's face and then he began to chuckle at himself. "I really do sound greedy, don't I?"

"Not at all!" the three women spoke in unison. Pam wrapped her arm around her husband's. The gesture was made in such a way that it was obvious that she wanted and needed to take the lead.

"As you can both see, Gary is a tender, big-hearted man. He feels deeply, thinks expansively, and is guided by a curiosity that is boundless. The only limited aspect that I see in him is his fear of overstepping undefined and or self-imposed boundaries. When Gar becomes excited about the wonders of our existence, his childlike enthusiasm leads him in ways that I cannot even imagine. He's phenomenal! And then, something is triggered and he stops himself. We've talked about this a lot, but the underlying agent still seems to elude him. I'm so glad that you two have witnessed his curious nature. You can attest to its power. I just want him to follow those avenues of curiosity that rev him up. I want him to accept the incredible person that he is." Pam leaned over and gave her Love a gentle kiss on the cheek.

"Now, that's inspiring," my words were softly spoken. "Your relationship truly is enviable, and you both are phenomenal. Pam, it was so touching to hear you speak about Gary's strengths and his limitations. You managed that in a tender and loving way. Gary, I hope you do not feel uncomfortable with this situation, because there is much for all of us to learn." He looked on curiously, and then admitted that he felt that he was in the hot seat. We all reassured him that each of us could easily step into his position.

"Oh Gary, I can so relate to the situation that Pam just divulged, and please hear me when I confess that I have similar issues. It's very frustrating to feel one's excitement erased in a flash. There are times when I feel so empowered about something that I can hardly wait to address whatever the topic is, and then in a blink of an eye, my energy is drained. Some thought, some idea, or some memory from the past squelches my enthusiasm. Some times I know what the cause was, but typically, I am clueless about it. It actually seems to be an unconscious experience. Does this make any sense?" Everyone nodded in agreement. We all related to Deb's comments but Gary particularly wanted to respond to her.

"Deb, you described my personal experiences amazingly accurately. These incidents happen so quickly that I often feel blindsided. Pam is wonderful, as you might imagine, when the experiences happen. She keeps me from sinking into an abyss, thank goodness. It was much worse in the past. These events could literally disrupt my mood for hours and sometimes days. I'm really tired of it, because it is such a waste of time, and quite frankly, it seems out of character for who I am today. You know, we all have issues, but enough is enough. Sometimes, I think we just need to greet these incidents as friends from the past; just thank them for the reminder, wish them well, and then proceed with our intentions." Gary paused briefly as he reviewed what he had just spoken. "Actually," he continued, "I think this is a good strategy, and I will add another component to the process. One needs to remember to trust oneself. If an issue surfaces that demands attention, trust that you will address it. The truth is, I'm always going to have some issue lurking about, and I have a good track record of facing these concerns. I can trust myself. But there comes a time when it's fair to say that the reminder from the past doesn't need immediate attention. It's a reminder that causes disruption rather than assistance.

"I hope this is making sense to you, my Friends, because I feeling my confidence coming back. I like the idea of considering these events as visits from old Friends, and I also like the idea of trusting myself regarding these old patterns. Geez! This feels big to me. Pam, what do you think? Can you give me some feedback?"

"I think you're brilliant, Dear! You idea is simple and profound, and it's workable. We are all of an age where we can trust ourselves to do the work that must be done. Your idea sounds healthy, gentle, kind, and resolute. It's a very emboldened strategy. I like it! And I'm going to join you in this new approach!"

"Me too!" announce Deb. "I think your idea is brilliant and a huge statement of self-trust. This is a powerful approach to monitoring one's vulnerabilities."

"I agree and I'm in! Gary, so how are you feeling about your earlier incident, now?" My question took Gary full circle. As he remembered his enthusiasm about wanting to understand everything about the 'more' that exists, a smile came to his face.

"I want to know more, which means more time with my nose in books, and lots more time in nature, where many truths await discovery, and much more time listening to these fascinating stories that broaden my awareness tremendously. I feel great!" We all applauded.

"What a lovely time this has been," acknowledged Pam. "We are so blessed and I believe we need to share our blessings with others. The heartfelt connection that the four of us are sharing is happening for a reason. We all know this. As lovely as it is to have these intimate gatherings, we must reach out to others. What's happening here is too important to be confined; we need to spread our wings. I must admit that part of me does not want to do this! I selfishly want to keep our Circle of Four just as it is, but that isn't why we've been brought together. Just look at what the four of us have to offer. These stories, our experiences, are important. Other folks will also feel validated when they hear them, just the way we have. My Friends, this is important. With blessings come responsibilities and we need to share our blessings." We all knew that Pam was right and we all shared a similar reluctance to do so.

"I agree, Pam! We need to do this, and let's take comfort in knowing that we can and will always make time for gatherings of just the four of us. We're not going to lose this! And we are going to benefit from this expansion as much as our guests will. No matter how we look at this, outreach is a win-win. I think we're experiencing anticipatory grief. Let's just acknowledge it for what it is and commit to one another that we will always nurture this foursome as needed." My words sounded more powerful than I was feeling, but they spoke a truth that we all needed to hear.

"Thank you for making that point, Sister!" interjected Deb. "Like you, Pam, I too have been hesitant about bringing in new folks. We have such a cozy, loving situation here that is hard to let go of it, and the point made is we don't have to. Yay! I promise all of you that I will abide by the commitment that was just suggested." Smiles brightened the faces among the Circle of Four as each individual vowed to maintain the special relationship that was shared. Then Pam turned business like, recommending a game plan.

"Okay, Friends," she announced, "let's commit to inviting four guests to our next meeting. We have several folks in mind and are leaning towards a lovely couple that just lives around the block from here. We're relatively certain that they will be interested, so we will make contact with them and see what unfolds. Do you two have some particular people in mind?"

Deb and I glanced at one another and both nodded. "Let us work on this and we will strive for two invitees as well. Pam, what's your target date for this?"

"Next week!" the couple replied. "We need to follow through with this," Gary continued, "or we will lapse into our comfort zone again." He briefly consulted with Pam and then announced that they would host the event.

"Thank you both for nudging us forward. We're taking the next step." The Circle of Four shared their appreciation for the evening, wished one another a good week, and exchanged huge hugs. Gary and Pam leisurely strolled across the street to their home while Deb and I observed them from the front porch. Once there, the couple waved goodbye before entering their abode.

"Another extraordinary evening!" noted Deb. "Sometimes, I have to pinch myself to realize that these conversations are really happening. It's a dream come true for me."

"Me too," I replied. "I feel as if we are characters in a play that are being masterminded by a source far greater than us. I find it all very curious, Deb...and I am so grateful to be part of this production. Cannot wait to see how this grand performance unfolds."

We discussed walking together in the morning, but mutually agreed not to. We each desired quality time with our respective journals and didn't want to place any restrictions upon that opportunity. A long hug was exchanged before Deb departed for the evening.

... *20* ...

A passage from
The Word
(Chapter One)

"Another truth that has been widely presented across all lands is the truth about the Earth's declining health. This crisis is real and the devastation that will be incurred if action is not immediately taken is too unthinkable to describe. The truth about the Earth's decline is known; it is indisputable, and still, lies about Earth's crisis situation continue to be presented for the sole purpose of confusing and distracting people from the truth. Unfortunately, it is highly unlikely that the perpetrators of misinformation about the Earth's failing health will alter their reckless behavior.

Dear Friend, two truths have come forward that require your attention. Hopefully, you will take both of them seriously. One truth informs a civilization of people that they are in peril. Another truth provides them with information that can resolve their planet's crisis. The truth is spoken truthfully, Dear Friend. Please ponder these truths carefully."

"Hello, Dear Friends, thank you for coming! And welcome to our backyard!" Gary graciously invited everyone to the circle of chairs that were arranged in the center of the garden. He and Pam had cleverly decided to have this initial session outdoors. It was a lovely setting for conversation that allowed for finger foods rather than the distraction of a culinary extravaganza. Scheduling the event on the weekend accommodated a daytime gathering. A buffet table was set up nearby for easy access. All was in order. It was time for the occasion to begin.

"Come, come, Dear Ones!" Pam encouraged everyone to choose

a chair. As one might imagine the invitees sat close to those who had extended the invitation. The usual moment of positioning and repositioning took place until we were all comfortably in place. "Ah," sighed Pam. "We are all here and it came about so easily." She glanced around the circle, and happily announced, "That's when you know that your intuition is correct. The four of us," she pointed towards Deb and me, "felt strongly that it was important for us to reach out to other folks about the conversations that we've been having recently. We've been having a lovely time together sharing our stories and experiences with one another, and we decided that the topics that were being discussed needed to be shared with others. So, we decided last week that we would invite some other people who we thought might be of like-mind to join us. And here we are! We are so, so happy that you all accepted our invitation to get together." Pam looked in my direction, and I took my turn at co-hosting.

"Well, I too wish to welcome all of you. We are delighted that everyone responded so quickly and positively. Basically, what has transpired among the four of us is sheer beauty. I think it is fair to say that we are all stunned, happily so, and extremely grateful. For those of you who don't know this, I live directly across the street from Pam and Gary. We've known each other for years, but just recently, our conversations turned to the unusual and precious events that we were experiencing. Then, the very next day, I enjoyed a different, but similar conversation with my Friend and colleague who has an office next door to mine. So, the four of us have met several times and found our conversations to be exhilarating. So much so, that we all agreed that these discussions were intended to be shared with others. We suspect that there are many more stories that also need to be told and we hope that this get together will facilitate that possibility.

"Our gatherings are bound by only two rules. We honor each other's experiences and we maintain confidentiality. Other than that, we all simply accept responsibility for participating, if and when it feels right to do so, and we all pitch in to facilitate the conversations. No one is in charge, and everyone is in charge. So far, this easy-going manner has worked well for us." I turned toward Deb urging her to share her point of view. She eagerly took over.

"Well, I think the first noteworthy item that I would like to share with our newcomers is the reality that we are all very nervous about this gathering." Her comment aroused a few chuckles among the Circle of Four and Pam teased Deb for revealing our deepest secret.

"The truth is the truth," admitted Gary.

"Yes, it is," continued Deb. "When I woke up this morning, my thoughts immediately took me to this rapidly approaching event. I found numerous concerns to worry about, and thoroughly did so, as I am wont to do, before it dawned upon me that I was so absorbed with my own perceived inadequacies that I had forgotten to put myself in our guests' shoes. So, New Friends, I tried on your shoes, and realized how remarkably brave you are. Invitations were extended, and you just said yes! As Pam indicated, this gathering came together so easily that we were all taken by surprise. And like Pam, I believe this happened for a reason. Having come to that conclusion inspired me to speak the truth about our apprehensions. We are so eager to be with you, to share some of our stories, to hear yours if you desire to share them with us, and most importantly to hear your viewpoints about the topics we intend to bring up today. So, please hear how excited we are to spend time with you and also know that we are a bit anxious. And if any of you are feeling a bit antsy as well, just know that you are in very good company." Deb appeared to be finished but before I could turn the facilitation duties back to Pam and Gary, she popped up with another idea.

"There's just one more thought I would like to share with you. Until this meeting began, I was the newcomer to this group, and I had all kinds of doubts and concerns before attending the first gathering. It was the easiest thing I've ever done…and probably the most important. Our conversations have changed my life. Welcome again, Friends! So glad that you are here." Deb's candor was well received. Not only did the newcomers relax, the original four did so as well. I glanced towards my neighbors and Gary took the lead.

"Well, Deb, we undoubtedly awoke with similar thoughts this morning, so I will elaborate upon the one that captured my attention. Interestingly enough, my concerns were not about the success of our gathering. I took that for granted, because it just seemed obvious to me that we are people of like mind and heart. I'm very confident that we are going to have an unforgettable experience today. But what concerned me early this morning, and still bothers me now, is how do we actually get started." Gary looked about the circle with his sparkling eyes and his boyish grin. "Not to worry, Friends! I have an idea." He paused again, took the deep breath that always moves one forward, and then he suggested that we all stand up and join hands. And this the Circle of Eight did!

"Dear Friends, we asked you here today to talk about topics that you may not have the luxury of talking about in other settings. Obviously, each of you was approached personally so you know a little bit about the purpose of our meetings. I think it is correct to say that our conversations are expansive. We have focused upon several themes thus far that include the wellness of the Earth, communications with other species, and let's just lump the rest of our stories into the category of our spiritual journeys. This is a very limited summation of what I personally feel has been the experience of a lifetime.

So, Dear Ones, let's join together now and spend a moment to honor our beautiful planet. Let's hold her in our hearts and reassure her that she is deeply loved and cherished." Gary remained silent as his simple prayer evolved into more within each participant in the circle. Unspoken words of gratitude and appreciation were expressed, deepening the level of connection immediately. "Thank you everyone, for joining me in that impromptu prayer for the Earth. I believe the first step has been taken. Pam, would you like to take the next step?"

"Yes, Dear, I would love to begin our conversation this afternoon with a story about an experience which occurred some time ago. Actually, it was a very long time ago, and it was an experience that I often return to because it was transformative. This particular incident is a reminder to me of all those little coincidences that happen in one's life, which are actually significant factors of relevance happening exactly at the right time in the right place, facilitating another growth spurt for the person involved." Pam paused as she recalled the incident that unfolded when she was a teenager. She wondered how that young girl managed to be present for the experience. That, in itself, was remarkable.

"I was a very curious youngster," she quietly began. "My mind was always working non-stop. Questions, ideas, suppositions, and more would race about in the chambers of my mind. Long before the notion of a computer came into play, my mind functioned like one. And I was interested in everything! There was no need for television or movies: I had Mother Nature! Even as a small child, I would go on great excursions (in the backyard) and return with a variety of found objects, which I referred to as artifacts. These relics demanded intensive scrutiny once they were collected and relocated to The Study that I had cleverly made in my bedroom. A much smaller version of my Grandfather's library, The Study was a special space for great learning. In addition to The Study, there was another space created with cardboard boxes that was designated The Laboratory. There, in that special space, samples of Earth, plant life, insects, etc. were gathered for research as well. My parents were very supportive of my creativity and always encouraged my curiosity." Listening to Pam's descriptions of her childhood made me smile. The image of her creating, in the limited space of a child's bedroom, not only a study but a laboratory as well was so in alignment with who she is today...orderly and persistent. Pam literally came out of the womb with an avid desire for knowledge. The lust to know everything about everything was in her genes.

"I have my parents and grandparents to thank for my curious nature." Her gratitude for her upbringing was obvious. You could hear the tenderness she held for her family. "I must admit," she chuckled, "my appetite for knowledge and information is large." Gary rolled his eyes and teased Pam about her comment.

"That's the understatement of the year!" he said grinning from ear to ear. "She's insatiable!" Their interaction with one another was delightful to watch, but Pam was still on task and she quickly returned to her story.

"Okay, Friends, so I ask you to picture this old woman here as a thirteen year old. No smirks now! Just imagine this kid in khaki shorts, a long sleeve T-Shirt, hiking boots, a backpack and a pith helmet. I was visiting my grandparents that summer at their cabin in the north woods and it was the first time my Grandfather saw me wearing the pith helmet that he had given me for my birthday. I'm not sure who was more excited about my explorer's outfit, but when he saw me wearing the hat, he immediately went to the small hall closet and grabbed his pith helmet from the shelf. We were quite a pair. He also grabbed two walking sticks, handed one to me, and announced that we were off. He told his beloved, my Grandmother, not to worry about us. We would be back when we were back. *"No limitations,"* he announced. She was accustomed to his long walks, so she showed no concern at all.

"Grandfather, who had been exploring the world for decades, steered us towards a path that was new to me. This was very exciting. On previous visits, I was not allowed to explore this particular trail because it was described as an adult-only trail. As you might well imagine that explanation never sat well with me. At last, the time had finally come. I was certain this was a sign that something really important was going to happen on this excursion. Before we actually entered the trail, I stopped, closed my eyes, and took a deep breath. My Grandfather stood quietly as he observed my behavior. When I opened my eyes, he was smiling at me. He asked where I had learned to do that, which really surprised me. I boldly announced that I had learned it from him. You and Grandmother always pause before entering a new adventure, I stated assertively. He seemed very pleased with my response, which of course, thrilled me.

"Walking with my Grandfather was like being in a movable classroom. Wherever your eyes focused, a new lesson unfolded. He knew something about everything, or so it seemed to someone who was just opening to the wonders of the world. On this particular morning, we appeared to be looking and talking more than we were walking. It was a wonderful time of day when the plant life was still heavily laden with dew. Grandfather said it was a time for the plants to quench their thirst and cleanse their beautiful forms at the same time. He taught me how to carefully touch without harming the various Life Beings in the forest. And even more importantly, he taught me how to notice everything…not just the biggest most conspicuous life forms, but everything! He would focus upon a specific plant, lovingly describe all its features, and then gently reach below the plant to see what other life forms resided underneath. 'Each layer of the forest has its own story,' he would tell me, and then continue to discuss each inhabitant that he observed. From a pill bug to the mightiest tree in the forest, my Grandfather treated every Life Being equally. 'Each member of the forest is essential to the whole,' he would say, 'and each one must be treated respectfully. They are all interconnected, Pamela, and without their presence, we will not survive. These Life Beings are our neighbors and we must treat them accordingly. We must do everything we can to maintain the health of the forest.'

"I could tell from the sincerity with which my Grandfather spoke to me that he was speaking the truth. Even in my youth there was already evidence that humankind was having a negative impact upon the planet. It was blatantly obvious in the form of trash that we saw along the trail, most of which we were able to carry back down to the cabin, but there were other ways in which the forest was also being affected. From one location to the next, my Grandfather pointed out signs of human negligence. Just a few feet off the pathway, we noticed where a campfire had been recently used. It was a remarkably reckless act. Not only were the plants tromped down all around the campsite, but the campfire itself was a gesture of absolute disrespect. How could anyone be so foolish to light a fire within the umbrella of the forest? My Grandfather, who was a very gentle man, was visibly upset by the carelessness of the unknown campers.

'People shouldn't treat the Earth like this, Pamela,' he said with his back turned to me. 'It's not right!' When he turned around to leave the area, I saw that tears were streaming down his cheeks. We left the site quickly, but just a few yards up the trail, my Grandfather came to an abrupt halt. He looked at me, and told me that we had to go back to the campsite. Obviously, I followed him. We stood together looking down at the ashes of the fire. 'Pamela, I want you to remember what we're witnessing here. This is wrong! Everything about this is wrong, and we need to make amends. Will you join me in a prayer for the Earth, Pamela?' I grabbed his hand and he proceeded to apologize for the act of unkindness that had been perpetrated at that site. And he promised the Earth that we would always treat her with love and respect. His words were so tender and loving and genuine that I knew I was listening to something that was divine. I think it was one of the most Holy experiences that I've ever had.

"That was the first time I learned that you could and should pray for the Earth. My Grandfather taught me the importance of doing that, and I've been doing it ever since." Pam sighed and took a moment to be with her Grandfather.

"I hope my story will in some way be of assistance to one or more of you this evening. It's a small event that had lasting results. On that hike, I came to understand the importance of honoring all other Life Beings, and the significance of being an honorable person. My Grandfather was a superb role model and he was a devout lover of life, all life. I am so grateful for everything that he taught me including the importance of prayer." She sighed again and then concluded her story.

"Thank you all for being such wonderful listeners. I am so grateful to be able to share this story with you." Gary reached over and squeezed his beloved's hand.

"Thank you, Pam. I feel like your Grandfather is here with us. I'm sure he is as proud of you, as you are of him. What a wonderful teacher he was!"

"He still is!" asserted Pam. "I know this may sound crazy, but I am absolutely convinced that my Grandfather continues to guide me." At first, Pam was surprised by her own candor, and then, decided not to worry about. "Please excuse my openness, Dear Ones, but it's simply my truth. I truly believe that Grandfather continues to assist me with my explorations."

"I believe it too, Pam," stated newcomer, Anne Marshall, "and it's refreshing to be in the presence of people who are open to such ideas. Thank you so much for sharing that lovely encounter with your Grandfather. I feel so privileged to be here and to hear your story." Anne paused briefly and glanced toward Deb. She seemed to be in conflict, but a look of reassurance from her friend provided the resolve she needed to continue. "I must admit that I almost cancelled earlier today. Truth is, when Deb invited me to come, excitement trumped my social anxiety, but as the weekend approached, I started having the jitters.

"As I was pacing back and forth this morning trying to muster up the courage to call Deb, I heard a noise in the kitchen. It sounded like something had fallen, so I immediately assumed that Twinkle Toes had once again knocked something off the counter. Trust me, previous experiences with my precious and somewhat feisty Persian cat warranted my suspicions. Whether she was responsible for this latest issue or not remains a mystery. She is swift to leave the scenes of her mischievous antics. Anyway, I arrived to an empty kitchen with my calendar resting upside down on the floor. Upon retrieving the displaced daily reminder, I tore off the top page to find today's inspirational message. It stopped me in my tracks. FACE YOUR FEARS! The message, written in bright colors, all caps, and bold letters, was too relevant and timely to be disregarded. Now, some might say it was a mere coincidence, but I don't believe in coincidences.

"I took the message to be a sign, thankfully. I am so glad to be here!" Before Anne finished, her eyes circled the group. "Just to be sure my intuition is correct, I have a question. You folks don't believe in coincidences, do you?" Reassurance came from every direction of the circle. The original four members were feeling very confident about their guest list, and the conversation was just in its beginning stage. Much more was to come.

"Anne, thank you for facing your fears," noted Pam. "I believe you are intended to be here!"

"Yes," replied Anne. "My intuition is telling me the same. And," she said tentatively and softly, "I think there is a story within me that needs to be shared. Is that okay?" She looked to the other members of the group for permission and received encouraging words and silent applause.

"Well, new Friends," she began with hands in prayerful position, "I consider this next step very similar to Pam's ritual when entering a pathway. Will you join me please as I pause for a deep breath?" The group did as requested. They all closed their eyes, took a deep breath, and without consultation, each participant held Anne in his or her heart. A smile crossed her face. As she opened her eyes, she thanked everyone for their warm support. "Pam, your story brought this old, old experience back to memory. It's a difficult memory for me, so I don't visit it very often, but it was an experience that profoundly impacted the rest of my life. I was very young, probably only five, when this event happened. Like you Pam, I loved the outdoors and could entertain myself for hours while my older brother was at school. One wonders how anyone so young could come up with these various fantasies, but children are very impressionable, and the movies of that time period were often about cowboys and Indians. I preferred imagining myself as an Indian because they seemed to know so much about the mysteries of the great outdoors.

"Well, one day, I sneaked into my brother's room and 'borrowed' his Red Ryder BB Gun. The gun was necessary because on that particular day, I had taken on the role of a great Indian Chief out on a mission to secure food for my tribe. I scurried about the yard from one tree to another pretending to be stalking some big game that would feed the entire tribe. This went on for some time, and eventually, my big game turned out to be a redbird. Just as I peeked around the corner of the house, I saw this magnificent cardinal sitting on a limb of the great oak tree that shaded the entire front of our house. Consumed by my role in this fantasy, I hoisted the BB gun from my side and pulled the trigger at the same time. Unfortunately, the target was hit. To this day, I do not know how that terrible incident occurred, but it did. And my five year old watched the beautiful redbird flutter to the ground. I can still feel the utter disbelief of that child. The bird was dead and I was responsible for its death. That was my first experience with death. And it was shattering! Even now as I remember that experience, it breaks my heart. That five year old had no idea that the game would end in such a tragedy. The reality of death became clear on that day. It was a very hard lesson.

"I've never shared this story with anyone before. I was too ashamed. The child had no idea what was going to happen. She was an innocent. But that sorrowful incident changed her life forever. It solidified my path of being a healer."

"Oh my goodness!" whispered Pam. "What a tremendous burden to shoulder all these years! Thank you for honoring us with your story. I hope you feel some sense of relief by finally sharing it with others." Nodding in agreement, Anne thanked everyone again for listening to her story.

"I'm curious, Anne, how did your parents help you through that tragic event?" My question caused more memories to surface. The look on Anne's face revealed more of the suffering that the child had experienced. "Oh, Anne, I'm so sorry to have stirred up more pain." She resorted to her self-healing skills taking another long deep breath to quiet herself.

"Not to worry," she finally replied. "I'm so sorry to burden all of you with this sad story, but it truly is a healing experience for me. I had totally forgotten the end of that story until you asked the question. The truth is I was so ashamed of what I had done that I buried the bird in the back of a flowerbed, and then sneaked back into the house to return the BB gun to my brother's room. I never told anyone about the incident." Anne released a long audible sigh. "How did that five year old manage all that suffering? Shame is an extraordinary emotion. There remains much more for me to learn from this sad story. Sharing this with you has made me appreciate the strength of that little girl who was able to bear all that pain. I am in debt to her and to the beautiful redbird. The two of them were the foundation for the rest of my life. I'm so sorry that she had to feel that shame by herself, but that experience awakened her, me, to the precious nature of life. I am so grateful to her. And I am grateful to all of you for helping me to finally process decades of grief and shame. Wow. This has been a powerful experience for me."

"Good work!" declared Deb. "Anne, may I ask you another question? I don't want to dwell on this, but this incident was so profoundly significant that it seems to be one of those experiences that was intended to happen. You mentioned that you don't believe in coincidences, and neither to I, and that's why I'm bringing this up. Do you believe that event happened for a reason?"

"Oh, yes, I do," answered Anne. "I've thought that for a very long time, and having the liberty to share this story confirms it for me. I believe..." Anne paused. One could tell that she was pondering her options. Should she or should she not continue to reveal herself to these strangers?

"Anne, trust yourself!" encouraged Deb. "We're not strangers. We're old friends meeting again for the first time." Deb's response to Anne's inner thoughts did not go unnoticed. Several individuals were poised waiting to hear Anne's reaction.

A smile came to Anne's face. "Thank you for that encouragement," she declared. "I do believe this group is a place where one's innermost feelings can be shared. Like you, Deb, I believe that incident happened for a reason. As said, I have wondered about this for years, and there are many questions, which remain unanswered, but I still believe it was an intentional act that was meant to steer me towards an intended path. In this lifetime, I am certain that my path is that of a healer. Even though that job description brings up all sorts of questions and opinions, the truth is we are all healers waiting to find our own personal direction. That act, so long ago, certainly got me on track at a very early age. Of course, I wonder why that beautiful creature had to die. Couldn't the lesson unfold in a different way? And why did it have to occur at such a youthful age? The answers still elude me, but the impact goes without question. That incident awakened the healing nature within me, which has manifested in numerous ways over the years. I am a student of nature, which led me to academic endeavors that expanded my understanding of the interconnectedness of all life on our planet and beyond. Then I became an energy worker and healing touch practitioner so that I could gain greater knowledge and understanding of that aspect of interconnection. And then, I got involved with volunteer work that includes educating children to the wonders of Mother Nature. All of this unfolded, as if I were following some cosmic script, and the play isn't over yet. I, like everyone else, am a piece of work, still in progress.

"Oh, I've gone on and on. You are such wonderful listeners. Thank you. I am so grateful to be here." Numerous participants, new and old, expressed their appreciation of Anne's story and her courage.

"Anne, you are an impressive woman. For someone who has social anxiety, you have certainly proven that you can stretch beyond your comfort zone. I am in awe of your strength and very grateful that you shared your story. It was very helpful to me." These comments came from another newcomer named Joan Andrews, who had been a friend of mine for many years. Her reactions to Anne's story didn't surprise me. I knew from years of conversations that she too had bouts with shyness and socializing. Just as I was thinking how easily the gathering was unfolding, Gary took the lead again.

"Isn't this wonderful? Stories are unfolding, interactions are happening, and the day is young. I hope everyone is feeling increasingly more comfortable, but I don't want to be presumptuous. We, meaning the old timers, definitely have more stories that we are ready to share; however, if anyone wants to take the next step, we are happy to be the listeners." The couple that was invited by Pam and Gary seemed ready to jump in, but there was a moment of hesitation. Gary nudged them forward with his lighthearted manner. "Come on, you two! We've been looking forward to hearing more about your adventures."

"Actually, Doug and I have several topics that we would like to address, but we're struggling over which one to share first." Laura Hanson elaborated upon their dilemma. "We talked about this last night, but couldn't make a decision, so we decided to wait until we heard some of the stories presented. And we're still confused."

"Let's just go with the retreat experience," declared Doug, who clearly wanted his wife to begin the story.

"Okay, new and old Friends, please join us as we indulge ourselves with a long deep breath. The group rallied around the Hansons. "Our story began a few years ago." Doug, raising his hand showing four fingers confirmed the timeline of their experience. "Yes, it was four years ago that both of us became very restless. It was odd: life was going really well. We were happy and actively involved in numerous projects that were very satisfying, and still, there seemed to be something missing. At the time, we had few words to describe our dilemma. We just knew that something was off. We tried to talk about our angst, but our attempts left us more confused."

Doug, indicating that he wished to make a comment, elaborated on Laura's remark. "Actually, our discussions heightened our confusion, and this too was extremely odd for us. Typically, whenever we're distracted by something, we talk about it, and we are able to gain clarity, but that was not happening with this angst, as Laura referred to it. At that point, we had our first unusual encounter." Doug turned to his spouse to see if she wanted to take over, but she urged him to continue. "I don't remember the time frame of our frustrations, but it seemed like our restlessness had been going on for months, and once again we found ourselves walking and talking on one of our favorite pathways about our sense of urgency and emptiness. Fortunately, at that point we had discerned that these two adjectives almost seemed to describe our predicament, albeit limitedly. It wasn't much, but it gave us hope that some progress was being made, even though we still didn't know what to do about our situation." Doug squeezed his beloved's hand and nodded in her direction.

"We were clinging to that tiny bit of hope. Everyday we would encourage each other to remember that something important was happening to us and we just had to hold on until it fully revealed itself. We were so lucky to have one another; I cannot imagine going through that period alone." Laura smiled at her husband and whispered that she loved him before returning to the story. "Well, after our conversation failed to answer our many questions, we decided to turn our attentions to a more positive topic. One of the ways we manage stressful times is to focus upon our blessings. We find this exercise very helpful. As we continued along the path that day, we took turns expressing our appreciation for the wonderful aspects of our lives, including having the privilege of walking that beautiful trail that we both enjoy so much.

"When we reached the southern-most point of the trail, the view of the ocean was just spectacular. We always pause there for a few minutes to fully embrace that seascape; it literally takes one's breath away. Just as we were about to move on, I noticed movement near the water's edge. At first, it looked like a huge sea turtle, but then the mound rose and stood upright. We were both startled and thought our eyes were playing tricks on us. And then, the man that had risen from what seemed to be tortoise shell turned around and stared at us. He moved gracefully across the large ocean boulders and with each step that he took, his appearance became clearer and brighter. What began, as a grayish brown mass, now appeared to be flowing white billowy fabrics that appeared to assist this fellow's movement rather than impeding it! The distance that he covered in just a few minutes was amazing. We moved closer to the rock formations as he approached, and then, there we were: the three of us standing face-to-face smiling at one another.

"We introduced ourselves to him, but he just kept smiling and nodding at us. He seemed to be absolutely delighted to see us. In fact, his eyes engaged with us as if we were old friends. Doug asked him if he was all right and his smile grew even bigger. He told us he was very happy to be in our presence again, which was a surprise since neither of us had any recollection of having met him before. Undoubtedly, he sensed our confusion, because he apologized for his exuberance. He said that he was so excited about seeing us again that he had forgotten that we were unable to remember our previous experiences. And then, he reassured us that we were very Old Friends who have shared many other life times together. As you might imagine, we were again surprised, but oddly enough, we were completely at ease with this gentleman.

"He invited us to sit down on the rocks with him, and we were delighted to do so. We talked for over an hour. He never told us his name, but repeatedly reminded us that we were Old Friends, and that he was here to assist us with our confusion. His exacts words were: *'The unrest you experience is the memory of old that calls to you.'* We, of course, wanted to know what memory he was referring to, and he embraced us with his eyes. Never before have we felt that level of compassion before; it was humbling. He told us that this was the first of more meetings to come, and that we did not need to worry anymore. *'Soon the memories of old will return and you will have clarity about the unrest that you currently experience. You are here for a reason, Old Friends, and the time is now!'* His words were riveting. We both knew that he was a messenger and that we were being called to duty. We watched the sunset together and then he bid us adieu. He turned toward the water again and with just a few steps taken, he faded into nothingness."

Tears glistened in Laura's eyes and Doug flicked one from his. Their story was mesmerizing.

The group looked on in amazement, wanting to hear more, and then finally realized that the account of the Hanson's experience was complete. What began with whispers of astonishment quickly led to questions spoken in unison! Pam efficiently took command, "Okay, everyone, let's give Laura and Doug some space. As you can see, you two have ignited the curious nature in all of us. What an amazing experience you had...and thank you for sharing this with us." Then she looked around the circle and invited Joan to go first.

"Joan, my eyes are drawn to you for some reason. Would you like to pose the first question?"

"Yes!" she replied eagerly and immediately turned towards the Hansons. "Thank you so much for sharing that experience with us. I have many questions! And I know others do as well, so I will tap into the one that is screaming inside of me." Laura leaned forward in her chair welcoming Joan's question.

"Has the gentleman connected with you again?" she inquired.

"Yes, he has, numerous times," replied Laura. Once again, the listeners were riveted by the exchange.

"Please tell us more, if you feel comfortable doing so," Joan's facilitation opened the door for more conversation.

"Goodness," declared Laura, "we are both so relieved by your acceptance of our story." Doug nodded in agreement. "As you might imagine, we were very concerned about sharing this unusual experience today. Your openheartedness is overwhelming and very healing. We've been afraid about sharing out relationship with the gentleman, even though we both agreed that it was absolutely necessary to do so. People need to know that encounters such as this are real. We know we aren't the only ones having theses encounters, but finding others who will open their hearts to this reality is not easy. We are so grateful to Pam and Gary for including us in this gathering today. Quite honestly, this invitation is as important to us as our encounter with the gentleman. This is happening for a reason!"

"Yes, that's true," added Doug, "and at some point, we would love to hear about how the four of you first came together. I doubt that it was a coincidence." His comment made us all chuckle and Gary reassured him that we would share the sequence of events that led to today's first effort of expanding our circle, and then he invited them to continue with their story.

"Well, the truth is," admitted Laura, "the gentleman is very present in our lives and he's been instrumental in our spiritual development. The unrest that we were struggling with has evolved into greater clarity about our purpose in this life. We still have many questions and I guess that's just part of life, but with his gentle presence, we seem to be moving forward. In fact, sharing this truth with you is part of our growth process. This is the first time that we've shared this part of our lives with anyone. So again, let me express our appreciation for your warm welcome and acceptance of our unusual story." My own enthusiasm forced me to raise my hand, but then, good manners stepped forward and quickly commanded the extended hand to return to my lap. My dear friends giggled and urged me to ask the next question. Embarrassed, but driven by my curiosity, I accepted the opportunity.

"I too have many questions, but for now, I am curious about the lessons you are learning. Is there a central theme that your messenger focuses upon?" Doug and Laura looked at each other as if they were strategizing how to answer the question. This time Doug took the lead.

"Actually there are numerous themes that are all interrelated. Essentially, this information is critical to the future of humankind. We are learning about the relationship of our species with all other species and the tragic impact we are having on other inhabitants on this planet, and upon the Earth herself. The information is frightening and disheartening; however, the gentleman repeatedly apprises us that we have the power to change what is happening. His messages are profoundly worrisome, and hopeful at the same time, as he reassures us that we have the ability to heal the Earth. He speaks bluntly of our role in the Earth's declining health and calls us to task. There is so much more that he has revealed to us, but the bottom line is this. We are responsible for the catastrophic events that are occurring all across the globe and we must significantly change our ways for the Earth to return to full health again. I apologize for speaking so forthrightly about this, but the truth is the truth. I suspect everyone in this gathering comprehends the reality of these messages. Please believe me when I say that there is reason for hope. The gentleman has been so kind in delivering the messages to us. He took such good care of us as he slowly educated us to the truth. I'm afraid my presentation probably feels like a slap in the face. Trust me, there is definitely reason for hope. And we are part of that equation; we can assist the Earth back to full vibrancy. She's a remarkable Life Being who has treated our species with the utmost respect and care, and she deserves the same from us. We're here for a reason…and Laura and I want to do our part." Doug took a deep breath and reached out to his beloved. He was exhausted. The outpouring of information had taken a toll on him. The group could see that and we all applauded his and Laura's courage. The couple hugged each other as they shared a few tears.

I turned to Deb and we immediately reached out to those next to us and soon hands were clasped around the circle. "Dear Friends, we are so blessed to be with one another. Let us breathe together and join as One." With hands tightly clenched, we shared numerous long breaths and with each one, we became more deeply united.

A passage from
The Word
(Chapter One)

"If changes are not made immediately, the issues of the Earth's failing health will become so tragically evident that even the harshest critics will be forced to silence their lies. In the meantime, the fate of this civilization is in the hands of those who do not have the Earth's best interest in mind. One wonders how long such foolishness will be tolerated. Lies will not solve her problems, regardless of how many times they are repeated. The Earth's health crisis is real and it is not going to magically disappear. No longer can the perpetrators of her problems be allowed to continue their outrageous acts of cruelty. Nor can they continue to disrupt and interfere with actions that are made on her behalf. Countries that refuse to participate in healing the Earth will fall into the darkness that they are creating, while those who focus their energies on saving the Earth will see their lands, skies, and waters recovering from the vile mistreatment that has been perpetrated against her. Rest assured every action taken on her behalf matters. No act of goodness is too small. Individuals, communities, nations, and global initiatives must take positive steps to assist her. Those who accept responsibility for assisting the Earth will benefit from their efforts; those who do not will suffer the consequences of their disrespect. Old Friend, these words are not spoken lightly. Hearts are heavy, but those who continue to violate the Earth can no longer keep others from doing what must be done.

The Earth has selflessly cared for all her inhabitants since they came into existence, and now she needs our help. This is a reality that does not demand debate. The planet is in serious trouble. The one who has generously and devotedly provided for countless generations is in need. Ignoring her situation is not an option. Continuing to abuse and misuse her is unthinkable. She is in need, and there is only one appropriate response to this situation.

Assistance must immediately be provided. To do anything less is unconscionable.

Everything that is required to be of assistance is available. All flora and fauna and sea life across the planet are already involved in helping her. Long have they been aware of her circumstances, and their efforts are substantial, but much more assistance is necessary. Those who are the offenders are the ones who must change their careless ways and return to a state of alignment with the energy of the Earth. As said before, everything that is required to be of assistance is available.

You are a Being with exceptional abilities,
and with these abilities,
you have the power to heal self and others.

This message previously delivered is the answer to assisting the Earth. All came into existence with this exceptional, yet natural ability. Please understand this reality. All Beings are naturally endowed with the ability to heal self and others. This is the way of existence. Unfortunately, not all Beings remember the ability that manifests within them. For this reason the message of truth is repeated. Often this message has been delivered over the ages, but few accept its truth, for reasons that vary from one Being to another. Dear Friend, please do not be one of those who discounts what is presented. Your assistance is needed and you can be of tremendous help to the planet Earth. For you to serve to your fullest potential you must accept this truth that lies within you. Your participation in assisting the Earth is critical for the success of her recovery. Do not forget, the Earth is a remarkably large Life Being and to achieve full recovery, she will need the assistance of the masses. Two factors are critical in her recovery process. First and foremost, the acts of unkindness must end immediately. She can no longer endure the senseless, disrespectful acts that are daily perpetrated against her. This requires the cooperation of everyone upon the planet. Secondly, she must be treated everyday with the healing powers of her inhabitants. Intentional acts of goodness, prayers for her well being, and healing sessions on her behalf must be initiated everyday. So little is asked of you, for someone who has done so much for you and your forebears."

"Dear Friends, let us be grateful for this reunion. We came together in hope of finding new friendships with others of similar minds and hearts. Little did we know that in taking this step we would find Friends of Old. We are so blessed! In such a short amount of time, kinship has evolved and there is still so much more to learn about each other and about our future roles. We have been brought together for a reason…and we are so grateful." With that said, an audible sigh reverberated through the Circle of Eight. Slowly, hands were released and we repositioned ourselves back into our chairs.

"Thank you, dear, for leading us into that warm space of connection. And thank you all for your participation in this gathering. I know there is much more to share, but perhaps, it is time for some munchies. Does that meet with your approval?" Pam's idea was definitely timely. Gary, who had the energy of a youngster, jumped up from his chair and invited everyone to meet him at the table. Nourishment was definitely needed and Pam had wisely included healthy protein options along with other temptations. We all milled about for about twenty minutes before settling back into our circle.

"Ah! Here we are again!" Pam graciously welcomed everyone back into the circle and then surprisingly turned to me for guidance. "What do you think, dear? How should we proceed at this point?" I took the necessary deep breath to give myself time to ponder our possibilities.

"Well, I think we should begin with grateful hearts. I, for one, am astonished by the heartfelt connections we've already experienced. Thank you! Thank you! Thank you!" Deb quickly tagged onto my train of thoughts by adding her own appreciations.

"Oh yes, same here! My heart is full!" Her eyes reached out to everyone as she elaborated upon her thoughts. "You know when we, the four of us, first began to talk about expanding our group, I was reluctant. Our relationships were deepening and we were very compatible. It felt very safe to share our adventures with one another and I didn't want that to change. My reasons were founded in selfishness and fear. We were such a cozy group and I didn't want to lose that. And now look at us! My goodness, the gifts of connection have multiplied, as has the level of connection. I truly believe this is happening for a reason, and I am so grateful to be part of this…whatever 'this' is." Other members of the group also shared similar comments before I led the group back to focus.

"Friends, I know we all have many more questions to ask one another, but before we take that path, does anyone else want to share a story?" I glanced around the circle hoping that Joan might be ready to gift us with one of her adventures, but as our eyes met, she pointed towards me.

"You go next," she said encouragingly. "And then, I'll follow you." Her suggestion was definitely appropriate, but it gave me pause. Pam was the only one from the original group, who had shared an experience thus far. It was time for one of us to address our own social anxiety.

"I think the best way for me to approach this is by acknowledging that Mother Nature has also captured my heart. It has been through nature that my heart has opened to the 'more' that exists around us. Like billions of others folks, I am a seeker. Admittedly, my search often leaves me baffled, but the wonders of this incredible existence that we live in are so bountiful and so present that even someone like me cannot help but notice. I am stunned by all the ways in which existence reaches out to us trying to get our attention, striving to remind us that there is more than the ordinary affairs of life. I fear we are so often distracted by our busy lives that we do not see the true vibrancy of life that is all around us. Fortunately, blessedly, existence did capture my attention long ago, and once that happens, the heart aches for more connection. The craving ebbs and flows, but with each new connection, the reality that there is more calls to you. The need to participate in this incredible experience of interrelatedness becomes a driving force within you, and no matter how many distractions deter you from your desire to connect with and understand The More that you seek, the source of the 'more' patiently awaits your return. The journey, as many people call it, is ongoing, never-ending. The source of your intention is always there, no matter how far you stray or how long you stay away, the source is ever-patient, ever-waiting, for the truth of existence is this: The source that you seek is also seeking connection with you, because you and the Source are One." A deep breath was necessary. I wondered if my words had many sense.

"I am sorry. Words fail me. It is difficult to speak about that which we know so little about. Still, the heart yearns to share its certainty that there is more. When I have an encounter with another species, I am absolutely certain that something remarkable is at work. It brings me great joy when these other beings reach out to me. And truthfully, I am also positive that these other species know much more about the mysteries of the world than humans do. We are so preoccupied with our distractions that we are not evolving with the same awareness, as are our other neighbors. We are surrounded by other Life Beings and we go about our lives as if they do not exist. Isn't that a shame?"

A passage from
The Word
(Chapter One)

*"For those who doubt the healing capabilities that
are suggested, please open the ears of your heart. What
is told is truth, and your doubts will never alter this truth.
You can choose to revel in your doubts and delay your
own progress or you can choose to open your heart to
this precious reality. Just because one is not in awareness
of a truth does not mean that truth does not exist. Your
healing abilities exist within you. If you open your heart to
this truth, the ability will surface. If you continue to scoff
at this reality, the ability will continue to lie in dormancy.
The choice is clear. Why would you deny yourself access to
this remarkable gift? Why would you resist an opportunity
to assist another with your healing powers? Ponder these
questions, Dear Friend. Give yourself time to discern your
decision. You have free will. Obviously, you can choose to
do whatever is your preference, but why would you turn
your back on an opportunity to help another?*

*Dear Friend, the healing powers within you are yours
to share. Simply visualize a small particle of your healing
energy igniting within you. And then visualize this particle
of healing energy exiting your body and transferring to
the recipient of your gift. The act is just that simple. It
requires so little of your time. The process of igniting
your healing energy and sending it to another is very
personal. Each individual creates and designs a method
that is unique.*

*Some individuals are hesitant to participate in this act
of kindness not because they do not want to, but because
they feel inept. They worry that the process of healing
another is beyond their means. This is a misunderstanding
and lack of confidence. When one first begins ministering
to another, one is naturally concerned and self-conscious
about the experience. One doubts his or her capability;
however, with practice, confidence and trust grow. Dear
Friend, this skill is one that everyone can access, and it is*

also one that cannot be misused. Healing powers simply are, and the energy of healing awaits its activation. The participant's role is to show up, open to the possibility, and engage with the process. In the beginning the new participant may feel awkward, but that will soon pass. With each healing session, one will refine and finesse the process until it is as comfortable as taking a deep breath.

The words spoken may sound too good to be true. They may seem to lack the grandiosity that one might presume a discussion of healing powers merits. The words are carefully chosen; they state a truth that is truth for all in existence. Is this an amazing realization? Yes indeed, it is, and still, it is an existential truth that simply is. Please accept this remarkable truth as the simple gift that it is."

"Dear Friends, what I really want you to know about me is that I believe that we are not alone in the world. Not only are we surrounded by other life beings on our planet that seem to be reaching out to us, but also, I believe that beings from other locations are also trying to capture our attention. The Hansons' encounter is an excellent example of that. And by the way, I want to thank you both again for sharing your story. Your courage was inspirational and gives me the confidence to share something new about my journey. Recently, for several months now, I have been receiving messages about the Earth's situation as well. This is still very new to me, but I trust what is happening and I will keep all of you posted as things move forward.

"There's one last thing that I feel compelled to say. It's been said several times this afternoon, but it bears repeating. These experiences that we're sharing with one another are real and they are happening for a reason. And the eight of us have been brought together for a reason as well. We need to keep this in mind, Friends. I suspect the days ahead are going to be very eventful, and I am so glad that we have come together.

"That's a summary about me folks, and I look forward to sharing specific events with you in the future. But now, let me turn this over to Joan."

"Wow," she sighed. "This is a day that will never be forgotten. I am so, so grateful to be here. I'm grateful for the invitation, I'm grateful for the heartfelt stories that have been shared, and I sit here now wondering, Why me? Why am I so lucky to be in the right place at the right time? Dear Ones, this gathering is an experience!" Her eyes met with every other group participant. "Think about it! In days to come, we will share this account with others and they will be as enamored with this story as we are with the ones that we are hearing today. This gathering is happening for a reason and I would love to see the cosmic script that orchestrated this event." Joan's comments made us all realize the importance of the moment. We truly were experiencing one of the unusual adventures that we all loved to encounter. Murmurs of confirmation and disbelief circled the group along with happy faces and quiet chuckles.

"I've been longing for people to have these kinds of conversations for a very long time. This is a dream come true. First, let me say that I believe every story that has been shared and I look forward to many more of these conversations. Like you, I have many adventures that have been unspoken for years. These stories occupy pages and pages in my journals, which of course, have never met another's eyes. These beautiful experiences have been relegated to secrecy because of their so-called unusual nature.

"My Friends, it is time to honor our stories and share them with the world—and then, we will find out just how ordinary these experiences really are. Our fears of being judged, discounted, and shamed have caused us to separate ourselves from others, and because of these decisions, we became isolated, which led to more worriment and concerns about speaking the truth. I understand why we did this, but we need to rethink those old decisions. My Friends, these experiences are not unusual. They are real experiences of connection that are unfolding in natural ways, but because people are afraid to speak the truth about these events, they appear to be rare and therefore are described as unusual. I believed this nonsense for a long time, but I don't anymore, and today's discussion confirms my new way of thinking.

"Friends, I think these efforts at connection are happening all the time all across the planet, and if we finally start speaking the truth about it, then these stories will become evidence of interspecies communication. We have neighbors of all shapes and sizes who are initiating contact with us. I mean no disrespect, but it seems to me that it is the human species that is lagging behind in this evolutionary process. It's time for us to listen to our neighbors because they have information to share about the Earth's crisis. These other species have been working in alignment with her since they came into being. They know so much more about the Earth than we do, and we can learn from them if only we will open our hearts to this reality. Please excuse me for going on and on about this, but I am an Earth enthusiast." Joan paused, took in the necessary deep breath and then refocused.

"Okay, let me back up and share a story with you that happened about a decade ago. I was going through one of those restless periods that Laura and Doug talked about and it was wearing me down. I had this intense sensation that something needed to be done, but I had no clue as to what that something was. I consumed books, went on retreats, meditated with little success, and walked and walked and walked. Walking became the most important part of my day, while my work, which I loved, felt as if it were intruding upon my life. It was as if I was leading two lives. The first was my ordinary life of getting up and going to work every day, which was necessary to sustain my livelihood, and then there was the other life that was anything but ordinary. That life consumed my thoughts. That life was filled with excitement, wonderment, and an insatiable desire to know more about the mysterious existence that was all around me. That life awakened me early in the morning, capturing my imagination for hours before the ordinary workday began, and it kept me awake long beyond my usual bedtime, reading, pondering, listening, and writing about the day's inexplicable events. It was a time of great expansion, and it was a time of great questioning. Reminiscing about this with you makes me realize what an extraordinary time it was for me. I was literally having the time of my life." Joan closed her eyes and sighed. "How sweet this is!"

"Back to my story," she said to herself. "So during this period of great angst and walking countless miles, my intuitive senses became more alive. Actually, the culmination of all that walking resulted in a more peaceful mind, which enabled me to be in the present, and living in the present awakens one to the world around us. It's amazing how much humans are missing! Life is going on all round us all of the time, but we are oblivious to this reality. We are so consumed by our own tiny part of life that we are clueless about the abundance of life with which we coexist.

"The point is, as I became more aware of what was happening around me, my world expanded. I started having delightful connections with animals, wild and domestic, on a regular basis. It wasn't just an occasional experience that one might discount as a coincidence, which of course, we don't believe in anyway. No, this was happening all the time. In fact, my friends were teasing me about it and started referring to me as an animal whisperer. Needless to say, I was enjoying every minute of attention from the animals. My heart was wide open to these experiences, but it didn't stop with animals. I started having connections with insects as well, which was more difficult for me to discern at first, but once again, it became blatantly obvious that these little creatures were reaching out to me.

"And then, another type of connection started." Joan paused for a minute and refreshed herself with the essential deep breath. We all joined her. A good listener needs to indulge in this exercise as much as the storyteller does.

"I believe the connection that was experienced with the animals and insects enabled me to engage with another level of connection. Perhaps, I'm wrong about that, but I don't think so. Once we open up to one level of connection, we gain confidence in the process. Essentially, we are prepared to open our hearts to more possibilities. Well, that's what happened to me. While I was absolutely delighted with all the wonderful incidents that were occurring, I also knew that there was more to come. In some ways, I felt like a selfish child always wanting more. But at the same time I realized that the 'more' that I was anticipating was calling me to come forward. It seemed as if an invitation was being extended, so I kept putting one step in front of the other until the invitation was blatantly received. It came to me in a dream that was as real as any encounter that I've had with another individual. In the dream there was an image of a place that my family had visited when I was just a child. I never forgot that setting and always longed to return to it, but as life unfolded, that travel experience was always delayed for another time. The dream was unusual in that I was witnessing it from afar. I saw the setting appear before my eyes, and observed a figure in the distance moving forward toward me. Once he was within easy view, he held his hands out towards me beckoning me to come closer. His exact words were: *'You must come home, Old Friend. It is time to return. You are needed. Please come home!'*

"As you might imagine, I took that as the undeniable invitation. I immediately got out of bed, started up the computer, and scheduled a flight to a place I hadn't seen in over forty years.

"Well, four days later, I found myself walking along the beach where our family had vacationed all those years before. And it was just as I remembered it! Can you imagine that? The beach was still clean, there were no housing developments at water's edge, and the most amazing thing was that the beach was empty except for me...and the wonderful shore birds that were enjoying the peace and quiet as much as I was. It was lovely!

"I quietly walked up the pristine beach for over an hour, just taking in the remarkable views in every direction. The seacoast, the skyline, the cloud formations, the precious beach treasures that are available when your footsteps are the first ones on the scene! Everything was perfect. No one could wish for more! I looked out over the ocean and just stood there for what seemed an eternity. Words cannot describe the serenity that was experienced; I felt a sense of peace never felt before. I wondered if this was heaven, and then instinctively looked up and down the beach to see if anyone else was about. The beach was still mine and mine alone, or so I thought. Within an instant of having that selfish thought, I felt a gentle tap on my shoulder. I quickly turned about and there was the man in the dream who had invited me to return to this beautiful setting. It goes without saying that I was at a loss for words. We stood there staring at each other for the longest time, or so it seemed. We seemed to be taking each other in as if we had known each other for a very long time. It was a very gentle moment. Although questions raced through my mind, I had no need to voice them. I was completely at ease in his presence. His face sported the most delightful smile, radiant and peaceful at the same time. Being in his presence was an experience that I will never forget, and even though I have no words to describe that moment in time, I will remember the essence of his presence forever. Eventually, he took the lead.

'I am most grateful that you are here. Your timing is perfect, Old Friend,' were his exact words. It became clear very quickly that he was fulfilling a commitment made long ago. Even though I did not remember this mutual commitment that we shared, he held the memories for both of us. He expressed appreciation that I responded so quickly to the dream and he apologized for interrupting my life, but he said confidently and firmly: *'I am here as was agreed long ago to remind you of the crisis that is unfolding upon the Earth and to assist you with the tasks that must be done on her behalf. The time is now, Old Friend. Her situation has worsened, and still the people do not accept the reality of the catastrophic events that are already occurring all across the planet. They do not realize the severity of their situation.'*

"Needless to say, his message was not pleasant to hear, but it confirmed the messages that I was receiving from other species. These beings are reaching out to us, trying to alert us to the truth of our circumstances. Why are we not paying attention to this? And why are we not heeding the advice of scientists from all across the planet? It doesn't make sense!"

A passage from
The Word
(Chapter One)

"In days ahead, new challenges will arise. These challenges will be like none experienced before. The times will require cooperation among the peoples of Earth. Based upon current global relationships, the hardships will be many, unless changes are immediately made. There is no longer time for the petty squabbles that presently plague this civilization. Please hear these words, for they speak a truth that demands your attention. You no longer have time for fighting amongst yourselves. The crisis situation that is unfolding upon the planet Earth demands compassion for all by all. Generosity, loving kindness, and selfless acts must be your guide. These words are a sound of alarm that action must be taken now. Your denial,

endless debates, and futile discussions have led you to this point. Enough! Preparations must begin now.

Dear Friend, this message is for all the Children of Earth. Take action now. We take no pleasure in delivering this news to you. We take no pleasure in speaking so forcefully to you, but what must be done must be done. The ramifications of a planet entering into a state of dormancy are beyond your scope of imagination. Already, your peoples have experienced the consequences of her raging winds, rains, fires, and eruptions. And still you ignore the evidence of her pain and suffering. What you have already witnessed is unbelievable, but it does not compare to what is coming. Please breathe deeply, Dear Friend. We are so very sorry to bring this message forward, but the truth must be spoken truthfully. If we were you at this moment, we would be inclined to trash this material. We would be outraged and terrified by the news, and we would be furious at those who brought it forward. We appreciate your fear and despair, and we regret having to be the bearer of such tragic news.

That which is spoken is the truth of your future unless action is instigated now. Dear Friend, please continue to read this message. Within you is the means to alter the future. Please hear us. Within you lies the ability to save the Earth and your civilization. Remember you are a Being with exceptional abilities, and with these abilities, you have the power to heal self and others.

You are a Being with exceptional abilities, and with these abilities, you have the power to heal self and others.

Please accept this message of truth, Dear Friend. Two profound messages have been presented to you. One informs you of truth of your planet's failing health, and the other provides you with the solution to this tragic situation. If you become paralyzed by the first message, the latter message will be in vain. The decline of your planet is real. The Earth is seriously ill and her only means of survival is to retreat into dormancy. She does

189

not wish to do this. This incredible Life Being is devoted to all her inhabitants. She continues for their sake, but she cannot continue for much longer.

You have the means to help her. Whether you believe in healing energy or not is irrelevant. All beings possess this natural ability and when it is activated, the process is restorative. When cooperation among all the inhabitants of Earth is secured, the combined and sustained energies can revitalize her back to full health. The process is not magical. Repeated treatments will be necessary. These treatments, combined with the elimination of the present abuses that continue to injure her, will result in a healthy Life Being once again.

Dear Friend, because the human species learns by repetition, a liberty is taken. In succinct form, the messages of truth are presented to you again. The Earth is seriously ill. This is the truth and anyone who says otherwise is spreading lies for their own personal gains. The Earth can be revitalized to full health by the elimination of all abuses currently perpetrated against her, combined with treatments of restorative energies provided by all the inhabitants of the planet.

The choice is yours. All in existence hope that you will choose to survive."

Joan closed her eyes and took another deep breath, and once again we all joined with her, benefitting from the restorative practice that helps us to ground ourselves with the Earth. I wondered if Mother Earth also benefitted from these brief, refreshing moments.

"Dear New Friends, this gathering is a blessing, and it came to me by way of an invitation. I mention that because I'm beginning to understand the importance of saying yes to invitations. My intuition tells me that we will face many more invitations in the future, and we need to be prepared to answer yes.

"So, I will conclude by saying, Thank You, once again. Thank you for this invitation, thank you for the stories shared, and thank you for being YOU! Each of you is here for a reason. I have an image in my mind of an old wagon wheel with all the spokes splaying out from its center. Each spoke is essential to the functionality of that wheel, just as we are all essential to the wellness of this Circle of Friends, and the wellness of the planet Earth, and the wellness of the Great Existence. We are all One and we must accept responsibility for each other. When one is vulnerable, all are vulnerable. When one is suffering, all are suffering. When one is in need, all must come to the rescue.

"My Friends, the Earth is in need and we must come to her rescue. The truth lies before us, and action must be taken on her behalf. The time is now!"

Joan's profound message of truth brought stillness to the group. We all recognized that we were being called to action. Each of us sat quietly contemplating the role that we were intended to accept. Silence prevailed, as the reality of our situation became increasingly more evident.

"We really are here for a reason," Pam broke the silence.

"Yes, we are," responded Joan softly, but firmly. "And thank goodness, we have each other to lean on for support, encouragement, and guidance. The idea of doing this alone was weighing heavily upon me, but now I feel strong and resolved to do whatever I can to help the Earth. I am so grateful for this reunion."

"When shall we meet again?" asked Anne. Another gathering was quickly scheduled, followed by more expressions of appreciation and sweet goodbyes. The Circle of Four lingered as the newcomers departed the backyard.

"Well, I think it is fair to say that the gathering was a success!" My comment brought about sighs of relief.

"Goodness!" declared Deb. "What just happened here?" she mused.

"Exactly what was intended!" interjected Pam. "Invitations were offered and accepted! And something very special transpired, just as it was supposed to. My Friends, we must remember what has happened here, and we must return to this moment whenever we are stricken by doubts or fear. What happened here happened for a reason, and we must never forget it. We are not alone! We are being assisted! Others are assisting us, and as a result, we are being reunited with folks who have similar purposes. This is amazing!" A group hug was shared and a prayer of gratitude was offered to those who enabled the gathering.

... *21* ...

A passage from
The Word
(Chapter Two)

"In the beginning of your existence, the planet upon which you came into existence graciously agreed to accept your seedlings. Because you were a species of great potential, she was eager to offer you residence. The relationship began with mutual acceptance and hopeful anticipation.

The planet, known by its astronomical location, was perfectly situated in a solar system faraway from the nearest populated galaxy. The Earth, as it came to be known, was an ideal Life Being, capable of hosting the new species that was transported to her. A loving and generous Life Being, the Earth accepted responsibility for hosting the new species. The agreement made so long ago seemed to be beneficial for all involved.

Initially, the relationship that developed between the Earth and the new species was harmonious. She provided hospitality, shelter, and sustenance, and the new species treated her with great respect, honoring her and the bounty that she provided. The relationship flourished, the species multiplied, and a healthy balance was maintained among the growing numbers and the large, benevolent Life Being. Everything that was needed by the new species was provided, but as the population continued to expand, their needs became greater than the Earth could manage. She extended herself as much as possible, but their needs grew exponentially.

Their lust for more supplies led the new species to behave in irresponsible and uncaring ways. They disregarded the consequences of their actions and continued to access the Earth's resources as if they would be endless. Their recklessness soon came to be a crisis for the planet, but the new species, the human species, ignored the seriousness of their disrespectful actions and continued to greedily strip her of resources that were vitally necessary for her personal health. Thrown into a state of imbalance, the Life Being Earth began to struggle. The new species, which had become an invasive species, continued to plunder her natural provisions without regard for the ramifications of their actions upon the planet and her other inhabitants. The selfishness of the human species was beyond any other action of disrespect that the Earth had experienced before. She attempted to provide warning signs in hopes that the beloved species would grasp the seriousness of their wrongdoings. Not only were they causing hardship to others, but they were also endangering their own futures. Their misguided behaviors were unthinkable. Each new tragic step taken hastened the new species' own destruction."

My mind was in a state, remembering every detail of every story that was shared at the gathering. It relived the stories, then marveled about the orchestration of the event itself, and then deliberated over the guest list that brought together the right people at the right time. It was an exceptional experience. I considered spending some quality time with the journal, but decided a seaside walk was necessary. Within minutes, clothes and shoes were changed, and I was out the door and on the way to my favorite walking trail. My mind was so preoccupied that the drive to the trailhead happened without my awareness. I simply arrived at the parking lot, having no memories of the drive itself. *How does the mind manage that?* Before an answer to that question could be revealed, the mind was off on another adventure of its own making. I decided to enjoy the walk without the company of my distracted mind.

Before entering the trailhead, I remembered Pam's story about her grandfather. I stopped at the entryway, took a deep breath, and sent a message of gratitude through the ether to both of them. As I moved forward, my footsteps captured my attention. *How many times have I walked this path? Why is it so important to me?* My mind quickly stepped in to rationalize my behavior. After all, this is a beautiful walk with ocean views, wonderful rock formations, and delightful wildlife. Why wouldn't you want to frequent this exceptional trail? Of course, my mind's assessment of the situation was accurate, but it didn't reach the depths of connection that I felt for this setting. I loved the area, for reasons that were beyond its beauty. While I didn't have clarity about the connection, I knew that it spoke to my soul. My visits to this setting were always restorative. Some day I hoped to have greater understanding about our relationship. The mind tried to intervene again, but I encouraged it to be quiet for a while. It reluctantly turned the volume down, which in itself was beneficial, allowing me to continue my walk without its blaring news alerts about topics of its own preference.

The trail ahead leading into a wooded area was empty, which was unusual for this time of day. I opened my heart to any and all encounters that might lie ahead, but also expressed appreciation for, and satisfaction with, the solitude. I was acutely aware in that moment that what was needed would be provided. And it was! The silence engulfed me; even the mind's murmurings were not heard. I walked without the sounds of my footsteps or the chirps and tweets of the wild birds that flitted about on both sides of the trail. Nothing was heard, but the silence. My walk continued without any sense of time. I simply was. I was one with the trail and the other Life Beings that surrounded me, but no communication was exchanged. The connection experienced through the silence was bountiful. No more was needed. The experience was ongoing, never-ending.

As the trail exited the wooded area and moved back into the bright sunlight, the ocean view took my breath away. *How inviting that view is! One can see forever!* As I took the seascape view in, the trail beckoned me to continue. It was easy to comply with this invitation, knowing that each step taken would bring me more views to enjoy. My eyes focused on a distant wave as it made its way to the shoreline. The dance of the rhythmic oceanic waters was mesmerizing; each movement renewed my energy and carried me further along the trail towards the southern point of the peninsula. How or why this blissful adventure was happening was a mystery to me. I simply knew that something, or someone, was taking very good care of me.

A passage from
The Word
(Chapter Two)

"As time went by, the Earth's health became increasingly more precarious, and she had no alternative

but to protect herself. More warnings were given. The signs of her illness became more and more prevalent. Temperatures were rising; the Artic ice was diminishing. Pollution of the land, waters, and skies were visible to the naked eye and documented by extensive scientific data. Winds and rains became unpredictable and fires ravaged the Earth. None of these events was mere happenstance; they were all cumulative effects of the maltreatment that she was enduring. The incidents of wrongdoing multiplied as natural resources were stripped for profit, all under the guise that humans had the right and privilege to do so. The selfishness demonstrated by the human species was unbelievable. Consumed by greed, their ravenous behavior appeared to be unstoppable. The blatant signs of the Earth's stress had little impact upon the majority of the human population. Scientific data was ignored, debated, and scoffed at by those who chose to believe in their presumed privileges. Both their denial of the truth and their lack of concern for others on the planet challenged the initial belief that the human species was one of great potential. Their lack of compassion for the Life Being Earth, as well as the other species that reside upon her, was astonishing. Selfishness seemed to be the primary force that drove them. Unless this treacherous trait could be conquered, the human species was not likely to reach their full potential. How sad this was. None in existence ever imagined this would be the fate of humanity."

The path finally ascended to a higher elevation that revealed even more beauty. To the west were tall grasses and small wind-shaped evergreens, which provided cover for several families of deer. This was not a good time for catching glimpses of the wonderful creatures, but hope springs eternal. To the east, the views of the ocean were even more magnificent than before, and it gave me pause. My thoughts were filled with questions. *Why? Why am I so blessed to have access to these remarkable sites?* No answers came forward through the silence. Nor did the authoritative mind offer any suggestions. The silence prevailed and my need for answers faded into oblivion.

As the trail continued southward, my shadow jumped ahead of me. This ever-present companion loved playing tricks, particularly when pathways were narrow and constantly changing directions. Sometimes, we walked side-by-side, other times it followed at a respectful distance, but always without doubt, the shadow's favorite position was to take the lead. I silently praised its antics but returned my gaze to seaside.

How lovely you are, Precious One. I am so grateful to be in your presence. As the waves captured my attention again, my shadow welcomed a visitor to the trail. The two led the way, as my focus embraced the ocean.

A passage from
The Word
(Chapter Two)

"When the human species came into existence, existence was so pleased. Although all species are cherished equally and each possesses a specific purpose, the human species brought a new dimension to the realm of existence. Created purposefully, the species had the potential for developing into beings of great compassion. All that was needed for this to transpire was provided. Great hope awaited the outcome of this burgeoning new species.

Within all species the element of compassion exists; however, all were hopeful that the human species would evolve to a leadership role in the implementation of this most desirable character trait. Loving-kindness is the way of existence. Appreciation and concern for others were the ways of existence. These traits that honor and respect all Beings in existence are the means and the way for a peaceable existence.

The new species was blessed with many gifts that would facilitate their evolutionary development. They were destined to be peaceable Beings who would exude their humanity to all they encountered. All in existence were deeply saddened by this most unfortunate development. It is regrettable, but no one is to blame. Natural circumstances were the cause of the new species' unfortunate misdirection."

The allure of the ocean waves held my attention, and again, I wondered why. It seemed odd to me that I could feel so connected to this area and to the sea itself. *Perhaps, I was a seaman in another life.* The thought captured my imagination, but was interrupted when a misstep abruptly returned my focus back to the nature trail. No harm was done. It was just a simple encounter with a protruding stone, but the incident reminded me that some modicum of caution was needed, even though this was an easy walking trail. My attention returned to the path, which was when I noticed the two shadows moving ahead of me. I immediately turned to the right to welcome the passerby, but much to my surprise, no one was there. My eyes reverted back to the path; the shadow was still merrily moving along with my own shadow. "What is going on here?" I looked to my side again and still there was no visible form beside me.

"You're here, aren't you?"

"Yes!" replied a gentle voice.

"How are you doing this? How can an invisible form cast a shadow? This makes no sense!"

"From your perspective, it seems mysterious, but for me, it is an easy way of attracting your attention. May I join you on your walk?"

"Yes, please do! I would love your company. You've been with me this entire walk, haven't you?"

"Yes, your intuition is correct. I have been at your side since you entered the trailhead. I hope my presence has not interfered with your time in the silence."

"Not at all," I reassured the invisible presence. "Your presence was most comforting. I wondered if you might appear, but then the silence engulfed me, and seemed to consume my time. I'm glad you're here. Do you prefer to remain invisible?"

"It is wise. There is a topic that must be discussed and it will allow us to practice communicating through our thoughts. Although you do not realize it, I am not speaking aloud to you now. I am actually communicating internally. You are capable of doing this as well, which will allow us to connect without attracting attention from others on the trail." The information shared took me aback. The Companion's voice was heard so clearly that I had not realized it was unspoken. The opportunity to communicate in this new way intrigued me, but reality quickly put me in my place.

"Hmm!" The sound made softly indicated that I was out of my depth. With a quick glance, I turned around to see if anyone was following us and then acknowledged that I had no idea how to communicate internally.

"Actually, you are very fluent in this form of communication, even though you are unaware of the scope of your abilities. My Friend, when you entered the trail earlier you were engaged in a conversation with your mind. You were addressing your mind internally. You heard your

internal voice speaking to the mind, and the conversation continued until you politely asked the mind to be quiet. That manner of internal speaking is what is desired now. You will speak from within and I will hear your words, and in turn, I will respond in like manner. All that is required is focus. Focus your words toward me, and then listen keenly. You are already communicating in this way when you receive messages during your journaling exercises. The principle is the same; we are simply connecting without the companionship of the written word." The Companion paused briefly and I imagined a deep breath was being taken so I did the same.

"Your intuition serves you well, Old Friend. I have a question to ask you, but before doing so, please prepare yourself to take a deep breath before responding. Remember, that the goal is to think your response rather than vocalizing it." I nodded in agreement and then focused all of my attention upon hearing the Companion's question.

"You need not strain yourself, Old Friend. Remember, you are already successfully hearing me. Just relax as we continue to enjoy our walk together." And this we did. It was a moment for me to practice patience and to trust that I could actually hear the unspoken question.

"Indeed, you will Friend. Many times have we had such experiences! I am delighted to share this moment with you now. Old Friend, I assume you have heard this acknowledgement. Am I correct?" The Companion was right! His words were heard as easily as the spoken word. As advised, I took a deep breath and thought my reply.

"Yes, I am delighted to share this moment with you as well. And someday, perhaps we can reminisce about previously shared experiences, but for now, shall we address the topic that is on the agenda?"

"You see, Old Friend, this form of communication is not complicated. It is the natural way of connecting throughout the Great Existence."

"Oh, my goodness. I had no idea sharing my thoughts would be such an easy experience. This is fascinating! Take the lead, Dear Friend. I will listen with the ears of my heart!"

"Your enthusiasm honors our relationship, Old Friend. I come to speak of the stories that were shared at the gathering today. You now have more evidence that others are having similar experiences across the planet. These connections are happening for a reason, and it is time that these events are made public. The truth must be spoken, so that the work that must be done can progress more rapidly." The sense of urgency was palpable. Questions raced through my mind, but I refrained from interrupting the Companion. Little did I know how quickly thoughts were conveyed!

"Your concerns are heard, Old Friend, and will be addressed. The reason it is imperative that individuals acknowledge their experiences with other species is so that people around the planet will be aware that these interactions are really happening and that they are occurring at a rapid

rate. *These incidents are not rare events; in truth, they are widespread. Species of all kinds are reaching out to humans in an attempt to educate them to the crisis that is transpiring on the planet. Efforts made thus far have fallen short. Although some humans are awakening to the crisis that is worsening, the majority of their species continues to be dismissive and negligent in their regard for the planet. While other species have mutually coexisted with the Earth since they came into existence, the human species has and continues to exist as if the Earth is theirs to dominate. This misguided sense of entitlement will not serve the human species. Those who cooperate and collaborate for the good of the planetary system will benefit from their efforts. Those who do not will unfortunately find themselves in an irreversible situation too tragic to contemplate."*

A passage from
The Word
(Chapter Two)

"Many attempts were made to assist the human species' development, but each attempt was overturned and/or misdirected by other natural circumstances resulting in a prolonged phase of development that was not in alignment with the way of existence. The misguided adventures led to more misguided behaviors, which have had tragic consequences upon the planet Earth and all her inhabitants. The misunderstandings that developed during this most unfortunate period led to many other misunderstandings that caused great confusion among the newly developing species. Unaware that they had entered an existence founded in kindness and goodness, the human species emerged with the misunderstanding that their survival depended upon a defensive and aggressive posture towards all new species that they encountered. From this initial misunderstanding, fear emerged, which distorted their perspective thereafter. So unfortunate this was. Within them is the power to quiet all others. The peace that dwells within each member of the human species has the potential for arousing the peaceful nature in another. Because fear overtook their consciousness, this innate human trait was not activated, and as a result, fear became the dominant trait that directs them.

What has happened is complicated. Fear was never intended to be the leader of the human species. When it was initially activated, the youthful species did not understand its purpose and was not prepared to manage the over-zealous nature that fear can command. As fear grew within them, it interfered with their peaceful nature, squelching it, and diminishing its potential to assist them. This situation can be reversed. The innate ability still resides within all members of the human species. With purposeful intention and commitment, humankind can become the peaceable Beings they are meant to be. Awareness is key; acceptance is essential. For this great transition to happen, the people of Earth must open their hearts to the truth of their very existence. They are more than they appear to be. This message has been delivered countless times before, and still, the masses do not give this message the attention and the respect that it deserves.

Dear Friend, please listen with the ears of your heart. Quiet yourself for this extremely important moment. Take several deep breaths and prepare yourself to hear one of the most powerful messages of your present life. Breathe deeply! Open your heart to the truth you are about to receive!

You are a Being with exceptional abilities!
You are more than you appear to be!

Awareness is the key! Acceptance is essential. This message is so important that it must be repeated. Dear Friend, the fear that dictates human behavior is not the leader of this marvelous species. You are people who were brought into existence with the ability to bring peace to all you encounter. It dwells within you, and 'you' are capable of spreading this remarkable blessing to others. Even though the development of this peaceable trait has been misdirected by fear, you and all other humans can reverse this unfortunate situation by reclaiming who you really are."

The news delivered by the invisible Companion was sobering. My heart was heavy. Although nothing that was presented was new, the reality of Earth's situation was more than I could bear. Part of me wanted the Companion to leave. I did not want to hear any more of this devastating reality. I tried to calm myself with deep breaths, but it didn't work. Tears streamed down my face, as fear and hopelessness engulfed me. The task seemed insurmountable!

"You are not alone, my Friend. I understand your heartache and the fears that rise up within you. The Earth's situation is frightening, and even the strongest, have moments of despair just as you have now. One cannot face this crisis without feeling the enormity of what is happening. She is in great peril, as are all the species that regard her as home. We must stand in unity, Old Friend. The task is too great for a few, but we are not a few! Billions inhabit this planet who are already actively assisting her and there are billions more from other locations who also work on her behalf. She is a cherished member of the Universe and her presence matters.

"As you witnessed today, many of your species are awakening to the reality that we are all intricately linked to one another. This is reason for hope! There remains time to restore the Earth back to good health. She is a very resilient Life Being and with love, respect, and proper care and stewardship of her resources, she will recover.

"Old Friend, the truth is difficult to bear, but it must be told and it must be heard if this mission to save the Earth is to be successful."

A passage from
The Word
(Chapter Two)

"As stated before, this message has been delivered to the peoples of Earth many times, and a few, only a few, have accepted it as their truth. As you review the current circumstances unfolding around this planet, it is evident that a 'few' are not enough. Unrest and fear dominate the human species, and the unpleasantness that this creates negatively impacts everyone on the planet, including the Earth herself. Life should not be lived under such unkind and terrifying circumstances. It need not be this way.

For those of you who are taken aback by the idea that you have exceptional abilities, perhaps it is wise for you to contemplate your doubts. The statement as provided is a truth of existence. You really are a Being with exceptional abilities! This simply is! You possess the ability to heal self and others, and you have the ability to bring peace to all others. Indeed, this may sound grandiose, but let us put this information in perspective. Your 'exceptional abilities' are innate. It is simply who you really are. You are not more than any other being, nor are you any less. You simply are.

However, the human species has evolved differently from other beings with the same innate abilities. Fear has overwhelmed you. Its grip upon your species has hampered your ability to tap into and access your peaceable capabilities; nevertheless, this evolutionary mishap can be reversed.

So address your doubts with an open heart. You are presented with this truth about your existence in hopes that you will take appropriate steps to reclaim your peaceable ways. You are capable of doing this, but be forewarned. Along with your open heart, you must exert diligence, commitment, and perseverance. Awareness is the key, but knowing that fear is interfering with your good intentions is not enough. You must accept the reality of your situation and you must confront your fear and learn to command it. How, you may ask, are you to command your fear? The answer is simple: open your heart to the truth of your existence.

You are more than you appear to be!
You are a Being with exceptional abilities,
and with these abilities,
you have the power to heal self and others.

Opening your heart to this truth is another essential element in reversing the horrific power that fear wields on the Earth. The heart is your guide. It is not the physical heart of which we speak, but of the Heart Space that is the center of your goodness and home of your peaceable ways. Opening your heart to who you really are is the first step for reclaiming your humanity. And then you must persistently practice monitoring your fear and activating your peaceable ways. This is doable. It is not an impossible feat. If only the people of Earth would open their hearts to their full potential, they could quickly address the serious issues of the Earth's declining health."

"Please forgive me, my Friend! My emotions are so strong that they have overcome me. The truth that you speak is difficult to hear, but I know it is necessary. Please continue. Do not allow my outburst to interfere with this process. It was just a moment of fear, but it is abating now. I'm okay; please tell me everything, so that I can prepare myself for the next step that must be taken." I turned in the direction of my Companion hoping that he would accept my apology, and then realized that my appeal had been spoken aloud. A quick glance in all directions revealed that no one was in listening range.

"I'm sorry! I didn't even realize that I was speaking aloud again." The apology conveyed telepathically was immediately accepted.

"No need is there for an apology, Dear One. Your reactions were appropriate. The truth of the Earth's situation is horrifying. I am so sorry that you must be subjected to this news, but as you well know, the truth must be delivered and it must be accepted. If only the people of Earth would listen to us. There is still time to save this planet. I apologize to you, my Friend, for burdening you with this information, but it is necessary. You are here to assist the Earth! You can save her, and by speaking the truth to others, just as I have to you, you will inspire others to participate on her behalf.

"My Friend, this conversation is happening for a reason. Although it is difficult, the reality of the Earth's crisis must be faced. She will not recover if the human species does not face the truth. They must face the truth, just as you have, and then they must accept responsibility for helping her, just as you have done. My Friend, you are not unique! Your fellow human beings are just as resilient as you are. They too will be shocked by the truth of the Earth's circumstances, and then, they will rebound, and they will want to assist her. Everyone, every being that resides on this planet, has something to offer, and each in their own way is capable of changing the course of the future. With the help of her family, the Earth can regain her full vibrancy once again.

"This may sound grandiose, but it is not. It is the truth! Everyone in existence has the power of healing self and others. This simple truth defines the reality of the Great Existence. The Life Being Earth is the host and guardian of countless Life Beings. She is in very good company. All who

call her Home must come to her aid. She requires the healing energy of all those who reside upon her. So little is required of those she has cared for since they came into existence."

A passage from
The Word
(Chapter Two)

"Attempting to understand the specifics of this bygone incident serves only to distract one from the issue at hand. What transpired is of the past. What lies ahead is what must be addressed. Dear Friend, it is time for you and the entire human species to reclaim your humanity. Have compassion for all those who experienced suffering and pain due to the influence of fear in their various experiences. Have compassion for those who presently suffer from the misdirection of fear. It is time to purposefully and intentionally alter the course of your evolutionary future.

Remember who you are. You are more than you appear to be, and you are Beings with exceptional abilities and with these abilities, you have the power to heal self and others. This truth is repeated again and will continue to be repeated until all of humankind has heard this message and accepted it. Although some of you who are receiving this message at this point in time may be skeptical, it is time for you to challenge your doubting minds. There is no longer time for doubting, skepticism, and critical judgment. Those who came before you suffered from these unhealthy characteristics as well. Birthed in their fears, these tendencies spread rapidly one to another and interfered in their development, and these same tendencies now impede your own development. This legacy of misunderstanding must stop. No longer can the misunderstandings of the past continue to mislead those of the present. Those who came before regret their role in the proliferation of misunderstandings and they wish to apprise their descendants that their fears were founded in misunderstandings. They are deeply sorry for the pain and suffering that is presently experienced, and they come forward to make the truth known, so that no other descendants will incur similar unnecessary suffering. Had they known before how to alter their misguided behavior, they would have done so. They do not wish future generations to experience similar discomfort; thus they make this appeal to you now.

'Please do not do as we did. Our belief in our fears misguided us, and we foolishly disregarded the message that you are presently receiving. Please do not make the same mistakes that we made. The current crisis situation on the planet cannot sustain more delays. Our misunderstandings greatly contributed to the Earth's declining health. Fears led us to believe that pain, suffering, and emotional discord was the way that life was. We were wrong. Please accept the message of truth that is presented to you. You truly are more than you appear to be! Everything this message asserts is true. Accept who you are and you will be able to alter the course of humankind, which will in turn heal the Earth. You are not alone. We are here to assist you.'

Dear Friend, we hope that the Children of Earth, the descendants of those who came before, will adhere to this heartfelt appeal. All in existence desire the highest good for the people of Earth. Efforts to inform you of your circumstances have been ongoing for millennia. Unfortunately, we have not succeeded in convincing you of your tragic situation. We will continue with great hopes that you will respond accordingly."

"I believe you. Your words resonate within me. I know you speak the truth." A loud sigh was audibly heard and reminded me to maintain my internal voice. Many thoughts rushed through my mind. I wanted to help the Earth, but doubts were large and present.

"Perhaps, I can be of assistance" His gentle voice quieted my racing mind. *"Do not blame yourself for having concerns, Dear One, but do not allow these concerns to paralyze you. It is easy to take action when one is feeling confident and strong, but one's potential is diminished when doubts intrude upon one's intentions. Having disdain for your doubts will not*

minimalize them, but having compassion for them will effectively reduce their power. When fears and doubts rise up within you, take a deep breath, pause for a moment, and lovingly reassure the mind that you are not in jeopardy. This strategy enables you to recover from the doubtful moment more rapidly. In situations when doubts linger, you may wish to focus your attention upon another task that feels more manageable. Sending healing energy to the Earth is always a wise option. Not only does it raise your spirits, but also, it is extremely beneficial. Likewise, praying for the Earth is an easy and effective means of assisting her as well. These generous acts distract the mind and allow you to continue your good works on behalf of the planet.

"As said before, each individual will contribute in a way that is appropriate for the giver and the recipient. However, as this process moves forward everyone will reach an understanding about the healing powers that exist within all in existence. By accessing these healing powers, assisting the Earth will transpire easily and rapidly, which will then afford time to create a sustainable strategy for the future. Old Friend, the crisis is real and it must be addressed now, but there is reason for hope."

A passage from
The Word
(Chapter Three)

"The time is now! So important are these four small words, and so often have they been disregarded. Perhaps they were repeated too often...to a point where they no longer held meaning for those who were intended to receive them. Nonetheless, these four words are of extreme importance and they will continue to be accessed. "The time is now" is an instructive message. It alerts the recipient to an agreement made long ago. Listen with the ears of your heart as your eyes capture the phrase again. Hear the words from within.

The Time Is Now! Be with these words as they echo within you...the time is now, the time is now, the time is now.

Old Friend, the message is real and it is delivered as was agreed so very long ago. If you are puzzled by this message, please just ponder it. Do not immediately disregard it. Just because you presently are not aware of its significance does not mean that it is not intended for you. Nothing more is required of you at this moment other than

> *your willingness to be open to the idea that this message*
> *has crossed your path at this specific time for a reason."*

The two walkers followed the winding trail towards the tip of the peninsula; each was lost in their respective thoughts. They arrived just in time. The visible one invited her invisible Friend to the best seat on the planet. The favorite bench, with its glimmering seacoast view accentuated by the descending sun, offered a performance that no one could resist. The moment, brief yet eternal, would never be forgotten. If another walker had passed by, he or she would have been too enamored with the sunset to notice the double shadow behind the single occupant on the bench.

"The time is now!" whispered the unseen viewer of the sunset.

"Yes, the time is now!" responded the walker, whose view of the world was much broader now than when she had entered the trailhead.

"**G**ood morning, Deb!" The greeting was accompanied by a hardy wave of the hand. Deb returned the gesture as she approached her Soul Sister.

"Don't you just love having the luxury of walking to work? We are so fortunate." We exchanged a big hug and walked arm-in-arm toward our side-by-side workplaces. By the time we reached the entryway to our respective offices, an evening walk and dinner had been planned. It was obvious that we both had topics we wanted to discuss, but neither of us had time before our first scheduled appointments. We shared another hug, wished each other a good day, and then disappeared into our separate professional worlds.

I was glad that we had arrived at the same time. Having a few minutes to check in with one another was satisfying, and I was looking forward to seeing her after work. Next door, in the adjacent office, Deb was having similar thoughts. She too was grateful for the brief encounter and for the after-work plans that had been made.

A few blocks away, Gary and Pam were just returning home from a sunrise walk. "That was a great walk, Gar! Thanks for getting up early with me. Sunrises just make my day."

"Yes, you're right, Dear! Early morning walks are the best! But the croissants that we just picked up from the bakery are going to make the day even better. Shall we have breakfast on the deck?" Within minutes, coffee was made and a beautiful table setting was perfected. As they sat down at the table, a buzzing sound was noticed, and much to their surprise, Madame Bumblebee was busily checking out the flower arrangement that Pam had placed in the center of the table.

"Welcome, Dear Friend! It's a pleasure to see you this morning. I just refilled your water dish, Dear One, and there are a few new stones for you to land on. I found them on the trail this morning. Make yourself at home, Dear." Gary watched attentively as his beloved spoke to the bumblebee.

"You know, Pam, the sound of her humming changed when you spoke to her. I'm certain this creature understands every word that you say."

"Of course, she does, Dear. She's a very intelligent being. It's good to see her again. So glad she joined us." As the bumblebee investigated every blossom in the arrangement, the couple also busily maneuvered about filling their plates and pouring the coffee. "So Gary, what's on your mind?

I know you're up to the something." Her husband blushed knowing full well that his wife's intuition was impeccable.

"Pam, your intuitive skills are so finely honed that it is impossible for me to have any secrets around you."

"That's not true, Dear! I actually haven't intuited anything. I simply made a deduction based upon our stop at the bakery. Typically, we make a bakery run when you're cogitating about something. And then, we discuss your plan while we enjoy the treats that facilitate our conversation." Gary blushed again. He hadn't made that connection before, but clearly his brilliant spouse was right again. "So, what is it, Dear? What wonderful idea have you come up with this time?" Pam loved her husband's creative mind. He was a genius, which he would deny, of course; but he truly had a mind that was enviable. She was energized by his ideas and she was eager to hear about the one that was presently brewing.

A passage from
The Word
(Chapter Three)

"Long ago, before any of today can remember, decisions were made on behalf of the human species. Volunteers came forward and willingly agreed to assist in the advancement of the species. Great plans were made, extensive research and explorations were done, and all who were of the original members of the human species agreed to participate in the translocation of their burgeoning species to another location in the Great Existence. Those who volunteered to leave did so for the greater good of the species, and those who remained behind also did so for the greater good of the species. The separation of families and friends was agonizing for all involved. Many discussions preceded this momentous decision and when all was said and done, all agreed that the decision to advance the human race forward was necessary. Great sacrifices were made by the Ones of Old that secured a future for the human race. Little did they know then that their descendants would make similar errors in their new location as were made in the previous location. The stories of old, documented and prepared for those who relocated to the new destination, were undoubtedly lost

in transition; and over time, the ways of the past were forgotten, and with those lost memories went the ideas for creating a more viable and sustainable future."

"Well, I'm not sure the idea has evolved yet, but my mind is definitely over-functioning, and I need to talk about it. Pam, something huge is happening and we seem to be in the middle of whatever is unfolding. Part of me is feeling a bit cautious, but another part of me is so excited that I am beside myself with curiosity. Pam, what is going on? Everywhere we turn, we meet someone who is having unusual experiences, which include communication with some other Life Being. That in itself is incredible, don't you agree." Pam quickly nodded in agreement.

"But these encounters that we're having are happening so rapidly that it gives me pause. Can this really be real, Pam? Don't get me wrong, please. I'm enjoying every minute of these unusual experiences, but it does seem odd that so many people are having similar unusual experiences.

"So, I just want us to talk about this, and be sure that we are thinking clearly about everything that is going on around us."

Once again, Pam sat in awe of her husband. His mind rarely rested. *How does he manage this?* "Gary, I know that wonderful mind of yours has already assessed every possible perspective about our unusual circumstances, so there is no need for me to duplicate your efforts. Perhaps, it would be beneficial if I shared my visceral reactions to recent events." Her suggestion met with approval.

"Yes," he cheered, while clapping his hands softly, "that's exactly what I want to hear. Tell me everything, Dear!" Giggles erupted from Pam.

"You are so demanding, Gar! I promise that I will share EVERYTHING that is meandering about in the chambers of my mind." Gary blushed again and Pam gently patted his hand. "I admire your enthusiasm! In fact, it's one of your most endearing characteristics." The sweet interaction did not go unnoticed. Madame Bumblebee, resting on one of the new stones in her water dish, observed them carefully. She enjoyed the tenderness that was shared between these two old friends. She had witnessed similar behavior before when the couple worked together in the garden. Madame Bumblebee had discerned that these humans were honorable beings. She enjoyed their company.

"Before continuing their conversation, Pam turned and focused her attention upon their small, hairy guest. "Thank you, Dear! We enjoy your company as well. Please know that you are always welcome in our garden." Then she turned back to husband. Her eyes were sparkling with joy.

"Our Friend approves of our behavior and she enjoys our company.

Isn't that lovely, Gar? We are so blessed that this connection is happening. It's a testament to all the other unusual connections that we're experiencing and hearing about. Gary, I believe we are witnessing and participating in a worldwide transformation. We, and others like us, are learning that these so-called unusual experiences are not unusual at all. I believe what we're seeing locally through our small circle of friends is evidence of what is going on all around the planet. These beings are making a greater effort to connect with us now because we are needed. Humans have to accept responsibility for the chaos that we've created on this planet. We have to change our ways, and that includes opening our hearts to these other remarkable Beings that are actually mutually coexisting with the Earth. We must learn to treat her with the same respect and high regard that other species already demonstrate." She turned to their small visitor and mused, "This little one does more for the Earth than we do." Pam's thoughts took her to other places as she imagined the challenges that this bumblebee faced. Her spouse watched several different emotions wash across her face before placing his hand upon hers.

"Come back, Dear." His voice was barely audible, but it helped Pam realign herself. "A penny for your thoughts, if you wish to share them."

"Oh, goodness! So many are racing through my mind, but the theme is the struggle that these creatures deal with on a regular basis. We humans have made such a mess, and all these remarkable species suffer the brunt of our recklessness. This cannot continue! That's why these incidents are occurring. Species of all kinds are trying to get our attention so that we will wake up and grasp the tragic situation that we are creating. And, the other lesson we're learning is that there are species involved in this wakeup call that are not Earth-bound. I find that very exciting, Gary, and I know you do as well. This is another reason that I feel as if a transformational event is in progress. For Beings from other dimensions to be involved in this awakening process tells me that the Earth's crisis is far worse than we imagined. I could go on and on about this for hours, Gar. You know how I am. But now, I want to hear your thoughts. Tell me what's going on in that remarkable mind of yours."

A passage from
The Word
(Chapter Three)

"Much more history has your species endured than is currently known to you. Because your species was believed

to have great potential, it was anticipated that you would make significant contributions to the Greater Existence. In many ways you surpassed expectations and all in existence remain most grateful for the ways in which you participated in serving the highest good. Advancements were made and all benefitted from your contributions. Unfortunately, there were also circumstances in which you participated that were puzzling and questionable. Initially, it was believed the choices that were being made were the result of immaturity, but sadly, the poor decisions persisted and the associated behaviors worsened. None understood how this unforeseen development occurred. It was most disturbing. Never before had a species demonstrated such callous disregard for other Life Beings, including those within their own species. So unusual was this behavior to other Beings in the Greater Existence. This was not the way of the Greater Existence, yet somehow the human species had evolved in a way that was not compatible with all others in existence.

So deeply saddened are we. We desire to help. Our faith in humankind remains steadfast. You are members of our Family and we wish to assist you with this most precarious situation. Our previous attempts to assist have not been successful. We strived to assist without interfering with your evolutionary development; however, the time has come for more direct communication. As your condition worsens, your evolutional path takes you in a direction that is unhealthy for your species and dangerous to others in existence. We bring this unfortunate news forward to you because you are capable of hearing this truth.

Within you is the means to discern right from wrong. You are intelligent Beings who are able to individually and collectively evaluate the behaviors of ill will in which you actively participate on a daily basis. Each of you must assess your personal proclivities towards ill will. Collectively you must accept responsibility for the horrendous and destructive behaviors that are commonplace among your peoples.

> *This is not a time for blaming others for the problems that plague your species. Each of you must actively participate by reviewing your own contributions to the crisis."*

"Actually that was the other topic that has been occupying my mind, and you're right, I am extremely curious about this, whatever 'this' is. What does it mean, Pam? Are we talking about those who have passed on, or those who are referred to as angels, or are we talking about aliens from other planets? Or are we talking about all of these possibilities? You know me, Dear, I choose to believe in all possibilities, but there is a part of me, albeit, a very small part, that doubts the validities of the connections. I'm embarrassed to say this aloud, but the truth is, there are many doubts and questions fleeting around the racetrack of my mind." Pam tried not to giggle, but she couldn't stop herself. The idea of a racetrack in Gary's expansive mind tickled her.

"Your racetrack spans across the galaxies, Dear." Her comment in turn tickled her husband and the two enjoyed a sweet moment of laughter. Madame Bumblebee reveled in the moment and celebrated with a quick flight around the flower arrangement. She then returned to her favorite new stone that was situated in the center of her personal water dish. It was the perfect location for listening to her new friends' conversation.

"Our companion is enjoying our discussion," explained Pam. "She is a very good listener." Gary turned to their guest and welcomed any feedback that she might have to offer. Pam listened carefully, but was not aware of any comments. She repeated her husband's invitation and also gave Madame Bumblebee permission to interrupt them at any time. Gary nodded in agreement and then turned back to his beloved.

"So, before we continue, there is one more factor that must be brought to the forefront. The truth is, Pam, I absolutely believe the stories that our friends have shared about their encounters. Our dear neighbor across the street is a person of integrity; she would never lie about this, nor would our neighbors down the street. These people are good people, who are having remarkable experiences, and I trust them! So here's my dilemma. On the one hand I believe that what has been shared is the truth, and I'm envious of their experiences. And on the other hand, I'm very frustrated with myself because doubts still rise up within me. Pam, I don't want to be one of those people who cannot believe something unless they have absolute proof about it. As far as I'm concerned, our friends' experiences are all the proof that is needed. Who am I to question this? Who am I to doubt this? Maybe I'm just jealous that they have had these experiences, and I haven't. Geez, it's hard to admit that out loud, but it rings true, Pam. Oh, dear, I am such a piece of work." Gary shook his head, judging himself harshly.

"Don't to this, Gary! You're being way too hard on yourself!" Her words were firm, as she tapped her right index finger on the table. "We're going to use this experience as a learning tool! We both know that we're going to be giving workshops in the future, so let's sort through this experience so that we will be able to help other folks when they encounter similar dilemmas." Gary agreed with his spouse and perked up. His self-judgment could be very bitter at times, but he was a very resilient and with Pam's aid, he could get back on track very quickly.

"This is what I would like to suggest, Gary." He listened with the ears of his heart. "We have a tendency to think in black or white, which doesn't work when you are talking about these unusual experiences. We need to be more open-minded and much more gentle when we are considering our possibilities. For instance, I believe that we, you and I, are capable of holding both aspects of this topic. We can accept these stories that we have heard with open hearts, and we can choose to believe and trust those who have shared their experiences with us. As you said, they are good people. Why would we judge them or their experiences? I don't want to take on that role.

"But at the same time, I want to feel free to wrangle with my doubts. When they come up, I want to face them honestly, forthrightly, and kindly. I don't want to beat up on myself, and I don't want you or anyone to resort to that either. Our doubting minds are here for a reason, Gary. They help us to discern our way in the world. We must trust ourselves, Dear! We must trust our doubting minds, and we must trust our dominion over them." Pam stopped abruptly and stared deeply into her beloved's eyes. "Does any of this make sense, Gar?"

"Yes, it does! As always, you help me to see things more clearly. My self-judgment derails me, and then I get lost in my shame and embarrassment. Thank you for bringing me back from that pit of misery. This is so helpful, Pam. We are capable of holding both aspects of the issue, and we will grow more rapidly because of this ability. You are a good teacher, Dear! In fact, you are an excellent teacher. This was a wonderful demonstration. By taking advantage of an unfolding issue, you lovingly created a teaching opportunity. Beautifully done! Your student is feeling very good about the experience!" Gary's demeanor had completely changed. He was feeling confident and strong again. "So, Pam, back to the original questions! Who are these Beings that our friends are communicating with and how can we reach out to them?" Pam rested back into her chair. She wondered what their visitor was thinking, and then a smile brightened up her face.

"We both know the answer, Gar. Your questions inform us of the truth. These other Beings include more than we can fathom. Some of the so-called unusual encounters are with those who have preceded us in departing this world, while others are Beings that reside in what is referred to as the angelic realm. And there are other Beings from other settings throughout the Universe who also are very invested in the Earth's recovery. They, too, are here to assist her. And there are more Gary that we, as yet, have no definition for…we are not alone, Love." Pam reached over and placed her hand on Gary's. They quietly relaxed into the moment, each accepting that what was known was true, and what was yet to be learned would unfold at the perfect time in the perfect place. A sense of peace overwhelmed the couple, and as they enjoyed the moment, the bumblebee circled the lovely centerpiece several times, and then, carefully landed atop their joined hands. The three friends savored the opportunity: connection, union, Oneness.

A passage from
The Word
(Chapter Four)

"The time for change is upon you. No longer can the human species linger in their phase of misunderstanding that corrupts its very core and has perilous effects upon other species around them. Perhaps the reader will be startled by these words and find great issue with the insinuation that your species is less than you imagine it to be. We are heartbroken to bring this news forward. We too are startled by the truth of humankind's situation.

The truth must be presented to those who have the ability to change what is transpiring within their species. We have faith in the human species and we believe that you will be dismayed by the information that we share with you. We hope you will be alarmed by this truth. And we pray you will take appropriate action to right the wrongs that you have created. For this to transpire, it will demand that the entire human race work collaboratively with one another. We speak to the entire human species, not to just a few. The presumed hierarchy that you mistakenly believe exists within your species does not exist. It has never existed except within the confines of your distorted minds. In truth, all members of the human domain are equal and all must be equally involved in the transformation that is required for the continuation of your species.

216

This news is not easy to receive, but the unrest within your species is evidence of the truth that must be accepted. Like so many other truths that are ignored and denied, this truth must be accepted. Your species is indeed one of remarkable potential, but you act irresponsibly. You must be the remarkable species you are intended to be. No species that denies the privileges of another species is a remarkable species. No species that deliberately savages other species is a remarkable species. No species that demonstrates selfishness before compassion is a remarkable species. It is time for the human species to evolve into their remarkable potential. Be the species you are intended to be. Be the species that emanates loving-kindness towards all others. Be the species that cares for and selflessly acts on behalf of others.

The time for change is upon you. Please change for the good of all. You are a species that is loved and cherished by all others in existence. Will you accept your role in the Greater Existence? Will you accept that you are One with all others in existence? Will you accept that being equal with all others is not a diminishment of who you really are?

In truth, this is who you have always been. The illusion that you are more than another is not your truth, and has never been your truth. This is an illusion that has led you down a path of destruction of Self and All Others with whom you exist. Dear Children of Earth, the time is now. The truth of your reality must finally be accepted. You are One with all others in existence, and your cooperation is necessary. You cannot continue your present way of being. As already stated, your current manner of being is founded in a misunderstanding that is perilous to you and all you encounter."

After the last client of the day departed, I prepared the space for the next morning. It was a simple task that gave me time to let go of the day's work and center myself for the remaining activities of the day. The journal, which for various reasons received no attention throughout the day, was replaced into its own special pocket in my shoulder bag for the trek home. A quick glance about the room confirmed that all was well in this sacred space. Before turning the light off, I paused, as always, for a moment to express my appreciation. *Oh, Beloved, thank you for this wonderful healing space. And thank you for assisting me throughout the day. I am so grateful.*

It will come as no surprise to you, Dear Reader, that a similar ritual also was unfolding in the Deb's office. Each friend ended the workday with a prayer: these two had much in common. Nor will it surprise you that they exited their respective offices at the same time, with a similar wish from the other. They exchanged hugs, and then simultaneously asked if the other would be disappointed if they skipped the walk. Each was relieved to learn that they were in the same place.

"Oh, yea!" responded Deb. "I'm just not up for exercise. It's been a long day."

"Me neither!" I replied, "But I am up for some good conversation. Would you like to join me now, and we can talk about dinner, as we relax with some delightful icy drink?"

"That sounds wonderful! Actually, it's a perfect alternative." Our stroll from the office complex through the quiet neighborhood to my house was unusual for us. Typically, we would talk nonstop when we were together, but today was different. We were both happy to retreat into the chambers of own minds. For me, it was a time to realign myself with the Earth. With each step taken, I felt increasingly more connected to her; it was a healing experience for me.

"Thank you, for this restorative stroll," Deb's voice sounded more relaxed. "It was just what I needed. Isn't it lovely to be able to walk in silence while in the company of another person? I think that's a sign of a very good relationship." Her comment pleased me, and it accurately described my feelings as well. As we turned up the sidewalk toward the house, Deb paused and just took in the view.

"Look at your front porch!" The setting sun, reflecting off the windows, was dazzling. We quickly turned around to witness the real event. "Oh my goodness!! What a view!" Arm in arm, we rushed towards the front porch and perched ourselves on the top step. Mesmerized by the sun's final performance for the day, we both fell into silence again. Deb was right. It was comforting to be in the company of another who appreciated the silence.

Across the street, Pam had just looked out the window at the same time that we were rushing for the porch. Her heart leaped, wanting to join us, but she decided that this was not the best time. Her sensitivity to our evolving relationship was a gift that we didn't even know was necessary. We remained on the top step until the curtain closed on the grand finale.

"So, Deb, what's your pleasure? Shall we adjourn to the living room or shall we relax out here on the porch?"

"Either setting will be lovely; however, it occurred to me that Pam and Gary may want to join us. I believe they need to talk about what is happening as much as we do." Without another word, I reached into my shoulder bag and retrieved the cellphone.

"Hello, Pam! Deb and I are sitting on the front porch and thought you two might want to join us?" Within minutes they were waving from their porch and moving in our direction. We both knew that another eventful evening was in the making.

Hugs and greetings were exchanged before we retreated to the kitchen. "We've only been home for a short while, so we haven't even thought about supper, but we're very thirsty. Shall we begin the evening with my famous icy spritzers?" That suggestion met with applause and then Gary announced that he had just finished preparing a small tray of fresh veggies with cucumber dip.

"We were just going to nibble our way through the evening. I'll go and fetch it." As he headed for the door, Pam reminded him to grab the key lime pie as well.

"Deb, will you get the cheese out of the fridge, and Pam, there should be a good selection of crackers in the pantry. Voila!" I proclaimed happily. "The repast is rapidly coming together."

By the time, Gary returned with his hands full, the cheese and cracker tray was ready for an award. And the spritzers were ready to be poured. "Okay, friends! We have a big decision to make. Where shall we park ourselves? Front porch, living room, dining room?

"Oh, can we please just be here in your breakfast nook?" asked Pam. "It's so cozy and intimate. I think it's the perfect setting for tonight's conversation."

"Good suggestion, Pam!" whispered Deb. "This is the ideal setting." In an instant the small table was appropriately dressed and ready for occupancy. The efficiency demonstrated by these four friends was a sight to behold. Others, from afar, observed their cooperative manner and were very pleased. The reunion was successful.

"Okay, everyone, choose a chair!" Although my manner was lighthearted, I was aware that something was brewing among us; an energy shift had occurred. "Dear Ones, before we sit down, perhaps we might enjoy a moment of silence. Hands were joined, eyes were closed, and deep breaths were heard. Silence prevailed until we all declared 'Amen' at precisely the same time. This set off a few giggles and comments of disbelief as we situated ourselves at the table.

Deb immediately raised her glass and announced, "To the future!" All replied in like manner to the thought-provoking toast.

"Would you like to elaborate upon that intriguing toast?" Gary's question gained momentum as Pam and I urged Deb to tell us EVERYTHING.

"EVERYTHING?" she mimicked our request. "Okay! I will!" she jovially replied. Deb put her glass down, took the necessary deep breath, and then reached out for support. "Isn't this wonderful? We are in elbow reach of one another." It was easy to hold hands around the small table. "Dear Ones, can you feel the energy in this room? Something huge is happening to us, and even though I don't know how to explain what is happening, I am certain that we are on the brink of a significant change.

"When I woke on this morning, a sense of anticipation and expectancy overwhelmed me. I could hardly wait to see my friend here because I desperately wanted to connect with her. But neither of us had any available time during the workday. And then, while we were sitting on the front step watching the sunset, I felt the same energy emanating from your house. We are supposed to be together this evening. We need to share our thoughts and our feelings and we need to hold on to each other, because we, the four of us, are here for a reason." Deb exhaled loudly, and relaxed back into her chair still maintaining the circle of hands.

"Whew!" declared Pam. "Thank goodness! I've been in a tizzy all day, and so has Gary."

A passage from
The Word
(Chapter Four)

"Please listen with the ears of your heart. You are loved and cherished by your Family in Existence. This is an impressive statement when you accept the extensive size of your Family. Suffice it to say, you have many who preceded you, and all these distant relatives love you dearly. They have patiently waited for you to join the family, and they stand ready now to assist you with the necessary changes that must be made. Do not fear the changes that must be faced. You are already all you need to be for this transition to transpire. You are people of goodness. This trait above all others is the avenue for your successful evolutionary step. Goodness exists within the inner core of humanity, but it must blossom into a state of ever being. Moments of goodness are helpful, but they are not enough. Goodness must be ever-present for it to reach its full potential. The time is now. This is the next great step for humankind to actualize. Goodness prevails in the Greater Existence and it awaits the coming of the energy of goodness from the human Children of Earth. It is long overdue. Those who

already live life in this way eagerly await the presence of
human goodness. Your essence will merge beautifully with
Those who already exist in this manner."

Gary confirmed Pam's statement by expanding upon their morning activities. He began by complimenting Deb's intuitive abilities and then proceeded to elaborate upon their breakfast conversation about transformation. "We have, as Pam alluded to, been in quite a state today. After our early morning walk, we had a riveting conversation, and I think it is accurate to say that we both are in agreement that we are in the middle of some type of grand transformation." Gary reacted to his own statement by clarifying his choice of words. "Perhaps, referring to whatever is happening as a 'grand transformation' sounds grandiose, but the idea that we are having a transformative experience is huge. Our thoughts are in alignment with yours, Deb. What we've been experiencing of late is not ordinary. And since none of us at this table is inclined to believe in coincidences, I think we must accept the reality that these remarkable encounters that we are experiencing are evidence of the transformation that is now in process."

"I agree, Gary. Like the three of you, I've been having similar thoughts. Let's face it! Meeting all these people who are having experiences similar to our own is exciting. For me, it's a dream come true. However, the fact is, a shift is happening and it's happening for a reason." There was much more that needed to be said, but my courage was waning. Fortunately, my wonderful intuitive friends sensed what was happening and challenged me to stay present.

Pam immediately reached out to me and squeezed my hand tightly. "Remember, we are all in this together! I suspect these messages that you have been receiving lately are relevant to this conversation. Am I correct in that assumption?"

"Yes, Pam, you are. The messages, which are stunningly beautiful and kind, speak a profound truth about our role in the Earth's health issues. I must admit that the messages are not always easy to receive. The truth can be painful to hear, but it is necessary. We have to accept our role in this terrible tragedy, which means we have to change our ways. And we have to take action now, because we're running out of time. Dear Ones, please understand I have no expertise in this area of knowledge, I'm just summarizing the messages that are being received. But generally speaking, we all know and accept the reality that the Earth is in crisis. We know this, but we don't really know how to change the situation. So, if my understanding is correct, this is why we are seeing an increase in communication from other species. They are trying to assist us. They already know how to mutually coexist with the planet; we are the ones who are clueless. They know and respect her as a Life Being, while we treat the Earth as if she is nothing more than a resource to fulfill our needs. The point is this: other species are trying to help us understand what is at stake here, and they are trying to educate us about various ways in which we can immediately provide her with assistance. Thus we are witnessing many more people who are interacting with other species around the globe. These interactions happened before, but much less often, and few people talked about it because it was regarded as unusual and they didn't want to be negatively judged."

A passage from
The Word
(Chapter Four)

"The time is now. So often have these words been shared. We hope this message will be heard and finally accepted as the reminder it is intended to be. The human species must embrace the reality of who you really are and you must do so now."

"It seems to me that we, meaning the human species, are being inundated by contact from various species around the planet and beyond, because we're reaching a point of no return." I took a deep breath, fearful of the message's impact upon my friends.

"Don't worry about us, Sister. You're right. This is not easy to hear, but we have to accept the truth of our situation." Deb shook her head in frustration. "Just look at what I said! This is an example of how self-absorbed humans are. This situation isn't just about us; it involves every living being on this planet and the planet herself. This is so much bigger than us, and yet, we are the primary culprits of the Earth's decline." Deb apologized for what she misperceived as an outburst, and then complimented her Friend's courage for speaking the truth.

"I'm grateful for both of you," inserted Pam. "The fact that we are having this conversation seems like a miracle to me." Pam reassured me that she had been curious about the messages that were coming through me and that she wanted to know the truth. "I am so grateful to hear the truth being spoken. Yes, it's unsettling, but it's better than listening to all the misinformation that is being presented. And Deb, I really appreciate how you handled that statement you made. You took a thought that could have been stated differently and turned it into a teaching opportunity. We had a similar experience at breakfast this morning. Honestly, I didn't even catch the slip, Deb, until you nailed it for us. Your acknowledgement was a wonderful way of bringing our limitations out into the open. Let's face it; none of us are experts about the Earth's crisis, but we care about her, and we want to do whatever we can to help her. And I think having these conversations is a strategic way of getting more people interested and involved."

A passage from
The Word
(Chapter Four)

"In simple words, humankind must reclaim its humanity. You must 'love thy neighbor' with your whole heart and you must place your neighbor before yourself. This message is not new to you, but it is one that has long ago fallen by the wayside. Selfishness has been the way of the human species for far too long, and this manner of being has proven that it is not a sustainable life path. As many of your species live in poverty, many others possess the riches that could easily alleviate the pain and suffering of those less fortunate. Those with open hearts assist as they can, but the masses turn their heads and disregard the truth that is blatantly obvious. These actions of unkindness, prevalent across the great lands of this planet, incite other actions of inhumanity, which over time have become the norm of a civilization. Where is decency? Where is goodness? When were these exceptional traits of humanity lost? The beginning of the fall of humanity does not need to be known. The point of relevance is that man's inhumanity to man exists now, and this is unacceptable."

"Once again, we are in agreement," stated Gary. "I must admit that the ease with which our relationships have developed surprises me. It is such a relief to be able to share one's innermost feelings without fear of reprisal. And we saw the same process unfold with our guests the other

223

day. Obviously, it makes sense that individuals with similar interests would find comfort in each other's company, but it seems to me that this is too easy. I know this is going to sound weird, but it feels like we are somehow being assisted..." Gary paused and Pam took advantage of the moment.

"It feels like someone is helping us find one another."

"Yes!" we all replied to Pam's comment. The mutual consensus brought us great pleasure. Gary's eyes were sparkling with excitement. He leaned closer to the table and admitted that he had many questions about this.

"So, is anyone receiving information about this?" He looked around the table to see if any answers were available. Deb and I exchanged glances and agreed that she would speak first.

"The communiques that I'm receiving definitely confirm that we are being aided."

"By whom?" The question asked by both Gary and Pam popped out so quickly that we all started giggling. It was a brief respite before the conversation continued.

"Oh, please forgive our ravenous curiosity! But we so believe that we are not alone, and it would be wonderful to have proof at last." The nods of agreement that circled the table indicated the Circle of Four was in alignment once again.

"The desire to have proof is an interesting concept," mused Deb. "Some must see to believe, while others believe without seeing. I fall in the latter category, but I would love to have visual proof. This is my interpretation of the messages that I receive, which by the way, I am happy to share with you. These messages are obviously for everyone, not just me.

"I am told that our predecessors who have passed over are very concerned about our situation and they are deeply involved in assisting us. And they are not alone. Other Beings from other dimensions and settings throughout the universe are also extremely concerned about the Earth's crisis. Their messages are informative and reassuring, and they encourage us to take action immediately. Pam, you will be glad to hear that the messengers affirm the scientific information that has been distributed and the sustainability strategies that are under way. They also are very disturbed by the misinformation that is causing delays in progress being made.

"Another issue that the messengers are adamant about is what they refer to as a reality of existence. They persistently and insistently state that all Beings in existence are innately endowed with healing abilities, including the human species. The messengers repeatedly declare that we are capable of healing the Earth with these innate abilities. Messages about sending healing energy to the Earth are abundant.

"They also speak of the similarities between our healing capabilities and our established methods of prayers, and encourage us to pray on the Earth's behalf daily and often until we perfect our ability to access our healing intentions. The point being: positive energy in the form of prayers, peace of mind, and acts of compassion, love, respect, goodness, and kindness are immediately beneficial to the planet. These acts of loving-kindness can and must begin now. They require no debate and no governance. There is no reason why these actions cannot begin immediately worldwide.

"The messengers also acknowledge with great appreciation those who are taking action on the Earth's behalf. They are not dismissive of the loving care that is being shown to her, but they insist that a few are not enough to stop her decline. We must all get involved! This means each of us must honestly assess the ways in which we harm her, and then, we must take the necessary steps to change our behavior. At the same time, we need to participate in her healing process by learning how to utilize and maximize our healing abilities.

"I know this may sound overwhelming, but if you break this down into small steps, it's very doable! We really are capable of turning this situation around. And I think this is why we've been brought together."

A passage from
The Word
(Chapter Four)

"Existing in peaceful harmony is such a desirable way to live. Why is the human species so resistant to practicing this gracious behavior? Species of all sizes, shapes, and forms accepted your species the moment you entered into existence. It is time that you reciprocated their loving, generous nature.

The time for reciprocity is upon you. Those who have assisted you since your beginning deserve to be treated with respect. Those who have existed with you upon this beautiful planet deserve your acknowledgement of their contributions to your existence. And the planet Earth, who has provided you residence since your arrival to her lands, also deserves a sign of gratitude. Of all those who have been mistreated by the human species, she is the one who has suffered the most. Not only has she experienced the outrageous acts of abuse perpetrated against her, but she has also witnessed every act of destruction that you have committed against all of her other inhabitants. Such unbelievable unkindness has the human race inflicted upon others and also upon their own kind. This trail of destruction is the legacy of humankind. And still, the Earth, all of her residents, and all existences within the Greater Existence continue to hold you in the highest regard. You are still loved and cherished by all Those Who Came Before.

Please awaken to your circumstances. You are not alone. You do not live in an existence that is your personal playground. In truth, you are merely one species living in a highly populated existence filled with countless other species who are equally cherished and regarded. Mutual coexistence has been the way of existence since existence came into existence. All in existence desire your presence in existence. Living peacefully with and respectfully of all others is not an unreasonable request to make of your species."

Face down and in deep thought, Gary sat on the edge of his chair. Without looking up he communicated telepathically to his beloved. *"Do you believe we can reverse the damage that has been done to the Earth and restore her back to her beautiful lush and vibrant self?"*

"Yes, I do," responded Pam in like manner.

"So do I," exclaimed Deb, showing off her new abilities.

"Count me in! I believe we can bring her back to full health!" And with my telepathic contribution made, the four of us burst into laughter. High fives were exchanged across the table as we celebrated our new means of communication.

"You two have been practicing!" teased Gary and Pam. Deb and I acknowledged that we were taking baby steps and looking forward to more exchanges with them. Then the focus went back to Gary's question.

"The messages that I receive repeatedly emphasize that there is reason for hope, and I choose to believe that. Let's remember what we have experienced in recent weeks. Among the four of us, there have been interactions with animals, plant life, insects, and Beings from unknown parts. And our four guests brought more experiences forward, all indicating that something very important is happening around us. We know these interactions are real! We feel it in our hearts and we must trust each other and ourselves. These events are not coincidences; they are signs that we are not alone, and they are evidence that we are here for a reason. We are here to assist the planet Earth."

A passage from
The Word
(Chapter Four)

"Many lifetimes have your kind experienced on the planet Earth, and still there remains the inclination towards violence and disregard for others. Time did not resolve the peculiar proclivity. Your actions placed others in great jeopardy and this shameless disregard for other Life Beings continues to be the path that you choose. This choice breaks the hearts of all in existence. Please reconsider what you are doing. Please accept the alternative that has always been available to you. Peaceful coexistence is yours to accept. Please understand that this is the way of existence and it is the way that existence will continue. Opening one's heart to another is an act of loving-kindness. Accepting another into your heart is the gift of endless lifetimes: a mutual gift that benefits the recipient and the initiator. All benefit from the diversity of existence; all benefit from mutual coexistence. Mutual acceptance of one another is so much easier than being the bearer of ill will.

Living with the misunderstanding that one is better than another is a terrible burden to carry. So much effort is wasted believing in this erroneous perception of existence. Relationships are cherished in existence, and they are far more expansive than the relational ideas of the human experience. In the Greater Existence, all existences live in awareness and acceptance that all in existence are family. Relationships include interspecies relationships founded in mutual love and respect. Everyone is loved and accepted! This is the way of existence.

Mutual coexistence has served the Greater Existence for a very, very long time. It is a way of being that has proven to be most satisfactory. It is very regrettable that the human species has not embraced the ideal of living in peace with all the other companions who occupy the Greater Existence.

Since existence began, all in existence came into existence knowing that they were not alone. This reality fostered the familial relationships that have continued since the earliest beginning. Our history is extensive and our love for one another warms the very essence of existence. This manner of being is so ingrained in the core of existence that it never occurred to anyone that a species would evolve without this inner knowingness. The spark of interconnectedness remains within your species, but those who reject the idea of living for the common good permeate your civilization resulting in chaotic thinking, which breeds fear among you.

Those who strive to live their lives in harmony with others are confronted and challenged by those who prefer a lifestyle that satiates their own personal advantage. The conflict in interest among the human species divides its populace, and as time passes, the barriers for congenial compromises strengthen, reducing the possibility for peaceful resolutions. Common sense has been replaced by selfish greed, which is leading the human race down a path of no return. The negative impact of your misguided ways on other species is clearly evident, and yet, the mistreatment continues.

The Family of Existence looks on in disbelief. Many attempts have been made on behalf of humankind, but the resilience of ill will seems to have a life of its own. With great sorrow, other members of existence have come to realize that the fate of the human species is of their own making. It is our most fervent wish that Your Kind will choose to join your congenial Family in existence. Our peaceable ways are yours to accept and enjoy. Our hearts remain open and our hands are reaching out to welcome you home, but we accept that the decision is yours. We so hope you make your decision before it is too late.

All that is required of you is that you choose to accept one another as equals. Mutual coexistence demands mutual acceptance of all. We hope that you will give careful consideration to your future, and we also hope you will hear our pleas. Please come home. Your Family awaits you. The time is now!"

"For a long time, Gary and I have felt helpless and hopeless about the Earth's environmental changes. We knew her health was waning. The signs are everywhere, if you open your eyes and pay attention. We tried to make our little plot of land a sanctuary for the plants and wildlife that reside there, but the truth is, it's just a little yard. Our hearts have been aching about this for a long time, but now, I'm feeling optimistic. We have something to offer. We have experiences to share, which may inspire others to open their hearts to all the other life beings with whom we coexist. These life beings are our neighbors! I suspect that most people don't give other species much thought, but the time has come for us to change our perspective. Not only do we need to acknowledge our neighbors' existence, but we also need to treat them as equals. Our attitude about equality on our planet needs to be seriously revised. We don't honor equality among our own species, much less other species that we simply disregard. We are so consumed by our own little worlds that we don't appreciate or even notice what happens to others. Forgive me for speaking in such general terms; I know there is goodness throughout our species, but it's time to bring that behavioral trait to the forefront. We need to reclaim our humanity and lay our ill will aside. The time has come for all of us to treat everyone, including all species, with the same love and respect that we wish to receive."

"That was beautifully stated, Dear!" The couple shared a sweet glance before Gary took the lead. "As my Beloved was sharing her truth, I realized that we are being given an opportunity to remake ourselves. Each of us has a chance to review his or her behavior and decide what improvements need to be made. This is a remarkable gift. I just hope people will take this opportunity seriously. And I hope we will all realize and accept the responsibility that comes with this gift. The truth is we must all participate in this personal review, not only for ourselves, but also for all those around us. As Deb said early, this situation is not just about us; it's about everyone.

"Some people may react obstinately to my viewpoints, but I hope, and I believe that most people will seek a humane response to this opportunity of a lifetime."

Pam reached out to her friends; everyone reacted immediately. With hands joined, eyes closed, and deep breaths, they rested in the silence. Time passed, as is its way, before another was heard.

"Dear Old Friends, so good it is to be in your company again. Long have I awaited this moment. Please remain as you are, Dear Ones, and simply be with me. As we are now, so too have we been many times before. This is not our first adventure together, my Friends. Let us enjoy each other's company through the breath that sustains us all. We are One, my Friends, as we have always been and will forever be. Let us cherish this precious moment in time." And this they did for an unknown amount of time. They simply relaxed in the revelry of their union. No more was needed;

the moment in time filled their hearts with the love and compassion that welled up within them. All were One with each other and with all others in Existence. No boundaries separated one from another. All were One.

"My Friends, I come to confirm that which you already know. You are indeed here to assist the Earth in her time of need. You are not alone! Please remember this. Turn to each other when you are in need and remember there are others like you who are also here on her behalf.

"Do not fear, Old Friends. Everything that is needed to assist this great Life Being resides within you. Accept the healing powers with which you are endowed and use them wisely. Each particle of your healing energy that you share with the Earth will assist her recovery process. Every prayer that you offer on her behalf will increase her strength and remind her that she is loved and cherished. The healing energy that resides within you has only one purpose. It was created and instilled into every Life Being in existence so that all in existence could assist all others in existence whenever one was in need. Never was it intended for any existence to suffer. Never was it intended for any existence to exist without awareness of its relationship with all other existences. All in existence are related to all others in existence. We are all One. This is how existence has always been and will always be. We are of the same Source regardless of our appearance. In essence, we are more than we appear to be, because we are intrinsically related to all others in existence. Because of our heartfelt connection with all others, we accept everyone as Family, and because we are Family, we accept responsibility for caring for one another.

"One of our own is presently in ill health. The Life Being Earth is loved and cherished by all in existence, and we are most concerned about her failing health. It is essential that we come to her aid. You, Dear Friends, and many, many more are here to rescue her. This is your reason for being, Dear Ones. This is not the first lifetime that you have dedicated your lives to service. Each of you has committed your existence to service, and your dedication to the Earth has involved numerous life experiences. The ache that burns within you is the call that reminds you that it is time to take action. The words, 'The Time is Now,' which you see and hear repeatedly speak a truth that ignites the ache within. As said before, I am here to confirm that you are here to assist the Earth.

"In recent weeks, you have experienced great changes and you have witnessed the power of sharing one's experiences with another. With each story told, another experiences the changes that are rapidly occurring around the planet. Life Beings of all kinds are focused upon saving the Earth. Humankind must take part in this process. It is essential! Without their participation, she will not recover. The human species is responsible for her ill health. No more need be said of this: it is simply the truth. Present behavioral patterns must change. Anger, hatred, violence, avarice, and

selfishness cause great suffering among the human species; and, this suffering sickens the planet. She absorbs every insult and every injury that is perpetrated. The pain of humankind's inhumanity becomes her pain. These ill-fated behaviors must stop.

"The cruel ways in which the human species has treated the Earth have greatly contributed to her downfall. Even though the news about her environmental crisis is slowly being recognized, the changes that are in motion will not reverse her declining health. Indeed, the development of sustainable practices is a necessity, but the proposed changes must advance forward much more rapidly. Other species that inhabit the Earth already mutually coexist with the Earth and they are increasing their efforts on her behalf. The human species must accept responsibility for their role in this tragic situation.

"All progressive actions presently underway must hasten their efforts. Proposed efforts must accelerate their timeframes; the time for dawdling is over. No other matter is of greater importance. The fate of Earth and all her inhabitants is at stake. Dear Friends, these words may seem harsh, but the truth must be spoken and action must be taken.

"For the Earth to survive, the species that is responsible for her ill health must change their ways. The path of cruelty and ill will towards one's fellow Beings is not a viable lifestyle. The crisis situation that envelops the planet is evidence of this reality. Many who read these words will be offended by this inference. We are sorry that the truth is difficult to hear. Those of you who already practice good will must expand your goodness. Your efforts are deeply appreciated and you must persevere. Regrettably, until your companions accept the truth of their ill-fated ways, you and others like you must carry the burden of Earth's failing health. Have compassion for her, because your kind thoughts will ease her pain. Hold your misguided fellow Beings in compassion as well, for they too are part of your family. Brooding about those who choose a different path will not assist the Earth's recovery. Focus your intentions upon positive, hopeful outcomes for these mindful actions are medicinal and extremely beneficial, while thoughts of unkindness, judgment, and ill will generate negative energy that worsens her situation.

"My Friends, the tasks ahead are challenging, but there is reason for hope. The Earth is a remarkable Life Being and she responds well to positive intentions. As you and others like you remind her that she is loved and cherished, her pain will diminish. As you enliven others with your good will and your good intentions, she will be uplifted by your efforts. As you honor and cherish all others, she will grow stronger. The process of healing the Earth is not complex. She is a Life Being that thrives upon peaceful relationships among all her inhabitants.

"Imagine, Dear Friends, what life would be like on this beautiful

planet if every life being graciously respected and accepted the needs of every other Life Being. Perhaps, some of you feel this is a ridiculous exercise that serves no purpose, but that is not true. This proposed image is the way life is intended to be. The state of unrest that has been endured for so long is an anomaly: it is not the normal way of being. Living in peace and harmony with all others is the intended way of living. Remember this, Dear Friends! If the people of Earth live in peace, the Earth will continue forevermore. It is that simple. Heal yourselves, and she will be healed."

The Time is Now!

Afterword

Dear Reader, the title of this book, *Love Thy Neighbor,* is a Message of Old. It was important when it first came into being so very long ago, and it is vitally important at this time when it is essential for Humankind to rise to their full potential.

Please read these three words aloud: LOVE THY NEIGHBOR. Listen with the ears of your heart as the three words are repeated over and over again. Love thy neighbor, love thy neighbor, love thy neighbor! As you now know from reading the book entitled *Love Thy Neighbor,* these words are much more expansive than was originally thought. You are indeed a member of a marvelous species existing within an existence filled with countless other species. Needless to say, you are not alone. Although you are not the center of existence, you are loved and cherished as are all others, and you are essential to the survival of all existences presently living on the Life Being Earth. As you discovered from reading this book, all species are intrinsically linked to one another and must work together for the good of the Whole. This means that all species are equally important and significant to the continuation of the entire planetary eco-system. This reality must be accepted.

Unfortunately long, long ago, a misunderstanding evolved on the Earth leading some members of your species to believe that they were more valued than others. This misunderstanding caused great pain and suffering to those residing upon the planet and continues to have devastating effects that are compromising the health of the Earth today.

Dear Reader, this book has crossed your path for a reason. The title was purposefully chosen with hopes that it would trigger a distant memory from many lifetimes ago. The misunderstanding that some individuals are more significant than others can no longer be the standard for the human species. All members of all species are equal. This truth is true throughout all existence and there are no exceptions to this reality.

When the Message of Old was introduced, it was intended to serve as a foundation from which all Beings would exist. Most existences embraced this divine guidance and have lived in this gracious manner ever since. Unfortunately, a small minority did not fully understand the concept of loving thy neighbor. Confusion led to more misunderstandings and soon those who resisted the idea of living harmoniously with their fellow Beings developed characteristics that were predominantly self-serving. As their misunderstandings grew, so too did their disregard for others.

No one imagined that this misguided attitude would lead to such tragic consequences. What is done is done; however, the past cannot be the guide for the future. The Message of Old, 'Love Thy Neighbor,' still remains the foundation for mutual coexistence. In essence the message means that one must accept responsibility for the well being of all others, and one must do so with an open heart.

Dear Reader, our neighborhood is large; it expands across this magnificent planet and beyond. We are so blessed! Let us not forget our neighbors with whom we share this expansive backyard. Let us not forget the gift of diversity that exists within our neighborhood. Let us not forget that we are intrinsically connected with all our neighbors. Let us not forget that we are all members of the same Family. Let us not forget that we are all One. Remember this, Dear Reader, for your future depends upon it.